The Empty Nesters

NINA BELL

D1426105

sphere

SPHERE

First published in Great Britain as a paperback original
in 2011 by Sphere

A CIP catalogue record for this book
is available from the British Library.

ISBN 978-0-7515-4366-7

Typeset in Bembo by M Rules
Printed and bound in Great Britain by
Clays Ltd, St Ives plc

Papers used by Sphere are from well-managed forests
and other responsible sources.

MIX
Paper from
responsible sources
FSC® C104740

Sphere
An imprint of
Little, Brown Book Group
100 Victoria Embankment
London EC4Y 0DY

An Hachette UK Company
www.hachette.co.uk

www.littlebrown.co.uk

To Sharon Wilden, with thanks for her support
for #authorsforjapan, raising money for the
Red Cross Japan Earthquake appeal.

Prologue

'I don't want to talk about Alice,' said Clover Jones to Laura Dangerfield.

They hesitated under the graceful porch. Clover read out the inscription on a brass plaque: 'Campbell, Brown. Solicitors. Purveyors in death, divorce and moving house.'

'Does it really say that?' Laura sounded startled.

'No, of course not. But those are the three reasons why anyone would visit a solicitor, aren't they?'

'I think there's something called tort as well,' said Laura.

'Tort is just an upmarket tart, as far as I'm concerned.'

'I see we're back to Alice again.' Laura smiled a wicked smile.

'Come on,' said Clover, acknowledging the remark with a grimace. 'If we're going in, we're going in.'

The front door had panels inset with strips of mirror glass. Clover could see slices of themselves – her own thick red hair tied up, and the neat dark edge of Laura's bob. They looked good in thin strips. The edge of Laura's jacket was camellia pink. And Clover, in the slivers of glass, wore the soft greys and creams of a pebble beach.

Perhaps everything – and everybody – looks good if you don't see the whole picture.

1

Behind them was a bustling street. People hurried about their ordinary lives, thinking about what they would buy for dinner.

With a final nod from Laura, Clover pressed the buzzer and the door swung open. In front of them was a quiet pastel hallway, its whispered secrets and pain all bundled up into neat files. This was where those ordinary lives were torn up into tiny pieces.

Behind them two mothers ushered a group of children across the road. 'Why aren't they at school?' asked Laura, perhaps still deferring the moment when words would finally have to be said. Written down. Turned into facts.

'Half term? Holidays? Remember them?' Clover wondered if she could change places with those women, their lives measured out in school runs, half terms, overladen supermarket trolleys and the need to get from work to sports day or the school play. Every moment was tightly scheduled but she could see, from the way one little girl held her mother's hand, and the way the two women spoke to each other, that their lives were full of love and friendship.

And if she could magically become one of those women again, would she?

'Come on,' one of the women shouted to a little boy who had stopped at a shop window. 'We haven't got time.'

Clover looked at her watch. 'Neither have we.'

They turned left, into a room where a receptionist sat at a big modern desk.

'Good morning,' she said with a polite, practised smile. She looked from one to the other, obviously trying to identify the client. 'Can I help you, Mrs . . .?'

Chapter 1

A Year Earlier

The arrangements for the last day of term were as complex as aircraft holding patterns over Heathrow at the height of summer. Five sets of parents would take a table at the St Crispian's leavers' ball and five children – no, not children any more, thought Clover – five *teenagers* would be on another table with their friends, as far as possible from their parents at the other end of the marquee.

Getting involved in the ball took Clover's mind off the yawning gap that was about to open up in her life. Today, and from now on, she would be a spectator in her daughter's life. She was no longer the cornerstone, the anchor ... the pivot around which Holly's existence revolved. But, on the other hand, there would always be milk in the fridge when she wanted a cup of tea. She would be able to find a pen when she wanted to write a note. And she and George might finally get to drive from the east coast of America to the west.

Clover dropped Holly, Lola and Jamie off at school for the last time, at eight o'clock in the morning on the last day, marking all the 'lasts' with a sense of foreboding. Clover, Laura and Lola's mother Alice had shared the school run for years. They had ferried Ben and Holly Jones, Jamie

Dangerfield and Lola Fanshawe to and from school, Cubs, Brownies, rehearsals, football, riding lessons and – increasingly – exams, parties and sleepovers. Alice and Laura were Clover's closest friends, and their children were also part of the same gang. It worked beautifully. They holidayed together. Exchanged childcare. It was like having a huge extended family.

Clover and Laura were the original core. Laura and Tim lived in an immaculate eighteenth-century yellow brick farmhouse on the slope of an idyllic valley. Their view consisted of fields, a half-timbered black and white medieval cottage, two barns, a herd of rare-breed cattle and a wood. Inside, their house was tastefully painted in shades of blue, terracotta and off-white with a Shaker kitchen and smart cream sofas.

Two miles away, in the raggle-taggle village of Pilgrim's Worthy, Clover and George lived at Fox Hollow, an extended Victorian cottage with a front door painted the grey-green of lichen. It shared a flint garden wall with St Mary's church, and was shaded by ecclesiastical yew trees and the Norman church's stone tower. The interior of Fox Hollow was a jumble of colour and pattern, with a scrubbed pine kitchen table, a claw-footed bath beneath a sunny window and apologetically squashy sofas, one of which was usually occupied by Diesel, a grey lurcher from a rescue kennels. The Joneses' cats, Bonnie and Clyde – formerly feral strays but now plump, smug and sleepy – occupied the high ground: perching on a Welsh dresser stacked with blue-and-white china, a distressed grey wooden settle or the top of a battered oak chest with dozens of small, carefully labelled drawers. Clover was a magpie, picking up anything – and anybody – that could be rescued.

Then, five years later, Alice had bought a dilapidated sixties bungalow at the other end of Pilgrim's Worthy. It had looked like a garage dropped at random on the edge of the village, but she had extended it into a much-photographed example of contemporary living with huge windows looking out on the hop gardens and pastures beyond.

Geography had drawn the three very different women together, as Pilgrim's Worthy was almost out of the St Crispian's catchment area. Although, as Laura often pointed out, Alice didn't figure in the school runs quite as often as the other two. Lola spent much of the time living with the Joneses, while Alice, who was a single mother, worked tirelessly and travelled the world setting up her mail-order clothing company, Shirts & Things. She needed help. So Alice and Lola joined Diesel, Bonnie and Clyde – and, of course, George, Ben and Holly – under Clover's wing.

As tradition dictated, the teenagers kicked off the elaborate set of Last Day of School rites with the exchange of boys' and girls' uniforms. They photographed each other, the boys in skirts, the girls striking poses in askew ties and blazers.

Then they shoehorned themselves into their leavers' uniforms, in a style unchanged since the eighteenth century. St Crispian's was one of the oldest grammar schools in the country and behaved like a private school. It had traditions, and these were encapsulated in thousands of tiny buttons, done up by a hundred and ten excited pairs of hands. Fifty-two pairs of newly hairy male legs tackled the intricacies of sock suspenders for the first – and probably only – time in their lives. More photographs were taken as groups formed and re-formed in the quadrangle: the boys, then the girls, the boys and the girls, the rugby team, the netball team, the drama group, the best friends, the jazz club, the Crew – Holly, Lola, Sandeep, Adam, Lucy and Jamie, plus about eight others, who'd been together, with a few exceptions, since they joined the school in Nursery.

They all shuffled in to the school hall for prize-giving. Laura bustled around, petite and trim in a neat turquoise jacket, buzzing with enthusiasm. 'Such a lovely brooch,' Clover heard her say to one woman. 'I love your hair,' to another, and 'Haven't you lost weight?' to a third. When Laura was nervous she went on a charm offensive but, occasionally, she dropped her voice and hissed to Clover: 'Where's Tim? I'll kill him if he's late. His only son's last-ever school assembly . . . '

Clover spotted Tim and George at the door, waiting at the back until the aisles were clearer. They reminded her of two very different kinds of dog, who nevertheless relaxed completely in each other's company. George was a friendly golden retriever, while Tim was a sleek, dark greyhound. Clover sometimes wondered if Laura had got him out of a catalogue of suitable husbands. He was smart and well-groomed, with classic, tapered dark hair – short, but not too short. He wore well-cut suits, always partnered with a crisp white shirt left open at the neck. Conventional but not quite, as befits a well-known architect.

George, taller and broader, often looked as if he might have dressed in a hurry, his brown hair slightly windblown. His expression was usually vague and amiable, hiding an intelligent and observant mind. Sometimes, when she looked at holiday snaps, Clover could see that she and George had come to look like each other: hair that only stayed neat for a few minutes, crumpled linens, cosy jumpers and slightly creased cottons in the colours of the sea, the sky and the countryside. Maybe that was what twenty years together did.

As parents and grandparents settled themselves in their seats, thinning the press in the aisles, Clover spotted her father.

'There you are,' he said, pinching her cheek affectionately. His startling blue eyes, framed by bristling white eyebrows that reminded her of a lobster's antennae, were almost on a level with hers. He took her elbow. 'Your mother would have loved to be here.'

'I wish she was here too. And George's parents. It's sad that you're the only grandparent who's made it this far.' She smiled at him, once again registering the unfamiliar change in height. Surely she'd always looked up at him? Colin Stewart had always been her strong, brave, wise father. The person she turned to for advice and consolation. Three years ago Clover's mother had died, and he had seemed instantly diminished. But, at eighty-two, he was still fiercely independent. He organised his strange, new existence with military precision and rebuffed all offers of help. He was still Dad. She occasionally detected the whiff of something not quite right in his kitchen but, as he always pointed out, she was no great respecter of 'use by' dates herself.

And now he seemed to be evaporating. She frowned. She'd heard of bones shrinking, but whole inches? Clover looked down at her shoes. She was wearing high heels. That must be it.

She often found the same sudden adjustment with Ben and Holly. Sometimes they seemed to come downstairs about two inches taller than they'd been when they went to bed. Clover always looked down at her feet, and then theirs, to see if the solution lay with the shoes they were each wearing, and had often been surprised to find that they were both barefoot.

Laura's parents – sprightly seventy-somethings who hiked in the Lake District and sat on charitable committees – followed Clover and her father in, and they all settled down. There was just one empty chair in their row.

Clover was saving it for Alice Fanshawe.

The headmaster stood up and welcomed them all. As he worked his way through the names and prizes, Clover could feel herself on the edge of her seat. Would Alice make it in time to see Lola pick up the Harding Prize, the main academic trophy? Surely she would? The other parents thought Alice was neglectful and careless, but in Clover's opinion she had a pin-sharp awareness of what Lola was doing at any time. She just wasn't always there to do it with her.

There was a scuffle at the back as the door opened and closed. The headmaster paused, as if to register the new arrival. Alice, tawny and golden, with olive skin that tanned easily and sharp, shiny hair the colour of autumn leaves, knew how to make an entrance. At five foot ten she dressed like the models in her catalogues: slubby silks and soft cashmere in muddy, subtle colours with little details that women noticed and men didn't. Chunky, pearly buttons or iridescent silk threads or a bias cut on a skirt. And very high heels. Alice was fast becoming the very image of success.

There was a certain amount of whispering and shuffling, then Alice glided down into the empty seat next to Clover. 'Phew, nearly didn't make it,' she whispered. 'Useless meeting went on for ever.'

'It's fine,' murmured Clover. George raised his hand in greeting and Laura leaned across them both, fizzing with warmth and fury as usual. 'How lovely to see you,' she whispered. 'Love your jacket!' She fingered the soft fabric. 'That colour is so great on your skin. Tim was late too! The traffic must be frightful.'

Clover wondered if she should point out that Tim had arrived only a few minutes after they had, along with George. But Tim could do no right, and Laura would only find something else to criticise.

The headmaster, clearing his throat, carried on.

The prize-giving was interminable, and Clover drifted off, remembering her own last day at her stuffy all-girls school.

There'd been no local nightclubs in those days, so they'd all driven to the beach with bottles of cider and wine, making a makeshift barbecue among the stones and preparing for their very first all-nighter.

By sunrise, there were only six of them left. At four-thirty, a sweep of glimmering pink illuminated the horizon, and the sea began to sparkle, as if tiny fairy lights were being switched on across its width.

Clover had tugged off her dress. 'Race you to that little boat. The one moored to the far buoy.' She'd stripped off her bra and knickers, and rolled her dress around them, tucking them into the side of the breakwater. Wading naked into the water, she was exhilarated by its champagne coldness.

She could hear a chorus of objections behind her. 'It's a long way away.' 'There might be currents.' 'What about jelly-fish?' 'It's a public beach, suppose someone sees us?'

But she didn't care. This was about an end to rules and reg-ulations, to the fear of being found in the wrong corridor in the wrong shoes. It was the beginning of freedom. When the water reached her knees she dived in.

'Come on,' she shouted, flicking her hair out of her eyes. She was almost breathless with shock. 'It's beautiful.' The water was like silk against her naked body. This was what free-dom felt like.

Chattering and giggling, the others followed, but as Clover ploughed steadily on she realised that they'd dropped behind. And when she stopped to tread water, the little boat on its mooring seemed no closer. The distance was deceptive.

'Clover, come back!' She could just hear the others shout-ing, worried.

But I am going to get there, she told herself. I am going to win. It didn't matter that there was no one else in the race. It was harder now, pushing against the waves, keeping her

9

breathing steady, and the buoy was still no closer. She could feel the current tugging her away, trying to drag her out to the sea.

I will get there, she promised herself. This is the beginning of the rest of my life. She began to count. In a hundred strokes I will get there.

But the current was strong.

In ten strokes I will get there.

In five strokes I will get there.

Freedom was hard, but worth fighting for. She swam towards the sunlight. Just a few more strokes. She would not turn back now.

Her hand touched the weathered wood of the little boat and the shore, with its five anxious dots, seemed a long way away.

Pausing to catch her breath, she raised her hand to them in a victory wave. She, Clover Stewart, was alone in the great wide sea. And it felt good. 'Yay!' she shouted, but her words disappeared into the breeze.

She began the swim back, working her way across the current rather than fighting it, emerging from the water tired and victorious.

'We were worried.' Her friends were drying themselves in the early morning sunshine, their hair tangled like seaweed. 'If you'd got into trouble, there was no one to help.'

'I don't need help.' Clover squeezed the water out of her long, red hair. She was often called Coppernob at school and had always shrugged off the insult. Clover, Coppernob, what did it matter?

Her beating heart and trembling legs told her that she had swum too far out, especially after a night of drinking, and that even these benign waters could easily be deadly. But she had survived. She would survive.

She sat down, enjoying the rare feeling of the rising sun on her long, white limbs. She wouldn't be able to lie on the beach in a few hours. She would burn almost instantly.

They lit cigarettes, sheltering their matches from the gentle breeze and laughing at how difficult it was to light them with wet hands. Then they spread their clothes on the stones to dry and lay back, letting the rising sun warm their bodies.

Clover awoke with a jerk at the sound of another burst of clapping. Someone had nudged her. Back in the auditorium, blinking, she saw her husband smile at the sight of Holly, taller and slimmer than Clover had ever been, but with her mother's mane of red hair, mounting the steps to accept a prize from the headmaster.

Clover's last day at school had been a generation ago. She had given up the cigarettes – finally – with her second pregnancy, and an extra stone had settled around her midriff. Her red hair had faded and she twisted it up into a loose chignon with a selection of scrappy clips. There was a little too much grey in it, except when Clover put a rinse through. The little boat moored near the beach had long since gone, and it had been years since Clover swam towards the sun. She not only listened to the voices on the beach, calling her back. The voices of common sense, of responsibility. She had become one of them.

She clapped as Holly took her book from the headmaster and descended the steps again.

Lola went up for her prize. Sandeep got the Walden Prize, for being head boy, and then, finally, the final words, and people began to trickle out of the huge hall. Alice smiled and texted someone. George squeezed Clover's hand. She looked up at his kind, slightly crumpled face. He looked down at her, with the sympathetic brown eyes that Holly had inherited, and she wondered – as she often did – how, between them, they'd managed to create someone as vibrantly different, and yet recognisably similar, as Holly. As the pupils shuffled out, faintly flushed with excitement (and probably, if the truth be known, the odd shot of vodka) Clover realised that that was it. They were out. Through. 'We did it,' whispered Alice. 'Thank God that's over.'

'Yes,' agreed Clover, her throat tightening. She looked for Holly's hair streaming out behind her, always distinctive however packed the crowd. She wanted to hold her daughter in her arms. 'We did it. Now it's up to them.'

Colin's blue eyes were watery in the hot sun. 'She's a fine girl,' he murmured as he watched Holly scream with laughter and hug her friends. 'She reminds me of you at that age. Determined. Feisty. Loving life.' He patted her arm again. 'This sun is a little hot for me. I might just pop off now and leave you all to it.' He bumbled over to Holly and kissed her cheek, and Clover saw it again. Holly was now so much taller than her grandfather.

Everyone seemed to be changing very quickly.

They could hear Laura, indignant as a terrier, berating Tim for his late appearance, as around two hundred parents shuffled out into the sunshine, some looking tearful, others checking their phones or clearly thinking about lunch.

Alice replied to a text, then stowed the phone in her bag.

'Have you told Lola's father that she won the Harding Prize?' Clover ventured with a sense that she was trespassing.

Alice responded with a deep, throaty laugh. 'Stop fishing. You know me better than that. He's had nothing to do with Lola's education so far; why would he want to know anything now?' She looked around and pulled some cigarettes out of her bag, shielding her light from the wind then blowing out rings of smoke. 'I promise you, dearest, that when Lola is ready to know who her father is, I'll tell you immediately after that. You will be number two to hear the news. But until then . . . ' She raised an eyebrow and took another drag of her cigarette. 'Life is full of secrets.'

'Your life may be full of secrets. Mine is really rather straightforward,' said Clover.

Alice laughed again. Loudly, as if Clover had been very witty.

Chapter 2

After more changes of clothing, followed by the ferrying of over-excited, slightly self-conscious teenagers from one place to another, retrieving items of clothing from lockers and classrooms, packing cars high with artwork, books, files and sports kit, Clover and George, Laura and Tim, and Alice, found themselves standing in a marquee on the sports field. It was a chilly July evening, and they were surrounded by the people who had dominated their lives for the past seven years. Or twelve years, in the case of those who had been there since Nursery.

'I can't think why the kids didn't bring most of the stuff back themselves,' said Alice. 'I mean, they've hardly had anything to do since the end of A levels. You'd have thought they could have cleared it all out a bit earlier.'

'I don't think retrieving manky sports bags from lost property has been high on their list of priorities.' Clover kept an eye out for the rest of their table. 'Too busy drinking White Lightning or cheap wine in the park and . . . Oh look, there's Sheila Lewis. And Nigel.'

Sheila Lewis kissed Clover and Laura with her usual anxious expression. The Lewises were a devout, hard-working couple with a teenage daughter and three older sons who had

14

left home. They had no idea what long-legged, exuberant Ruby really got up to.

Sheila scanned the marquee with a furrowed brow. 'You don't suppose the children will get … well, you know … drunk tonight? Ruby is practically unconscious after two glasses of wine. We don't drink much at home, you see.'

Clover and Alice exchanged glances. Unlike Sheila, they did see. And what they often saw was Ruby Lewis teetering around, vodka in hand, laughing, dancing, wrapping herself round some gawky boy. Ruby, at thirteen, had been the first of the Crew to get drunk-sick. The reason she passed out after a couple of glasses of wine was probably because she'd drunk a couple of bottles beforehand.

But how could you tell another parent that their daughter was drinking too much, probably smoking dope and maybe even sleeping around?

After an uneasy hello in Alice's direction Sheila and Nigel formed a tight knot with George and two other parents from their church. Laura trotted round the marquee, kissing everyone. 'You're so clever,' Clover heard her say. 'What gorgeous shoes.' 'Didn't you think the headmaster's speech was wonderful?' 'Yes, Jamie's going to do law at Leeds. We're looking into internships for him.'

'Laura is such a people-pleaser,' observed Alice. She occasionally had flashes of malice.

'She's just nice.' Clover often found herself defending one friend to the other. There was a certain rivalry between Alice and Laura. Or maybe it was resentment? It was something that chilled the air, anyway. Laura kept a very beady eye out when Alice leaned into Tim, talking about returns, and customer profiles, and 'bounce'. But it might just have been the age-old animosity between Alice, the archetypal working mother, with her taxi account and cleaning lady, and Laura, the stay-at-home mum who spent half her life ferrying her own and other people's children about. Clover enjoyed her middle ground, working as an assistant art teacher at the junior school three days a week. It meant she belonged in both camps, although she suspected that that was cheating.

'So who else are we expecting?' asked Alice, surveying the crowd over her glass.

'The Baxters and the Marchandanis. And there's a spare man, Duncan Hesketh. His son, Joe, joined in Sixth Form and got friendly with the rest of the Crew. Look, there's Duncan.'

A rangy, muscular man with a shock of pepper-and-salt hair appeared at the entrance to the marquee, peering over the tops of people's heads, looking bemused. Clover waved. 'That's Duncan.'

'He looks like Diesel,' commented Alice, adding: 'You know, your dog.'

'What, a cross between a greyhound and a Brillo pad?' But Clover could see what Alice meant.

'Clover,' he said, ambling over and kissing her on the cheek. 'I didn't think I'd find you in this crowd.'

Clover ran through the introductions, pulling George back into the group: 'This is George, my husband. And Tim. He and Laura, who is busy charming everyone in the marquee, are Jamie's parents, and Tim's a conservation architect. Nigel and Sheila are Ruby's parents. Nigel works for Packpac and Sheila does amazing volunteering at the charity shop on King's Mile.'

Duncan smiled and shook hands all round. 'I hope you're not going to test me later. I might have trouble remembering all that.'

'And this is Alice, Lola's mother.' Clover suddenly realised that Duncan probably had no idea who their children were.

The labels that had defined them all for so long were suddenly redundant.

As Clover added that Alice was also MD of Shirts & Things Alice extended a slender hand, be-ringed and braceleted in Indian silver. Assessing Duncan with a half-amused look, she added, 'As we're going for full job descriptions, I might add that Clover is too modest to tell you that she's a very talented painter. She's been hiding her talents by working as a part-time art assistant at the school for how long now, Clover?'

'Eleven years,' she admitted. 'But they're re-jigging the Art Department so I'm taking voluntary redundancy. I'd been there long enough.'

'So this is a big, big goodbye for you?' asked Duncan. 'Having been so very involved with the school, not just as a parent like the rest of us?'

Clover nodded. 'A major change in my life. But exciting. I get to leave school along with my children.'

'Just as long as you don't leave home along with them.' George put an arm round her. 'That's all I ask.' He grinned at her before turning his attention to Duncan. 'So what do you do, Duncan?'

'I'm a decorator. I put paint on walls. Or film sets.' He smiled, easy-going and friendly. 'What about you?'

'George is marketing director of Petfast, the animal medical and feed experts,' Alice took his arm, and fluttered her eyelashes at him.

'And this is Deepak and Leila Marchandani,' Clover said. 'Their son, Sandeep, was head boy this year, so you've probably seen him about. He's going to Oxford to read medicine.'

Leila Marchandani tilted her head with a gentle smile. 'If he gets his A levels.'

'Come on Leila, he's got two already,' drawled Alice. 'At

the highest possible grades. He was only taking the last three so as not to be bored.'

Leila smiled in acknowledgement. 'Yes, Sandeep is a good boy.' She placed a hand on her heart. 'And we will miss him when he goes. When Rajesh – that's his elder brother,' she added to Duncan, 'when Rajesh left home it was like a bereavement. But we have the other three who are younger, so we are still busy.'

'Deepak and Leila are both doctors too,' Clover told Duncan. 'So they've got very full lives as well as a still-full nest. Oh, and here are Ken and Sarah Baxter. They're just about to turn their whole life upside down and go round the world.'

Ken and Sarah looked like male and female versions of each other: medium height, brown-haired, pleasant-faced and fit-looking. 'We're selling up,' said Ken to Duncan.

'And we've already bought our round-the-world tickets,' added Sarah. 'Now that Adam is off to uni, and Milly – his elder sister – is about to start her last year at Cardiff we're just going to take off. The kids don't need us any more, so we're free. We've both retired early.' She beamed at everyone, then introduced herself to Duncan. 'What about you? Is this empty-nest time for you?'

'Absolutely.' He sounded wistful. 'Joe is our – my – only son, and my . . . wife had two daughters by her first marriage, but they left home several years ago. He's going straight to university. He didn't want a gap year.'

'No, neither did Holly,' said Clover. 'Our son, Ben, left school last year but he did take a gap year – he's off in Thailand now – so Ben and Holly will be leaving for uni together. If she gets the grades, of course.' August lay ahead like a storm brewing on the horizon. So much rested on those few grades.

'What about your . . .?' Duncan turned to Alice. Clover noted that he was one of the few men who could look down on her when she was wearing heels.

'Lola's got an offer from Oxford.' Alice smiled in satisfaction.

Duncan moved so that he and Alice were cut off from the group and Alice, in turn, leant in a little closer.

Clover turned back to the Marchandanis to talk about the summer, which Leila and the children would be spending in France. 'Near us!' exclaimed Clover on hearing where in France. 'We must all get together for a lunch or something.' Over Leila's shoulder, Clover could see George, who was staring across the marquee as if it was completely empty. She was struck, for one moment, by the desolation in the folds of his face. He was usually so solidly cheerful. But, before she could go to him, Alice buttonholed her once more. Duncan had gone to say goodbye to one of his son's teachers.

'Really, Clover, only you could find a relatively hunky single man for the leavers' ball,' said Alice with a laugh in her voice. 'Are you match-making, by any chance?'

'Not really. But after his wife died of cancer, Joe came here for A levels. Duncan doesn't really know any of the other parents – you just don't meet anyone if you come that late. So I thought it would be nice to invite him to join our table.'

'Mm.' Alice contemplated his back over her glass. 'He looks strong. And he's got his own hair. It's gone a bit steel-grey and looks a bit shaggy, but at least it's not a wig.'

'A wig?'

'I went out last night with a man who looked like he wore a wig. Up in London,' confided Alice. 'It was a very good wig, but I'm betting it was a wig all the same.'

'No! That's awful.' A small voice at the back of Clover's head murmured that Alice should have set aside that evening –

the last of Lola's schooldays – for her daughter, rather than going out with a man in a toupee. But the kids had all gone out together, to Pizza Express and a club, and none of the adults had seen any of them anyway. Lola, as usual, had spent the night – if you could call four-thirty until seven in the morning 'a night' – on the spare bed in Holly's room. And Alice, with her easy view of parenting, had been right all along. The children no longer needed them.

'I quite like his clothes,' said Alice, still looking at Duncan. 'Quite', for her, was approbation. 'He'd make a good older-man model for one of my catalogues, don't you think? With that lived-in face, and that pirate colouring. I bet if someone was to lure him into bed they'd find he was still pretty lean and mean.' Alice's voice suggested that she might be that someone. Possibly even before the night was over.

'Mind you,' she added. 'I've always rather wanted to put George in the catalogue, because there's nothing quite like that very English country look. As if someone should be tucking his shirt-tails in.'

'George modelling?' Clover couldn't help laughing.

'But I wonder if Duncan *might* consider being in our next catalogue?' mused Alice, always working. 'We're thinking it could be good to introduce a few "real" men. Slightly older ones.'

Sets of parents drifted past asking each other the same questions. What universities are they going to? What are their gap year plans? And what are you going to do? The air was peppered with names of towns in the north of England – York, Durham, Leeds, Lancaster, Sheffield . . .

'Don't we have universities down here in the south?' asked Clover.

'All our kids are just trying to get as far away from us as possible,' Alice replied. 'Presumably there's a leavers' ball up in

Yorkshire somewhere, where all you can hear is Brighton, Bristol, Bath, Kent, Cardiff, Oxford Brookes . . . '

'It's all so competitive,' observed Clover. 'Like some great card game. With everyone knowing the rank of absolutely every university and exactly how difficult it is to get a place on which course. Last year we definitely had the four of clubs because poor old Ben didn't get any offers and we had to go through Clearing. You'd have thought one of us had just been diagnosed with a terminal illness, the way people expressed sympathy. Holly's Leeds offer has definitely moved us up the game a bit.'

Alice smiled.

'It's all right for you: you've got the ace of spades – English at Oxford. You've got bragging rights.'

'It's not just the kids that seem to be up for bragging rights,' Alice pointed out after a few more exchanges with other parents. '*We've* got to be stunningly interesting too. There's no question of just growing old gracefully any longer.'

All around them the air vibrated with plans.

The crowd of people ebbing and thickening, like waves around rocks, carried the words 'always been our dream', 'writing', and 'Canada'. From the roar, Ken and Sarah's voices emerged most clearly. 'We'll start off in India at the end of September,' said Ken. 'And we thought we'd take a houseboat in Kashmir, then see how far we can get up Everest,' added Sarah. 'We're not expecting to make it past base camp or anything like that, but we'd never forgive ourselves if we didn't at least try.'

'I feel I ought to be cycling to China. Or going into politics to change the world. Everyone seems to have such plans,' Clover muttered. 'They know what they're going to do.'

Alice contemplated the crowd over her glass and took a sip of white wine. 'Nah.' She looked at Clover with amusement

21

in her eyes. 'They're all terrified. None of us has the least idea of what we're going to do now we're no longer anchored by school runs and filling fridges.'

Clover laughed. She could have added that Alice had never exactly been anchored by school runs and filling fridges. Somehow she'd always managed to pay or cajole someone else into doing it all for her.

'So you'll stay on down here? Or will you be more based in London?' Clover had complete trust in Alice. They spoke on the phone or saw each other almost every day. But now that Lola was no longer at school in Kent, might Alice not spend more time in her tiny one-room pied-à-terre in London? And Lola would also be gone. Clover felt that she wasn't just losing Holly, but all of Holly's friends too.

Alice laughed again. 'You must be joking. I'd go mad if I spent any more time in London. No, my long-term plan is to hang on until we go public, make a killing with my shares and then retire while I'm still young enough to enjoy it.' She smiled at Clover. 'I'll base myself in dear old Kent and travel the world. And finally write my novel, and take up gardening.'

'You see, even you've got a plan.'

'And you've got your painting. This is when you break into the big time. Come on, Clover, you're one of the most talented artists I've ever met. You've been putting the children first for far too long. You gotta get out there.'

People only saw the hedonistic, selfish Alice. They didn't see the loyal friend who supported and encouraged, who made you believe in yourself and, well, who made you laugh. That was why Clover loved Alice. She turned everything into a joke.

But Clover didn't want to talk about painting. She felt she had lost sight of who she was and, in the busyness of organising the children's lives, that didn't matter. There was an easel that stood untouched in her studio, reproaching her for a loss of nerve.

Alice surveyed the packed marquee again, a smile on her lips. 'Anyway, you know what they say about the best-laid plans. I was doing some research today on when women get divorced. To see if it might affect our marketing strategy.' She raised a finger. 'Now, the number-one age for getting divorced is exactly what you'd expect. Late twenties. People get married when they're too young and then regret it. It's called a starter marriage. But if you look at the rest of the ages you can see that about a third of divorces happen between forty and sixty, which is exactly where we all are.'

'What do you mean, about a third of us are about to get divorced?' Clover was shocked.

Alice rolled her eyes. 'No, dear. One-third of all divorces happen around the time the kids leave home. That's not the same thing.'

Clover found numbers and statistics bewildering, while Alice could see a figure and instantly understand where it was going.

'Say there are about a hundred marriages here in this room,' explained Alice, who developed her argument, counting off on her long, perfectly manicured fingers, until Clover lost track of the statistical probabilities. Alice could see her puzzlement. 'Clover, can't you count at *all*?'

'Nope. And I don't want to hear about fractions and percentages. They mean nothing to me.'

'I'll make it easy for you,' Alice sighed. 'How many tables of parents are there at this ball? I know you were part of the organisation. Along with everything else you do for the school.'

'Um. Twenty tables. Almost all the parents are coming.'

Alice narrowed her eyes. 'And ten on every table, I presume?'

Clover nodded.

'That's it. One couple on each table, on average, will divorce between the ages of forty and sixty.'

'Are you sure?' Clover felt anxious. 'One couple on each table of parents is going to get divorced? Probably in the next ten years or so?'

'Statistically,' corrected Alice. 'Which means in reality, of course, that some tables will have two sets of divorcing parents, or maybe more, and others none.'

'It still seems an awful lot.'

'On our table, I think the odds have got to be on—'

'Laura and Tim Dangerfield!' They both laughed. They often finished each other's sentences.

Alice sipped her wine thoughtfully. 'On the other hand, sometimes those up-and-down marriages are surprisingly resilient. Fewer illusions, I suppose.'

'But Tim is hardly ever there. He's always working late. Never at home.'

'I'm always working late,' Alice pointed out, 'and I'm hardly ever at home. That doesn't mean I have affairs. Not that it would matter if I did, I suppose, because I'm a free woman. I'm just saying that sometimes a lot of work is just that. A lot of work. On the other hand, they haven't had sex for five years.'

Clover almost choked over her wine. 'What? How do you know that?'

'Tim told me.'

'When?' Clover studied her friend's face. This didn't sound good.

'Oh, I don't know. It just came up somehow.' Alice's eyes danced with amusement. 'I told him TMI. Too Much Information. We changed the subject.'

'Well, Laura has never said anything about it to me.' Clover thought they talked about everything. But obviously not.

'He's an attractive man in that sexy-politician way, don't you think?' mused Alice. 'Nice even features, goes around in great clean gusts of lime and lavender, has well-sculpted hair . . .'

Clover couldn't help giggling because it described Tim's hair beautifully. 'You're making him sound quite creepy. His hair's fine. Properly shaped. All his own. Quite a nice shade of steel grey.'

'He is a bit of a smoothy-chops,' agreed Alice. 'But he's an OK guy underneath it all, and Laura will drive him away if she keeps going on at him like that. Not to mention that the sex thing is a relationship-breaker, so if we were putting bets on they'd be favourites at about two to one. But we have to consider the outsiders, too . . . the Lewises. Perhaps one or other of them has got a secret life. '

Clover giggled at the thought of Nigel and Sheila Lewis having a secret life. 'Anyway, not the Baxters. Too busy trekking the Hindu Kush and bungee-jumping in New Zealand, don't you think?'

'And you're sound with George,' said Alice. It was a statement.

Clover knew you could never take anything for granted. 'I hope so. I think . . . well, divorce is unthinkable to George. He's such a family man. He really is.'

But his family is about to be cut in half, when Ben and Holly go. It was a little niggle in Clover's mind, that she and George would be on their own together for the first time in almost twenty years. Would they have anything to say to each other?

Still, there was the summer to come. The Jones and Dangerfield families were going away on one last family holiday together, with Lola, to France. Alice, who could rarely get away for long, was going to join them for most of it.

'Believe me,' Alice reiterated. 'You're sound with George. He's a really solid man. The way my father used to be. Able to fix shelves and screw on doorknobs. Someone you can rely on.' She looked wistful. 'I envy you,' she said suddenly. 'I really do.'

Clover was embarrassed. 'I can't imagine ... you ... well ... you've got everything. You look gorgeous. You're incredibly clever ... you're really successful ... you've got a great relationship with Lola ...'

'Yeah.' The old Alice, cynical and confident, was back. 'I'm just perfect.'

Clover looked across the marquee for George, and caught his eye. He came over. 'Are you marshalling us all to sit down?'

'Are you all right?' Clover looked at him carefully.

'Of course. Why shouldn't I be?'

'I saw you. Across the room. You looked sad.'

He put his arm round her shoulders and squeezed her tightly. 'Not me. I'm so proud of Holly, aren't you? She looked so pretty up there, picking up her prize.'

Clover continued to search his face. In the background she heard Sarah Baxter tell someone that they might rent a place in South Africa for Christmas, so the kids could join them. 'Or maybe we'll have got to Malaysia by then. We're going to live for the moment—'

'—and see where life takes us.' Her husband completed her sentence.

'George?' Clover took his hand. 'Are you OK?'

'Perhaps a touch of indigestion,' he added. 'I ate my sandwich too fast, and it was quite a spicy pickle.' He sighed, and there it was again. A whisper of sadness. But he smiled. 'Now, are you going to boss us into sitting down? Have you done place cards?'

'Am I too bossy?'

'We love you for it,' he said, kissing her briefly on the lips. 'I love you for it.'

Chapter 3

Laura counted out nine neatly ironed T-shirts and laid them in Jamie's suitcase. Seven pairs of white socks, rolled into balls. Seven pairs of boxer shorts, all ironed. Two pairs of cargo shorts. Swimming kecks. She would have to buy him some new goggles. It would probably be the last time she packed a case for him – except for uni, of course – and she didn't really want to admit, not even to Clover, that she still did it. Clover had stopped packing Ben and Holly's cases when they hit thirteen and eleven respectively, and Alice, of course, had no idea what Lola took on holiday. 'I've never packed a case for her,' she'd drawled. 'She just had to do it herself. It's how they learn.'

Well, that was hardly likely to be true, was it? That was the trouble with Alice Fanshawe. She was not truthful: what Laura's mother had often referred to as a 'holy friar'.

In rhyming slang, a liar. Clover couldn't see it. She thought Alice was just colourful. 'She doesn't really mean it,' she'd say, laughing.

Alice had moved to Kent when Lola was ten, to take advantage of the good schools, around the time it first seemed that Shirts & Things might really take off. She'd met Clover, presumably spotted that she was an easy target and pretty much installed Lola in her house. Within months Alice had been travelling all round Europe, visiting suppliers two or three nights a week ('So that's what lovers are called these days,' Tim had chortled) while Lola ate supper, did her homework and was tucked up in the spare bed beside Holly's in Clover and George's cottage. 'I don't mind,' Clover always said. 'One extra is no trouble.'

But it was one extra for Laura as well, when it was her turn for the school run. Nobody thought about that, did they? As Laura did up the straps of Jamie's case and ticked 'pack for Jamie' off her to-do list, she allowed herself to feel irritation about the holiday ahead.

It had been Laura's turn to choose. Clover had found them a delightful Portuguese villa the year before, but it had been a bit expensive, and too far from the shops, so Laura had looked forward to finding something much better. She'd picked out Chez Vous, a nice purpose-built holiday villa in a well-designed and tasteful complex not too far away from Nice – but just far enough to be out of the sky-high price range. It was quite basic, but had a good modern kitchen and was only twenty minutes' drive from the beach. The complex had a shared pool with a bar, so the children could socialise with other kids. She'd e-mailed Clover, George and Alice. 'This is perfect for our price range,' she'd said. 'If you're all fine with that I'll put the deposit down immediately, so that no one else snaps it up.'

Alice had responded with links to the websites of several companies, all of which had faux-chic names like Secret Châteaux or Private Places of Distinction (the latter sounded positively pornographic, in Laura's opinion), pointing out five different houses, all of which were, naturally, more expensive than Chez Vous, but had their own swimming pools and bigger beds. She'd offered to pay extra if cost was a problem, but, of course, George and Tim had refused.

So now they were each going to pay several hundred pounds more, for something that was apparently a château, with a swimming pool, a billiards room and a tennis court. It was twenty minutes' drive from the nearest town, but with no immediate neighbours. It was ridiculous – what were the kids going to do for amusement? And what about breakages?

Then Laura had somehow lost control of the bedroom allocation. She wasn't quite sure how it had happened, but 'from her BlackBerry' on the other side of the Atlantic, Alice had managed to bag the en suite double in the turret: 'Not really big enough for two, so better for a single' had been her reasoning, along with 'by the stairs so I can get up early to do a bit of work without disturbing anyone'.

At that point Laura had made a bid to bring everything to a halt by citing her asthma. A seventeenth-century house with all those curtains, beams and dust-harbouring cornices would be a health hazard. Alice, however, replied that the stable block extension was modern, with horrid red tiles and blinds (she hadn't actually said they were horrid, but you could see from the pictures on the website that they were). Perfect for an asthmatic. So now Laura and Tim were in hard, new twin beds in the ground-floor extension as if they were staff, while Clover and George luxuriated with glorious views in the main en suite double, and Alice had the romantic room, with its little private terrace, in the turret.

It was supposed to be Laura's year to be in charge! The couple who organise the house were meant to get first choice of rooms. The whole thing would probably be a complete disaster and, anyway, Alice wasn't even going to be there for more than a few days. She was going to arrive three days into the fortnight (naturally, because it would get her out of the hard work of unpacking and provisioning the house at the beginning). She had an important meeting in New York, apparently. She would also be leaving forty-eight hours early, thus getting out of the clearing up, because there was an important board meeting about a possible takeover. And now Tim, too, was going to leave early for some idiotic business reason. They would be on the same plane. It made Laura feel quite wheezy just thinking about it.

She sat down on Jamie's bed and picked up his ragged stuffed bear. Jamie always had Bearie on his bed, and even took him on holiday. Occasionally other kids teased him, but both Ruby and Lola had teddy bears, so it was tolerated within the easy camaraderie of the Crew.

He probably wouldn't take Bearie to university, though. He would finally grow out of the worn bear. Laura held him close to the searing pain in her heart. She wept jerky, glass-sharp tears for the threadbare teddy that would lie alone in an unheated bedroom, waiting for a little boy who would never come back.

Chapter 4

The Joneses and the Dangerfields drove down to Bordeaux over two days, in convoy and in high spirits, sharing the driving and navigating between the four parents – George and Clover, then George with Tim and Laura with Clover, and so on. Ben would be picked up at Bordeaux airport on Sunday, while the other three Crew members – Jamie, Holly and Lola – stayed together in either car, plugged into their music or dozing, or occasionally taking out their headphones and demanding to know what 'this crap' was.

'Our music,' said Clover firmly. 'Drivers get to choose the music.'

'Well, they don't have to choose old Woodstock tracks, do they?' asked Holly peevishly.

'Your dad works extremely hard and this is his holiday too.'

'Yeuch. I tell you, I am never doing another car journey with you again. Never. I'll get a cheap flight.'

'If you earn the money, you can get a cheap flight,' said George. 'It's up to you from now on.'

Holly looked thoughtful. Her father usually indulged her. Mile after mile of motorway flew past, the green of northern France giving way to the flat brown of the hotter south.

They stopped for lunch, then tea, and the heat shimmered

up from the tarmac as soon as they opened the car door. The baguettes, hard, pre-packaged and tasteless, were a disappointment.

'I don't know what's happened to French service stations,' said Clover. 'Do you remember when we first started coming down, you could get the most delicious meals, beautifully served and really inexpensive, at a French service station? They're worse than English ones now.'

'Much worse,' agreed Laura, picking bits out of her baguette with a frown, 'but I do love their benches. It's so lovely to sit at a picnic table in the open air surrounded by trees. You could never do that at an English one.'

'You say *everything* is lovely, Mum,' said Jamie. 'It's just a crap service station, OK?'

'Well, it's better than saying everything is awful,' retorted Laura. 'I'm not the sort of person who goes around complaining all the time.'

'Yes, you are,' replied Jamie. 'You're always complaining about Dad, and now you're leaving half that baguette.'

'Jamie.' Clover touched his arm briefly. 'Your mum does a lot for you. Give her a break.'

'Yes, bet you'd never have got into Leeds if she hadn't written your personal statement for you,' jibed Holly, giving Jamie a mischievous look. 'My mum didn't even look at mine.'

'I didn't know you were doing it,' said Clover. 'But, let's face it: a mother's place is in the wrong.'

'You lot' – George looked at the three teenagers over his baguette – 'less lip. Your mothers do the best they can for you, and you're bloody lucky to have them.'

Jamie, Holly and Lola exchanged amused glances, but subsided.

'Do you remember . . .' Tim began, looking relaxed and suave, as usual, in an open-necked white shirt and cream safari shorts, '. . . when they were doing that tyre check, and that mechanic literally sucked his back teeth and shook his head at our tyres, like someone in a comedy sketch? And then he proposed that—'

'—we spend four hundred pounds on a set of new tyres?' Laura cut across him. 'And you nearly did. If I hadn't stopped you, that would have been our holiday budget cut in half.'

And they were off on 'do you remember . . . that awful woman who was on a fearsome diet . . . that little dog who adopted us . . . the time we played boules against the old men of the village . . . that beach in Spain that was utterly deserted . . . the villa in Italy that didn't have a corkscrew?'

George got up first. 'Right, you lot. Time to get going.' He shook out the map and laid it on the bonnet of the car, so that he and Tim could confer over the route. Clover watched them: George pointing out the route, his check shirt hanging loose over a battered pair of jeans, his hair ruffled by the slight breeze. Tim leaning forward to inspect George's suggestion, then throwing his head back in laughter at something George had said, his teeth gleaming white. Then George bending towards Tim, as Tim pointed out an alternative, and their heads dropped into a huddle. Tim's route won. They laughed again, touched each other briefly on the arm or the shoulder in acknowledgement, and began to gather their families up.

'Let's swap drivers,' suggested Laura. 'You two go together, and me and Clover.'

Tim and George exchanged glances. They were obviously thinking the same thing: that Laura and Clover would get lost.

'Come on,' said Clover with a smile. 'Just because I'm a woman it doesn't mean I can't read a map.'

'Really, you two are being quite ridiculous.' Laura got up, shovelling all the sandwich detritus into an empty carrier bag.

Both men, scenting trouble, backed off, but George insisted on explaining the route to them three times.

'I don't know why they think we're such idiots,' grumbled Laura.

Holly, Jamie and Lola were instructed to travel with George and Tim, so that Laura and Clover could stock up at the supermarket.

'I wonder what we've forgotten. I never forget the corkscrew now, but there must be something,' mused Clover. 'I've forgotten literally everything else at some point – I even forgot all my knickers once, because they were drying in the back garden at home, but I still had the corkscrew.'

'If it's a choice between knickers and corkscrew, I'd choose the corkscrew too.' Laura paused. 'And I'm sure Alice would.'

'She doesn't drink much.' Clover knew that the Alice conversation would have to be had. 'She's OK, you know. I'm sorry about the bedrooms. Are you sure you don't want ours? We don't mind the stable block.'

Laura shook her head. 'No good for my asthma. But thanks anyway.'

They settled into a few minutes' companionable silence until Laura started up again. 'It's just that I think she's using you. You've had Lola to stay for weeks and weeks this holidays, and now you're driving her down with the rest of us.'

'She'd do the same for me if the tables were turned, I know she would. Lola's taking up the spare place in the car because Ben's flying in separately. And Alice does contribute, in her own way . . . I actually think she's paying more than she really ought for the rent, considering there are only two of them, three of you and four of us.'

'I think she *should* pay proportionately more,' said Laura in a tight voice. 'And we divvy the food up according to how many eat it, so it's all fine. Really fine.' After a few miles she spoke up again. 'But could you make sure that she doesn't get us all going out to expensive restaurants when it's her turn to cook? I don't think she realises what life's like for people who don't earn squillions. I made a decision to give up acting when I had Jamie, and I'm proud of that. I don't appreciate being looked down on by people like Alice, who's barely there for her own child. She's missed out so much of Lola's growing up.'

'She doesn't look down on you, and she was pretty broke when we first met her, don't forget. She's had to work really hard to keep them both going. It was just her and Lola in that awful bungalow.'

'Which has now been extended and extended, so that the original sitting room is now the boot room,' grinned Laura. 'It reminds me of a very smart multi-storey car park.'

'She's done it very well,' said Clover. 'If you like modern design. It's got wonderful views.'

'Do you think she gets all the money from Shirts & Things or is Lola's father contributing?'

'Must be the company. I don't think Lola's father features at all. Although she was texting someone during prize-giving.'

'It could have been her parents.'

'Alice doesn't have parents. They're both dead.'

'Or she was beamed down from another planet. Sent to take over the world. And, you know, it's not really fair on Lola. Children need fathers. That's why I put up with Tim.'

'How is Tim?' Clover peered at the signs. 'I do hate the Bordeaux ring road, it's so easy to get lost. Do you remember that time we missed our exit and ended up going right round it? It added three-quarters of an hour to a ten-hour drive.'

'Wasn't that the time Holly was sick and we couldn't stop? Just don't follow the signs for the airport, that's where we went wrong last time.' Laura bent over the map. 'Look, there, this one.'

They left the tangle of junctions with a sigh of relief. There was woodland on either side of the motorway, and lavender down the central reservation. 'Off at the next junction, sign-posted St Etienne, I think,' said Laura. 'Tim's OK.' She sighed. 'He's travelling a lot. He gets up at about five in the morning and is out of the house by half-past. Then not back till about ten.'

'Poor Tim.' Clover wondered, as everyone did, whether he was having an affair. She wished she could ask about the sex thing, but it wasn't something you could just come out with.

With practised unity they shopped at a supermarket, Clover buying the fresh food, Laura getting drinks and staples, meeting at the checkout just three-quarters of an hour later with their trolleys stacked so high that the loo rolls threatened to slide off. 'I always forget that French supermarkets often don't do disposable carrier bags, only reusables,' said Clover, relishing the newness of being abroad.

They pushed the trolleys out into the blazing sunshine, stacked the bulging bags high on the now-baking back seats, and found their way on to a road bordered by sunflower fields. 'Look, a prune museum.' Clover pointed out a single small sign. 'We must go some time.'

'Unmissable. I look forward to suggesting it to the kids – what would you like to do today? Play tennis, swim or go to the prune museum?'

'There'll be a stampede.' The road began to climb, and the occasional house appeared, shuttered and apparently deserted, although they saw a dog, barking on its chain. Nothing moved in the sunlit landscape, except for a giant sprinkler system working its way up and down a huge field. 'You'd never think it was the height of summer,' said Clover. 'Trust

Alice to find somewhere that hasn't been discovered by tourists.'

'I just worry that the Crew won't find enough to do. At that age they want nightclubs, not the sound of owls hooting. But it'll be lovely for us, of course.'

'Look – Château St Etienne. Down that driveway.'

They bumped along the last few miles of rough track, past an old stone wall and found the farmhouse where the key was stored. 'I don't know what's happened to the rest of them,' grumbled Laura. 'I bet they're in a bar.' A corpulent French farmer handed it to them with a few guttural words of instruction.

'Did you understand that?' hissed Clover, as they got back into the car.

Laura shook her head. 'Accent too strong. But I don't suppose it matters. We've got the instructions in English on how the house works.'

They turned right into a courtyard. 'Wow,' said Clover. 'It's like something out of Grimm's fairytales. I love the turrets, and look – gargoyles and dragons on the guttering.'

Laura didn't say anything.

Clover worked the huge key into the lock and pushed open the front door. It was about fourteen feet high and painted a weathered blue. Inside, the château was cool and dark.

They went from room to room, pushing open tall doors to reveal a pretty blue-painted dining room with a huge gilt mirror, a vast farmhouse kitchen with a dresser stacked with blue-and-white plates, and a stiff formal drawing room ('Don't the French ever have comfortable sofas?' asked Laura). Clover's spirits rose. The stable extension was just beyond the kitchen and even Laura had to admit that it had been done beautifully, with old brick and beams and a vaulted ceiling. The terracotta floor tiles didn't look as new and harsh as they'd seemed in the pictures on the internet, and each of the twin beds was a four-poster. There was a grey leather sofa and matching armchair. 'Almost like a bed-sitting room,' said Clover. 'And your sofa at last.'

Back through the house they threw shutters and doors open, and found a long stone balcony running along the back, overlooking a delightfully overgrown garden and a path to the swimming pool. They climbed the attic stairs to a long, low corridor under the eaves, off which were several little rooms that had obviously once been occupied by servants. 'The terrace downstairs will be perfect for drinks at sunset,' conceded Laura, looking out of a window at a small wood around the château, and the sunflower fields undulating beyond. 'I suppose finding special things is part of Alice's job. Naturally, she's good at it.'

'She probably found it when she was looking for somewhere to shoot a catalogue. She keeps a file of everything she comes across that she likes. Oh look, we've even got mobile reception up here.' Clover clambered on to a chair and waved her phone around. 'Just. If you stand on a chair and stick your hand up as high as you can.'

'Results day will be fun, then. We'll all be up here balancing on chairs at seven in the morning.'

There was a beep as Clover's phone received a message. 'Can you imagine how the children would have loved this when they were about ten? And I think they'll love it now, but you could be right about them needing nightclubs as well.'

Laura looked pleased. 'I'm sorry I'm so grumpy. I just can't believe that it's actually happening: that Jamie's left school, is going to go away to university, and that it's the end of us being his home.'

'They do come back for about six months of the year, you know. And just think of all the new things you'll be able to do. Or you can go back to acting.' Clover's heart contracted painfully. She too was trying not to think about September. Well, obviously results day had to come first, but Holly had an insurance offer and surely she couldn't fail both. 'And there are all sorts of exciting things we can do that we couldn't before.'

'I just don't know how I'm going to cope. I can't bear the thought of Jamie not being there when I get up in the morning. It must be all right for Alice, she's practically never in the same house as Lola anyway.'

Clover ignored the latest dig at Alice. 'You get used to it. Ben's been away for seven months, and we've survived.'

She remembered the day they'd taken Ben to the airport. It had been the most painful thing she had ever done. Usually, as parents, they divided trips. You take Holly to riding, I'll take Ben to rugby. You pick Holly up, I'll get Ben later. But this time neither had wanted to miss their last precious minutes with Ben, although he'd been snappish and nervous in the car, and had said that he didn't know when he'd be able to get in touch. At the airport they'd met up with his travelling companion, Kieran, so he'd rushed their last hugs. He wanted to be off, and not to seem childish.

She and George had waited beside security, watching Ben shuffle forward in the queue, deep in conversation with Kieran. Just before he stepped through the scanner he turned round and waved, stopping for a second as if reluctant to go. Then, with one last lopsided grin and one more wave, her beautiful boy had stepped through the scanner and was gone. That had been seven months ago. It seemed for ever ago. And just yesterday.

Neither George nor Clover had spoken on their way back to the car park. As they got into the car George had smiled. 'Well, one down. One to go.'

He and Ben had a sparky father–son relationship. Ben was a disappointment to George, who had been a scientist and an athlete. Captain of his school's cricket team and still a Sunday player. In the first team for rugby at both his school and at university. Ben was clumsy and wrapped up in computers. George had gone to veterinary college in London, Ben had been rejected for most of his choices, settling eventually on media studies at York. 'Such a good university!' Clover had said. 'Well done!'

'If he'd worked a bit harder and applied himself more, he'd have a few more choices,' George had muttered. 'Media studies isn't a serious degree.'

'Yes it is. And it's so difficult to get an offer anywhere these days. It was so much easier for us, in our generation.'

But, driving away from the airport, Clover could see the lines of his face drawing downwards with sadness that Ben had gone. Or perhaps it was regret that Ben would never now be the son he could cheer on from the touchline.

Clover had been unable to speak for the rest of the journey, and had walked around in stunned shock until she got a text from Mumbai fifteen hours later. 'Just arrived! Amazing colours and very crowded. XXX'. He had survived. He would survive. She had done her job as a mother.

Since then, she had kept her mobile phone with her at all times, even placing it under her pillow while she slept. If there was to be a call from India, from Thailand, from New Zealand or Australia, she wasn't going to miss it.

And every day she scoured the papers, the TV and the internet for news of air crashes, bus crashes, insurrections and storms. In newspapers the faces of young men who died abroad jumped out at her – the tanned, open smiles of the soldiers killed in action, the fuzzy prom photos of the teenagers killed in climbing accidents, the innocent Facebook pictures of the victims of car crashes. Her eyes always blurred with tears at the lost lives, turning the boys' faces into Ben's over and over again. It would be lovely not to have newspapers on holiday, and to have Ben there, well and safe.

'It was fine when Ben went,' she lied to Laura. 'You get used to it.' She hid her face, checking the text message. 'Oh. It's Alice.'

'They're here.' Laura sounded excited. 'Look, from here you can see our car turning into the drive.'

Alice's text was forgotten in the cries of astonishment at the fairytale turrets and the height and scale of the rooms. 'Isn't it lovely,' shrieked Laura, hugging them all as if she hadn't seen any of them for days. 'Don't you think it's the prettiest place ever? Now bring your case straight upstairs, Jamie, so I can get you unpacked before we have supper.'

Chapter 5

Clover and George met Ben at the airport the following morning. He was taller, tanned and had filled out, with a wispy goatee. His unruly light brown hair, which had been exactly the same shade as George's, was bleached by the sun. He seemed very much more than seven months older.

When Clover eventually stopped hugging him, George clapped Ben on the shoulder. Clover was struck again by how alike they were. Ben was lanky, while George was solid, but their skin had a similar olive undertone. They went brown almost immediately. There was nothing distinctive about either of them – none of Tim's sculptured good looks or Duncan's gypsy cool – but they were faces that were easy to like.

'What's this bumfluff, then?' joked George, chucking his son under the chin.

Ben grinned sheepishly. 'A bet we made at the full-moon party on Koh Samui. Who could grow the biggest beard in time for getting home. Kieran won: he looks like Captain Birdseye.'

Back at Château St Etienne, over salad and French bread eaten at a long table under a vine-covered pergola, Jamie,

Holly and Lola all questioned him at once about the beaches he'd camped on, the ashram he'd spent a week in, the surfing festival under the stars and the work he'd managed to find picking melons in Australia. George nodded approval, uncritical of his son for once. Laura told him, over and over again, how gorgeous he looked with his hair longer and that lovely tan, and how much they had all missed him. Clover sat back and listened, sipping white wine and basking in the warmth reflected off the grey stone of the château walls and the knowledge that Ben could find his way around the world alone.

'Where's Tim?' she asked.

'The reception is hopeless here,' said Laura crossly. 'He went off to find an internet café. Or somewhere he can get into his e-mails.'

'Oh, I knew I'd forgotten something.' Clover hastily pulled her mobile out of her pocket. 'I got a message from Alice yesterday, when we were upstairs in the attic.'

'What did she say?'

'Oh ...' Clover scrolled through it '... she wants to bring Duncan and his son down with her. She says, is it OK if they have the spare twin room? And to text her back within twenty-four hours if it's no, because she's hoping they can all drive down together. They should be with us this evening.'

'Really!' exclaimed Laura. 'It's a bit much. She can't just turn up unannounced like that with two men in tow. I'd thought Ben would like to have that room to himself, as he's older—'

'I'm cool sharing with Jamie,' interrupted Ben.

'And I'm cool sharing with Ben.' Jamie's eyes gleamed with amusement. 'Mum can tidy both our sock drawers.'

'Clover can tidy Ben's sock drawer,' snapped Laura.

'Ben can tidy his own sock drawer,' Clover replied. 'If he's got any socks left, that is.'

'I've got a sock left,' conceded Ben. 'A white one, with a hole in the toe.'

'And you started out with how many pairs?' asked George, the old edge in his voice.

'They're only socks, Dad, I'm wearing flip flops most of the time anyway.'

'Children, children,' said Holly, banging the table with a spoon. 'Can we all concentrate on the extremely exciting news that Joe Hesketh, hottest dude at St Crispian's, is actually joining *our* family holiday. If there's any problem with room sharing he can certainly bunk up with me and Lola. All that cool sophistication you've picked up on your travels . . .' Holly snapped her fingers at her brother ' . . . is to no avail. You look like a dork next to Joe.'

Out of the corner of her eye Clover saw George frown. 'I thought Alice was supposed to have a meeting in New York. Wasn't that why she couldn't come at the beginning like the rest of us?'

'Mummy's meetings are often getting cancelled.' Lola spoke for the first time. She looked like a carbon copy of her mother, slim and honey-coloured, with big grey-green eyes and long shiny hair, but she was quiet and studious. Clover often worried about her.

'Even so,' said Laura. 'It's leaving it very late to find out if anyone objects.'

'That's my fault,' admitted Clover. 'I turned my mobile off and forgot to turn it on again until we got here, and then there was only reception up in the roof. Alice sent the text two days ago, just after we left.'

'Oh, I'm not blaming you.' Catching sight of Lola's anxious face, Laura softened. 'It's all fine. It'll be lovely. We'll have such fun, won't we? And I gather Duncan's brother is a top-flight barrister, so he might be useful in getting Jamie a really good internship next summer.'

Jamie rolled his eyes in embarrassment.

Chapter 6

A week into the holiday, Laura put all the Dangerfield clothes through the wash and stacked them up for ironing. She could hear the soft pop of a tennis ball bouncing and landing, and Tim's odd shout of 'well played' or Jamie's 'Dad, you're an arsehole', as they played Joe and George in a men's doubles. A murmur of voices and the occasional laugh from the kitchen signalled that Alice and Clover were putting lunch together. The girls and Ben were working on their tans by the pool. She wasn't sure where Duncan was, but he'd shown a tendency to go off exploring and come back with the news that there was a 'good bar' just next to a 'promising-looking restaurant'. He usually seemed to feel it was necessary to assess the restaurant by having a lager at the bar. Tim and George always agreed with him, and the three men would disappear for an hour or so.

Laura felt very alone, as she methodically picked up one garment after another and worked the tip of the iron into every little crease, comforted by the crisp edges and sense of control that ironing gave her. Alice, with her throwaway lines and casual warmth ('Darling, what heaven!' was her most frequent exclamation), seemed to have commandeered Clover's attention, and Tim, as always, was remote. Pleasant. Bland.

Hidden behind the busyness of his life. Seemingly compliant. If she told him it was his turn to do the washing up, he did it. When they'd run out of balsamic vinegar she'd asked him to get some more and he'd got into the car and returned with it an hour later (An hour? Where had he been? At the internet café or phoning from the top of the hill?). But she had no idea what he was thinking, and if she asked him, he just smiled and said, 'Nothing much. Just a project I'm on.'

It was like having a relationship with a sheet of glass. You could see life on the other side, but you couldn't touch it or feel it. A large tear plopped on to a pair of Jamie's boxer shorts, and Laura furiously ironed it away.

She'd never told anyone – not even Clover – that Tim had had an affair five years ago. They'd talked. They'd been to couples' counselling. They'd looked at the finances. And they'd looked at Jamie. And agreed that if they divorced Jamie would suffer, and that there wasn't enough in the pot to fund two lifestyles anyway.

So Laura was trapped. Tim had spoilt everything. He more or less slept in his 'dressing room', the small single room beside theirs, ever since, and she had made it clear that she couldn't contemplate sex with him, not after he'd been with someone else. She had some self-respect, even if he didn't.

They had started out with such dreams. The fashionable conservation architect and the well-known actress had recognised ambition in each other from the start. They were engaged three months after meeting, and married in six. He was going to be the face of restoration in Britain. She was going to be one of those actresses who do a few high-profile jobs a year, prioritising motherhood over being a star. They would have four children. She would bring them up beautifully: no television, lots of music and sport, and they would never, ever have fast food. They would live in a house in the country, with fields and ponies, and dogs, and each child would have its own vegetable patch, and she would ensure that they fulfilled their potential by putting aside plenty of time for homework, music practice and reading. It would all be so different from her own miserable childhood, with a bullying father and a defeated, frightened mother.

She would be proud of her children and would cheer them on. There would be treats for good reports (never chocolate, of course). Not like when her report used to arrive. Her heart always jumped when she heard the thud of the envelopes as they hit the doormat. The air in the house immediately became thick with tension. Laura was usually top of the class, while her brother struggled not to end up bottom, to her father's fury. He didn't think it was worth educating girls. 'The boy's got to earn his living,' he'd say, alternately shouting at her brother for his string of failures or, less often, praising him for getting a B minus in geography. He would open Laura's report with its stream of As and highly commendeds, read it silently, then tear it up and throw it in the waste-paper basket. 'Well, what are you standing there for?' he'd snap. 'Why aren't you helping your mother in the kitchen?'

When Laura met Tim she knew she could give her children the childhood she'd never had. They'd taken out a mortgage they couldn't really afford to buy the farmhouse with five acres just outside Canterbury, among gently rolling orchards and fields. Laura got pregnant immediately. And miscarried. And miscarried and miscarried, until finally, one day, two months early, darling Jamie was born, clinging on to life.

She always told herself that she'd given up a successful career as an actress for Jamie and all the other little Jamies she'd hoped would be come after him. Then there had been an ectopic pregnancy, a haemorrhage and, finally, a hysterectomy. With just one precious, fragile child she dared not take her eye off him for a second. And now here she was, with a husband who barely spoke to her and a son who was clearly irritated by her, ironing fourteen pairs of boxer shorts on what ought to be her holiday.

Alice and Clover were lounging in the kitchen chairs, drinking wine. Alice was idly slicing some local ham into wafer-thin shards. Everything Alice did looked easy.

Laura sat down with a thump. 'I seem to have been working all morning.'

'Well, at least Tim's cooking supper tonight. You can take a back seat,' said Alice.

Laura rolled her eyes. 'Yeah, that means that he waves a few ingredients around while I scurry about chopping and washing up. You know me, I'm the sort of person who can't sit down until absolutely everything is cleared up. It'll be like being at home but without the well-equipped kitchen.' This, as well as being unfair to Tim, who was an excellent cook, was a dig at Alice as the château kitchen was certainly quite rickety. There was a large – usually warm – fridge with a door that didn't shut properly, and an oven with two temperatures: On (very hot) and Nearly Off (very low). Laura had had to abandon several of her fail-safe recipes because she knew they would turn out raw or charred.

'Perhaps we ought to split the couples up for cooking,' suggested Clover. 'Why doesn't Alice help ... er ... George, I'll help Tim and you can work with Duncan?'

Laura suppressed annoyance at Clover's cheerful common sense, but couldn't think of a reason to object to her suggestion. Eventually she shrugged. 'That would be lovely. If neither of you mind.'

'It seems a good way of giving you a break from having to partner Tim, and, as you said, you have been working all morning.' Alice seemed amused by the arrangements. And, of course, she would always back Clover up. It was like going on holiday with a double act.

'Perhaps that would be a good idea. I don't feel all that well,' admitted Laura.

'We were talking about what we were going to do with our new-found freedom once the kids have gone,' said Clover. 'Will you go back to acting?'

'Yes, I rang my former agency the other day,' Laura improvised. 'They asked me to come in in September, after Jamie goes, and they might have a few auditions lined up.' In fact, Laura had gone to her agent's retirement party and the phone call she had made had merely been to clarify the dress code. There had been no mention of auditions. But there might have been.

Alice never seemed to realise that she, Laura Dangerfield, had, as Laura Winter, been really quite a big name. 'Of course, my original agent has retired now, but her assistant has taken over and is now very senior. She remembers loving me in *Bottoms Up*, which she saw when she came home from school in the summer.' She could see Alice looking perplexed. 'You know, that long-running veterinary series. I played the second lead, the sexy receptionist who everyone kept falling in love with.'

Alice nodded vaguely. Probably didn't like anyone else being in the limelight. 'When was that?'

'Oh, around fifteen years ago.' Laura did a quick calculation. 'Actually, a bit longer than that because it had just finished when Tim and I met. So . . . '

'You had your twenty-fifth wedding anniversary last year,' Clover reminded her. 'It was a great party.'

'Oh. Of course. Well, twenty-five, maybe twenty-six years ago.' Laura had seen a video of *Bottoms Up* for sale in a charity shop. Her face – and the other faces on the cover – seemed bland, unformed and blurry. Their hair seemed extraordinarily bouffant.

'I must have missed it. That was when I was living in Kabul,' said Alice, and they all had to hear about how she'd trekked across India and then Afghanistan, and had started her retail career by bringing back a suitcase full of smelly coats. As if the Sunday supplements hadn't done that story to death already.

'So.' When Alice finished, she cocked her head at Laura, as if she was really interested. 'Did you give up acting when Jamie was born?'

'I went on for a bit – I used to take him to auditions in his buggy, but casting directors don't want mothers, you know. They think that if there's a crisis with the baby you'll be off. I only discovered later that some actresses were taking off their wedding rings and keeping the fact they had a baby secret when they went for an audition.' She remembered getting the odd job, an advertisement for rubber gloves and a small part in a West End play. She had felt lumpen and awkward, her body permanently distorted by motherhood. The easy confidence she'd had as a young actress had been stripped away too, as she had become terrifyingly aware of life's fragility and how precious it was. She could see how much could go wrong, and the awareness followed her on stage, making her sound frightened and wooden.

'I decided Jamie needed me,' she concluded, determined to show Alice what real values were. 'There's no more important a job than motherhood and my agent told me she could get me parts any time once Jamie was at school.'

What her agent had actually said was 'Darling, you're not getting enough sleep and it shows. There's no make-up for that red-eye look, your hair is like straw and you look exhausted. Come back when Baby is sleeping through the night.'

Which, as it happened, was when Jamie was five and went to school. By that time Laura knew that bringing up this little person, making him the very best he could be, was the only job she wanted. It also meant that Tim could concentrate on building his business. 'Even once they go to school,' she told Alice, 'your children need you when they need you, and you can't always predict when that will be.'

'Hello girls.' George shambled into the kitchen like a big bear. 'Or, sorry, am I not supposed to call you that these days?'

Laura looked up at him. Despite the untidiness, there was something very masculine about him. He was good at changing a tyre but hopeless in the kitchen, unlike Tim's even-featured metrosexual ability to bake his own bread and stuff chickens with olives. 'You can certainly call *me* a girl,' she said. 'But Alice is quite an important businesswoman, so she may find it demeaning.'

Alice responded with one of her big, surprisingly dirty-sounding laughs. Laura felt wrong-footed again, as Duncan, in safari shorts and aviator sunglasses, drifted into the kitchen. Now there was a man who really was easy on the eye. Laura noticed that his brown, sinewy legs had a fine dusting of hair, placing him in just the right point on the spectrum between man and monkey. 'There's a lot of laughing going on in here,' he said. 'Am I missing a joke?'

'We were just discussing whether we should split couples up for cooking in the evening,' said Clover. 'So that husbands and wives are less tempted to hack each other to death with the meat cleaver.'

'I don't really know any of you well enough to hack you to

death with the meat cleaver. So fit me in wherever you like. I do a mean chilli con carne, but the rest of my culinary repertoire is a bit limited. Although I can barbecue.'

A real man, thought Laura, smiling at him.

'Laura was telling us about her career as a star of stage and screen,' said Alice.

Was she teasing? Laura blushed. 'I used to be Samantha on *Bottoms Up*.'

'Of course! I *thought* your face looked familiar. Every red-blooded male in Britain was mad about you.' Duncan appraised her. 'I should have recognised you immediately, you've hardly changed.'

He was flattering her, but it was still nice. Laura felt tears start behind her eyes. It seemed so long since anyone had complimented her. It was always her making the running, telling everyone how marvellous they were, cheering everyone up. No one ever turned round and told *her* how wonderful she was.

'Well,' he added. 'I can't wait. Making chilli con carne with Samantha from *Bottoms Up*. It's every man's dream.' He opened the fridge and took out a lager. 'Anyone else? No?' He picked up his book – a thriller, Laura noticed, not like Tim's award-winning tomes with long names and terrifyingly serious reviews – and drifted off.

Laura flashed a quick look at Alice, who was presumably having some kind of affair with this man – although he seemed to be occupying his own room as far as anyone could tell – to see if she minded, but Alice had leant forward to whisper something to Clover. She felt the tears start again. Clover was her friend, and Alice had bewitched her. Neither of them was thinking about Laura.

She put a hand to her head. 'Actually, if you don't mind me missing lunch I think I'll have a lie-down.' She sniffed. 'It must be the dust in the curtains or maybe I'm going down with something.'

They let her go with cries of concern, but she could hear them all laughing again as she lay in bed. The stable extension was so close to the kitchen.

Chapter 7

On the evening before results day – the second to last of the holiday – it was Duncan's turn to cook, assisted by Laura. Afterwards, the Crew were going to go into town to find a nightclub.

'We won't be able to sleep,' said Holly. 'We might as well dance.'

'That's a good philosophy for life.' George gazed at his daughter approvingly.

Laura, who had spent most of the previous day in bed and appeared in the morning in a fragile state, declining coffee and croissants ('Wheat allergy, darlings' she had said reproachfully, her fingers pressed to her forehead) and turning the kitchen over in search of a herbal tea, came to life. She sat drinking white wine at the table as Duncan chopped and stirred.

Every so often Clover put her head round the kitchen door. 'Do you need any help in here?'

'No, no,' said Laura. 'We're absolutely fine. You have a nice relaxing time. Duncan is helping me decide how I'm going to repaint Jamie's room when he goes off to uni. Jamie doesn't seem to mind at all, but obviously I want to it to be appropriate. Duncan thinks that as it's a south-facing room I could probably get away with pale grey rather than cream.'

Clover sighed with relief and went back to the long stone terrace, where Alice was enjoying an evening drink.

'She's furious with me, isn't she?' said Alice. 'Was it because I suggested this place rather than the one she originally chose?'

'No, really not. I think she's been genuinely ill. She told me several times how much she loves this place and how perfect the extension is for her.'

'Hmm.' Alice was not convinced. 'Is it the nude sunbathing? That's why I wanted the private terrace, so I could tan in the buff without anyone noticing.'

Clover spluttered with laughter. 'Every single one of the men, and especially Joe, Jamie and Ben, finds about a hundred reasons why they have to walk from the swimming pool to the house and back a million times while you're on your "private" terrace.' She wiggled her fingers to emphasise the word 'private'. 'When you stand up to rearrange your towel or get another drink, I'm afraid there's not a lot left to the imagination.'

Alice looked abashed. 'Sorry. Do you mind?'

'Of course not.' But Clover suppressed a twinge of unease. 'And Laura?'

Clover hesitated. What Laura had actually said was, 'I'm worried that seeing an older woman naked will traumatise the boys. You know, Alice is not in the first flush of youth, and the sight of all that wrinkled flesh may well put them off sex, with dreadful consequences in the long run.'

Tim had made the matter worse by looking up from the latest Booker Prize winner and saying 'Alice's flesh is not wrinkled.'

George had added that nothing could put an eighteen-year-old boy off sex.

Laura had stormed off without comment, and had spent the next three hours lying down in her room.

'Laura will be fine,' Clover said, deciding that passing any of this on would only make things worse. 'Don't take any notice. What she's really upset about is Jamie leaving home, and that's why she's in such a grump with us all. She's never normally like this.' She paused. 'Well, not often anyway. She's usually charming, and very positive. The first person to say something nice about anyone.'

Alice nodded. 'Yeah. I think the kids' going is affecting us all, so maybe none of us are exactly at our best.' She stretched out her legs in the sun. 'But poor Tim is freezing to death out there. Have you noticed that Laura never, ever speaks to him, except to snap at him or cut across him? And, you know, he's a nice, intelligent person.'

'Yes, you certainly seemed to be enjoying his company last night.' Clover fixed Alice with a firm look. 'But I think that if you do all that laughing and asking interested questions again tonight, then Laura, in her present mood, may well tip the chilli con carne over your head.'

'I don't want to steal Tim,' said Alice with gleam in her eye. 'I'd just like to play with him for a bit.'

'Well don't.'

'We're going running together. He says he prefers to go with someone – he has a running buddy at home.'

'Alice. Do. Not. Cause. Trouble. With. Laura. OK?'

Alice laughed her wild, mischievous laugh. 'I promise.'

'Hmm,' Clover replied. 'I think you've got your fingers crossed behind your back. Concentrate on Duncan. I like him.'

'I do too, but he's after a wife, and I'm not exactly wife material.'

'Well, as you said, we're all going to be different after the kids have gone. You might find you have room in your life for a husband.'

Alice looked genuinely surprised, as if she'd never thought of that.

But it was George who was worrying Clover. Apart from telling Duncan and Laura that it was a great chilli con carne, he barely spoke at supper. From time to time Clover saw his expression harden as he looked at Joe and Holly, who always seemed to be either giggling with him or hanging on his every word.

Joe seemed more mature than the rest of the Crew, perhaps because he'd flunked his first AS year of A levels when his mother had died, so he'd come to St Crispian's to start the whole two-year course again. As a result, Joe was nearly twenty, older even than Ben, and seemed to have a permanent five o'clock shadow. Maybe his mother's death had made him grow up faster, too. You could see real strength in his sinewy body. His dark eyes, almost hidden by the shock of dark hair that kept falling across them, made his face seem brilliantly intense. Studying Duncan, Clover could see what Joe would look like in thirty years' time. Duncan caught her eye and held it for a second before smiling. Clover quickly looked away.

Around Joe's neck was a leather thong with a silver charm, which he occasionally touched – the only sign, perhaps, that he ever got nervous. Even when the rest of the Crew – usually very quick to criticise or taunt an adult – hesitated or deferred, he was always challenging and confident. Duncan said that Joe got this from his mother. 'Once she got an idea in her head, there was never any telling her.'

George did not like Joe. You could see it in the way he always addressed Joe if he had to reprove any of the Crew: 'Joe, there's damp swimming kit strewn all over the furniture, you need to clear it up before it causes any damage', or 'Joe, have you kids finished off a whole bottle of vodka in three days?' Clover hoped that the others weren't picking up on the tension between them.

'It must have been awful for him, losing his mother when he was only seventeen,' she pleaded with George. 'And I know he looks older, but he's still a child.'

'He is not a child. Unlike Holly, who really is very innocent in spite of her pretending that she isn't.'

'Holly can look after herself. She's no fool.'

'She's a very bright girl, but those are often the ones that fall the hardest. She's used to people who play straight, and I can tell that Joe Hesketh is a manipulator.'

'Are you sure? What makes you think that?'

But George just shook his head, his brow furrowed. Now he'd withdrawn, with a cigar (offered to him by Duncan), to the far corner of the terrace. He smoked and looked out into the blackness of the trees.

'Smoking?' Clover placed a hand on his shoulder, and he reached up to cover it with his.

'Once a year is OK. Trust me, I'm a scientist. Or I was, anyway, before Petfast got me in their clutches. Thinking about the kids' degrees makes me remember my own. I'm not sure I expected to end up in middle management.' He liked to complain that Petfast cut too many corners and that they should spend more on research and less on marketing.

Clover sat down beside him. 'Are you worried about Holly's results?'

He didn't answer. But he didn't deny it.

'You seem much more worried than you were about Ben's. Holly will be all right, I know she will.' Although, of course, she didn't know anything of the sort. 'Unless there's something else wrong?'

'Mm?'

She could hear the loud chirruping of the cicadas, and the

low murmur of voices from inside. Touching his arm, she repeated her question. 'Is there anything wrong?'

George seemed to come back from distant thoughts, and gave her a brief smile. 'What? No, no, it's fine.' He inhaled and blew the smoke out in a slow, careful ring. 'Yes. Holly's results. Tomorrow morning at six. Seven o'clock French time. A verdict on our success as parents, don't you think?'

'No!' Clover was surprised. George wasn't usually introspective. 'It's ... it's not a verdict on anyone or anything. They're just results.'

'It's all such a big deal, isn't it? Holly is such a great girl, she's clever, she's hardworking. And she wants to go to Leeds so much.'

'I'm sure she'll get her A and two Bs. Easily. But Ben is clever too. You never give him credit.' Clover knew that this was several glasses of wine talking, its corrosive action stripping away common sense to expose her barely buried resentment that Ben so rarely got approval from his father.

'He's certainly bright,' said George, 'but he doesn't work. He's idle, and he will miss out on his chances in life unless he pulls himself together.'

'He worked hard to get the money for his gap year together. He was doing double shifts at the bar.' Clover took George's hand in hers. His skin was thinner and softer these days. The hand she'd held for so many years seemed less strong.

Clover and George had been at neighbouring schools, something that both Holly and Ben claimed to find difficult to live up to. 'You guys have known each other for ever,' wept Holly on being dumped by her first serious boyfriend. 'I thought it would be like that with me and Matt.' Ben, too, had been dumped, although he hadn't spoken about it, retiring to his room to play *Grand Theft Auto* and snarling at anyone who tried to cheer him up. Eventually Holly had interpreted his grief to Clover and George. 'He feels a failure. At his age, you two were already an item.'

'No, we weren't,' said George. 'Your mother was part of the cool gang, the arty set, and I was a science geek. I was terrified of her. I kissed her once, after a school disco, and didn't dare try again for five years.'

'But you were all part of the same gang. You must have known you'd finish up together. You shared a common language,' wailed Holly, determined to believe that no one had ever suffered as she had.

'Yes. It's called English. And you're part of a group too, Miss Misery.' It was pointless for Clover to explain that, although they had become roughly part of the same crowd, they'd both had liaisons with other people that had culminated in either boredom or heartbreak. It wasn't until ten years later when they were both working in London – George as a junior vet and Clover at a graphic design studio – that they'd got talking and discovered that they both wanted to walk Hadrian's Wall. The bed and breakfast George had booked them into had double-booked its second room. They agreed to share a double bed.

Even after that, their affair had progressed slowly. They'd even split up for eighteen rather miserable months. George had gone into small-animal practice outside London. Clover worked at the design studio and continued to party with her girlfriends until one day she discovered she was pregnant.

Life had suddenly, thrillingly, become crystal clear. Of course they were in love. They couldn't imagine their lives without each other. Unable to afford to buy in London, George had got a job with Petfast in Canterbury and they'd bought a tiny two-bedroom terraced house in Faversham, where Ben had been born, followed by Holly. Clover gave up graphic design but managed to combine some painting and art teaching with motherhood, and here they were. Sitting on a terrace in the South of France, their children grown up, listening to the cicadas and each knowing exactly what the other was thinking.

Or did they? 'We've never really been alone together, have we?' said Clover.

But George knew what she meant. 'We went out for quite a long time. Five years. Minus eighteen months, I suppose.'

'Not living together. Not as a couple. We were both still pretty independent.'

'But you were always the one. I never doubted that.' He squeezed her hand.

Clover had known that. She'd always known she could rely on George's love but, secretly, she hadn't been quite sure that it was what she wanted.

But when she looked back on the early days of their life together – the small, crowded terrace, the sleepless nights and interminable days with a small baby, and then a toddler and a baby, their little hands constantly clutching at her, the excitement of the move to the rural Fox Hollow with its four bedrooms, and the sense, constantly, of growth and development and going somewhere, she remembered happiness.

'It's easier for you,' she said. 'You've got your job. That won't change. But the whole of my life will be different. No school runs. No giant weekly shops. No teaching or sitting on committees at school.' She tried to think what else she might lose. Hugs. A constant barrage of being told how annoying she was. 'Perhaps we should do that drive across the States?'

But George was back in his private world, studying the brilliance of the distant stars in the sky. 'What with AS results and all the predictions they get, and all the care the school takes' – he seemed to be talking to himself – 'it would be extraordinary for any of them not to get their grades.' He came back to earth and stubbed out his cigar. 'I'm going to sort something out in the attic so we can get on to the internet in the morning rather than having to wait for the café to open,' he said, getting up. 'Tim and Duncan will help.'

He seemed to have more to say to Tim – or even Duncan – than he did to her these days. She heard the men laughing as they took a bottle of brandy upstairs to drink while they rigged up a way of getting a signal.

The following morning, all the parents were up well before seven, gazing sightlessly into cups of coffee. Clover saw Laura surreptitiously stuff a croissant into her mouth. Holly, Lola, Jamie and Joe were strewn around the ground floor like discarded toys. Holly and Lola were propped up against each other on the hard upright sofa, and the boys sprawled on chairs, their mouths open and their arms dangling. Ben, without the pressure of results day, had made it to his bed. 'Wake up.' Clover touched them each gently and they started.

'I don't want to know,' Holly moaned. 'I know I've failed everything! Please don't make me find out.'

Alice put her hand out and Lola took it. 'Come on, let's get it over and done with.' They walked upstairs, hand in hand, as if Lola were five.

In the attic, George, Tim and Duncan had set up an old bookcase with a table propped against it. 'You climb up there, so you can get a signal on George's laptop. It's got a dongle. Who's going to go first?'

'Not me!' shrieked Holly. 'I'd rather die.'

'I think you might well die.' Laura frowned at the contraption. 'That doesn't look at all safe to me. Lola, would you like to go first?'

Lola shook her head furiously. She was ashen.

'Joe?' George glared at him.

He shrugged and jumped nimbly up on the table, tapping in his codes in seconds. Then, in one sinuous movement, he came down, raising one hand to his father, his face unreadable. Duncan raised his hand in return and father and son high-fived. 'Gotcha,' said Joe. 'I'm in. Imperial College, London here I come.'

Laura shrieked and threw her arms around him. 'You're such a clever boy. Your mother would love to be—' She drew back, 'I'm sorry, I've no right to say that. I didn't know her.'

'I'm glad you did,' said Joe, picking her up and whirling her round in the crowded attic.

'Stop,' she shrieked. 'You'll hurt your back.' But she was laughing.

Behind them, Alice and Lola were cautiously picking their way up on to the table. 'Look, there,' said Alice as the room fell silent.

Lola made a surprised noise. 'I'm not sure what it means.'

Alice frowned. 'It's OK, darling, you've done it. Well done.' She put her arm round her daughter. 'Well done. Oxford for you. Now get down carefully.' Clover had never heard Alice tell Lola to be careful before.

Lola, half-sobbing, kissed each adult in turn.

'I suppose I'd better look,' muttered Holly, clambering up with something that looked like eagerness. They all fell silent as she punched in her codes. 'Yay!' She jumped down, and bounced round the room shouting 'We are the champions! We are the champions!' so noisily that no one – except Laura, who was hovering anxiously – noticed Jamie manoeuvring his gawky frame up on to the table.

'Well, darling?' Laura's high voice cut through Holly's. The room was suddenly still, although Clover could hear George whisper to Holly that he was very proud of her.

'Uh, you'd better check that, Dad. I'm not sure . . .'

'Jamie is so modest,' murmured Laura to Clover. 'He just can't believe he's got the grades.'

The table creaked as Tim stepped up and studied the screen carefully. He put an arm round Jamie. 'Let's get down.'

'Well?'

Jamie ignored Laura until they were both standing on the ground. 'Jamie, this is your news to tell,' murmured Tim, putting an arm around Jamie's shoulders.

Clover caught Alice's eye and they gently pushed everyone out of the room as Laura's face turned grey. She didn't have time to close the door before they heard a shriek.

'Jamie, how could you do this to me?' Laura cried. 'This is your fault, Tim, distracting him with sport when he should have been revising.'

Chapter 8

September was the worst month of Laura's life. Jamie's disastrous results – only one A, and that was in art – had meant that he had not just failed to get into Leeds, but also his insurance choice, Gwent. They'd rung the school and found out that the whole geography class had dropped a grade and, after further to-ing and fro-ing between the school and the examination board, it was conceded that there had been some kind of administrative error. This meant that Jamie's grades, along with some frantic negotiations, had at least got him into Gwent. Suppressing the thought that top law firms didn't recruit from the old polytechnics, unless they were outstanding – and Gwent's only claim to fame was the vast amount of money the government had spent on its buildings – Laura put on a brave face. She spent her time telling everyone that academic achievement wasn't everything, and that she was so proud of Jamie for being a well-rounded person.

It was her job to make sure that this early setback didn't dent Jamie's confidence. She told him that Gwent was really great so often that he finally turned round and told her that he'd wanted to go to Leeds and was still upset that he couldn't go, but that the least he could ask for is that she would allow him to be upset.

'Jamie is so mature,' Laura told Clover. 'He'll make a great lawyer. This whole rotten system is so unfair on them, don't you think?'

Then there had been the question of driving Jamie up to Gwent. It was around four hours away, including stops. Laura had made a bid for her and Jamie to go up on their own: 'There won't be room for all the stuff in the car if there are three of us. You should have seen Holly going off to Leeds last week. The car was so full that George couldn't see out of the rear window. Both Holly and Clover had bags on their laps.'

'Holly is a girl – they always take loads of stuff. What is Jamie taking? His clothes. His guitar. His laptop. The university supplies bedding in hall, so he doesn't even have to take a duvet or pillows. And our car is certainly big enough.'

It was true that Jamie seemed curiously unattached to possessions. Laura's suggestions that he might like to take a rug, or posters, a few cushions or even framed photographs, had been met with indifference: 'I can't be bothered.' Laura hoped that this wasn't hiding despair at having to go to Gwent rather than Leeds. You heard so many stories about students committing suicide. Cold fingers clutched at her heart.

She tried emotional blackmail on Tim. 'I've spent the whole of Jamie's childhood driving him around in the car. I deserve to do this one last journey with him.'

'That's why I want to be with you. I don't want you to drive all that way, and then to have to come all the way back on your own.'

Tim didn't care about her, of course, he just wanted to be there to say goodbye to Jamie. They settled on driving up, taking it in turns, in one day, starting out early, then staying in a smart hotel and taking the journey back more slowly. What were they going to talk about?

Jamie, a talking book, Radio 4 and an interminable international cricket match sorted out the problem of conversation on the way up, but on the way back, there wouldn't be any sport and they'd finished the talking book. And Laura felt as if someone had punched her in the solar plexus. How was she to live without Jamie?

He hadn't wanted them to hang around, couldn't wait to push them out the door once he'd let Laura unpack for him. The room was small and modern, but well thought out with a single bed, a wardrobe, drawers and a basin. And a big cork board. 'For your photography. You will join the photography club, won't you?' begged Laura. 'It's so important to keep up with hobbies.'

Jamie just grunted.

As they walked away from the glittering glass towers, Tim muttering that some architects could obviously get money for old rope, Laura could barely breathe with pain.

Tim put an arm round her shoulders. 'He's just nervous. I remember when my parents dropped me off at Bristol. I was so terrified I just wanted them to go before they spotted it and started fussing.'

Normally she would have shaken Tim off, but she didn't have the strength. As he drove them to the hotel she withdrew inside her current daydream.

On results day, Tim and Jamie had gone to the top of the hill to pick up mobile reception in order to call the headmaster of St Crispian's and to get on to Clearing. After around half an hour they'd then returned to say they were going to spend the morning at the internet café and drove off again.

Laura, exhausted and sick at heart, had claimed that she'd had a reaction to the wheat in the croissant. Unable to face the other parents, including the Marchandanis, all seven of whom had driven over for a celebratory lunch, she lay down on her bed, pulling off her T-shirt and shorts, lying on top of the sheets to try to cool down in the still, heavy heat. Sandeep, of course, had got three more A stars. Laura had barely been able to congratulate Deepak and Leila.

She was drifting off when she heard the doorknob turn softly. Not wanting to have to talk to Tim, she lay still with her eyes almost closed. But through the fringes of her lashes she could soon see that the man walking quietly across the room towards her bed was not Tim.

She never knew why she didn't sit up and pull her sheet around her, or why she still pretended to be asleep. The sound of his breathing echoed her heartbeat as he stood over her bed and looked at her. Deep down, she knew that he knew she was aware of him, and that she was faking sleep.

But she lay there, in her peach silk bra and matching knickers, and let him look.

'I wanted to say' – his voice was hoarse – 'that you're very beautiful. In case that helps.'

Laura lay still and felt the warmth of his breath against her stomach as he knelt beside the bed, slipping one bra strap down to expose her breast. Then the other. His breath, warm, deliberate, roved over her body.

This is not happening, she told herself. If I seem to be asleep I can pretend it never happened. If I don't even think his name I can pretend I thought it was Tim all along.

His mouth fixed on one nipple, and she began to find it hard to breathe. He must have noticed that her chest rose and fell more quickly, and she could hear her own breaths alternating with his. But still she lay there, eyes closed and her arms by her sides. His mouth brushed against her ear.

'If you ever need me . . .' She felt him slip his hand across her stomach and beneath the silk over her hipbones, leaving something tucked into the lace. 'Call me,' he said. 'Call me any time.' And he dropped his mouth on to hers and she let herself respond. Just a kiss. Just his mouth against hers.

Not her body. Not her quivering, desperate body. She forced her limbs to lie still and straight. She kept her eyes closed. It was a game that they both understood.

She knew who it was but she would never acknowledge it. She would never call him. It would be a secret between them for ever.

He drew back, slid each bra strap up slowly, adjusting the silk to cover her breasts, and stood up. If she had opened her eyes she would have begged him to stay. Her body was starved of physical affection. It wanted him. It couldn't have him. She was Tim's wife and Jamie's mother. And doing . . . anything would have terrible repercussions, for her friendships and her family's friendships. It could rip her world apart. This moment was a dream, something that stood outside time. As long as she kept her eyes closed and lay as still as a doll.

'I'll see you,' he said softly, and the door closed behind him.

She was beautiful. She was still beautiful. After Tim's infidelity and Jamie's impatience, and the way her back and hips ached when she got out of bed in the morning, and how people's eyes now slid over her – Alice's, in particular – she drank in the words.

But it must never happen again. It had been a dream. The fantasy of a middle-aged woman. It had been a hot day and she had drifted off without noticing it.

But that didn't explain why she had a mobile phone number scrawled on a scrunched-up piece of paper inside her beautiful La Perla knickers, or why her legs trembled when she finally got up to join the others for dinner. She was careful not

71

to look at him over supper, not even when she could feel his eyes on her.

Driving away from the agony of leaving Jamie, she thought about the anonymous hands and the hunger inside herself. There was a huge, empty hole at her core.

Tim parked in front of an Elizabethan building draped in Virginia creeper, its scarlet September foliage just discernible in the fading light. A uniformed flunkey stepped forward to open the car door and, for one moment, Laura felt like a star again.

Tim's eyes met hers over the top of the car. 'Truce?' he suggested. 'Just for one night?'

She shrugged, and walked up the stone steps to find that Tim had booked the honeymoon suite. Which meant he wanted sex.

On the other hand, she realised as she pressed her hand down to check the softness of the huge four-poster bed, so did she. The encounter in France had left her liquid with desire. And she didn't care who it was with. If she could pretend in France, she could pretend here. She could pretend that Tim was someone else.

At dinner, they drank champagne and Laura constructed a story inside her head that Tim was a salesman she'd met in the lobby. She steered the conversation away from Jamie – it hurt too much to think about him anyway – and used some of her tricks from the old dating days, such as asking a man about his work and faking an interest in it. 'Really,' she murmured, sliding an oyster into her mouth, 'so it's better to use new, traditionally made roof tiles than to look for salvaged ones, because the salvaged ones might have been stolen?'

Under her lashes she thought he might have twigged, but no, men really were very easy to lead. Even husbands. 'The

Nottingham Project is six weeks late and over budget?' she echoed.

The waiter asked if they'd like coffee, and Laura dabbed her lips with her napkin. 'No, thank you. I'm exhausted, aren't you ... er ... darling?' She wondered if the waiter thought she was Tim's mistress, not his wife, because the look she had flashed him was not very wifely.

The thought was exciting. She would rather be a mistress than a wife.

'Well, that was nice.' Tim threw himself down on the bed and picked up his yachting magazine. 'We haven't been out for dinner for ages.'

She slowly unbuttoned her blouse and took as long as possible about taking it off, then slipped out of her skirt, discreetly unrolling her tights at the same time, before casually sliding her shoes on again. If she'd planned this she might have thought about suspenders. Not that Tim, his nose in *Yachting Monthly*, seemed to notice.

She walked across the room in high heels and matching La Perla.

'Navionics software is now available as an app,' said Tim. 'Interesting.'

Was he winding her up? He seemed completely unaware of her leisurely striptease. She decided to switch fantasies. Now she was a spy, and Tim was an important personage from a foreign power, whom she had to seduce. There were secrets that could destroy the world inside *Yachting Monthly*, and it was her job to make sure she got hold of them without him noticing.

She sat on the bed beside him and removed his shoes.

'There's a piece here saying the LORAN system is making a remarkable comeback. It would give us protection against the MOD's GPS-jamming trials.'

Tim seemed remote and impossible to reach. Surely he couldn't be a man she'd been married to for twenty years? He might as well have been a foreign dignitary in possession of state secrets. Perhaps he no longer found her attractive.

Perhaps he was not desperate for sex after all, because he was getting it somewhere else. For a moment Laura froze. Then she remembered the feeling of a man's breath on her belly, moving across her body. This didn't have to mean anything. It could be anonymous. Tim's remoteness, and the gaps between them, meant she could take this as a slice out of time, unrelated to anything else.

She leant across him, and took *Yachting Monthly* out of his hands. 'You've got me interested,' she said. 'I can't wait.'

Tim looked surprised.

'I'll read the article while you get undressed.' Laura stuck her nose into the magazine and tried to concentrate on a small news item about new chains and whether the ductility was lower with galvanised or marine stainless steel. In her head, the memory of a hot, still day in France ticked away.

After brushing his teeth and folding up his clothing Tim finally got into bed, switched out the light and reached towards her. In the dark, she finally allowed herself to respond, thinking of Tim as a strange man in a strange bed.

Her hand trailed down his muscled torso, and she thought of another torso, tanned and strong in the French sunshine. Tim's body, too, was firm and strong. It could be anyone's. Her hand slid down.

'What's this?' She sat up abruptly. Her fingers had circled over something that she hadn't expected to feel.

'What?' Tim sounded lazy and curious.

She leant across him and turned on the lamp. 'This swelling here. In your groin.'

He peered down. 'Is that a swelling?'

'Of course, it's a swelling, you idiot. You didn't have something the size of a banana tucked into the top of your leg when I last felt down there.'

'And how long ago was that?' asked Tim sharply. 'It's fine. It's nothing. I'm just getting older. And it's equal on either side, so there can't be anything funny about it.'

Cold fear washed over Laura. 'I'm not a doctor,' she said, 'but we need to get this looked at.'

'When I've got time.' Tim was defensive. 'You don't seem to realise that I'm actually quite busy at the moment. Especially with having had to take days off to drive Jamie up here.'

'You said you had time. I offered to do it on my own.'

'For Christ's sake.' Tim switched off the light and turned away from her.

'Tim,' she spoke softly into the dark, touching his shoulder. 'This is important. We have to get it checked out.'

'I'll see what I can do.' He sighed. 'Now let's get some sleep.'

Laura lay awake, icy cold inside. But, she told herself, she wasn't a doctor. It wasn't a lump. More of a sort of swelling thing. And perhaps Tim was right. Maybe they'd always been there, and neither of them had noticed before.

They would go to the doctor together, and the doctor would say that they were wasting his time.

Tim began to snore.

Chapter 9

In the run-up to their departure, Clover felt as if she had three children going off to university because Alice was away for three weeks, sorting out new suppliers in China and India. Lola stayed with the Joneses and did her shopping for uni – coffee mugs, student cookery book, a new coat – with Holly. Ben rolled his eyes at the idea of buying anything new, but eventually the girls dragged him off and made him buy two pairs of jeans and a leather jacket. Clover thought he might have a new girlfriend he was keeping very quiet about. But that was Ben. He was very private. Diesel whined softly as suitcases and backpacks were brought out of the loft, and the cats tried to get into them as soon as they were opened up. 'They know what suitcases mean,' said George. Diesel looked up at him adoringly. Animals always loved George.

Holly was the first to go, piling the car up with everything, alternately sobbing that she was going to hate it and that she was leaving her best friends behind and admitting that she was really quite excited. Afterwards, apart from a single text there was no news, and when Clover eventually got through to her Holly gabbled that she'd met some great people but was a bit too busy to talk.

Alice returned to Kent for a few days with Lola before

taking her for a 'last' mother–daughter holiday of shopping in Paris. First they stayed at Fox Hollow for Ben's last night. They went off in the morning, squeezing Lola's suitcases into the back of Alice's sports car while the Joneses packed their own car with Ben's things.

It was another long drive up to York, with Diesel almost on Ben's lap and the cats left behind with a neighbour looking in. George softened towards his son, hugging him.

'The gap year was a good idea,' he said as they left Ben's college. 'He does look a bit older than the others now, and he always seemed so young before. He'll be able to hold his own.'

'Were you afraid he couldn't? Is that why you've always been a bit harder on him than on Holly?' Clover knew she shouldn't bring up this argument now, because she felt shocked and numb. She was determined not to cry.

George took one hand off the steering wheel and squeezed her knee. 'Maybe. At least you're not like Laura, shoehorning poor Jamie into law when it's quite clear that nothing could be less suitable.' He laughed. 'Laura tries so hard to be the perfect mother.'

'I just can't imagine her without Jamie to fuss around. And what do you think will happen to her and Tim?'

George started to answer when his phone beeped. He read the message, frowning, and tucked it back into his pocket.

'Is there a problem?'

'No,' he said. 'Not at all.'

'Who was it?'

'Work.' He concentrated on the road ahead.

After a long drive – during which they'd talked about Holly and Ben, and Lola, and even Jamie, then about politics and what the government was doing, and then films they'd like to see – they got home to a quiet, still house. George sat down on the sofa and patted it. 'Amazing.' Diesel jumped up beside him, circled a few times and lowered himself down with a whine.

'*What?*' Clover opened the cupboard and found a tin of baked beans.

'Absolutely amazing,' he repeated, picking up the remote control.

'What?' Irritated, she put her head round the door to see what he'd found.

'I can sit on my own sofa,' he said. 'And watch my own TV.'

Clover sat down beside him and giggled. 'I see what you mean. In fact, we can *both* sit on the sofa. Together. Without anyone else getting in on the act. I don't think that's happened since 1998.' She took the remote control from him and waved it at the set. 'Do you think we can watch anything we like? Not just *America's Next Top Model*, *House* and *Family Guy*?'

'It seems very odd,' George conceded. 'But I think that may be the case.'

'Well.' Clover got up to do the beans on toast, handing the remote control back to him. 'We'd better familiarise ourselves with the TV schedules again. I feel like a battery chicken let out to roam. Not quite sure what to do with my freedom.'

'I will miss them,' said George, 'but it seems there are compensations.'

She came back a few minutes later. 'Actually, it's just baked beans. Ben ate the last of the bread before he left.'

'There certainly will be compensations,' said George, smiling up at her.

Beside him, Diesel let out a long sigh.

'We're so lucky, aren't we?' said Clover as they got into bed that night.

George put a hand out to touch hers. 'We are.'

'Lots of people are worried about not having enough to say to each other. And then there are the ones that have stayed together because of the children. Like Tim and Laura. God knows how their relationship is going to survive.'

George drew her towards him and she tucked up in the crook of his arm, happy with its familiarity. 'We should celebrate.' There was laughter in his voice.

'We should,' she agreed, knowing what he meant and running her hand down his dear, familiar chest.

He switched the light off. 'We haven't done this for a bit, have we?'

'Been too busy,' she murmured, kissing his ear. 'But that's all going to change.'

'Shall we go away somewhere?' He spoke softly, tracing his lips down her neck.

'Mmm. Somewhere nice.' She rolled towards him.

'Somewhere very, very nice.' His voice was like treacle, warm and sweet.

Chapter 10

Baxtersblog. 3 November

Hi everyone! Thanks for following this blog as we make
our way across the world in search of adventure. We'll
have to admit we had the odd tear in our eyes as we
packed up the old house. Some of the stuff will go
straight to Adam and Milly when they get their own
places, some of it will come back to us wherever we
decide to settle in the end (New Zealand? The Orkneys?
Just down the road? Who knows? That's what's so
exciting about it all!) Quite a lot of it went to the tip or
the charity shop! After twenty years in the same place
you do accumulate and it's been very freeing to know
that we've got everything we need in two suitcases and
a backpack. And Sarah's bottomless handbag, of
course!

For those of you who are new to Baxtersblog, here's
how it happened. Now that our son, Adam, is 18 and off
to uni, and our daughter Milly is just about to complete
her degree and join the world of work, we realised that
we had about ten or so more years of good health. And

we reckon it'll probably be at least that long before Adam and Milly have families of their own, and might need us to be hands-on grandparents, so now is Our Time! We both took early retirement from our jobs. The house is too big for us – and we'd like to think of another young family growing up and being happy in it – so we put everything we own on the market (including Ken's boat, at last!), and completed at the end of September, after dropping Adam off at Leeds. He and Milly will join us for Christmas – wherever we are. They think it's really cool to have parents who don't plan ahead.

We started off with a last luxury family holiday in the Seychelles, and Sarah and Milly really enjoyed the spa. Sarah knows that it'll be youth hostels and cheap hotels from now on (we really want to experience the places we see, not to be insulated in tourist air conditioning!). Then, with the house sold and our stuff in storage, we headed off to Mumbai, which has to be the most hectic city on earth! Sixteen million people jostle each other on what is really just a narrow spit of land and, in spite of all those call centres run for British banks, the poverty is still pretty dreadful. But we loved its energy and the flamboyant architecture, and the way twenty-first-century tower blocks and old-fashioned street vendors stand side by side. We couldn't resist trying some of the street food, and as a result poor Sarah had the dreaded 'Delhi Belly' for a few days, but she's fine now. From here we're going to sun ourselves on a beach in Goa, then head off to the Sun Temple of Konark, and then to Kolkata (Calcutta to you sofa surfers back home!)

Hope the M25 isn't too gridlocked and that leaves on the line aren't bringing your commuter trains to a halt! Oh, and if you want a really free-form holiday, then why not join us for a week or two? We don't know where we'll be, but if you can take off at a moment's notice get in touch. We'd love to share our adventure with you!

Clover scrolled down to read five comments, along the lines of 'Thanks, you guys. I was feeling too old to travel, but you've inspired me' and 'Now I know what to do when ours leave home.'

She forwarded it to Alice, commenting, 'The Baxters have actually done it.'

An e-mail came straight back. 'They obviously haven't heard that exclamation marks should be used sparingly!!!!'

Clover giggled as the doorbell rang. It was Laura, looking pale and strained. 'Are you busy? I was just passing after doing my shopping in town. It's weirdly light. Less than fifty pounds and only two carrier bags. So odd.'

'Yes, I find myself still cooking for four. Then George and I eat too much. Our waistbands are getting tight.'

They sat down at the kitchen table. The way they had always done. Clover pushed her laptop across the table to show Laura the blog. 'It makes me feel as if we ought to be doing the same. Making the most of life.'

Laura's nose wrinkled as she scrolled down. 'If I'm going to make the most of life, it would have to be in five-star hotels, thank you very much. And I wonder how they can afford to retire so early?'

'Well, Ken was a dentist and Sarah commuted to the City for years. They've probably got quite a nest egg.' Clover looked around at her beloved kitchen, with its years of children's pictures, and the message 'bye bye hope u miss us xxx' spelt out in wonky magnetic letters on the fridge. It was a big, friendly room – a typical opened-out back extension with cream Shaker units, and glass doors on to the garden. Clover loved it. 'I would hate to sell this house. I can't think of anything worse.'

'It's looking so gorgeous. Incredibly tidy,' commented Laura.

'Holly used to shed her clothing as she came in the door and trail it all the way through the hall, the sitting room and up the stairs. And Ben's stuff was spread all over the sofa and the kitchen table. So it's easy keeping it all tidy now.'

But Laura didn't seem to be listening.

Clover made them both mugs of tea. One mug, given for her birthday five years earlier, said 'The World's Best Mum'. The other was inscribed 'She is too fond of books, and it has turned her brain'. A later present. Laura appeared to read the inscriptions on both mugs carefully, even though she had seen them hundreds of times before.

Clover proffered a large tin of Quality Street. Laura took one absent-mindedly. 'Eat them up,' Clover urged. 'I only got them in for trick or treating, but no one knocked at the door. I've been eating them all myself. I asked the kids down the road why they hadn't come, and they said it was because we didn't have a pumpkin in the window. But I was hardly going to sit there on my own carving a pumpkin, was I? It's been almost ridiculous doing it with teenagers as it is.'

'I carved a pumpkin on my own this year,' said Laura dully. 'One of the ones from my garden. And I drove it to his uni and used it as an excuse to take Jamie out to lunch.' She tried to smile.

'Are you all right?' Clover was worried. 'It's three and a half hours to Gwent. Did you drive there and back in one day?'

'Jamie's friends obviously thought he had a very stalkerish mother.' Laura's eyes glimmered with tears.

'Laura, what's wrong?'

'Nothing. Everything's fine.' Laura seemed to drift off then come back to the present. 'I just had to see him. I had to know he was all right. But I'm fine. And how are you?' She suddenly seemed very keen to know. 'And how's George?'

Clover sighed. 'George is . . . well, he's basically fine. But I hadn't expected him to miss Holly quite so much. If that's what's wrong. He wasn't like this when Ben went travelling. But he used to do a lot of revision and stuff with her, because she was doing sciences, which, of course, is what he did too for A levels. She can tease him and wind him round her little finger, whereas Ben just irritates him.' It hurt. It still hurt to see Ben look at his father for approval then turn away.

'Funnily enough, I just saw Sheila Lewis in Tesco and she says that Nigel is just the same. She says that, to him, Ruby is the perfect girl, like Sheila was when they first met. Only shaped by him. I think she's a bit cross about it, actually.'

'I don't see how Ruby can possibly be like Sheila was when Nigel first met her. Or how even the most doting father could consider her the perfect girl. Although under all that make-up she's often a sweetie.'

Laura looked very pale. 'Seems extraordinary, doesn't it?' she said vaguely. 'Funky, loud Ruby with her endless legs and teeny-tiny skirts coming out of mousy, meek Sheila. Do you think you and I have changed that much?'

Clover shrugged. 'I can hardly remember myself before the children. I suppose that all I had to do was earn a living and amuse myself, both of which were quite fun, and that's about it.'

'Aren't we supposed to be sneaking into our departed children's bedrooms and pressing old shirts to our noses just to remember the smell of them?' Laura poured some more tea and split some on the table. 'Sorry. Sorry.'

'I'd pass out if I pressed anything of Ben's to my nose, so I rushed in, scraped everything off the floor and bunged it in the wash. No time for nostalgia.' Clover wiped the tea away and noted that Laura's hand was shaking. She kept her tone even and jokey. 'And I can't penetrate Holly's room at all: there are so many little ornaments, framed photographs, invitations, scrunchies and bits of make-up on every surface. She's pinned a notice on the door saying "This Is NOT a Guest Room. No Lodgers Allowed". Apparently they all circulate horror stories about parents who put a lodger in their rooms without telling them.'

Laura began to laugh, then burst into tears.

'What is it?' Clover touched her arm.

'You can't tell anyone. Not even George. And definitely not the kids.' Laura fumbled for a tissue and blew her nose. 'This mustn't mustn't mustn't get out to anyone.'

'OK.' Clover told George everything. But maybe there was a time for secrets.

'It's Tim.'

'Is he having an affair?' asked Clover before she could stop herself.

'No! I mean, well . . .' Laura stared at her in horror. 'Well, I don't think so anyway. Why did you assume that was what it would be?'

'It's kind of logical. Wife crying. Husband having affair. I mean, I presume he hasn't been arrested or anything? Or has he lost his job?'

'Worse than that. He's got . . . something.'

'What?'

85

'Possibly leukaemia. Or lymphoma. Or maybe even …' Laura blew her nose again. 'Maybe even Aids. They're the only three things that would account for him being … covered in swellings. He's had loads of tests, and we're waiting for the results of most of them.'

'Is there any chance that it could be something less awful?'

Laura shook her head. 'No. From the start it was clear that the doctor was worried. The GP examined him all over, then called in a colleague who also examined him. Tim said he'd never been probed and prodded so thoroughly in all his life. Then he was referred to a specialist at the hospital. And it took ten days for various appointments to come through. Even privately.' She blew her nose again. 'I know that sounds really quick, but I didn't sleep or eat properly. I kept trying to tell myself it would all be fine. I'd believe it for one moment, then the next all I could think about was Tim dying and what it would do to Jamie.' She covered her face with her hands. 'Sorry,' she murmured. 'Sorry. It's like being trapped in some terrible dark dungeon and you can't call out to anyone. I didn't go with him to the GP, but we went to the specialist together. He says there's no other possible explanation except for some very obscure jungle bug, and Tim hasn't been abroad for ages. So now Tim's had a biopsy, and loads more blood tests, and a CT scan, and we get the final verdict on Monday. I've been telling myself it's going to be fine, but I don't see how it can be.'

'Laura, I'm so sorry.' Clover didn't want to ask Laura if she was worried for herself.

But Laura answered her unspoken question. 'If it is Aids, I suppose I'll have to be tested too, but I don't have any symptoms. And we haven't … well, basically we haven't done it since I discovered he was having an affair. Five years ago. Thank God. It will be her fault, I presume. Someone who sleeps with someone else's husband is probably very promiscuous. The murderess. The absolute murderess.'

'If there's anything I can to do help . . . ' Clover's voice trailed off. Nothing would help.

'The doctor says we mustn't go on the internet, that we don't have a diagnosis until we have a diagnosis, but I couldn't help it. It was awful. Some of the leukaemias and lymphomas are curable or treatable, but some could kill him in a matter of months. And there's treatment for Aids now but it doesn't always work.'

'I don't think you should take any notice of the internet,' urged Clover. 'It's too broad-brush. Even if he's got one of the bad ones he hasn't necessarily got it badly. Like the doctor says, you haven't got a diagnosis until you've got a diagnosis. And there are huge medical advances now that can happen quite quickly.'

'I know.' Laura looked around, as if to find something else to talk about. 'I know.' She sighed. 'So what do you think of Alice's new flat?'

'What new flat?' Clover was shocked.

'Oh, sorry, I'd have thought she'd have told you.' Laura looked uneasy. 'Tim bumped into her at a conference on sustainability the other day and she said she was just completing on a two-bedroom flat in Borough. I'd have thought you'd have known, but—'

'Is he still working?'

'Oh yes. He says he feels fine. He still insists, sometimes, that it's all a stupid mistake. And he says he'd go mad if he didn't keep working.'

'Anyway, Alice has been very busy since the holiday.' Clover tried not to feel hurt. 'We haven't really spoken – not for a long chat – for weeks. Last time was after she dropped Lola at Oxford.'

'She probably thinks she's told you,' said Laura, and Clover could see that she was trying to smooth it over. 'You're one of her closest friends.'

There was a silence between them as Clover, trying not to feel excluded, also wondered whether Tim and Alice could seriously have been at the same conference on sustainability. An architect and a fashion designer? Presumably it was the only conference they could conceivably have both been at. And should she warn Alice that Tim might have Aids?

But it was ridiculous. Tim would never sleep with anyone with this hanging over him. Surely?

'So what are you going to do about George being miserable?' asked Laura. 'Ride it out?'

'Oh, it's nothing. Compared to what you're going through.' Clover suddenly felt very loving towards George. 'So what if he's a bit bad-tempered and remote? He's here, and that's all that matters. There are various things we've always talked about doing together. Not the full Baxtersblog-type adventure, but we did say that we'd take a month out and drive across America, from the east coast to the west.'

Clover struggled to focus on the subject of George, rather than the painful thought that Alice had not bothered to tell her about something as major as moving house.

'Why don't you?'

'I can't get him to concentrate on it. One minute he seems keen on us doing something special together, and the next he says "mm" and "I'm a bit busy at the moment". Or "I don't think we should go too far until we know Holly is absolutely settled".'

'I know what you mean. Tim is impossible about anything like that. We decided to sit down and list the things we wanted to do. Before all this happened, of course. His were so insular. He wants to do more sailing. Learn more about sports photography. And go on cycling holidays. All the stuff we've been doing for ever with Jamie anyway. I want to broaden our horizons and enjoy some culture for a change. I'd like to go to Florence, to art galleries. I'd like to see the great sights of the world, like the Niagara Falls. I don't want to stand at Twickenham while he takes photographs of enormous muddy men landing on top of other enormous muddy men. At least that's what I told him when we discussed it ages ago.' Laura took another tissue out and began to cry again. 'He can photograph every rugby player in the universe now, as far as I'm concerned.'

'Well, couldn't you combine it? Go to see great sporting events and then go to the galleries in that city or country afterwards?'

But Laura's phone had pinged. She took it out and studied the message.

'Bad news?' Clover's antennae were well tuned to Laura's expressions.

'Sorry? No. No, no. It's fine.' Laura put the phone away without answering the message. 'It was . . . a tree surgeon I've been trying to get hold of. The garden has got so overgrown.'

After a few more exchanges, she gathered her shopping and left. 'Don't worry about Alice not telling you about the flat,' she said. 'You know what she's like. So busy.'

'Let me know about Tim,' said Clover, hugging Laura. 'Good luck.'

'Please,' she replied. 'Not a word to anyone. Not even to George. Not till we know what we're facing.'

'But surely Tim would tell George?' Clover couldn't imagine keeping such a secret from him.

Laura shook her head. 'He's behaving as if everything was absolutely normal. Almost as if this was a matter of bunions or wisdom teeth. I don't think he wants to talk about it. Not to anyone.'

'How lonely for you,' said Clover.

Laura's eyes filled with tears, and she nodded.

Chapter 11

Laura recognised the number on the screen. Not because it had ever called her before, but because she had studied a piece of paper with a number on it until she knew it by heart. There were three 7s, and three 6s. The mark of the beast. A very distinctive number.

She would not be tempted while Tim's life was in danger. She deleted the message without opening it. A fantasy was a fantasy. Affairs could ruin lives. As Tim should have realised before he embarked on his. He might die because of it.

The days to Monday inched by. Tim wanted to catch up on work, in case he needed urgent treatment. He seemed outwardly confident. 'I'll beat this,' he said. 'Once we get the results of the tests it'll all be so much easier.'

Laura scrubbed out already clean cupboards. She longed for a frost, so that the dahlias would die and she could clear them away. But they remained, a stubborn blaze of blood orange and crimson against the flaming red, copper and gold of the autumn trees. Sometimes she found herself in the potting shed with no idea of how two hours had passed. Every time the phone rang she seized it, hoping that it would be the hospital to say that it had all been a mistake. Then, almost immediately, she was terrified that it might be the hospital saying that Tim was far more ill than expected, and that he must go in immediately. But it was usually someone like Sheila Lewis, suggesting a wine-and-wisdom in aid of something that sounded like Outer Mongolia, because Nigel had got interested in Mongolian goats. Surprisingly often, it was her beloved Jamie.

Who said he was not enjoying Gwent.

'That's perfectly normal, darling,' she explained. 'The first few weeks are always hard. Everybody's trying to find their feet.'

'No, they're not,' he replied. 'They're trying to get so drunk they can hardly stand. Every night. I've been drunk before, Mum, it's not very interesting.'

'Sweetheart, it's just that you're very mature for your age. But they will catch up. Once everyone's settled down I'm sure you'll find some kindred spirits. Have you joined any clubs?'

He conceded that he had joined the rugby club.

Laura winced. She hated rugby, it was so dangerous. 'There you are, darling. How's the course itself?'

'Awful. I'm useless at it.'

'No! You are *not* useless. You have an excellent brain, it's just a question of applying yourself. And getting used to the course. Have you talked to your tutor?'

'I hardly ever see him. We have two lectures a week and a seminar once a fortnight.'

'Are you sure? It doesn't sound enough.'

'I'd like to change course. I've been thinking about—'

Laura cut him off. 'No darling, that would be silly.' It was bad enough doing a degree at a university that no one had ever heard of. If Jamie transferred to the kind of no-hoper subject that Ben Jones was doing, what chance did he have of ever getting a job? Worse still, Ben was at a great uni, while Jamie was only at Gwent.

Eventually the hours crawled by and it was nearly eleven o'clock on Monday morning. Laura's eyes felt like sandpaper and her mouth was dry. Tim seemed calm, knotting his tie neatly as usual, touching his always-immaculate hair with a brush one last time, and straightening his jacket. Laura picked a hair off it, assessing it quickly before flicking it away. Was it blonde?

But Laura knew she was going grey herself, so a pale hair was not necessarily out of place on Tim's jacket. Not that it mattered. Not now.

'Do you want me to drive?' Laura hoped he'd say no, because her hands were shaking.

'I'm fine.' He gave her his crooked, half smile, the one she'd fallen in love with over twenty-five years ago.

'You're being very good about this.'

'Making a fuss isn't going to change anything.' Tim was always pragmatic.

Tim's health insurance meant that the hospital was private, with peach-coloured walls and an upmarket coffee machine. People sat in pairs – sisters, friends, mothers and daughters, husbands and wives – flicking through the *English Garden*, *Harper's Bazaar* and *Orchid Collector's Monthly*.

Tim had brought a copy of the *Architects' Journal*. He seemed much younger and fitter than any of the other men in the room. She could see the women looking at him, and the men assessing him before they retreated back into their own private hells. Tim sat easily in his chair, one leg crossed over the other, looking like a successful businessman waiting for his private jet to be called.

At eleven, one of the nurses came out and looked round the room. Laura fixed her eyes on her, willing her to say the name Dangerfield.

'Mrs Ford?' called the nurse. Laura slumped back in her chair as the mother-and-daughter pair got up.

Four other patients were called, and the clock ticked round to eleven-fifteen. 'You'd think private hospitals could stick to time slots,' whispered Laura to Tim, who smiled vaguely.

Her phone beeped with an incoming text message. 'Good Luck.' It was from Clover. Laura hastily shut her phone down.

'Who was it?'

'Clover ... er ... wondering if I wanted a walk later.' Laura suddenly realised that the nurse had called the name Dangerfield several times. Her stomach lurched, as if she was in an out-of-control lift that had suddenly plunged towards the ground. Jumping up, she dropped her handbag. The contents — a lipstick, a notebook, half a bar of chocolate — scattered out across the floor.

Tim helped her pick them up and squeezed her hand. 'It's going to be fine,' he whispered. 'Don't worry.'

Laura immediately felt calm. Tim was right. There would be treatment, but it would only last a few months, and then they could have their old life back. Neither cancer nor Aids were the death sentence they once had been.

They shook hands with the consultant, who introduced himself as David Craven, and sat down on two chairs facing him across his desk.

'Well,' he said, and began to talk about stages, development and prognosis, pulling up scans and showing them where the cancer was, and where it was clear.

'Cancer?' Laura eventually picked up on the word. At least it wasn't Aids, she thought.

'Lymphoma. There are over twenty different kinds of lymphoma, and this is ... '

David Craven's words went in and out of range like a badly tuned radio. 'But it is all going to be all right, isn't it?' asked Laura. 'It's not serious, is it?'

'It's Stage Four. That is always serious,' he replied. 'Stage One is the lowest.'

'And what happens after that? What about Stage Five?' She looked from the consultant to Tim and back again.

Tim took her hand, smiling gently, the lines around his eyes crinkling in regret and, somehow, amusement. 'There isn't a Stage Five.'

Chapter 12

Clover's first instinct was to tell George. Tim was his closest friend. But Laura said not to. She had promised. And it would be OK. Modern medicine was amazing.

She was also puzzled by Alice's behaviour. It was odd to buy a flat without mentioning it. If that, indeed, was what she'd done. She dialled, and Alice answered immediately.

'Howdy.'

'It's Clover.'

'Yes, I know it's Clover.' Alice sounded amused. 'We have spoken to each other almost every day for nearly eight years.'

'Laura says that Tim said you'd bought a flat.' Clover waited for Alice to tell her that, as usual, Laura had got the wrong end of the stick. That the Kent countryside was always reverberating with the sound of Laura barking up the wrong tree.

'Sure have. I can't wait to show you. It is a serious flat. With a capital F.'

'Wasn't that a bit sudden?' Not, of course, that there was any reason why Alice should tell them everything. Clover reminded herself that this was nothing to do with her.

'I'd been finding the studio a bit tight for quite a long time, and with Lola at Oxford she might want her own room in London. And then this came up. Someone I've done some work with was about to put it on the market, but I snaffled it first. When are you coming up to see it?'

So that was all right then. 'Any time,' said Clover. 'Things are quite quiet here.'

Alice laughed, as if that was a great joke, and suggested the following Friday. 'Bring George, and ask him to bring his toolbox. And stay the night. I'd adore to see you both.'

Clover and George drove up to London, and it took them ages to find somewhere to park. Alice kissed them both noisily. 'It is so great that you're here. You're my first-ever guests.' She was wearing a long gold brocade tunic with a mandarin collar, floaty trousers and huge dangly earrings. She seemed lit from within with enthusiasm.

The flat was on the second floor of an old warehouse. It was a vast, high-ceilinged space with bare brick walls and huge industrial windows.

'Well?' said Alice, looking delighted. 'What do you think? A serious flat or what?'

'A very serious flat,' said George, grinning. 'Well done, Alice.'

'And this isn't all.' She led them across the room – the footprint of Fox Hollow would have fitted into it twice over – and down a corridor with two bedrooms – one en suite – a bathroom and a sliver of an office area. Alice's bedroom had a bed, but there were clothes and boxes all over the floor. Lola's room was empty; the office area already had a computer connected up, and files arranged on shelves up to the ceiling.

'You've furnished it incredibly quickly,' said Clover as Alice led them proudly back to the main room.

'It may sound freaky,' replied Alice, 'but I bought most of the furniture off the people who sold the flat. There's no way this stuff would fit in a normal home, and they wanted to get

97

rid of it.' She waved at the room. It contained two oversized L-shaped sofas in dark grey, a coffee table the size of a front door, a kitchen with a central island that extended into a seemingly endless long table ('It seats eighteen,' whispered Alice), and two other sofas, each huge, with accompanying side tables or coffee tables.

'Alice, this is amazing. Oh, and look, you've got *Fields* up here, too.' A large abstract in green and yellow hung on the wall. It had been the focal point of Alice's living room in Pilgrim's Worthy.

'It needed a big space.'

'It had a big space,' said Clover. 'Although you're right. I thought your lovely extended place down in Kent was big enough, but this is . . . well, it's wonderful. Did you manage to sell the studio?'

'I'm renting it out. Now, champagne, anybody? I've asked a few of the neighbours in. I want you to meet them. On the ground floor there are four flats, but two are apparently only lived in for a few months a year. There's this amazing older couple who are just so cool, and another couple who seem really nice, plus one or two single people, then, on this floor, the other flat is owned by someone who lives in China and the whole of the penthouse is owned by a merchant banker who is . . . ' she lowered her voice, as if he could hear ' . . . well, shall we say, somewhat up himself. He's called Josiah. Messiah, if you ask me. In his own mind, that is.'

As if on cue, the doorbell rang and people poured in, all dressed smartly. Clover felt lumpen in her country sweater. She, Alice and George worked together in their old familiar way, opening bottles, handing out glasses, passing round peanuts.

'This is Clover and George,' Alice told the older couple from downstairs, whom she introduced as Ralph and Barbara.

'Clover and George are absolutely my closest friends and the perfect couple.'

Clover opened her mouth but Alice went on, listing their accomplishments. 'Clover is just the ideal mother *and* she paints. She was so clever, teaching three days a week when the children were at school, was on every single committee and—'

'That makes me sound terribly boring,' protested Clover, embarrassed.

'And her house is just so pretty. She's got an artist's eye, so even a jug of flowers looks just divine. And, as for cooking, well . . . ' She dropped her voice. 'You definitely need to be invited to Clover's house. If you enjoy good food, that is.'

'I'm not really . . . ' Clover could see Ralph and Barbara looking quite startled.

'And George is, of course, the perfect husband,' Alice continued. 'This is a man who knows what a u-bend is, and how to unblock it.' She put an arm round his waist. 'And isn't he hunky? People think that what women want are George Clooney lookalikes, but what we really want is a real man. Solid. Lived-in. Capable. Someone to look after us.'

Ralph and Barbara stood open-mouthed. They were both small, dressed conventionally in neat beige, tan and cream, and their eyes flickered from Alice to Clover, then to George and back again.

Alice turned her attention to them. 'And Ralph and Barbara are just the coolest guys on this block. They had a lovely house in Hampshire and they sold it so that they could live in London in their retirement, and enjoy all the theatres. Don't you think that's . . . er . . . cool. Oh, Josiah!' She flowed, as if on a current, towards the banker, leaving Ralph and Barbara looking warily at George and Clover.

'It's a bit difficult to live up to that introduction.' Clover tried to make a joke of it, but Ralph and Barbara's eyebrows went up. She realised they might take offence if they thought she was laughing at them. 'At least, what you two have done is really interesting but we . . . '

Alice's arm snaked out to lasso George. 'George, darling, Josiah is desperate to meet you. He covers pharmaceuticals and wants to hear how the animal veterinary side is doing at the moment.'

'So you lived in Hampshire?' Clover, left with the two bewildered-looking pensioners, decided to start from the beginning.

Forty-five minutes later, they were still in Hampshire and Clover knew all about their five children – one had already been divorced – the nine grandchildren, including the one that might be dyslexic and the other who was in line to be a champion rower, and how three of the married children lived in London and the other two abroad, so it made sense . . . Clover found herself bending forward slightly to listen to Ralph, and it made her back ache. Every now and then she heard a shout of laughter from Alice.

Out of the corner of her eye, she saw the 'really nice' couple from downstairs say goodbye, and a few other people, and then, finally, just as Ralph was getting to how they'd viewed their flat, but that four other people were after it, Josiah appeared in the group.

'Just off, Babs, me darlin'.' He put on a mockney accent, while shaking Ralph's hand and kissing Barbara on the cheek.

'I was just telling Clover here how we found the flat,' quavered Ralph.

'Fascinating story,' said Josiah, not bothering to acknowledge Clover. 'You two are the mainstay of the block. Alice, if you ever want anything delivered when you're out, Ralph and Babs here will ride to the rescue and take it in.'

'Would you?' asked Alice, her eyes shining. 'That would be just so kind of you.'

'Anyway,' Ralph resumed his story, eventually reaching a point where Clover could interject. 'That is such an amazing coincidence, but I must help Alice with the clearing up.' She picked up all the glasses and began to wash them, but Barbara followed her.

'I'll help you, my dear.'

In fact, Barbara, out from under Ralph's relentless narrative, turned out to be sweet and gently interrogative. Between them they washed up all the glasses.

'I get the feeling Alice isn't too practical, would that be right?' whispered Barbara as they looked across the room to see George explaining how the giant blinds worked, and fixing a small fault in one.

'She's an amazingly good businesswoman, so she must be quite practical in some ways,' conceded Clover. 'But I think her mind is often on higher things.'

They both looked across the room to where Alice had looped her arms round George's neck and dropped a kiss on what looked like his lips. 'You angel, you darling man,' they heard her say.

'She's rather ... well, shall we say "flamboyant"?' murmured Barbara, as if she was being very daring even saying the word.

'We're very old friends,' explained Clover hastily, in case Barbara thought she was worried.

It was nearly ten o'clock by the time Alice managed to gently propel Ralph, tugged by Barbara, out the door.

'We'd better order a pizza,' she said. 'I'm starving. What did you think of Ralph and Barbara? Aren't they sweethearts?'

'She was delightful, but he was rather On Transmit,' said Clover.

'What does that mean?' asked George.

'You know – talking as if you were a radio, not stopping for any response,' said Alice with a smile. 'I am sorry, I looked over to see if you were OK a few times, but you looked fascinated.'

'Oh, it was fine.' Clover hastened to reassure her.

Alice let out a sudden shout of laughter. 'Oh God, I've just realised. I don't know where you're going to sleep. I haven't bought any beds except mine yet. But the people I bought the flat from said they always put guests up on the sofas. They're so huge, and very, very comfortable, apparently.'

It was like an overnight transatlantic flight. Clover woke up almost every hour, either because her arm was cramped against the back of the sofa, or she was hot (the flat had fierce central heating), or, later, when the heating went off, cold. Alice hadn't found any spare bedding as such, just a big sheet for each of them, plus some cashmere throws she dug out from one of the packing cases. They left their toes sticking out. Clover got up to put her tights on, and then her coat. George, on the other sofa, snored contentedly.

They drove back the following morning, after George had fixed Alice's washing machine, and they'd bought breakfast from a bakery near the river. The three of them sat on the bank of the Thames, dipping their croissants in their takeaway coffees as they watched the occasional riverboat chug gently down the water, and the big wheel of the London Eye turn slowly round.

'You can see so many famous landmarks from here,' said Clover. 'It's like being at the heart of things.'

'That's why I love it. I'm so glad you feel the same. You must come up lots, especially when the children are up at uni and I've furnished Lola's room.' Their friendship shimmered between them, still full of shared opinions and laughter.

But as they drove home Clover felt hurt. Almost physically. Something was wrong. Something was missing.

'I still think it's a bit weird how she bought that flat so quickly without mentioning it to us at all,' she confided in George.

'It probably all happened very suddenly, which was why she was too busy to get in touch.'

'And she invited us up without thinking about what we'd sleep on, or eat, or anything.'

'She's just moved in. She'd done an amazing job to get the flat that organised.'

'Which shows that she *can* organise domestically.' Clover pinpointed the source of her pain. 'But she didn't consider *us* important enough to be organised *for*.'

'We're just old friends. You expect to be a bit relaxed with old friends. Not to have to fuss over them too much.'

'I just feel that she didn't think about us and our comfort at all. She knew we were driving; we could have brought our own bedding up from home if she'd warned us. I mean, she remembered to ask you to bring your toolbox.'

'You are being a bit girly about this, as Ben and Jamie would no doubt say. Yes, she didn't manage to provide hotel-quality bedding and towels, but she's achieved an amazing amount in a very short time, and I think it's quite sweet that she wanted to show it to us before she was really ready. No, Clover, I think you've got to let this one go.'

Clover swallowed back tears. Have faith in the Alice you know, even if her lifestyle is now very different from that of the poverty-stricken single mother in an ugly bungalow who you first befriended at the school gate.

'Anyway, I think Alice has lined up her Borough helpers, don't you?' said George, sounding amused. 'Ralph and Barbara are going to find themselves taking in an awful lot of

103

parcels, looking after door keys, putting out the rubbish when Alice is away . . . '

'Do you think that's what we were? The Kent helpers? Laura always says that Alice used us.'

'I don't see why you're worrying about it. We did what we did because we wanted to. How did you find that Josiah guy?'

'He didn't even acknowledge me. I felt like a real country bumpkin, and completely invisible.'

'I think you've got to ask people questions about themselves,' suggested George. 'I find that they usually relax after a bit if you do that.'

'He wasn't unrelaxed,' shrieked Clover. 'And I know all about asking people about themselves. It's just that he never looked me in the eye. How could I ask him anything?'

'OK, OK, keep your hair on. I was just trying to be helpful.'

'What would have been helpful was if either you or Alice had rescued me from an hour's monologue from Ralph about their house in Hampshire.'

'Clover, I do not know what has got into you.' George decelerated off the motorway and turned on to the Ashford Road. 'We've just had a really nice break in London, we've met some new people, we've stayed in Alice's stunning flat and sat on the banks of the greatest river in the world with the most delicious coffee and croissants. And you're making out it's all some great insult to you.'

'I know. I'm sorry. I'm just worried about how our friends are changing. And I miss the kids. And I don't know what I'm doing with my life.'

George reached over to touch her knee affectionately. 'And absolutely none of that is Alice's fault, is it?'

Clover shook her head. 'Although one reason why I'm grouchy is probably because I had such a bad night's sleep. And that is down to Alice.'

She said it with a smile, and meant it as a joke, but a look of irritation crossed George's face. 'Women! You get yourself into such a froth over absolutely nothing.'

Clover was too tired to retaliate. It was no good turning this into a big argument, so she closed her eyes against the bright November sunlight.

'In terms of doing something with your life, by the way,' he said, as they parked outside their house. 'It needs to involve earning some money.'

'Are we in trouble?' Clover's heart quickened.

'We're OK for the time being, just.' He smiled at her to take the sting out of his words. 'But none of the financial planning we've done is going to turn out quite as well as we hoped, and the kids are going to cost more at university than we'd thought. So if we're to stay in this house in our retirement, or even do things the way the Baxters are, we need to put aside more.'

Chapter 13

Laura left the hospital in a daze. Tim would spend all day having more tests, and she wanted to get away. To flee the pain and fear, and the unfairness of it. To find a way back, however briefly, to her old life again. Tim was a healthy person. He didn't smoke or drink too much. It didn't make sense. They'd always bought low-fat milk and healthy spreads. Used sunscreen. He took regular exercise. Lots of jogging. Why had this happened?

Her car, of its own volition, made its way to the comforting familiarity of Clover's road and she parked in the usual slot under the chestnut tree guarding the gate to the Joneses' house.

By the time the front door opened she was leaning on it, and nearly fell into the hall. Clover hugged her. Laura felt how strange it was to be held by a soft, seemingly boneless woman, redolent of gardenia soap, rather than Tim's hard strength and citrus aftershave.

'Tim's got Stage Four non-Hodgkin lymphoma,' she said, finally pulling away. 'It hasn't got an "s", apparently, although everybody thinks it has.'

'What?' Clover couldn't understand what Laura was talking about.

'Everybody calls it non-Hodgkin's lymphoma,' she said,

'but once you've got it, you learn how to spell it.' She tried a wobbly smile. 'I can't remember the exact name of the strain he's got, but it's pretty incurable. If he didn't have treatment he'd have about eighteen months to live.'

'But that's ridiculous,' exclaimed Clover. 'It doesn't make sense. He looks so well. He was jogging five miles a day in August. And swimming.'

Laura followed her through the narrow hallway to the sunny kitchen at the back. 'When I look back on it I realise he probably did seem a bit more tired than usual.' She had a sudden memory of seeing him dozing on the sofa at eleven in the morning, and feeling a twinge of unease. But in that far-away world in France she had suppressed any tenderness towards Tim in her permanent, now-seemingly futile, indignation over his affair. 'If only I'd noticed earlier,' she said, sitting down at Clover's pine table. 'If I'd . . . if we hadn't . . . I might have realised something was wrong before it got this far. It's my fault. For being a rotten wife.'

'You can't say that.' Clover put the kettle on. 'If you see someone all the time, you don't always notice small changes. And they can become big changes before you know it.'

'Do you think so?' Laura seized upon her chance of redemption. 'Do you think that . . . sorry . . . we haven't been exactly what you might call "intimate" for rather a long time, and I, well, I just didn't see him naked. Or if I did, I didn't look. And certainly didn't feel. Until we spent a night in the honeymoon suite of that hotel after dropping Jamie at Gwent, and I . . . well, found these huge swellings in his groin.'

'Which you might not have noticed if they'd grown slowly and you'd been feeling round there on a regular basis,' Clover pointed out. 'Maybe you would have found out even later.'

'Do you think so? Do you really think so?' Laura tried to shake off the terrible guilt. If it wasn't something Tim had done – and how could it be? – it must be her. The memory of lying in the hot room in France as a man's breath roamed over her bare flesh, feeling the lightest flutter of his lips as they skimmed across her body, flashed into her mind. Was this her punishment? But she had not done anything.

Not yet.

She pushed the word 'yet' out of her brain.

'Anyway, he is going to have treatment, isn't he?' Clover put out a plate of biscuits. 'When did you last eat, by the way? You look ashen.'

'I . . . um . . . food tastes like cardboard. I can't swallow. It chokes me.' But she picked up a biscuit and nibbled the edge. 'Yes, he's got five months of various chemotherapies, and after that he's going to have a stem-cell transplant. It used to be very pioneering, but now it's more common. It's his only hope of seeing his grandchildren. Living to retirement. Doing any of those things that the Baxters seem to be doing.' She tried to smile.

Clover nodded. 'What sort of operation is it?'

'He'll have a lot of blood taken, out of which stem cells will be harvested, then six days of really fierce chemotherapy to kill practically everything except him. Then, when he's at his lowest, the stem cells will be re-introduced and, with any luck, they'll make their way into his immune system and grow again.'

'Is it painful?'

Laura hesitated. They had been warned that it was a phys- ically tough operation and that Tim, fit and strong apart from his cancer, was at the top end of the age bracket in terms of being able to cope with it. 'It's not so much painful as very, very demanding on the body. As Tim's in his mid-fifties he's only eligible because he's so fit. And there's a risk of other cancers developing as a side effect, later on, but normally those can be dealt with when and if they arise.' She rubbed her eyes, feeling exhausted. 'David Craven, the specialist, has asked us to think quite carefully about what we want to do, because it's also quite dangerous. He could die of the operation itself, if he gets an infection at a critical time.'

Clover handed her a mug of tea, and milk in a pretty little floral jug. Clover's kitchen seemed so safe and warm.

'He'll do it, though,' added Laura. 'He's prepared to take any risks.'

'Brave of him.'

'I think he feels "brave" is when you have an option. But he's being amazing. I wish I was able to cope as well as he seems to be. By the way, we've got to keep it a secret until we tell Jamie.'

'Of course. But we have to tell George.' Clover didn't like to say that keeping a secret, even for the best of reasons, was widening the gap between her and George. They snapped at each other now, for no reason. The house seemed empty and shabby, and the cats were off their food. Diesel, always so bouncy, no longer grinned, but walked reluctantly behind her, his head hanging down. Clover often found him sleeping on Holly's bed, which he knew was forbidden. She hadn't the heart to turn him off. 'I miss her too, Diesel.' His wiry grey tail thumped in acknowledgement.

'I'll get Tim to go out for a drink with George. Meanwhile, there's Jamie. He's not enjoying Gwent, and I don't want to mess up his first term. But he'll be home in three weeks.'

'Three weeks! That means Holly and Ben will be back soon too.' Clover was surprised it had gone so quickly.

'How are they?'

'Holly's buzzing with it all as usual. When we manage to speak to her, which isn't often. And Ben is pretty silent. Also as usual.'

'He's grown into a very attractive young man,' mused Laura. 'That gap year gave him a confidence that he didn't have before. I bet the girls are after him.'

Clover smiled. 'I wouldn't know. But these weeks have gone by so quickly and I haven't done anything with my life.'

'You don't have to do anything with your life. It's enough just to have one.'

Chapter 14

'We need to talk about money,' said Tim after supper, three days after his diagnosis. 'I've been talking to my partners at the practice.'

Laura's heart nearly stopped. 'I don't want to talk about money,' she said. 'It doesn't matter. Not compared to—'

'We have to. The financial side of this is major.' Tim's voice, as ever, was calm, as if he was discussing what to have for breakfast tomorrow, or a proposal for a listed building.

Laura stood up and pushed her chair back. 'I don't care about the money,' she hissed. 'I only care about you. You obviously think I'm some kind of money-grabbing, venal . . . ' She couldn't think of a suitably venomous noun, so she stamped upstairs and hurled herself down on her bed.

Tim tapped softly at the door, then came in. 'I don't think you're in the least venal. That wasn't what I meant.' He sat on the edge of the bed and she shifted her body over to give him space.

But the rage was still boiling. 'I know what everyone thinks of me. That I'm some high-maintenance bitch who has to have cashmere and organic cotton, and who's fussy about everything.' She stared at the ceiling, unwilling to meet his eye. 'Who'll only be interested in the life insurance and shopping.'

Tim picked up her hand. 'I don't think you're a high-maintenance bitch,' he said softly. 'I think you're a wonderful, loving mother.'

'And a crap wife.' She snatched her hand away.

'We've both made mistakes. And I regret mine. Very much. We've had a difficult time over the last five years—'

'Yes. Because of your affair.' Laura wasn't sure that she was going to admit to any mistakes.

Tim didn't retaliate. He just took her hand again, and this time she left it there. 'I need to talk about the money,' he said. 'Because I care about what happens to you and Jamie after I've gone.'

'You're not going. You're going to have the stem-cell transplant, and everything will be all right.'

'Yes, but if anything does happen we need to be prepared. I'm going to go on working during the first phase of chemo. If and when I can. But it's agreed that I'll still probably be earning my full salary. Then I'll go on sick leave for six months, for the stem-cell transplant. We've got insurances in place in the partnership to cover that, and provided I can return to work our income won't be affected. We've got a long-term sick leave provision, if I'm never able to return to work I'll get fifty per cent of my salary until . . . until I die. Then there would be a lump sum after that.'

'You're not going to die.' Laura stared at the ceiling. 'I won't let you.'

'That means a lot to me,' he said softly. 'That you still care about me.'

'Of course I still care.' She tried to keep the tears from bubbling up. 'But how was I going to compete with *her*? You'd been sleeping with a woman who's younger than me, and cleverer and . . .' The old jealousy – the corroding fear that someone else would steal the love that was rightfully hers –

rose up like bile in her throat. Until she remembered that it wasn't another woman she had to fear. It was a collection of malignant cells.

'Laura. Stop comparing yourself with other people. You're my . . . ' he fumbled for her hand and clutched it ' . . . you're my beloved Laura. You're beautiful and fun and loyal.'

'And difficult,' she conceded, trying to swallow the jealousy. It wedged in her throat like a large piece of glass. If they got through this she would never be jealous again, she promised a vague, amorphous Being up there.

She could hear the vague amorphous Being laugh. She'd have to do an awful lot better than that. She clung to the only thing she knew, which was that Tim was here, now, and she had another chance with him. The piece of glass turned out only to be ice. It melted and slipped away. 'I'm sorry for being so difficult,' she whispered, forcing the words out.

She could hear the smile in his voice. 'You are bloody difficult,' he agreed. 'But there's no one like you, so I don't compare you with anyone else.'

A wave of sadness and relief engulfed her, and she held her arms out as she moved across the bed to let him lie down. They lay there, holding each other, drifting in and out of a doze until Laura realised that it was nearly midnight and Tim had to work in the morning. 'Come on,' she said, pulling him up. 'You need to get undressed.'

He drew her down again. 'It would be so terrible to lose each other just as we've found each other again.'

'We're not going to lose anything.' Laura was determined. She snuggled back into his arms after they undressed. They were warm and strong, the way they'd been all those years ago. Between them they could do anything.

113

She had suddenly seen it, just briefly, like a flash of sun between the clouds. A new thought. You could think differently. You didn't have to go on treading the same old painful path.

Chapter 15

Hi guys. There's no doubt that seeing India by train is
Seeing India! With Capital Letters and lots of
exclamation marks!! We've learned how to negotiate the
maze of tickets and classes on Indian trains: there are
eight different classes, and First Class is really not the
best! You have to pick one with an AC prefix for Air
Conditioning if you want anything we would call luxury.

Who would have thought that the welcome cry of 'Chai,
Chai, Chai' of the tea-seller coming down the aisle would
now feel as familiar as the address system at Canterbury
East informing us that 'there are delays due to late
arrivals'? Of course, there are delays on Indian trains
too, but we don't have meetings to make.

The Marudhar Express from Agra to Jaipur is probably
our favourite, because it's a day journey and we can see
the Real India flash by – although only just, as the
windows can be quite grimy. Jaipur –'The Pink City' – is
one of the most stunning sights in India, but Agra is

tourists, tourists, tourists. But The Taj Mahal was everything we imagined and the lesser-known 'Baby Taj' is well worth a visit too.

The kids will be back soon, and we're meeting them in Kerala, to enjoy the stunning mix of cultures the 'spice port' has to offer. Sarah's back is acting up a bit after so many nights spent on Indian trains – the sleeper bunks are great, but quite hard – so we're looking forward to a little luxury: two weeks idling in a four-star hotel then, once the kids have gone back, we're going to spend a week in an ashram.

Meanwhile, we've found the Indian people amazing and diverse, and just to give you a taster of what our daily life now involves, here's a video of a really unique boy we met in Jaipur. Enjoy!

Clover clicked on a YouTube video showing an Indian boy of about eleven in front of a market stall selling vegetables. With Ken's encouraging commentary in the background, the camera panned over every vegetable on the stall in turn, as the boy gave it its Hindi name. 'Wow,' said Ken. 'We are just learning so much now. I tell you, back home in dear old Blighty you really need to open your minds.'

No, thought Clover, what I really need is for Tim's treatment to be successful. She felt mildly depressed as she switched off her computer.

Tim was, well, Tim. He was so much a part of their lives that the idea he might not be around in a few years' time was incomprehensible. Where Laura was fiery and demonstrative, he was always calm and rational. How many times had he taken a look at a scene of domestic chaos – at toddlers throwing toys all over the floor or at teenagers making themselves sick-drunk – and had quietly taken charge? 'Come on, kids,' he'd say. 'Time to tidy up.' And they did.

He was a fantastic father to Jamie, encouraging his sporting ability with quiet enthusiasm. Laura professed to be furious when they 'wasted' weekends, sitting on the sofa watching sport on Sky. George often joined them, and tried to encourage Ben to come too, but after ten minutes he usually sidled off to play PlayStation with headphones on. As Holly grew up she tagged along with her father, and was now very knowledgeable about football and rugby. Tim had season tickets for Chelsea, and he and Jamie, George and Holly often made a foursome.

George and Tim went out to the pub on Saturday lunchtime, and George came back pale and grim-faced. 'You knew,' he said. 'Tim was ill and you knew.'

'Laura told me not to tell.'

'Great to know how much everyone trusts me.'

'I do trust you,' said Clover, but her voice came out thin and reedy. 'They're going to treat it. It'll be all right, I'm sure.' She wanted to make everything better for him.

'I don't see how you can be sure.' George began to make himself a sandwich. 'And he's healthy,' he protested, as he assessed the freshness of the bread. 'He doesn't smoke. He doesn't even drink much.'

'I know. That's why he can have this operation.'

They went round and round the same questions until George had finished eating, throwing away half of his sandwich with a sigh. He rubbed his face in his hands. 'And they've announced five per cent redundancies at Petfast,' he said. 'I'm not in line – not yet, I suppose – but I've got to decide who goes in my department.'

'But you'll be all right?'

'I've survived two mergers, but every time a big company swallows up another company, jobs go. Everything's getting more centralised. In the old James Herriot days, it used to be that a vet bought into a practice and stayed there till he dropped. But now the mergers mean that the reps change constantly, and the vets' practices are merging too, so everything's bought centrally.'

Clover didn't want to hear. There was enough to worry about without looking for problems. 'Yes, but they're still buying, aren't they? Petfast is a well-known name and—'

He shook his head. 'On top of that, people are cutting back on pet care. Where five years ago they might have had three horses, now they've got one. They're also trying to treat their animals themselves, with cheaper drugs bought off the internet. And on it goes, chipping away at the business.'

'But surely they don't know what they're getting?' Clover was horrified. 'Suppose the animals are harmed? Or, at the very least, not helped?'

'Sometimes that's what happens.' George drummed his fingers on the table. 'I'm not sure what else I could do, to be honest, if I lost my job. I think it's too late to go back into practice – I'm not up-to-date enough. But we're fine for the time being. I just wanted to flag it up with you.' He cocked an eye at her. 'Have you thought about what you'd like to do next?'

Clover immediately felt guilty for not earning. 'I suppose if things were bad I could go into supply teaching. Although there are quite a few teachers around now.'

'Take your time. Don't rush into anything. But I think it would be well worth having another income coming in. By the way, Alice is thinking of launching an upmarket pet mail-order arm, Pets & Things, and she wanted my advice. Is that OK?'

'Of course it's OK.'

'She and her business partner would like me to pop up for dinner next week.'

'Just you?'

'I think so, don't you? You wouldn't have any input on a pet mail-order company, would you?'

'Are they going to pay you for your advice?'

'Well, if they want any major input then yes, I will ask them to pay me a consultancy fee. But, no, I wouldn't charge for any initial consultation. No one would. Alice is a friend.'

'Be careful about how much advice you give for free.'

George looked at her sharply. 'What's all this about? You don't normally say things like that.'

'Maybe I should. I can't help feeling that Alice has used us a bit.'

'If this is about her and the night at her flat, you've got to let it go. It's ridiculous to attach any great meaning to a bit of bedding and a few pizzas.'

'And a party for the neighbours that we conveniently helped with.' Clover got that one in before George's face could shut down in irritation. 'But yes, you're right. Time to let it go. Though I do find it slightly odd that she hasn't discussed your getting involved with her business with me. We always used to speak all the time, but now that Lola's not at school here any more I never hear from her.'

George looked exasperated. 'What else did you expect? Of course she would call here a lot if we're looking after her daughter. And, of course, when life changes, there'd be fewer calls. That's what any man would call sensible.'

'But Alice isn't a man.'

George's eyes sparkled in amusement. 'She is, in a way. Why not think of her as a man in a woman's body? It would all make much more sense that way. The easy attitude to one-night stands. The driven way she works . . .'

119

Clover laughed, and let the topic go. She didn't want to fight. 'Back to Tim's being ill – we can't talk to anyone about it until they tell Jamie at Christmas.'

'So Tim said.' George shook his head and sighed. 'When exactly did Laura tell you?'

'Last week, but asked me not to say anything.'

'That's ridiculous. Didn't you trust me?'

'Of course I trust you, but—'

'You're always keeping secrets. You release information to me only when you think it's right for me to have it.'

'That's not true.' Clover was indignant. 'When did I last keep a secret? I thought you were always saying how bad I am at being discreet.'

George started to say something, then stopped. 'It doesn't matter. All that matters is Tim. How's Laura taking it?'

Clover tamped down her anger. 'She's fine.' She didn't know what she was really angry at: George's attitude, Tim's illness, the apparent withering of her friendship with Alice. It was easiest to focus on Tim: 'Laura says she can't believe how brave he's being. In fact, I think they're closer than they have been for ages. She's distraught. I really think she loves him after all.'

But George hardly seemed to be listening. 'I can't believe it. It just shows you,' he said, shaking his head and getting up to look out of the window, as if searching for something. 'You've got to live every moment. I still don't understand why you didn't talk to me about it, though.'

'I'm talking about it now. I couldn't earlier.' But Clover knew she wasn't being quite truthful. There had been a time when they never kept secrets from each other, no matter how important. And she wasn't quite sure how that time had gone. Another little brick was added to the wall being built between them.

An hour later Alice called her mobile. 'Hi there. I'm kidnapping your husband. Are you cool about that?'

'You can have him as long as you like.' Clover was relieved to hear from Alice. There had been something hard about the silence. Or was she imagining it, just as it occasionally crossed her mind that the lack of warmth and hospitality at her flat had been a deliberate attempt to punish her for something? She shook the thought out of her head. George really would be furious if she produced that little theory.

But Alice's voice sounded like the same old Alice, asking to borrow George because her car had a flat tyre, or she couldn't start the lawn mower, or the one hundred other things that George could do so competently.

'Do borrow him,' said Clover, keeping her voice light. 'Just give him back in one piece.'

Alice's loud laugh echoed down the line. 'I promise not to break him. How's life?'

Clover admitted that it was quiet. 'But nice. How's yours?'

Alice's trawl from Hong Kong to China to the Philippines to Milan was as breathless as ever. 'Can't wait to see you. How are Tim and Laura?'

Clover stifled the desire to tell Alice about the cancer. 'Fine,' she said. 'Getting on all right, anyway. When are you coming down for Christmas?'

'Josiah – you know, the man who lives upstairs – has got a chalet in Switzerland, in Gstaad actually, and he's invited Lola and me to join him for Christmas. He's got a god-daughter and a niece around her age, plus some other friends who sound fun. So, as Lola's never skied I thought I couldn't turn it down. Although he is a bit of a bore: I'd much rather be with you in Kent. But hey, what are you doing for New Year?'

By the end of the conversation it had been established that

Alice would join them for New Year, with Lola if any of their teenagers were about, although they both agreed that the chances were that they'd all be off partying somewhere.

George and Tim went out for a pint together a few days later. They didn't talk about the cancer much, according to George when he returned.

'Is he really as OK as Laura says he is?'

George shrugged. 'Tim's pretty pragmatic. He says he doesn't mind dying, but he does mind leaving Laura and Jamie to cope on their own.'

'What? He said that? What else did he say?'

'Just that he hoped he'd be able to get the racing on the hospital television. At least the Six Nations and the FA Cup will be over by the time he has his stem-cell transplant.'

And that was that. Provided they could watch some sport, Tim and George were adamant they were fine. Clover felt like a cat scratching at a door. She knew she should support George. His best friend might be dying. And she knew she should find another job. Maybe some supply teaching, just to bring the money in.

But instead she lingered in the silent house after George left in the morning, taking an hour to get up. Instead of the mad scramble to find backpacks, stray homework books and games socks, she lingered over a fragrant cup of tea, often patrolling the garden with a coat pulled over her pyjamas. The telephone, once ringing with innumerable changes of plan ('If you can do Thursday, can I do Tuesday ... ') was silent. Instead Clover heard the chink-chink-chink and 'chup!' of the birds beginning their early morning song. It was a stolen pleasure, like a surreptitious chocolate sliding down the throat with reviving sweetness.

The garden was wrapped round the house, and the end

bordered on open fields. Clover had planted fruit trees when they first moved in and, even this late in the season, she could pick an apple from her own tree as she passed. It was satisfyingly crunchy and sweet. The leaves drifted down over the grass, leaving the trees outlined like charcoal sketches, and a thin frosting of ice outlined the dark hollies. The air, clean and clear, was as exhilarating as champagne.

Somewhere in that silence was the answer to the question. Who am I?

Chapter 16

Laura came round for lunch after Tim's first session of chemotherapy. She went with him for the morning, and stayed in the treatment room for a few hours. George had promised to drop in to the hospital over his lunch hour, then Laura would return to pick him up at three.

'He's still being amazing,' said Laura. 'For some reason it's very difficult to find his veins so the nurse had to have three stabs at it – literally – but he hardly even winces. He's got a series of five chemos, one every three weeks, plus various other things he has to take. We've definitely decided to go ahead with the stem-cell transplant, so that'll be in May some time, we think.'

They talked about Tim for a while. 'He's so amazing,' said Laura, for the tenth time. 'There are two biggish rooms, with all the patients in comfy chairs round the sides and a visitor chair next to each one. They sit there for hours, with a drip in their vein, and every so often a nurse comes and changes one bag of poison for another bag of poison. But it all seems quite cheerful. And he's got to know one or two of the other patients already. On one side there was a woman of about our age, Cathy somebody-or-other, who's got leukaemia and is on much the same cycle and drugs that he's on, although I don't think she's having the stem-cell transplant. And then a much younger guy on the other side, who was on one of his last treatments. It's so awful to see someone who's not much older than Jamie completely bald.'

It was a sobering thought.

'Tim's trying to work as well. It's absolutely manic in architects' offices just before Christmas because everyone wants drawings and budgets and whatever in on their desks before the construction industry stops for about three weeks. I don't know how he can keep it up.' Laura sighed. 'Let's change the subject. Who have you seen recently? It's so impossible for us to go out because what do you say when they ask how you are, and what you're doing with your new-found freedom? I'm the worst person in the world at keeping secrets, so we're avoiding people.'

Clover couldn't help smiling. Alice had once described Laura as the sort of person who thinks a secret is something you only tell one person at a time. 'But, tell me,' she continued, 'how are you? Have you seen Alice at all?'

'We went to the new flat. It was stunning.' Clover hadn't wanted to bring up the night at Alice's flat with Laura, partly because it would be spoilt to obsess over minor inconveniences like sleeping on a sofa when Tim was so ill, and partly because she felt foolish about it all. Alice couldn't be expected to think about them as well as about moving in, meeting new neighbours and running an internationally successful company. As George always said, one of the privileges of being an old friend was being able to be taken for granted. On the other hand, perhaps Laura would understand.

Clover described the flat, and went on to talk about the evening. 'Immediately we got there she had all the neighbours round, including this quite sweet old couple, but the husband banged on and on for hours and I got completely trapped.

And there was a merchant banker there who completely ignored me. You know how middle-aged women sometimes feel completely invisible? Well, that's how I felt, which I don't normally.'

'Do you think she wanted you there so that she didn't have to entertain on her own?'

'Maybe. I wouldn't mind if she did. I mean, friends do help each other, don't they? I think most people are happy to get stuck in if someone needs a hand passing round drinks.'

Laura's sideways glance was knowing. 'Except that it's always you two helping Alice, never the other way around.'

'That's not entirely true.' Clover tried to think of a particular instance as proof. 'For example, she booked and paid for taxis for all our kids after the leavers' ball. Most other parents were up all night scraping half-conscious kids off the streets of Canterbury.'

'Thus ensuring she herself got a decent night's sleep. It wasn't entirely altruistic.' Laura wasn't going to let it go. 'Quite apart from anything else, you and I have saved her a fortune over the years by driving Lola to and from school when Alice herself has hardly ever been able to do a school run. A few late-night taxis, expensive as they are, can hardly be considered full compensation for seven years of regular ferrying.' She snorted in indignation. 'Did she ask George to bring his toolbox up?'

'She did, actually, but I think it was a sort of a joke, really. I mean, we did take it, but—'

Laura laughed. 'I knew it! She's always talking about his toolbox. I take it that the toolbox was used?'

'Well, only to install the washing machine. And a bit of fiddling about with some blinds. And a drawer handle. But, once again, I don't think people mind doing stuff for friends. You do stuff for friends, they do stuff for other people, other people do stuff for you. It's a kind of pay-it-forward principle.'

'If you say so.' Laura took a sip of coffee. 'I take it you cleared everything from the party away and did the washing up, by the way?'

'Only to get away from volume two of Ralph's interminable life story. And his wife, Barbara, helped me.' Clover couldn't help a small smile. 'Although George says that Alice has Ralph and Barbara marked out as her Borough helpers, presumably the London equivalent of us.'

'It's unusual for George to say anything even slightly negative about Alice. He's really got a soft spot for her, hasn't he?' There was an edge to Laura's tone. 'Where did you eat?'

'We had a takeaway pizza.'

Laura's eyebrows shot up. 'You're in the middle of one of the most gastronomic cities in the world and you have a takeaway pizza? When Alice has had so many amazing meals at your house?' She shook her head. 'Alice seems to have got two helpers for a drinks do for the neighbours, plus her washing machine and various other bits fixed. All she's had to do in return is buy a few pizzas.'

'Er, I think George paid, actually.' Clover had a sudden recollection of him answering the door and pulling out his wallet. 'But that's what George is like. He wouldn't dream of letting a woman, and certainly not a woman on her own, pay for him.'

Laura spluttered with laughter. 'And you think Alice doesn't know that? That's presumably why she let him answer the door.'

'No! Really, that's going too far. George just happened to be closest at the time. Alice protested and tried to pay. But he wouldn't let her.'

'Doormat, Clover, doormat.' Laura wagged her finger at Clover.

'I don't think that's entirely fair. I'm sure it wasn't that cal-culating. And she does sometimes cook for us down here, so it's not always one way.'

'How often? Hmm? As far as I can see, she gives about one dinner party a year, while having eaten at your house almost every weekend for the past seven.'

As this was probably about right, they sat in silence for a few minutes. 'Actually, the thing that really did upset me,' Clover could resist no longer, 'is that, although she remem-bered to ask us to bring the toolbox, she never told us that she didn't have any bedding for us. Or a bed. So we had to sleep on the sofas – which weren't in themselves too bad, but still not that comfortable – under a sheet and a cashmere throw. I kept waking up absolutely freezing. It's not that I needed to have a beautifully made bed, but if only she'd thought to tell us we could have brought our own bedclothes up. I know I'm being silly about this, but I felt it showed she didn't care about us. But she does have a lot on her mind, and she probably just didn't think.'

Laura let out a shriek. 'But this is the woman whose com-pany opened another arm last year – Sheets & Things is *famous* for its sheets and super luxury duvets! Are you telling me that the renowned bedding supremo, Alice Fanshawe, didn't have enough sheets or any duvets or blankets for her guests? And what about pillows?'

Laura could be very satisfactory at times. It would never have occurred to George to worry about pillows.

'We used the sofa cushions. I was a bit worried about drib-bling on some very lovely purple damask,' admitted Clover. 'But I don't suppose she keeps stock at home. It'll all be at the warehouse, or I suppose samples in the office.'

'Towels?'

'There was a rather limp hand-towel the size of a postage

stamp in the bathroom, which I used, and George waited till we got home to shower. But I should have asked, I suppose.'

'I won't even mention soap. Clover, I think you have got to get out of the habit of needing to be needed. People like Alice can spot people like you a mile off. I've said it before and I'll say it again: she's a user.'

'No. I always felt that I was helping her and that she'd help me in return, whenever she could or if I needed it.'

'But somehow she never has.'

'She has, sometimes. And I'm sure that that's not what our friendship is about.' Clover couldn't bear to think that Alice was that calculating, or that she herself was so stupid. 'She's a friend, and friends do things for each other in different ways. We don't always have to count everything out, then pay it exactly back.'

'No, we don't, but sometimes a rough tally might be a good idea. For the sake of your self-respect.'

'Not everyone cares about the same things,' Clover pointed out. 'Some people just don't mind or notice about their own comfort, let alone anyone else's.'

'Alice minds about her own comfort a great deal,' retorted Laura. 'And she's made a lot of money out of pandering to other people's.'

'Oh well, if I think she's using me, I can always say no.'

'Except that now Lola has left St Crispian's you may not have that opportunity.' Laura got up. 'I must go and pick up Tim, but being able to get really stuck in to a good bit of indignation has cheered me up.' She kissed Clover. 'You're a lovely friend. Don't let Alice get you down. As you said, I'm sure we're over-analysing it all.'

She turned round and waved as she went down the garden path. 'But a bit of bitching is always such fun. Better than anti-depressants any day.'

As Clover said to George later, as they got into bed, Laura was surprising. 'People always think she's very wrapped up in herself and rather high-maintenance, but this whole thing with Tim's illness has brought out the best in her. She's not just thinking about herself. She was very interested and sympathetic when I told her about our night at Alice's.'

'For God's sake,' snapped George, who had been even more preoccupied since seeing Tim in hospital. 'You're not still obsessing about that, are you? The trouble with you, Clover, is that you don't have enough to do. Alice, unlike you and Laura, actually earns a living. She works very hard, and I really don't think you can judge her until you've walked in her shoes.'

'Or slept in her sheets,' muttered Clover to herself, very quietly, as she turned her back on him and switched out the light.

Chapter 17

Laura felt the weight of secrecy on her shoulders, dragging her down like a bag of rocks. Tim's cancer was the biggest thing that had happened to their marriage, and it infected every moment of her life. Every time someone asked how she was, she would push it to the back of her mind, leaving a great big gap of nothingness in the foreground. 'Fine,' she'd say, injecting as much brightness into her voice as possible. 'Don't you look gorgeous? I love that brooch. That colour suits your eyes.'

Eventually she would run out of ways to keep the conversation at bay. As soon as anyone asked after Tim she fled, murmuring that he was fine, but very, very busy.

Laura was aware of Alice's remark that she, Laura, thought a secret was something you only told one person at a time, but she could keep a secret. She could. As long as she didn't have to talk to anyone for too long. So she avoided parties. Just until Jamie came back. She and Tim stayed in together, watching DVDs and re-runs of old favourites, sitting together on the sofa, her toes tucked under his warm body.

'You know I've been talking about re-painting Jamie's bedroom? Can I go ahead?' she asked. 'It really needs it.'

Tim rarely said no to her requests these days, but he hesitated.

'I'm really reluctant to spend any money,' he said. 'We just don't know where we'll be in six months' time.'

Laura would usually have argued. Maybe even slammed a door or stopped talking to Tim for a few days. Now she couldn't do that. 'OK.'

'Tell you what.' He treated her to his crinkly smile. 'If I die, you can do it on the insurance, OK?'

'It's a deal.' She smiled back. They did a lot of that these days. Occasionally she saw that flash of sunlight again. You can think differently.

'But,' as she said over a coffee to Clover, the secrecy was the most difficult thing. 'The chemotherapy is in an open room and someone who knows Tim is bound to come in, and then it'll be all over Kent. That Cathy woman who sat next to him, I'm sure she knows people we know. She seemed the type.'

'I'm sure it won't,' soothed Clover. 'I'm sure anyone would understand. And Tim's next treatment is a few days after Jamie comes back. Nobody's going to hear anything until then.'

'Oh, and there's another thing. I wanted to paint his room, because it's really tatty, but Tim doesn't want us to spend the money.'

'I'll help,' said Clover. 'Then it'll only cost as much as the paint. And it'll be fun, both of us doing it together.'

They bought cheap white overalls from the DIY shop and took turns up a ladder. Clover was careful and meticulous, as she rejected a cream that was just slightly too yellow and picked out a grey-white that wasn't too cool.

'I've looked up talking to children on the Macmillan website,' said Laura, sanding away at a piece of skirting board. 'You know, about cancer.'

Clover, filling in a couple of thin plaster cracks near the ceiling, looked down at her. 'Do you think Jamie is still a child? I mean, does it still apply?'

'He's a child to me. And I think he's a child in relation to Tim.' Laura sat back on her heels and sighed. 'You know, however much I've complained about Tim, he's been an amazing father. It just isn't fair that he might not even get to see Jamie graduate. And I can't bear to think of what it will do to Jamie. Do you think we ought to leave it until after Christmas?'

'The treatment has got a good track record, so I'm sure he will be around for Jamie's graduation. And if you don't tell him, he'll probably pick up that something's wrong. He'll worry about it, or maybe draw the wrong conclusions. Telling him just as he's going back to uni probably wouldn't be the best time to do it either.'

'I'm dreading it. Just dreading it. And I wish he was enjoying uni a bit more too.'

They painted in silence for twenty minutes, working steadily. Laura found her mind tracking back and forth, going over the same old ground and occasionally identifying something new. Such as Alice. Clover hadn't mentioned her for a while. 'How's Alice?'

Clover sighed. 'George went up to see her last night, to talk about a new line for her company. They're thinking of moving into the top-end pet market: diamond dog collars, faux leather pet beds, that sort of thing. And they wanted to pick George's brains about the area.'

'Good old Alice. Still on the take.' Laura straightened up. 'It's funny to think that just last summer I was worried that she was after Tim. On holiday. But now all that seems so petty.'

'Oh, I'm not worried about that sort of thing. If she fancied George, or he fancied her, they'd presumably have done something about it by now.' Clover continued painting. 'The only thing I mind, a bit, is that he's really interested and excited when he talks to her, or about her, over this Pets &

Things business. But he's absent-minded or snappish with me.'

Laura didn't like the sound of that. 'Did she give him supper or did they go out?'

'They had supper at hers. Something she picked up at Borough Market.'

'So it was Alice, George and Alice's business partner?'

There was a silence from Clover. 'Actually, at the last minute, the partner couldn't make it, so it was just Alice and George,' she said eventually.

Laura put her sander down and looked at Clover.

Clover stopped filling cracks and looked round. 'It's fine. I trust George.'

'Of course,' said Laura. There was no point going out looking for pain. It would find you soon enough.

Tim went up to collect Jamie, on his own. He'd asked to do it, because it was towards the end of the three-week cycle, when he'd be feeling at his strongest.

Laura had let him, spending the extra time cooking Jamie's favourite dish and opening the bedroom windows to let the smell of paint out. 'It seems ridiculous,' she said, when Clover called round. 'We get on so well now. I let him do whatever he wants, and he lets me do what I want. Our marriage used to be like a tug-of-war. Every time we discussed anything one of us was left victorious, and the other bruised and bashed about. I never realised how easy it was just to say yes.' She sighed. 'The room looks great, by the way. We did a good job. Thanks.'

'Any time,' said Clover. 'I enjoyed it.'

'And I've got you the tiniest present to say thank-you.' To Clover's cries of 'You shouldn't have', Laura handed her a beautifully wrapped present of a silver bangle. It fitted

134

perfectly. 'I haven't had a treat like this for so long,' said Clover, looking pleased.

After Clover had left, Laura's ears strained for the sound of Tim's car on the gravel. She was at the front door before he'd braked. When Jamie got out – seemingly taller yet again – and wrapped her tightly in a hug, it was as if he'd never been gone. She inhaled the very essence of him. 'It's so good to have you back.'

'And it's good to be back.' He pulled away from her, and studied her carefully. 'Hey? What's up?'

Laura ran a hand through her hair, tidying it after the hug. 'Nothing. Why?'

'Mother.' It was a command. He only called her Mother when it was serious. 'Tell me.'

'Tim! You've told him. Or you've dropped clues.'

'I haven't said anything.' Tim hefted the last suitcase, along with Jamie's sports bag, into the hall. 'It's your face. Everything is written in it.'

'What haven't you told me?' Jamie's face paled.

'We weren't going to do it like this,' said Laura, panicking. 'This is all going wrong.'

'Tell me now,' demanded Jamie. 'Whatever it is, I need to know.'

Tim put his hand on Jamie's shoulder. 'I've got cancer, son,' he said gently. 'It's non-Hodgkin lymphoma – a cancer of the immune system. But it's being treated.'

Jamie stood still, his face blank.

'I'm sorry, darling,' Laura tried to reach around him again in a hug. His arms hung, motionless, by his sides.

'We didn't want to tell you like this,' she said desperately. 'We had it all planned. Your favourite meal and a proper home-coming tonight, and then we'd leave it till the morning . . .' her voice began to break ' . . . leave it till the morning . . . ' She swallowed back tears. 'We were going to leave it till the morning to tell you.' The last few words were a whisper.

Jamie put his arms round her, his parka rustling against her nose. She could no longer hold back the tears. 'It's all right, Mum.' He stroked her hair. 'I can handle it. You don't have to treat me like a baby any more. I want to know what you know.'

Laura put a hand out to Tim, drawing him into their embrace. They stood there, hugging each other, a solid unit of intertwined arms and chests and faces, a family united at last. Everything she had ever wanted.

Chapter 18

It snowed. In the middle of what the weather forecasters were calling the 'coldest week in December for seven years', Fox Hollow began to fill with noise and clutter. First Holly returned from Leeds, shedding bags and clothing all the way along the hall as she unpacked, draping every chair and sofa with a scarf, a discarded jumper or a woolly hat. Ben had fewer possessions – a battered pair of smelly trainers, a navy hoody and a wallet – but they seemed to be wherever you were.

Clover loved it all. She made lists, filled the fridge, store-cupboard and freezer, wound decorations round the tree and hung the stairs with lights and garlands. Holly perched like a starling in the kitchen, nibbling brownies, then flying off to meet up with friends, returning with them, re-forming into a different group, then flying off again. Ben slept or occasionally joined them. He occasionally wrapped Clover in a giant hug, or ate a whole loaf of bread at a time.

'So how are you, Mum?' asked Holly one morning as she peeled a tangerine.

Clover stopped. She wasn't used to being asked how she was by her children. She ran through a mental inventory of how she was – Alice still out of contact, heartache over Tim, joy at the children's return, mild worry over how she was going to earn money (but that could be a New Year issue) – and finally pronounced herself fine.

'But you had to think about it,' observed Holly.

'Er . . . no . . . I was just surprised to be asked, that's all.'

'Are we such selfish louts?' Holly's eyes were bright and clear.

'No. It's just that . . . '

Holly fiddled with her hair. 'I just wondered how you two were feeling about Tim's cancer. It must be quite upsetting for you.'

'Oh. Well.' Clover sat down. 'I think, oddly enough, that Dad's more shocked than I am. In a way I haven't seen before. How do you think he is?'

'A bit missing,' agreed Holly. 'As if he was worried about something, or maybe distracted.'

Clover hesitated. 'He might be a little bit concerned about work too. There have been so many mergers in the vet profession – but he'll be all right. He's a great survivor.'

'That sounds like a rather carefully worded "don't worry the children", but what you might not have noticed, Mother dear, is that we're not children any more. We can vote. We can fight in wars. We can drive. We could, if we weren't studying, earn money.'

Clover smiled at her, proud. 'So you can. But I miss the children you once were. Have you seen Lola at all, by the way, or been in touch?'

'I went to the new flat for a sleepover on her birthday. About three weeks ago. Alice took us all to a show, and then a restaurant. It was mostly Lola's new friends from Oxford, plus two of us from school. And Ben, of course. We had drinks at the beginning in an amazing penthouse flat. It belonged to some banker person who lives upstairs from Alice. Josiah somebody or other.'

'Oh, *no*, I forgot Lola's birthday.' She felt another twinge of separation. Last year – Lola's eighteenth – she and Alice had organised a trip to the ten-pin bowling alley together, followed by dinner in a restaurant. 'Do you think Alice is having some kind of affair with Josiah? They're going to his place in Switzerland for Christmas.'

Holly shrugged. 'Alice flirts with everyone. There was a funny little old man there, who popped in for a very quick drink, and she was exactly the same with him. He keeps Alice's spare keys for her.'

'Oh, you must mean Ralph. And his wife, Barbara.'

Holly shrugged, uninterested.

'I must send Lola a present,' said Clover. 'How's she enjoying Oxford?'

Holly frowned. 'I think the first term has been quite difficult. She said she was homesick.'

Clover was puzzled. 'Which home was she sick for? Surely not the studio in London, and she hadn't even been to the Borough flat. So presumably she misses being down here, but it's not as if even then she spent much time in one house. She and Alice dotted around all over the place, and she spent half the time here.'

'Apparently, at one point Alice went down and had a meeting with the Master of her college. Alice thinks they're not looking after Lola properly. But I think she's settled a bit since then. She came up to Leeds one weekend, and saw Ben in York, too, I think.'

'Poor Lola. It's funny that Alice never said.'

'I think Alice was rather cross with her. The whole Oxford thing seems really important to her. She makes Lola e-mail her essays over to her, then she corrects them before Lola gives them in.'

'No!' Clover was pleasantly appalled. 'But how is Lola ever

going to find her own style with her mother leaning over her shoulder the whole time?'

Holly shrugged. 'The flat in Borough's amazing, though. I've got some pictures on Facebook.'

Clover let herself be shown endless photos of girls with flushed and shiny faces holding glasses or bottles up to the camera. 'There. That's us on Lola's enormous new bed in London.'

Clover peered at the tiny picture. 'Lola is looking gorgeous. Has she got a boyfriend, do you know?'

Holly closed down her Facebook page and snapped her laptop shut. 'What's with the questioning? Has Alice asked you to try to find out?'

'No! I've hardly spoken to Alice, if you must know.'

Holly's eyes sharpened. 'You always used to talk every day. Have you had an argument?'

'No, of course not. Alice has been travelling a lot. She's busy.'

'That never stopped you talking before.'

Clover hadn't confided in Holly before. Not about being upset. She believed that adults should sort themselves out. But ... She told her how little she'd heard from Alice and about the unsatisfactory evening in the flat.

'Laura has always said that Alice used me while Lola was at school. But I always felt we were just friends supporting each other. Now, since that evening in Borough, I've felt that maybe Laura's right. Perhaps Alice was using us. Worse still, I even feel that treating us in that off-hand way was deliberate, that she wanted to take some kind of revenge on me. I definitely have the feeling that it wasn't just carelessness – that there was an element of malice in it. But why, I can't imagine, and I'm not quite sure why I even think that. It makes me think I must be going mad. If she had a problem with something I'd

140

done, then surely she'd discuss it? What would she take revenge for?'

'Being happy when she's so bloody miserable?' suggested Holly.

Clover laughed. 'Alice isn't miserable. She's a great success.'

Holly gave her wise look. 'Alice is one of the unhappiest people I've ever met.'

Clover decided not to tell Holly about Pets & Things. George had come back from his dinner with Alice, eyes bright, and had regaled Clover with every single detail of what they'd talked about, pacing the room in an excited fashion. 'If the business does take off, there might well be a job there,' he'd said. But Clover was reluctant to relay it all to Holly. It would muddy the waters.

'But, you know, it's probably not deliberate,' Holly went on. 'I get the feeling that Alice is pretty ruthless – she has to be to make that company work – but I know she genuinely likes you. You make her laugh.'

'Everyone makes her laugh.'

'Not like you.' Holly touched her arm. 'Really, Mum, you've been a great friend to Alice, and I'm sure that she thinks of you as one. But just now she's focused on other things, and she's also worried about Lola. I think you should let it go. And don't listen to Laura: she always sees the worst in everyone.'

The fog cleared. 'You're right,' said Clover. 'It sounds so much better when you say it than when Dad does. There's that tone of male irritation in there, that "you're just being silly".'

'I don't think you're being silly.' Holly smiled up at her. 'I wouldn't like it if one of my friends behaved like that. But I think it's probably just her being busy and carelessness. She's coming for New Year, isn't she? That'll be fun. Can I invite Joe Hesketh?'

141

Clover assessed her daughter. 'The two of you from school who went to Alice's birthday party – was one of them Joe?'

'What if it was? He's just a friend.' Holly rolled her eyes and pulled out her mobile phone.

Chapter 19

Baxtersblog. 17 December

Hi guys. Just to show that us Baxters can always surprise you, we decided to get to Kerala earlier than we'd planned. When you're an empty-nester, plans are for changing! Most of you probably know Kerala – if you know it at all, that is – for its network of lakes, canals and lagoons, and we have indeed rented one of its legendary houseboats for the festive season. But Kerala is also a vibrant mix of churches, synagogues, temples and mosques – and you'll be surprised to hear that Christianity got here in AD52. Vizhinjam harbour is a mishmash of traditionally painted wooden boats in dazzling reds, blues and yellows. It's famous as a trading post for Indian spices.

After a week exploring, we met the kids at the main railway station, and took them 'home' to the houseboat. They were blown away by it all. But before we all set out to explore the network of canals and lagoons between the Arabian sea and the Western Ghats, we had a day inland exploring the tea plantations. Women still work traditionally here, clipping and hand-picking the tea bushes, only occasionally disturbed by marauding wild elephants! As you're sitting drinking your cuppa, think about where it all comes from!

Sarah has a bit of an infected foot from the day's climb – a blister went septic! – but she wouldn't have missed it for the world. Adam and Milly have both had a successful term at uni – Adam has taken up rowing, and is apparently showing great promise, and Milly has her head down. This'll be her last break before finals as she'll be revising through her Easter holidays, so it's great to know that we're giving her such a memorable one.

Before we sign off, we have to share sad news about our great friend, Tim Dangerfield, who has just been diagnosed with the Big C. What can we say, Tim? There are no words. There are just no words.

Except that the more pain there is, the greater the cracks through which joy can seep. There's nothing more to say.

Clover blinked at the last paragraph, but otherwise skimmed the blog quickly. She was late for her father. He lived just over three-quarters of an hour away, near Tunbridge Wells, which he always described as being 'within striking distance – should you ever need to strike me'. But it wasn't exactly round the corner and Clover wondered, as he got older, whether she should try to convince him to sell his cottage and move into sheltered accommodation nearer her. It was not a conversation she would enjoy having. He was ferociously independent, and only just accepted that she should visit him every Wednesday morning to see if there was anything he needed.

He always prepared fresh coffee, in the best gold-rimmed china, neatly arranged on a tray with a doily, the milk in a rosy jug, just as her mother had always done. As he poured out the milk, agonisingly slowly, his hand trembled slightly.

Finally they settled down, Colin in his own upright chair, Clover perched on the sofa. 'So how's George?' he asked.

'I don't know.' Clover surprised herself with the sudden honesty of her answer. 'He seemed surprisingly bereft when Holly and Ben went off, but they came back last week and he almost doesn't seem to have noticed. It's lovely having the house full of their noise and mess again. I was wondering if this business of Tim having cancer had affected him.'

Colin took so long to reply that she thought he'd dropped off to sleep. He occasionally did that. 'Well,' he said eventually, 'when your mother was ill, people always said "How is she?", never "How are you?" And I was so tied up with it all that I forgot to say "How are you?" back.' He nodded sadly. 'So, if that's what your instinct is telling you, then that's probably what it is.'

Clover was indignant. 'I'm always asking him how he is. And there's a lot of insecurity at work. Maybe it's that.'

The blue eyes watered with all their old directness. 'George is used to a lot of insecurity at work. It's how it is these days. You've got good instincts, Clover, listen to them. If you think it's Tim's illness, then it probably is.'

Clover sighed. 'So what have you been doing this week? Did you play bridge yesterday?'

His eyebrows beetled at her. 'Why are you asking?'

Clover was taken aback. 'Well . . . I always ask, don't I?' She peered at him. 'Are you all right?'

'Of course, I'm all right,' he snapped. 'I'm not dead yet, you know.'

'No, I didn't think you were, but if you didn't go to bridge . . . I mean, you haven't been ill or anything, have you?

145

How's umm . . . ' she rummaged in her mind for the name of one of his group of friends. 'How's Gerald?'

'You're like one of those do-gooders we get round here. People who think us old folk are lonely. I'm not lonely. And whether I'm doing what I always did is my business.'

'Dad, I didn't . . . ' Clover was worried that her father's mind might be slipping. It was very unlike him to be snappish, and wasn't that an early sign of Alzheimer's? 'Have you given up bridge?'

'I'm not playing so much,' he conceded.

Clover didn't quite dare ask why not. Bridge dates were planned a long time in advance. When her mother had realised her illness was terminal she had kept it secret for a while in case people decided it wasn't worth including her in a bridge four seven months ahead.

Clover's heart dropped. She knew that as soon as your children left home your parents fell apart. At least that's what everyone said.

'Dad, I just wondered if it might be time to think about shel—'

He stood up. 'Whatever it is you're going to suggest, the answer is no. Now, isn't there anyone else you could busybody?' He sighed and began a slow shuffle towards the door. 'We all know that as soon as the kids leave home you all start poking your noses into our lives. All my friends are having the same problem. Suddenly they've got their adult children trying to stuff them into sheltered accommodation or get them new double glazing or stair lifts. Couldn't you all take up budgerigar breeding or something to keep you occupied?' But his blue eyes watered with humour.

If he was joking, he presumably couldn't be terminal?

'Dad, you will promise that if anything's wrong you'll let me know?'

146

'And what if anything's right?'

She wasn't quite sure what he meant. 'Well, that too. Do you need anything doing while I'm here?'

Colin shook his head. 'I'm able to cope.'

'I know. You're a very good coper. But not everyone can do everything themselves.' Clover looked round. Her father did seem very able to do everything. The house and garden were the same as they had always been. In summer, the same flowers were planted in the same beds. Her mother had decided what to plant twenty years ago, and her father had followed her plans to the letter ever since she died. In the winter the fragrance of a pot of forced hyacinths blew over the coffee table. 'Did you plant those, Dad? And keep them in the cellar like Mum always did?'

He nodded.

She noticed a poinsettia on the windowsill. 'Mum never used to have poinsettias.'

'I fancied a bit of a change.' He folded his arms.

Clover folded her own arms and faced him down. Colin was not a man who ever fancied a change. Nor was he someone who bought flowers. Clover's mother had been the gardener; her father did the lawn and took out the rubbish. When she died, he'd taken over her side of the bargain, but did everything exactly as she had.

'Oh all right. A visitor brought them.'

'What visitor?'

'I can't remember,' he said, irritated. 'You know what it's like at my age. No short-term memory.'

Clover had a feeling he was winding her up, retaliating for her having said the first syllable of 'sheltered accommodation'. His short-term memory had, so far, been pin-sharp. 'Are you sure you don't want to stay with us over Christmas?'

He shook his head with a smile. 'At my age, lunch is quite enough. I'll see you at midday on Christmas Day.'

He showed her to the door, landing each foot slowly and precisely in front of him, as if walking to the door was a balancing act. As he held the door open to say goodbye to her she hugged him, wanting to know he was still the strong father who had all the answers. She could feel his bones. The core of him hadn't changed. It was just the flesh around them that had loosened. He held her tight.

As she drew away he stopped her, his grip still surprisingly strong. 'I love you very much, Clover.'

She kissed him goodbye. 'I love you too, Dad.' She looked up at the sky with a shiver. Did her father know something she didn't? Might this be the last time she saw him? 'They say it's going to snow again. Now, you won't shovel your path, will you? Call us and we'll drive over and do it. Pensioners have been dying, falling over in the snow.'

He pinched her cheek with an affectionate smile. 'I'll have to go some time, you know.' But his eyes twinkled. 'I won't do anything silly. Now be off with you.'

Chapter 20

It was snowing again on New Year's Eve, the tiny white flecks drifting gently down, deceptively soft, yet covering the ground as ruthlessly as any blizzard. Hour after hour, centimetre piled on to centimetre. Some of the steps in the Fox Hollow garden disappeared entirely.

People burst in through the door elated to have arrived, each with a tale of complicated journeys and narrow escapes. Tim, Laura and Jamie, who were staying the night, helped pass around glasses of wine and plates of dates stuffed with cream cheese, little squares of smoked salmon and chipolata sausages with mustard. Giant shepherd's pies were stacked up in Clover's oven.

The Lewises had asked if they could bring a house guest who was going to be on her own that New Year. 'She's got cancer.' On the telephone, the day before the party, Sheila lowered her voice, as if imparting scandal. 'And do you know, her husband upped and left her. Don't you think that's disgusting? So we're making sure she's got company for the evening at least. How are Tim and Laura, by the way?'

Clover wondered if Sheila was implying that Laura might be 'upping and leaving' Tim. 'It's still early days in terms of knowing how the treatment works, but Tim seems to be holding up pretty well. He says he doesn't feel too sick, and he isn't losing his hair.'

'Isn't that wonderful!'

'And Laura and Tim are great together. If anything, I think it's brought them closer together.'

'How marvellous,' breathed Sheila. 'Of course, sometimes you don't know what you've got till it's gone. Laura must be finding that.'

'Tim hasn't gone yet. His cancer is treatable.'

'He was always such a wonderful man. It's so sad.' It was clear that, to Sheila Lewis, Tim was a dead man walking.

Now, somewhat predictably, the Lewises had arrived first. Sheila and the friend stood on the snowy doorstep with Ruby behind them in a teeny-tiny skirt and huge fur hat, her face glowing with cold. Ruby and Holly shrieked and fell into each other's arms before rushing off to find a drink, both talking at once.

'This is Cathy Parker,' said Sheila, drawing the newcomer forward. 'We're keeping an eye on her over Christmas.'

A petite dark-haired woman offered a slim, cold hand. 'This is so kind of you.'

'I'm so glad you could come,' replied Clover.

'Shall I take coats?' offered Tim. 'Cathy! What are you doing here? This is extraordinary. Cathy's on the same chemo cycle as I am,' he explained to Sheila, who looked slightly shocked, as if he might be talking about enemas or venereal disease.

'Oh dear,' she murmured. 'How awful, I shouldn't have . . .'

'Laura darling,' Tim called into the room. 'Look who's here. Cathy!'

Laura, wearing a silver top and – for some mysterious reason – a white fur headband, burst into the hall and kissed Cathy effusively on both cheeks. 'Oh my goodness, what an amazing coincidence. I love that darling top of yours. Is it Issey? It looks like it. Terribly smart for down here.' She bore Cathy away, talking nineteen to the dozen. 'Would you like a glass of fizz? It's a very good Cava. Or are you off booze? Tim has barely touched a drop, he says he's got a funny metallic taste in his mouth.'

'Where's Nigel?' asked Clover.

'He says he's very sorry, but one of us has to stay at home to keep an eye on the Mongolian goats. You know we've taken up breeding them?' Sheila's face became animated. 'And, of course, we don't want to leave them on their own at New Year, because of the fireworks.'

Clover thought that Mongolian goats were probably quite hardy creatures, but she'd noticed that every time either Sheila or Nigel mentioned them they seemed besotted. Perhaps they had filled the hole left by Ruby's departure.

The doorbell rang again.

It was Alice. 'You're so clever, Clover, you've even managed designer snowflakes.' She pulled off a huge faux-fur hat, her eyes shining. 'Isn't it just heart-breakingly pretty down here? Mwah! Mwah! And where's that lovely man?' She seized George's face and kissed him full on the lips. Sheila Lewis, pressed against the hall mirror by the sheer force of Alice's presence, looked even more appalled.

Clover wished she could explain to Sheila that that was just how Alice was. She had been kissing George on the lips for as long as she could remember. It didn't mean anything. She, Clover, didn't mind at all. But she did object to Sheila looking as if someone had stuffed a sprig of holly up her bum.

'Alice!' Laura's head re-appeared. 'That red velvet really suits you. Turn round – is it really backless?'

Alice managed a half-turn as she handed her coat to George over Clover's head.

'It is! You are so brave, wearing so few clothes in this weather. But it's gorgeous.' Her hand snaked out. 'Shall I take that? We're helping Clover and George with the drinks.' She removed a prettily packaged gold bottle carrier from Alice's manicured fingers.

Behind Alice was a press of people coming up the path – Duncan and Joe Hesketh, Deepak, Leila and Sandeep Marchandani and Adam Baxter.

Clover tried to push everyone through to the kitchen. 'George, can you get everyone a drink in the kitchen … drinks through there … Sandeep, how are you enjoying medical school? Deepak, Leila, how lovely to see you, do go through … yes, hello Duncan, isn't it snowy?' Duncan pressed a bottle into her hand. 'Oh, thank you so much … Do go through to the back … Joe, how lovely to see you! Holly and Ben are in the kitchen, do go through … oh, hello Adam!'

Adam Baxter, presumably just back from his parents' empty-nesting tour of India, towered over her, tanned and smiling.

'What are you doing here? I thought you were in Kerala. Or was it Goa?'

He smiled. 'I was, but I came back. Holly said I could stay.'

'Of course. It'll be lovely to have you. How was it? We're all enjoying your parents' blog.'

'It's great.' He nodded and smiled, while at the same time looking over everyone's heads for someone. Holly? Lola? You never knew who was with whom at any time.

'Now, you need a drink.' She gently steered him down the passage.

The flurry of activity finally died down. Clover edged past people and wiggled into the kitchen to get some bottles. Laura seemed to be managing a production line. She seized the bottle Duncan had brought from Clover's hands and unwrapped it. 'Look, vintage champagne. I'll stash that in your salad drawer so that you can enjoy it with George some other time.'

'No, we should open it. Other people have brought champagne too – we'll bring it out at midnight.'

Laura pulled Alice's bottle out of its gold carrier and inspected it with disdain. 'Hmph. Chardonnay. Not even a very good one. This one's two-for-five-pounds at Tesco. You know, Alice is as tight as a duck's arse. It's all show with her. All fur coat and no knickers, as my old nanny used to say.'

'Your nanny must have been quite a character.' Clover had decided that her New Year's resolution was not to listen to Laura when she was getting at Alice.

But it wasn't just Laura's words. Somehow she couldn't help looking at Alice differently either. Yet Alice was the same as she'd always been. Bringing a cheap bottle of wine wasn't necessarily meanness. More likely, she'd left it too late to buy anything and had grabbed the first bottle that came to hand, thrusting it into whatever packaging was left over from Christmas. Clover had seen her get ready hundreds of times: 'Bugger, bugger, bugger, I'd better take something.' She'd pick up a bottle of wine while threading an earring in, then rootle around in a pile of clothes – she was very untidy – to come up with a smart carrier bag or a piece of tissue paper. She often wrapped it in the taxi on the way to the party, while still applying her make-up.

Alice had a lot on her plate. But a little voice inside Clover said that she would like her friend to make a special effort for once. Clover told the little voice to stop being so self-centred.

'Hiya doll.' It was Alice, with a packet of cigarettes in her hand. 'Just popping out for a fag. Apparently, it's stopped snowing. Come and keep me company? I'm longing to know how you all got on without me at Christmas. I thought of you, having a good laugh, while I was stuck with Josiah, Josiah's dreary sister and her stuffed-shirt husband.'

They stumped outside and shivered in the garden as Alice smoked. A little questioning elicited the information that Josiah's chalet had ten bedrooms and was fully staffed. 'It must have been very relaxing,' suggested Clover. 'Not having to do any cooking.'

'Darling, I nearly died of boredom. I'd much rather have been here peeling sprouts. But it was worth it to have Lola learn to ski. Josiah hired a ski instructor for the week, so that anyone who wanted to could have lessons whenever they liked.' She took a drag of her cigarette. 'He's an ace skier himself; I wouldn't have dared to go out with him. I read lots of lovely books and drank hot chocolate all day. I put on two pounds.' She patted her narrow hips.

'Romance?' Clover raised an eyebrow.

'Not exactly romance. But . . . ' She shrugged, a mischievous glint in her eye.

Clover knew she was unlikely to get any more out of her. 'By the way, George seemed very excited by the possibilities of Pets & Things.'

Alice blew smoke and contemplated Clover carefully. 'Was he really? It's hard to tell with George. But I really respect his opinion, so if he thinks Pets & Things has a chance it gives me a lot of confidence.'

Clover started to reply, then jumped as Duncan, muffled up, came out carrying two coats. 'You two must be freezing,' he said, mainly to Alice. 'I don't know who these belong to, but I'm sure they won't mind lending them.'

Clover took one coat, and Alice fluttered her gratitude at him as she let him drape the other over her shoulders. She offered him a cigarette. 'Fag? I'm giving up at midnight, so I've got to smoke as many as possible until then. Even if I die of hypothermia trying.'

He took one. 'I gave up last New Year's Eve and I've lasted until now, but I've got to have something to give up tomorrow.' He coughed as he lit it.

'What are you all doing out here in the snow?' Laura joined them, blowing on her hands and rubbing her arms. 'Did you have a good Christmas, Duncan?'

He turned to Laura. The back garden was illuminated with fairy lights, the moon, and the general yellow glow of Pilgrim's Worthy's lamplight. It threw his features into relief. He looked like his son – all bone and sinew, with a shock of hair. Only the deepest lines, crinkling around his eyes, were visible. 'Christmas was good. What about you? I'm sorry to hear about Tim.'

Laura nodded an acknowledgement, with a quick smile, and changed the subject. 'These fairy lights in the garden look so pretty, Clover.'

'The whole house looks gorgeous,' said Alice. 'The bits of it you can see through all the people, that is. Clever Clover. That's what I always say, isn't it?' Was that an edge to her voice? And if so, why?

'I'm not clever at all, compared to you.' She heard her own voice squeak, as if in deference.

Alice put an arm around her, almost knocking the coats off. 'Clover is the perfect woman, don't you think, Duncan? Talented, nice, lovely children, lovely house . . .'

'No lovely career, don't forget.' Clover felt increasingly uncomfortable. There was some message here, but she couldn't decipher it.

'You wouldn't want a career, would you?' Alice made it sound ridiculous.

'Well, I've got to earn some money. That's my goal for next year.'

Alice laughed.

'You could always be a decorator,' said Laura. She turned to Duncan. 'Clover and I painted Jamie's room, and I thought the finish was as professional as any I've ever had. And I'm fussy.' She sparkled a small, wicked laugh, her breath pluming out in the cold. '*Hideously* fussy, as you might imagine.'

'Really?' Duncan turned to Clover. 'Who did the painting here, by the way? In your kitchen, for example?'

'That was me,' admitted Clover.

He nodded. 'Good quality work, I thought.'

'How can you tell?' asked Alice, quite sharply.

He grinned ruefully. 'Old decorator's habit, I'm afraid. I'm always running the back of my hand discreetly along someone's walls, or a finger over the glosswork. Can't help myself. But I spotted your kitchen had been painted well, certainly unusually well for an amateur. Kitchens are not easy, especially when you're trying to paint mass-market units.'

'You really have noticed everything. That's exactly what we did. We bought some cheap DIY units. George put them in, then I painted them in Farrow & Ball and we added some nice handles.' She laughed. 'We rather hoped everyone would think we had a designer kitchen.'

'You see,' drawled Alice. 'George and Clover are the perfect partnership.'

'Everyone except me *would* think you had a designer kitchen,' said Duncan. 'But I work with all these brands the whole time, so I can always tell. But, seriously, if you do want to earn some money one of my lads has just broken his wrist in three places falling over on the ice outside a pub when he was drunk. He'll be off for at least three months, if not longer. If you wanted to give decorating a go, it'd be great to have you on board. It's only preparation and drudgery, though, I warn you, and the pay is horrendous.' He laughed, as if joking, but she could see that his eyes were watching her carefully.

Clover was about to say no. It would be too embarrassing to work for a friend. She might not be any good. But she suddenly thought of the girl who had dived into the ice-cold sea and had swum towards the sun.

It was time to go back into the water. She raised her chin. 'I can't promise that I'll be as useful as your lad, but I'll give it a try. I can't do anything until mid-January when the kids go back. Maybe that's too late for you?'

'It's perfect. We've got a big job which re-starts on the sixteenth. I'll pick you up at seven-thirty.'

'You must sack me if I'm no good,' warned Clover.

'He won't need to.' Alice turned to Duncan: 'Clover does everything well.'

'So I can see,' he smiled, stamping his feet to keep warm.

'I think we'd better be getting back.' Alice threw her cigarette stub into the border. They looked back at the house. One of the windows was half-open. A party roar blasted from it. Clover could see dozens of heads, crammed together in the lamplight, everyone shouting louder and louder to be heard.

As they walked back towards the kitchen Alice put an arm round Clover. 'Do you really like painting? As in decorating rather than as in art?'

'Of course. It's kind of meditative sometimes. It gives you a chance to think.'

'It's just that I wondered ... Well, I'm taking some time off in the first week of January. Do you all fancy coming up to Borough, and we could paint Lola's room together? Then we could have some fun in the evening? It would be like old times.'

Clover hesitated.

'Forget it. You've probably got everything organised for that week.'

'No, really. I'd like to. I don't think we've got anything on, but I must check with George and the others. But if they're

157

free, yes, that would be great.' She smiled and the old Alice – warm, conspiratorial, irreverent – smiled back as she quickly scanned the kitchen worktop for another drink. It was crowded with half-empty and unopened bottles. 'Well, in that case, let's drink to a great first week in January. Oh look – a decent champagne. I do love people who bring proper bottles to parties, don't you?' She filled her glass and Clover's. 'Hey ho.' She sighed. 'Nearly the end of the year. And next year I shall be fifty.'

It occurred to Clover, with a start, that Alice's new sharp persona might not be a figment of Clover's imagination after all. For a few seconds the eyes that met hers, ringed with eye-liner and desperation, reminded her of an animal peering out of a gilded cage, haunted by fear and insecurity.

Clover immediately wanted to smooth it all away. 'We could have a party,' she said. 'For your fiftieth. Just let us know what we can do.'

'Not everything in life can be sorted with a party.' Alice laughed her big, outgoing laugh. 'But it's certainly a good place to start.'

Chapter 21

In the garden, Laura looked up at Duncan. Tiny, pretty flakes of snow began to drift innocently down again. Laura put out a hand to catch them. 'They seem so real, then as soon as you touch them they dissolve.'

'How are you doing? Over Tim, I mean.'

Laura had a sudden desire to burst into tears. Everybody always asked after Tim. She had begun to feel that she herself, as a person, barely existed. 'I'm OK.' She shivered.

'Good.' He seemed to mean it.

'Clover will be great, by the way,' Laura said. 'Her confidence might need boosting, but she's meticulous. You were so clever to think of taking her on.'

'I was only picking up on your recommendation. I have the greatest respect for your judgement.' His face was very close to hers, and she could almost feel the warmth of his body.

'We should go inside. Before we freeze to death.' But she couldn't quite move.

The kitchen door opened again and the volume of sound increased. Holly, Lola and Joe came out, Joe fumbling for his cigarettes. Ben followed them, languid and silent, his eyes sweeping over Laura. He hadn't shaved, and Laura couldn't help thinking how like his father he looked. He'd have the same lived-in, rumpled face in twenty years' time.

Holly caught Laura's eye. 'Don't worry, *I* don't smoke.' Her eyes sparkled as she jumped up and down to stay warm. 'We're just keeping Joe company. And it's so hot in there. Mum's log-burner is certainly doing its thing.' Lola, swathed in someone's fake-fur scarf, and wearing fingerless gloves, smiled and whispered something to Ben.

Laura's feet were so icy she wasn't sure if she could walk. 'We were just going in. I'm sure the women clustering round Tim are just being sympathetic, but all sensible wives have to circulate at parties with a blunt instrument from time to time, if they want to beat off the opposition. Remember that, Holly, won't you, when you grow up?' She didn't want the Crew wondering what she and Duncan were doing out there. 'See you later, kids.' She carefully hobbled back inside on freezing toes and high heels, feeling their eyes on her back. Duncan stayed behind to exchange a few words with his son and Ben. Something about football drifted through the crisp, cold air.

For the rest of the party she had the sense that someone was watching her. It wasn't an unpleasant feeling, just a prickling of awareness that made her smile and stand up straighter. She could feel herself glittering more brightly, and people responding to her as if she was a fire or a shooting star.

She needed to find Tim, to anchor herself. He was sitting on the sofa with Cathy. Sheila Lewis, looking saintly and protective, was sitting in a chair beside them, fetching non-alcoholic drinks and pressing dishes of peanuts on them. Tim looked fine, although Laura suspected that he was sitting down because he was more tired than he let on. Cathy didn't look as if she'd make it to midnight.

Cathy was very slight. Laura could tell – just – that she was wearing a wig, although it was a very good one. Tim's hair had thinned slightly, but nothing too obvious. Cathy had obviously had that fine, dead-straight hair that was never thick at the best of times. Sheila had told her that she had three children, aged nineteen, twenty-one and twenty-seven, all of whom were 'doing their own thing' for New Year. Laura admired her bravery. She would have wanted to scream at them. Tell them that there might not be many more New Years to spend with her. And how could that husband leave her when she needed him so badly?

She sort of knew why. The new-year kiss was going to be difficult. There would be a pair of lips she needed to avoid, a hand she shouldn't take. A body she should not feel the warmth of. She should make sure she was next to Tim for 'Auld Lang Syne', and she would keep her fingers firmly interlaced with his, throughout all the kissing. Because if she left the room – to go to the loo, or to find another drink – she knew who would follow. She would be lost. If he touched her anywhere, she would melt.

Sheila was still sitting next to Cathy and Tim. 'Do you want to sit down?' Her voice dropped, to express her sympathy and respect for Laura's situation as Wife of Cancer Sufferer. 'Here, have my seat.'

Laura took her place, thanking her. She looked at Cathy, whose skin was grey. 'Are you all right? We're staying here tonight, so you could lie down on our bed if you aren't feeling up to all this.'

Cathy smiled. 'Actually, I do feel pretty awful. I was thinking of getting a taxi home but it's so difficult to find them on New Year's Eve.'

'I'm not drinking,' said Tim. 'And I don't seem to be getting quite the degree of the side effects from the chemo. I could run you home.' He looked at Laura. 'It's only about twenty minutes away.'

'I would do it myself, but I'm over the limit,' Laura admitted. 'But are you OK to drive? Are you sure?'

'Don't worry. If I need to, I'll stop and have a doze.'

'There are blankets in the boot, remember,' she urged. 'And water. And drive very slowly. It's still snowing.'

'Sheila is trying to recruit for her church,' added Tim as he helped Cathy up. 'She keeps suggesting that we'd get so much comfort if we only let Jesus into our lives.'

'I've tried to explain that Jesus is in my life,' said Cathy, looking exhausted. 'I'm a practising Catholic. Sheila's view is that it's not surprising I'm ill if I subscribe to the Devil's message.' She tried to smile. 'But she has been very kind in lots of other ways.'

'And I've told her we're Jehovah's Witnesses,' said Tim. 'I'm not sure if she believed me, though.'

Laura tried not to giggle at the thought of Sheila's expression as she helped Cathy find her bag and coat, and promised that she would pass on her goodbyes. 'You're lucky that she's not trying to recruit you for the Mongolian goats. They seem to have rather replaced the Church as Sheila and Nigel's religion.'

Tim kissed her goodbye. 'It's only ten o'clock. I'll probably be back for New Year. But don't worry if I'm not: I'll stop to rest if I need to.'

Laura felt so weak that she had to lean against the door frame as she waved them off. It was down to fate now. If Tim came back in time she would be with him at New Year.

And if he didn't . . .

Chapter 22

The following morning, picking her way through empty bottles and retrieving the last few plates that had been stashed under chairs and forgotten, Clover tried to ring her father to wish him a happy new year.

He didn't answer. She rang his neighbours and got their answering machine, then remembered that they were away for Christmas.

'I'm a bit worried that Dad might have hurt himself,' she said to George, who was gathering up plates and stacking them in the dishwasher. 'He's in quite a strange mood these days, and I think maybe he's not quite as sharp as he was.'

'He seemed completely fine at Christmas,' observed George. 'Totally on the ball.'

'Hm. When I saw him just before he was complaining about do-gooders and he had a strange poinsettia hanging around.'

George burst out laughing. 'That does it. A strange poinsettia. Very sinister. Shall I drive straight over or should we call the emergency services?'

Clover was horrified to feel tears start behind her eyes. She turned away to hide them, but George put an arm round her. 'Hey? What's this?'

'It was just something about the way he said goodbye to me when he left after Christmas lunch,' she mumbled. 'It was like it was for the last time.' She brushed a tear away with the back of her hand and tried to smile. 'But I often think that. When someone's eighty-two you never know whether you'll see them again.'

George drew her to him. 'I'll go over.'

She struggled away. 'But it's miles away.'

'So what? I told Alice I'd drop round, but that won't take more than about half an hour. I don't have anything else to do today.'

'Why are you going to Alice's?' Clover didn't like the sudden lurch she felt, as her lungs seemed to run out of breath and collide with her heart.

'We're going to talk about Pets & Things. She's only here for today, then she and Lola are flying out to see her aunt in New York.'

This, too, was news to Clover. Alice had said nothing about New York. 'She suggested we all go up there for a few days in the first week of January. She and I can paint Lola's room, and we can all do some shopping, take in some exhibitions . . . what do you think?'

'Yeah, fine. Sounds good to me. I can help with the painting too.'

'You can take your toolbox.' She watched to see if he would react in any way, but he just murmured agreement and continued with the washing up.

'George?' A terrible sense of foreboding crept over her.

'Mm?'

'You and Alice.' She had to force the words out. 'There isn't anything I ought to know, is there? I mean, it is just business?'

He swung round. 'Clover, what is up with you? You're

imagining that your father's dead, that Alice has some kind of . . . I don't know, some kind of vendetta against you . . . and now this.' His normally good-natured face held a mix of concern and irritation. 'Is that really what you think of me? That I'd have an affair with my wife's best friend?'

'Well . . .'

'Is it? Is that seriously what you think of me after twenty-two years of marriage? Shit, Clover, I thought we had some trust here.'

'We do, we do, but she's *always* kissing you full on the lips and . . .'

'Yes! She's always kissing me full on the lips. She always has. As she does to Duncan, Tim . . .' He broke off.

'She doesn't do it to Tim any more. Not since he got ill.'

'What the fuck does that mean?'

'Laura and I have both noticed it. She used to flirt with him. Now she more or less ignores him.' Clover felt disloyal even saying it.

'Alice doesn't fancy my husband any more, now he's ill,' Laura had said in one of their long chats. 'She's one of those people who, deep down, really believes cancer's contagious. Do you know, I'd trade anything to go back to the days when all I had to worry about was whether Tim was getting into her knickers.'

'I'm sure he wasn't.' But Clover had seen it too. No more flirtatious laughs with Tim. And Alice had barely mentioned either Laura or Tim to Clover. She had never rung to see how either of them were. It was as if they had been erased from her thoughts. She tried to explain it to George. 'Alice hasn't contacted Tim and Laura at all. Not even a card. She's dropped them completely.'

Upstairs, seven or eight teenagers were draped across mattresses and Clover thought she could hear sounds of

165

movement. She closed the door so that none of them would walk in on the argument. 'The thing is ...' she added, knowing that she shouldn't but unable to stop herself. 'I'd just like to feel that my husband was on my side whatever. That you would support me.'

'I *am* on your side,' he told the washing-up bowl. 'I've always been on your side. But how I'm expected to support you in this latest campaign of yours, I can't imagine.' He turned round again. 'Shall I ring Alice now and say I can't come and talk about Pets & Things? My wife is feeling a bit used. Stuff your job. Eh?'

'What do you mean, job?' asked Clover, her heart and lungs suddenly shifting again.

'At this stage, of course, there's not necessarily a job. We're talking in a very preliminary way. It will probably never happen.' George spoke slowly, as if she were about six. 'But if it does, and if the money's right, Alice has promised that I'd be first choice for MD of the spin-off company.'

'You never said.'

'You never asked.'

'I feel worried about you going into business with friends.'

'The way you're talking, Alice can scarcely be classified as a friend.'

'That's not true. And you know what I mean.'

'No, Clover. I do *not* know what you mean any more.' He put the washing-up brush down and turned to her. He opened his arms and half of Clover wanted to bury herself in them. The other half wanted him to say that yes, he understood what was worrying her. That Alice was great fun but that it was Clover's judgement he trusted, and that he would be careful. Most of all, she did not want her whole future, her mortgage, her house and her husband tied up in Alice's business. The thought was more frightening than anything else so far.

'Please don't leave your job for Alice's company,' she said. 'Please don't.'

Irritation crossed his face again as he dropped his arms. 'Of course I won't. What do you think I am? But if the writing's on the wall at Petfast – and it could so easily be – I'll jump before I'm pushed. There aren't many jobs for a fifty-five-year-old man these days. I'd be a fool to turn down an opportunity to run my own show.'

They eyeballed each other. Clover was the first to change the subject. 'By the way, Duncan has offered me a stint as a junior junior *junior* decorator.'

'I thought you didn't believe in going into business with friends.'

'It's different. I'm working for him, not going into business with him. And I won't be giving anything up to do it.'

'Did you think of asking me whether I minded my wife working as a manual labourer for one of our friends?'

'I suppose I'm asking you now. But I didn't think you'd mind.'

'I didn't think you'd mind if I worked for Alice.' His shoulders dropped. 'Look, I'm sorry. If you really want to do this, of course I'm happy for you. But it won't be like painting with Laura or Alice, and I don't want you to be disappointed when it doesn't work out. It's hard physical work, and you won't be among people like you.'

'I know. But I thought it was worth a go.' Clover sighed. 'And I'm sorry, too. I don't mean to argue. We're both tired. It was a late night.'

George sighed in exasperation and stacked the flan dish on the rack. 'Just let me finish this, and I'll have a quick shower. Then I'll drop Lola off, have a quick meeting with

Alice and check on your father. I'll be back mid-afternoon some time.'

'Thank you. And sorry.' Clover stood on tiptoe to kiss his cheek.

He acknowledged the kiss with a rueful grin, let the water out of the sink and mopped up around it. 'It's a good idea, this thing with Duncan. It'll take your mind off the kids not being around.'

Still rubbing their eyes and stretching as they came, one by one, downstairs to the kitchen, the Crew slowly woke up: Adam first, then Holly, Sandeep, Ruby and Joe.

'Where are Lola and Ben?' asked Clover.

Adam, Holly and Joe looked at each other.

'Oh no,' said Clover. 'Don't tell me. Just don't tell me. How long has this been going on?'

'You said not to tell you.' Holly pulled some croissants out of the bread bin. 'Breakfast, anyone?'

'Well, Dad is just about to leave for Alice's, so I suggest someone gets Lola up and out so she can have a lift home. They're going to New York tomorrow, apparently.'

Holly, her hair a witch's tangle and eyes huge with smudged mascara, grinned at her. 'Who's got out of bed on the wrong side this morning?'

Around mid-afternoon, just as Clover was beginning to wonder whether she should ring George, he called to say that Colin was fine, but that he'd had some problems with his phone line. 'I'm fixing a couple of things for him around the house. I'll be back about six.' The tone of his voice was conciliatory.

Clover was determined to be conciliatory too, and not to ask how long he'd spent at Alice's or what he'd talked about. And, most definitely, it wasn't a good time to tell him about Ben and Lola. If, indeed, there was anything much to tell.

They did seem to be keeping quite a lot from each other these days.

Chapter 23

At half-past five in the morning, Laura couldn't sleep. She crept downstairs, made herself a cup of tea and decided to get ahead with removing the Christmas decorations. It was the fifth of January, and it was bad luck to leave them up past Twelfth Night. The Dangerfield family really didn't need any more bad luck.

With a knot of tension tightening in her stomach she worked her way methodically round the tree, placing each bauble carefully in its box, tugging the lights off and piling the boxes up. She then struggled to get the Christmas tree down, removing it from the iron grip of its stand – breaking two fingernails – and dragging it through the house to the garden. Outside there was a murky gloom, with dawn still over an hour away. She sniffed the air. Not so cold this morning. There were still a few patches of snow on the fields across the valley, but everything in the garden was muddy and soggy.

She set about cutting the Christmas tree up for kindling, and suddenly felt a deep pain crunching at the tip of her little finger. She had cut herself with the secateurs.

She ran her finger under the tap and tried not to cry. She was trying so hard. At everything. And she was hopeless. She would be useless without Tim.

'What's up?' Tim, already dressed, switched on the kitchen light, illuminating the morning gloom.

Laura blinked away tears. 'I was just cutting up the Christmas tree for kindling and nicked my finger. It'll be fine.'

Tim took her hand. 'That's nasty. Do you think it might need stitches?'

Laura shook her head. 'This family spends too much time in hospitals as it is. We've got plenty of bandages.'

Tim helped her. 'But why were you doing the Christmas tree anyway? It's always my job.' He looked at her intently.

'I couldn't sleep,' she said, not looking at him. 'I thought I might as well.' A little voice inside her spelt out the real answer. Tim might not be there next Christmas. She had to learn to survive alone. Without Tim or Jamie.

'You must ask for help. If you need it.'

Was he reading her thoughts? Laura nodded, still not looking at him. 'I will.'

'We need to leave in fifteen minutes.'

Laura sped upstairs. She wasn't dressed yet. It was the day for the results of the scan following the first two rounds of chemo. To see if it had worked.

They sat nervously in front of the consultant, David Craven, as he leafed through papers. 'Hm. Hm. Good. Good. Nmm . . . '

Laura wasn't sure if he was talking to himself, and whether 'good' applied to Tim's results or he was just speaking generally. She leaned forward, anxious.

He looked up at them with a smile of satisfaction. 'In fact, very good. Let me show you.' As Laura sagged back into her chair with relief, he pulled his laptop round. 'Here you can see a reduction in . . . ' Laura tuned the rest of it out. It was working. Tim would be fine. Next week's chemo would go ahead as planned.

'You see,' said Tim as they left. 'I'm going to be around to cut up Christmas trees for a few more years after all.'

She smiled back at him, weak with relief. 'Really. I know. I was only doing it to fill in time, not because I thought you couldn't do it.'

'Liar.' But he grinned back.

Jamie met them at the front door. 'Was it OK?'

'Was what OK?' They hadn't told him about the appointment.

'Come on, Dad. Both of you going out together at nine in the morning, looking smart. What do you think I am? An idiot? Or a child? Or both? I want to know, did that appointment or whatever it was, go OK?'

'It went very well.' Laura put a hand on his arm. 'Your father is responding very well to treatment, and the tumours have shrunk by almost half already.'

Jamie sighed in relief. 'You could have trusted me, you know.'

'We didn't want to worry you.'

'I'd be a lot less worried if I didn't think you two were keeping stuff from me.' Jamie folded his arms and looked down at her from six foot one inches above the ground, his rugby-player shoulders broader than she remembered. Had he grown again?

Tim put a hand on Laura's arm. 'Perhaps it's time we were all a bit more honest. I know we're trying to protect each other, but maybe we're not going about it in the best way.'

'Yeah, I'd agree with that,' said Jamie. 'I'm nineteen. I live away from home – well, at least part of the time. Hell, in many societies I'd be married with kids of my own by now. I think you could trust me with basic information, OK?'

Laura felt another layer of childhood being torn off him, like a worn, fraying baby blanket snatched away by the wind.

She wanted to clutch at it and wrap it tightly in her arms, feeling its soft familiarity. She wanted to protect him. She looked at Tim, who nodded his agreement.

'OK, darling. No more secrets.' She reached up to Jamie for a hug and a kiss, but couldn't reach him until he bent down.

'It's a deal. Mum – no more secrets. Dad? If you know something, I want to know it.'

Tim slapped Jamie on the back. They embraced. 'No more secrets,' he echoed.

Laura tried to stretch her arms round both men. *Not many more secrets, anyway. There is just one little thing I might not be sharing with you both.* She didn't even feel guilty.

She had to have something that was completely separate from all this, somewhere she could be Laura again, where there was always light and sparkle. A place where she could survive on her own, even if it was mainly inside her head.

Chapter 24

The Jones family arrived in Borough and found a parking space near Alice's flat.

Alice buzzed them up and was standing with the front door open. 'Welcome. Welcome. How heavenly to see you all. Bring your things in. Holly and Ben, you're on the sofas tonight. George and Clover, you're upstairs in the mezzanine.'

This was an area that Clover hadn't even noticed before, up a spiral staircase from the main big room. It had a double bed but no other furniture.

'The sheets have only been slept in by one person, Ekaterina – you know, the model? We've just hired her as the face of Shirts & Things so she was over for the latest shoot. But she's terribly clean, and she was only here for one night, so I knew you wouldn't mind.' Alice waved a hand at the bed. Clover put her bag down on the floor.

'I've booked a table for us all at a tapas bar nearby. And I've got some paint charts so we can talk about colours over supper.'

It was midnight before they got to bed. It was a restless night, partly due to Clover having had at least one glass of wine too many. And every time she turned over, she was assaulted by musky human smells, and the occasional whiff of cigar smoke. Did Ekaterina smoke cigars? Or had she smuggled a lover up to the mezzanine without Alice knowing? Neither seemed terribly likely. If Ekaterina had indeed only spent one night in these sheets, it must have been quite a night. Clover wondered if it would be very provincial of her to launder the sheets the following day. And how would she broach the subject with Alice?

Three times she tiptoed awkwardly down the spiral staircase to go to the loo and, the last time, noticed that the sofa on which Ben had been sleeping was empty. Presumably he was with Lola.

But Ben was back, stretched out on the sofa, by the time she awakened, filled with excitement at the thought of painting. The sheets would be fine for the second night – they'd have got used to them.

By six-thirty, she couldn't sleep any longer, and got up. Duncan had told her about a decorator's merchant not far from Alice's, where she could buy paint, brushes and any equipment. 'I go there almost every day,' he'd said, 'if I've got a job in London. It opens at seven.'

She might as well get on with getting sample pots of the three paint shades they'd identified as possibles, plus some filler, sandpaper and brushes. It would be easier to find the place if she went now, before the traffic built up.

The decorators' merchant was under three railway arches, and at ten past seven was buzzing with men of all ages in jeans and overalls. Everyone seemed to know exactly what they were doing. They all turned round as if to assess Clover, who felt out of place, provincial and very female. Was she really allowed here if she wasn't a professional?

The boys behind the counter treated her indulgently, as if

she were a particularly funny joke, and she thought she heard a certain amount of joshing behind her, but she got everything she needed. As she was leaving, she almost crashed into a familiar wiry body with a shock of steel-grey hair.

'Duncan!'

He held the door open. 'Clover.' He smiled at her. 'What are you doing here?'

'You told me about this place, remember?'

'Oh yes, you're painting Alice's flat. Look, I've got to pick up some filler, but I'm off to breakfast at the caff opposite. Join me?'

Clover hesitated. 'Oh, why not? Everyone else is sound asleep.'

They ordered greasy fried eggs, pink slabs of bacon and crisp, golden triangles of fried bread, eating hungrily as they talked about paint colours and sandpaper. Duncan slapped two huge white mugs of tea down on the table. It was strong – almost bitter.

'Delicious,' declared Clover as she put her knife and fork together, feeling the excitement of being alive, in a strange city on a misty morning, eating breakfast with an attractive man. Intermittently there was a whoosh and a roar as a train rattled overhead. As the winter sun warmed the grimy window she could hear the mounting hum of traffic. Each figure hurrying past seemed to have a purpose, their heads bent against the sunlight as the mist evaporated. It was like being abroad. 'I usually only have a piece of toast,' she said. The bacon and eggs felt like rocket fuel, and she could feel her energy levels soar.

'Nothing beats a proper breakfast. It's scientifically proven.' Duncan leant his elbows on the table, his sleeves rolled up to reveal powerful forearms. 'How are the kids?'

'They're great. Holly loves Leeds, and Ben . . . well, I never really know with Ben, but he seems fine. How's Joe?'

Duncan frowned. 'It's difficult to tell. I think losing his mum at that age hit him hard.'

'It must have done.' Clover thought of how vulnerable Ben had been at seventeen, and how he still needed her. Just occasionally — even if he pretended he didn't.

'There was something I wanted to ask you.' Duncan suddenly began to search his pockets, as his mobile phone rang. 'Yes? Yes? OK, I'll be right there.' He snapped the phone shut. 'Sorry about that. The client's just arrived, a good hour before we were expecting him.' He slammed the empty mug down on his plate. 'Don't let me rush you, though.'

'Don't worry, I've finished.'

When Clover got back to Alice's flat it smelt of burnt toast. 'Where've you been?' asked Alice. 'You weren't around for breakfast. We had to do it by ourselves.'

There was a peevish note to her voice.

'I went out early to get some paint samples. And the stuff we need to prep the room with.' Clover decided not to say that she'd had breakfast with Duncan. A line of disapproval was already deepening between Alice's brows, and Clover had a feeling that owning up to something that could be categorised as 'having fun' would not go down well. 'So, did everyone sleep well?' She kissed the top of Ben's head, and he acknowledged it with a small shaking-off nod.

'*I* slept well,' said Holly, with a wicked smile, 'but . . . '

Clover glared at her over Ben's head and Holly subsided into her glass of orange juice.

Alice sighed. 'One forgets how much there is to *do* once they're all back, don't you find, Clover? Breakfast for six is quite an undertaking.'

177

'Five,' said Holly, her eyes sparkling. 'Mum wasn't here, remember?'

'It's rather a lovely part of London, isn't it, under the arches where the paint shop is? With all those trains rattling over-head?' suggested Clover, hoping to change the subject. 'It's so atmospheric. Almost Dickensian.'

'What are you talking about?' Alice sounded astonished. 'It's really grotty.'

They decided on a pale, almost silvery mushroom shade, with barely there grey paintwork. It took the whole of the first day to wash the walls with sugar soap, gouging out cracks in the plasterwork and re-filling them. George did the high-up work from the top of the ladder. Every half-hour Alice checked her e-mails or took a long, complicated phone call, which usually ended up with her issuing orders. 'It's all right for some,' she said to Clover. 'You're so lucky being able to concentrate on the job in hand.' With the children out shopping, they talked about them and how they were finding university.

'Holly is just going for it,' said Clover. 'I'm so proud of her. She's joined the entertainments committee and is getting involved with putting on bands. She's signed herself up for practically everything and seems to have a huge group of friends. It's harder to tell with Ben.'

There was a pause. Clover wondered if Alice knew about Ben and Lola, and, if so, whether she minded. But it was difficult to ask with George present.

'It's a bit harder at Oxford,' said Alice. 'They have to work so hard. Leeds is party central, everyone knows that.'

'Is Lola finding it difficult?'

Alice's eyes flashed. 'Not difficult, of course not. She's

178

having a great time. But there's a lot of pressure, and people whose children go to easier universities don't always understand that.'

There didn't seem to be any reply to that, so Clover concentrated on filling a crack.

'The trouble is,' said Alice, in a more conciliatory voice, 'I think Lola is desperate to find her real father.'

'Isn't it time to tell her, then?'

'It's not that simple.' Alice squeezed out a sponge and looked at her bucket. 'I'm just off to change this water.' When she came back, George had left the room.

'I'm not sure that this ... thing ... with Ben is helping, actually,' she whispered. 'I was wondering if you could have a word with him. It's so important that she doesn't get distracted from this amazing opportunity of being at Oxford. It would be a shame if Ben spoilt it for her.'

Clover was shaken. She couldn't believe that Alice had actually said that about Ben. Her beautiful boy would not 'spoil' anything for anyone. 'I'm sure he won't. But don't you think they'll go all star-crossed lovers if either of us says anything? It might make it worse.'

'Well, you've always had a very relaxed attitude to what your children get up to, but it's not so easy for me because I'm on my own. There's only me and Lola.'

'Well, um ...' Clover tried to decide how to reply. 'I've only just found out about it myself. Maybe George can say something, man to man.'

'Thank you,' said Alice. 'I knew I could rely on you. It's just not great that she's going up to York at weekends instead of getting involved in what's going on at Oxford. I'm sure you understand that.'

'Is she? I didn't realise.' Clover wondered whether the reason why they'd seen so little of Alice was that she was deliberately cutting her ties with Kent in order to get Lola out of Ben's range. It was quite possible.

Alice's phone went again. 'Sorry,' she mouthed at Clover. 'Important call.' She retired to the cubbyhole where her desk and computer were, and remained there for most of the afternoon.

That evening the Crew had all arranged to meet to go clubbing while their parents looked at what was in the fridge. Not a lot.

'I don't know about you,' said Alice, 'but I'm exhausted. You two go out, though, don't worry about me.'

George yawned. 'I'm bushed. But there was a company I found on the internet who are doing something similar to Pets & Things – I've brought my laptop. Shall we go through it?'

'If Clover doesn't mind.' Alice leant forward with interest.

Clover opted to go out to buy some food and cook it, while Alice and George sat on the huge L-shaped sofa, poring over washable velveteen pet beds, diamond collars for rabbits and personalised diets for goldfish, Alice's huge laugh ringing out every time George made a comment. Clover saw George's tiredness drain away, and his face come alive with enthusiasm.

Clover found a DVD of a film she hadn't seen and slotted it into the machine at the other end of the room, turning the sound down as low as she could manage. Alice was clearly stressed about Lola. But it was not Ben's fault. Clover, curled up on one of the massive sofas, her feet tucked under her and a glass of wine in her hand, decided to say so. It might be best to wait until Alice was in a better mood, though. In the meantime, Kevin Spacey and Tom Hanks on the widescreen TV reminded her that spending time with attractive men was a very pleasant experience. Breakfast had been fun. It was her little secret.

She got the chance to defend Ben as they were stacking the dishwasher.

'Alice, Ben is certainly not doing anything deliberately to harm Lola. They're both very reserved, and perhaps they need each other at the moment.'

Alice put a hand on Clover's arm. 'I hope I haven't upset you, Clover. I just thought you ought to know what was going on, that's all. Especially as Lola is just that bit younger than Ben, and is easily led.'

'I really don't think that Ben can be held responsible for any problems she's having settling in at uni.'

Alice threw her head back and laughed. 'Clover, Clover, you are such a gem. Forget I said anything. The last thing I want to do is upset you.' She put an arm round Clover's shoulders and squeezed.

The next day they opened up the cans of paint and began the first coat. After an hour, Alice went to the bathroom and vomited.

Clover was alarmed. 'Are you all right?'

Alice, ashen, clung onto the frame of the bathroom door for support. 'Fine. It must have been something we ate last night.'

'George and I are both fine.'

'Or maybe paint fumes.' She closed her eyes and looked as if she were about to collapse.

Clover thought of saying that she didn't think paint had fumes any more, but Alice was so pale that it didn't seem like a particularly helpful remark.

Alice spent the morning asleep in bed, while George and Clover painted Lola's room.

By the afternoon her face was still grey, but she was sitting up with her laptop open.

'Are you feeling better?' Clover asked.

Alice grimaced. 'A bit. An effing e-mail has just come in that I need to respond to immediately. It's extremely difficult to think about supply chains if you feel sick.'

Clover and George went on painting late into the night. 'We might as well,' said George. 'Then, if Alice is better tomorrow, we can finish off early and do something together.'

Alice was still pale and unable to eat anything the following morning. She lay back among her pillows looking as if she were about to die. Clover was worried. 'Why don't I call a doctor? I think that might be sensible.'

'Yes, but they don't do house calls these days, and I couldn't possibly go in a car.'

'Well, I could phone NHS Direct or something?'

'You could, but I'm sure it's just an allergy of some kind. I've had it before. Was there any kiwi fruit in that salad you did?'

'No, I'm sure there wasn't.'

'The headache's the worst of it now. I think the sickness has pretty much gone.'

'I've got some ibuprofen. Why don't you take some of that?'

Alice flapped her hand. 'I'm even more allergic to ibuprofen than I am to kiwi fruit.'

Clover suggested paracetamol instead.

'That won't do any good. It's pointless. It never has any effect on me.'

Clover offered aspirin and, in desperation, even echinacea and Rescue Remedy in turn, but Alice rejected them all for various reasons. 'Really, it's very kind of you. You two just have a nice time. Don't worry about me.'

Alice closed her eyes and Clover crept away. In the end, she and George finished painting Lola's room, got the Crew to put all the furniture back and packed up their possessions.

She tapped on Alice's bedroom door.

'Come in.' Alice's voice was still faint. 'Hi. I hope you're having a bit of fun.'

'We've just finished the painting, and then we'll be off,' said Clover.

'That's so sweet of you.' Alice sounded very weak and faded.

'But I'm worried that you're still ill. Do you promise you'll call a doctor if you don't get better tomorrow?'

Alice nodded. 'I promise. And Lola will look after me.'

Lola had asked to come back down to Kent with the Joneses for a few days. Clover sent her in to discuss it with her mother, and she came out shaking her head. 'I think I'd better stay with Mum.'

Clover let Ben and Lola say goodbye quietly, sending Holly off with George to get the car.

Once home Holly declared that she wanted to make brownies.

Clover decided to help her, and to see if she knew what was going on. 'Alice said that Lola pops up to see Ben at weekends.'

'She went *once*.' Holly sounded scathing. She measured out ingredients on Clover's old-fashioned scales.

'Alice is worried that she's not settling in because she's being distracted by Ben. And that she's going to miss out.'

'Alice needs to get off Lola's back. She's down there almost every weekend, chivvying her into joining things – that's why Lola keeps telling her she's going up to York.' Holly sifted and added ingredients into a large mixing bowl, one eye on the recipe. 'And she thinks Lola should be writing for the college newsletter or some student arts paper. But the worst of it is the friends business. She thinks Lola's too shy to make friends. She turned up one day and demanded to see the Master, to talk about whether Lola was socialising properly or being bullied, but he said he wouldn't talk to her without Lola's permission, because she's an adult. Alice was furious.'

'I can imagine she was. But maybe she's just having trouble understanding the transition from schoolgirl to student. It's quite odd for us all, you know. And Alice hasn't got a partner so there's no one she can talk it over with. It's not surprising that it can get a bit out of control.'

'She could talk it over with you. You don't hover over us with helpful advice and insist on checking our essays before we give them in.'

Clover was warmed by the implicit compliment. 'She seems to be very critical of me at the moment. I don't understand it: Alice is usually very laid back. She must be worried about something, and it's coming out in over-protectiveness and criticism.'

Holly shrugged. 'I've never thought of Alice as laid back. She just doesn't care about some things, but she can be quite fierce if it's anything to do with Lola.'

'Are Ben and Lola serious, do you know?'

Holly turned on the electric whisk, and a loud rattling filled the room.

Clover waited, putting away the packets of flour, cocoa powder and sugar.

Eventually Holly stopped and tested the cake mixture. 'If they want to talk to you about their relationship they can. But I'm not going to be used as a spy. There. Do you think that's about right?'

Clover tasted it. 'Delicious.' She hugged Holly, comforted by her daughter's good sense.

The phone rang. It was Laura, to say that Tim's scan showed that the chemo had begun to work. 'They're so pleased that they're probably going to give him even more chemo than they'd planned. Apparently that's what's known as good news in the world of cancer.'

'Fantastic.' Clover took the phone into the sitting room so that Holly couldn't hear, and recounted the story of the last few days.

'Do you mean to say,' demanded Laura 'that she lay in bed sending e-mails while you and George painted her daughter's bedroom?'

'No, really, it wasn't like that. She was clearly very ill, absolutely grey. I heard her vomiting – she could hardly fake that. We didn't do any more than any friend would have done in that situation. I mean, you'd hardly walk out, would you? Come on, tell me: would you have downed your paint-brushes, saying you'd come back when she was well enough? No, you wouldn't.'

'Hmm.' Laura's tone was cynical. 'Did you ever find out what was wrong?'

'No, I haven't heard from her. Maybe she just collapsed because she could. Whatever you say, it's pretty tough running a company and bringing up a child all on your own. Maybe she knew she could relax once George and I were there.'

There was another snort of laughter from Laura. 'Her Christmas sounded like a pretty relaxed situation to me.'

Clover went on to explain about Ben and Lola, and Alice's concern. 'I hadn't pegged Alice for a helicopter parent, though. She's always seemed so casual.'

'Mm. As in a crocodile is "casual" when it creeps out of the river to snaffle your leg. She's absolutely focused about everything, and you know it.'

'Laura!'

'I mean it. She could act all carefree and laid back while they were at school, because she had you to pick up the pieces. How many times did she "forget" about dressing-up days, home-clothes days or making things for the school fair? Always. Because she knew she had someone to remind her. But she knows she can't get anyone else to hover over Lola and chivvy her along now, so she's doing it herself.'

'Laura, this is just going over old ground. I think we both have to move on, don't you?'

'Well, as long as you realise that Lola being unhappy at Oxford is not Ben's fault. And it's not up to you to make it right.'

'No, don't worry. Of course it's not Ben's fault. And I feel cross that she's making it his fault.'

'And you don't like feeling cross, do you? You would only feel cross on Ben's behalf, and not on your own. You're Clover, who hates confrontation. Have you thought about getting some help? You know, professional counselling?'

'Not you too. George thinks I'm going mad.'

'I don't think you're mad, but I do think that some of the old questions that we all had before we had children haven't gone away. They were just muffled by the whole frantic looking-after-kids thing.'

'I don't have any questions. Except about what I am going to do to earn a living.'

'Clover Jones,' said Laura with mock severity. 'You have not stopped asking questions since you closed the door on your children when they first left for uni.'

Clover laughed. 'Rubbish.' But, as she put the phone down, she realised that a lump of resentment had lodged in her throat, choking her. She would not have wanted to confide it to anyone, not even Laura.

Alice had not thanked them for painting the room, nor had

she apologised for being too ill to help or to entertain them. Just as she hadn't thanked them for helping with her drinks party, or apologised for the lack of a comfortable bed. 'Thank you' and 'sorry' were the simplest words of friendship. And, once again, they had not been spoken.

Chapter 25

Baxtersblog. 15 January

After the commercialism of Christmas, the Baxters are turning their eyes towards the spiritual side of life. We've said goodbye to the kids and, although it was great to see them, it's also always great to see them go. All parents should remember that their job in life is to give their young both roots and wings. As you pile up your car to take them back to uni, fortified with instructions and extra tuck, remember that today's parents are far, far too protective. It doesn't make our children feel any more secure or any more able to survive in the world today. We're proud that Milly and Adam are making their own way back to uni from halfway across the world, with nothing more than a backpack. We know our kids will be able to stand on their own two feet.

We'll be offline for a few weeks while we retreat to the ashram of . . .

Clover read half of the Baxters' latest instalment after dropping Ben back at York, having spent a night at an old friend's house on the way back down. Home felt cold and dark, with an unused smell about it. Bonnie and Clyde unwound themselves from the airing cupboard, where they had taken up permanent residence, mewing with indignation at having been left for forty-eight hours with only a neighbour popping in to feed them. Diesel, stretching himself after the long car journey, looked at her reproachfully and whined. He bounded upstairs, and she could hear him checking first Holly's and then Ben's rooms.

She opened windows and made herself some coffee. This was freedom. Nobody to cook meals for. No more staggering round the supermarket with a trolley that was trying to go in a different direction from the one she wanted to go in. No lying awake at three in the morning, waiting to hear the sound of their car door slamming.

But everything felt wrong, as if her skin no longer fitted. She fretted over it. First, Ben, she thought, had not really wanted to go. They'd chatted happily about everything – TV shows, books, music – on the way up. Being able to talk to him as an adult was a joy. But she rarely asked him personal questions because it made him shut down. She'd risked just one.

'So, are you looking forward to getting back?' she asked brightly.

'Not really.' He gazed out of the window.

'But you've got some nice friends. And you said the course was all right ...' Clover was alarmed. The most important thing about university was that it should be fun. Wasn't it?

'It's OK, Mum, don't get your knickers in a twist.' He gave her a grin that was so like George's that she almost laughed. 'I'll be fine.'

'Um, what about Lola?' It was the first time she'd dared mention it, but he was trapped in the passenger seat of the car and they were going at seventy-five miles an hour down the motorway. He couldn't storm out.

She gripped the steering wheel in anticipation of being sworn at.

But he just grinned at her again and put his headphones back in.

'Alice thinks you should both settle in to your own universities a bit more, and really get to know people there. She thinks that Lola leaving Oxford at weekends means she isn't really settling in.' Clover raised her voice so that he could hear her, but Ben didn't respond. He closed his eyes and nodded his head in time with the music; she could just hear a tinny 'shakah shakah shakah' over the sound of the engine.

George would be back that evening, having dropped Holly off at Leeds. Tomorrow she was starting as Duncan's apprentice. She looked at her phone. It would be nice to talk to someone.

She'd like to talk to Alice. The old Alice, who turned everything into a joke, and was so sure about everything. But Alice would be busy, dismissive and bossy, and their recent encounters had added a note of restraint between them. Clover felt bruised. Angry.

She reminded herself that she had a new job. Even if it was only as a temporary decorating assistant. So she opened up her e-mails, and enjoyed being irritated by the way the Baxters seemed to think they had the secrets of the universe worked out. So delivering your children back to uni was cosseting them, was it? Well, perhaps Adam and Milly deserved a bit more cosseting.

When George returned he was grey and tired.

'Did Holly go off all right?'

'Yeah, she was fine. Couldn't wait.' He hung up his coat.

'I thought Ben wasn't all that keen.' She allowed a note of anxiety to creep into her voice.

George sighed. 'He's got to learn.'

'What has he got to learn?' The note was sharper this time, and she could feel her anger flashing up.

George swung round. 'Just give it a break, OK? Give me a break.'

Clover was stung by the irritation in his voice. 'Fine.' She went out into the garden. The air was warmer now, although the trees were still charcoal sketches against a parchment sky.

The following morning Duncan, looking lean and grizzled in a leather jacket, rang the doorbell at seven-thirty. 'Ready?'

Clover felt nervous. 'Of course. Am I dressed OK?' She was wearing the cheap white overalls she'd bought from the builder's merchants but, not made for bosoms, they were too tight across her chest. She felt self-conscious.

'Perfect.' They got into a battered estate car and Duncan removed the remains of a muffin from the passenger seat. 'Sorry. Breakfast.' He ate it with one hand while driving with the other, and talking.

'This is my favourite kind of job – the clients haven't moved in yet. They're a Mr and Mrs Dundy. Bit difficult. New money, but interested in old houses. She's . . . ' He turned to grin at her. 'Well, you won't have to deal with her unless you're very unlucky.' He ran through the project – a listed Georgian town house that had been offices but was being converted back into a home, with rigorous conditions from the conservation officer and the need to use traditional methods and materials. 'It's quite a headache to find a good lime plasterer or a first-class tiler.' The lines around Duncan's mouth crinkled up to his eyes as he smiled again.

When they arrived at the house – a classical double-fronted house in a small Canterbury side street – Duncan introduced her to the rest of the team. 'Chris is the chief carpenter and jack of all trades. He's in charge when I'm not here, as I'm usually project-managing at least two jobs at once. Dave is doing first- and second-fix plumbing, Stanislaus is on electrics, Mac is the lime plasterer and Lee does the heavy work.' His voice echoed in the big, empty room. Clover found herself looking at all the ages of man, from sixteen to seventy.

Lee, clearly a teenager, grinned impishly at her. 'Hallo Miss.'

Dave, a heavyset man in his mid-fifties, looked her up and down. 'So you fancy doing a bit of decoratin' then, Poppy?'

'It's Clover,' she murmured, trying not to blush.

'Chris, Clover here is an artist and has done some great decorating in her own home, but she probably doesn't know much about the way we work, so I'm going to give her some basic guidance, and otherwise leave her in your hands.'

'You can leave her in our hands, all right,' leered Dave, winking at Clover.

Chris was a mild-looking man in his thirties. 'That's enough, Dave. Leave the lady alone. Dave's our resident expert on sexual harassment.'

'I don't do 'arassment, I'm a ladies' man,' grumbled Dave. 'Ladies appreciate banter, don't they, Daisy?'

'It's Clover,' said Chris.

'I knew it was a flower.' He winked at her again and lumbered out of the room, whistling.

'Sorry about Dave. He's a bit unreconstructed,' said Duncan. 'But he's a first-rate plumber. One of the best. Come through here. We're going to start with this little study.'

Clover thought he probably wanted to see how she worked before letting her loose on a larger area.

'We need to gouge out any cracks . . . ' – he knelt down and demonstrated on a plaster crack close to the floor – 'and fill with the appropriate filler. We use a French make called

Toupret. Then you sand it down. Prepping this room should keep you busy.'

'And out of Dave's way,' muttered Chris, standing behind them.

Clover worked around the room, from floor to ceiling. Behind her, in the next room, she could hear Lee and Stanislaus over the sound of Radio One. From time to time Chris came in and checked what she was doing. He crouched down, felt the filled cracks with his fingers and went off without saying anything. Her knees, back and arm began to ache.

Duncan, who was working elsewhere in the house, reappeared. 'Hm. Good. Just here though . . . '

Clover let her thoughts drift as she worked. George. He was worried about his job, she knew that. It made him short-tempered. It was also why he was so interested in Pets & Things. And he missed Holly.

Then there was Alice. In terms of Alice and George. She hadn't told Laura too much about how George seemed when he was around Alice, because she would immediately jump to the wrong conclusions. Clover was sure they were wrong. Why would Alice bother with a provincial executive? Judging by a few comments she'd dropped, she was now partying with people like Ekaterina and some of London's A-list businessmen. George was rumpled, chunky and practical. The people Alice mixed with glittered.

Clover took out her mobile and looked at it. Every day she expected a text, an e-mail or a call from Alice to thank them for painting Lola's room, and suggesting another date for the good time in London they hadn't been able to have because she had been unwell. But it never came. And, sitting in an empty room, methodically scraping out old plaster repairs and renewing them, Clover could see that everything had a lifespan. Even friendship.

Her friendship with Alice had reached the end of its life when Alice had said that a relationship between Ben and Lola would 'hold Lola back'. It was a solid, heavy feeling. Like a bereavement.

She straightened up, and her knees protested. A loo visit would stretch her legs. Chris had shown her where it was – a small cupboard at the back of the house, which had been retained while the rest of the building was being ripped out. Clover wondered who was responsible for cleaning it. There was a distinct watermark in the bowl and a certain stickiness over everything. An old topless calendar hung on the back of the door and, when she washed her hands, she couldn't find a towel.

Picking her way back over paint pots and lengths of timber, she could hear Dave and Chris working in the room above, their voices echoing in the emptiness. 'So Duncan's installed 'is latest lady friend, I see,' Dave guffawed.

'I don't think she's necessarily a lady friend,' said Chris.

'Have you seen how he looks at her. Phwoar . . . '

'Well, yeah, I think he does fancy her. But that don't mean she fancies him. And don't go taking it out on her. She's not likely to last long, but he won't like you frightening her away.'

'I won't 'ave to frighten her away.' Dave sounded confident. 'I give her till the end of the week, and then she'll be bored of playing decorators.'

Clover heard Chris laugh, and shut the door. There was some further murmuring. Her cheeks flamed red. She couldn't imagine Duncan fancying a fifty-five year old housewife. But it was humiliating to think that that's why they thought she had the job.

She wasn't sure whether to join the others for lunch, but decided not to seem standoffish. Chris and Dave had each brought a folding chair, some sandwiches and a thermos.

Clover sat on the floor, her back against the wall, and unwrapped the sandwiches she'd brought from home.

'Here, have my seat.' Chris jumped up.

She shook her head. She didn't want any special treatment. There was an awkward silence, and Dave shook out his copy of the *Sun*, folding it and leaving it face up on the floor at page 3. She wasn't certain if the sight of a pair of pneumatic breasts was intended to make her uncomfortable. If so, Dave had picked the wrong tactics. She wasn't going to be frightened off by a pair of airbrushed boobs.

Chris asked her a few questions, establishing that she was married and had a family. When she mentioned George, he and Dave exchanged a meaningful glance – presumably over Duncan – which she pretended not to have noticed. At one point Lee, talking in an undertone to Stanislaus about football, said 'fuckin' 'ell'.

'Oi, oi, ladies present,' snapped Dave, winking at her.

'Don't worry. I don't fucking mind.' She treated Dave to her sweetest smile.

They all looked appalled. She folded up her sandwich wrapper and looked at her watch. 'Is that the time? I'd better get back to work.'

On her way back to the study she saw a mobile on the stairs as she walked past. It began ringing. She picked it up, and saw that the image of a horned devil had come up as the caller identification. 'Whose phone?' she called.

'Oh, it's mine.' Chris put a hand out to reclaim it. A moment later she heard him saying 'Yes, Mrs Dundy. No, Mrs Dundy.'

'She saw the devil on the phone,' Lee commented as Chris put it back in his pocket.

Chris went pink. 'Don't tell the boss, OK?'

'I didn't see anything,' she assured him.

At four o'clock they started to pack up. Chris checked her work again, still without comment. 'Tomorrow you can give that an undercoat. Then Duncan's doing one of his specialist treatments on it. They want it marbled.' He snorted. 'A marbled study! You see some funny sights in this business, you do.'

'So we'll be seeing you tomorrow then?' called Dave. It was a challenge. He placed a slight, but unmistakeable, emphasis on 'seeing'.

'See you then,' agreed Clover, resolving to bring a folding chair, a cushion to kneel on, a small radio, a thermos. Oh, and a towel. Possibly some Domestos. Loo paper certainly. She was beginning to see why Duncan drove an estate car.

'Want a lift home, Clover?' Duncan was last out, locking up the house.

Clover tried not to blush. 'Oh, er, yes, very kind. But I can bring my own car tomorrow if there's somewhere to park it.'

'That's a tricky one on this job, because it's in town. You'd have to use the public car park. But I don't mind picking you up on my way past and dropping you off.'

The public car park charges – for a whole day – would eat into her seven pounds an hour. 'Thanks.'

'I hope Dave was OK. You won't have to deal with him much. Usually the wet trades – the plumbers and the plasterers – are out of the way before the painters come along. But it's a big house and we got the ground floor done first.'

'That's OK. I'll survive.' Clover smiled at him. If they thought a dirty loo and a few page-three breasts could frighten her off, they were much mistaken.

They drove in silence for a few miles. The thought that Duncan might fancy her echoed in her brain. She struggled to find a topic of conversation.

Eventually she thought of one: 'Has Joe gone back to uni?'

'He's going back tomorrow. Although, being in London,

he pops back down quite regularly. It doesn't seem too much of a hole in my life. What about Ben and Holly?'

'Back yesterday.'

Duncan must have picked up a note of desolation in her voice. 'You sound as if you need cheering up. How about we celebrate working together with a drink?'

'Now? It's only half-past four.'

'It's dark,' he said. 'The sun has gone over the yardarm. And we start early on building sites.'

'Oh, why not?' Clover was sick of being sensible.

After ten minutes Duncan turned off the main road. 'My favourite pub overlooks Oare Creek,' he said. 'Is that OK by you?'

It had a roaring fire and painted tongue-and-groove panelling. Clover let the wine warm her as she talked to Duncan about Ben and Holly, Ben and George, and Ben, Lola and Alice. Then Laura and Tim, and how the cancer seemed to have brought them closer together as a couple.

He listened carefully, and with sympathy. 'Now that I've heard all about everyone else,' he said finally, 'what about you?'

'What do you mean? I've been talking about me.'

He touched the back of her hand briefly, a barely perceptible contact. 'No, you haven't.' His eyes met hers. 'You haven't told me how you felt about today.'

'In fact, I really enjoyed it. I'd like to learn more.' She decided not to tell him about the devil image on the phone. She didn't want to get Chris into trouble.

'Well,' he grinned. 'That works just fine for me. You did well. Even Chris said so, and he doesn't approve of women on site.'

'*Chris* doesn't approve of women on site? I thought it was Dave!'

'They all disapprove. If it's approval you want, you've chosen the wrong industry.' He watched her carefully.

'I don't give a stuff about approval,' she lied. 'I just want to work.'

'Good girl.' He looked at his empty wine glass. 'Now what about the other half?'

'The same again? Let me get it.' She stood up. Drinking at five o'clock in the evening made her feel very drunk.

'Duncan,' she said as she sat down with their drinks. 'I overheard Chris and Dave talking about me upstairs. They seemed to think that you'd engaged me because you ... um ... well, you and I were ... um ...'

His eyes gleamed in amusement. 'You and me, eh? Are you worried?'

'About them talking about it?' Clover wasn't sure if she was right to raise the subject.

'Or me finding you attractive?'

'Well, you don't ... I presume.'

'No, of course not,' he said, roaring with laughter. 'Not in the slightest. Do you find me attractive?'

'Of course not,' she echoed. Somehow it seemed very funny.

'Well, that's got that sorted.' They both laughed until their sides hurt. You had to be there, she decided later, when considering whether or not she would tell Laura. Not, she thought.

Chapter 26

Five weeks later, Laura drove Tim to his fourth chemo session, dropping him outside the hospital and kissing him goodbye. He said there was no need for her to come in. He had some work to do. Cathy would be there, and one or two others who were on a three-week cycle.

She was almost sorry. The chemo room was the one place where Tim was normal. It was his world, the way school had been Jamie's, and where she, Laura, was on the sidelines but nonetheless had a role. Nobody looked at her with pity or spoke in hushed voices. In the chemotherapy day unit she and Tim were an ordinary couple.

She couldn't even drop in on Clover for a comforting cup of tea. Clover was in her fifth week at work, still prepping surfaces at the town house in Canterbury. And she was beginning to learn specialist paint techniques from Duncan.

Everybody's lives were diverging. She had the sense that she and Tim had been on parallel tracks for years, but that the cancer had thrown them back onto the same path. But now, several months into his treatment and with more to come, she could see Tim taking the high road, getting close to people that Laura knew nothing of and settling into routines that she could not possibly envy, but which left her standing uselessly on one side. While she was on the low road. The very lowest of all roads. Betrayal.

You take the high road and I'll take the low road. It echoed in her mind. She ached for Jamie, and for the simplicity of a life that revolved round him. Or whatever, as Jamie would say. Or would have said. He was so much more sensible now. And she still missed him so much. She couldn't believe that he would now only come home intermittently, and that the next step would be a flat of his own. Perhaps she would be a different person by then. A better, more loyal one. Tim would get well, and they could go back to their life as it was before his affair. The cancer had brought them so much closer together.

Laura parked the car and went into a coffee shop. She had to do something.

Or she would make a call.

And she must not make that call. She ought to throw her phone in the river.

Tim had not returned in time on New Year's Eve. The snow was deeper where Cathy lived, so he had gone home after dropping her, because it was much nearer and he was tired. He'd come over to the Joneses' house at Pilgrim's Worthy in the morning of New Year's Day to pick Laura up. She plunged her face into her hands at the memory of that night, careless of whoever might be watching.

'Can I help you?' asked a voice.

It took several repetitions before she realised she was only being asked for her coffee order. For a moment, for a blessed, precious moment, she thought someone might actually be offering to help her. That they could take away the pain and the longing. 'Oh, er, yes . . . of course. A skinny cappuccino. Thanks.' She picked up a newspaper to give herself something to do, flicking through the pages without seeing them.

But New Year's Eve didn't count. It was meaningless. Completely irrelevant. Just two bodies, a fumbling of zips and buttons, an urgency of lips and thighs, of hard against soft, of strength against weakness, of limbs that fitted together perfectly and others that were just in the way. She had hardly been able to breathe, hadn't been able to keep her gasps silent although she had tried. Desperately. She had clutched at him as he'd grasped at her, as if they'd been swept together and tossed about in the irresistible current of life.

When they finished she had, finally, dared to look into his eyes, still fighting for breath. 'We shouldn't do this.'

'Should and shouldn't don't exist for us.' He cupped her head in his hands and she could feel their strength, his hot breath against her lips.

'There is no "us",' she whispered.

'There is always us. There always has been and there always will be.' He cocked his head, and placed a finger on her lips. 'Shh, someone's coming.'

It seemed impossible that whoever the footsteps belonged to could fail to hear their breath, still coming in ragged gasps, but they passed and went into the bathroom.

He quickly bent his head and kissed her. 'I'll see you,' he said. And was gone.

The memory burned through her entire body, filling her with liquid desire. She must focus. On things. Like getting some work. Yes. Work. Like Clover.

The paper was a tabloid, and not one she usually read. It was all gossip. Film stars and their divorces and pregnancies. She noted, with a brief flash of dissatisfaction, a story about an actress she'd been at drama school with, who was now considered a national treasure. Her latest film was bound to lead to an Oscar nomination, according to the gushing interview. No one had ever rated her, thought Laura, as she turned the page with a sniff. They were all completely baffled as to how she'd done so well for herself.

But then, like a slap in the face, she saw a picture of Alice and Lola under the headline 'Tycoon's daughter finds long-lost dad'. Beside it was a picture of someone called John Wright, a wealthy West Country landowner. Across his chest was splashed the banner 'the hands-off dad'.

'Lola Fanshawe, 19, was brought up by her single mother, attractive blonde catalogue tycoon Alice Fanshawe, 49. When brainy Lola won a place at Oxford ...' Laura read on. It seemed that Lola, 'desperate to know who her father was', had approached the newspaper with various documents – bank statements and diaries – she'd found in Alice's desk and managed to photocopy. The newspaper had done some more digging and had eventually taken Lola to challenge her father as he left church last Sunday morning. His words were reported to have been: 'I pay your mother good money to keep this story quiet. That's the end of anything you'll ever get from me.' Alice, on a business trip to Shanghai, made 'no comment'.

Laura dialled Clover. 'I need to see you.'

'I'm working.'

'I'll come to the site. I won't be more than ten minutes, but there's something you have to see.'

Half an hour later Laura handed the newspaper to Clover.

'What an unpleasant man,' commented Clover after reading it. 'This will hurt Lola much more than simply not knowing ever could. I can see why Alice said it wasn't simple.'

'She always led us to believe that she'd had no financial support from the father. That she was struggling.'

'It probably wasn't very much. I always thought it either must be someone very famous, who needed to keep it a secret for, say, political reasons, or else a holiday romance. A Greek fisherman or a French waiter, or something. But he's not particularly special.'

'Just rich. And respectable.' Laura read the story again. 'His own children are Lola's age. So presumably that's why he paid Alice to keep quiet.'

'It's a rather sad and sordid story, don't you think? A rich, married man and what must have been an impoverished young woman without any family to help her. You have to give Alice credit for not having an abortion, and for going it alone. She's very brave. I must call her. Do you mind if I quickly do it now? I'll just leave a message – she hardly ever picks up during the working day.' Laura could hear the tinny tones of voicemail as Clover left a message. 'So sorry to hear about Lola's father, and that it all came out so publicly like that. I hope you and she are OK. Lots of love, Clover.'

She clicked the phone off. 'Thanks for telling me. How's Tim?'

'Fourth chemo. Doing fine, apparently. They're giving him something different today, because he's responded so well so far.' Laura forced herself to concentrate on the thought of her husband.

Because the fire still burned. Even though she was holding a newspaper in her hands, filled with stories that showed how much damage affairs could do, she knew she couldn't help herself. It was wrong.

'Are you all right, Laura?' Clover's voice seemed very far away.

'Yes. Yes, of course. Just, you know . . . Tim's cancer.'

You are a liar, Laura Dangerfield. A scheming, unfaithful liar who would betray your friends and your ill husband.

Sometimes Laura didn't think she deserved to live.

203

Chapter 27

For the first time in the five weeks since she'd started working for Duncan, Clover found herself hanging around.

'Chris, what do you want me to do now?' Dave and Stanislaus had long since left the site, leaving it entirely to her and Chris, Lee and – for a couple of hours a day – Duncan.

'We need to get on with the painting the bedroom,' said Chris. 'But Mrs Dundy hasn't made up her mind what colour she wants. It's the last room. Then we're finished.'

As if on cue, there was the sound of a key in the lock. 'Hello everybody!' A woman in cream trousers, a camel-coloured trench coat and expensive blonde highlights stepped into the hall, looking out of place among the planks, ladders and pots of paint. It was clearly Mrs Dundy who, until that point, had been nothing more to Clover than a devil image on Chris's phone.

Chris cleared his throat. 'Have you decided what colour you want the spare bedroom? We need to get on with it today.'

'Dark,' she said with a tight smile. 'Very dark and moody. I want a boudoir feel.'

'You were going to do it pale cream,' warned Chris.

'I've got too many pale colours as it is. I want something

204

with a bit more oomph.' Her heels echoed on the bare wood as she began to climb the stairs. 'I was thinking black.'

'Black?' echoed Chris, exchanging glances with Clover.

Duncan came upstairs from the basement. 'Hello, Mrs Dundy.'

She looked over the banisters. 'I was just telling Chris that I'd like that last bedroom to be dark.'

'Dark,' repeated Duncan.

The heels clicked up to the top of the stairs, and they heard the sound of the door opening.

'It's an east-facing room,' said Clover. 'It'd do well with something with a blue or green base.'

'You go up there and talk to her.' Duncan gestured up the stairs. 'Take some paint charts.'

'Hello.' Clover entered the room with a tentative knock.

'Yes? Who are you?'

'I'm one of Duncan's assistants. I've brought the paint charts up.'

Mrs Dundy held out a hand.

'There's often quite a blue light in an east-facing room,' Clover went on. 'So I thought you might think about something with a blue tone. Such as Farrow & Ball's Pelt. It's purple.'

'Purple?' Mrs Dundy clicked her fingers. 'Let me see.' She almost snatched the card from Clover's hand.

'It would work well with Charleston Grey and a light blue. And you've got quite a lot of Charleston Grey around the house, so it ties it all together nicely.'

'Have you got a design qualification?'

'I went to the Chelsea College of Art.'

'Hmm.' Mrs Dundy gave her a sharp look, but was obviously listening.

Clover fished out a Paint Library chart from her handbag. 'Or you could try an almost-black if you were feeling very brave. It can look great if you've got a lot of very strong pictures.'

'Hmm. OK. Get Duncan to paint a large swatch of each on the walls. I'll decide over the weekend.'

She stalked round the house, opening cupboards and doors, beckoning Clover to follow. Then she sighed. 'Well, what are you hanging around for?'

Clover passed the message on. Chris sighed. 'I'll get the sample pots in and paint them myself. You might as well knock off,' he said, neatly packing the tools and paints into one corner of the room and covering them with a dust sheet.

'I've got a meeting in town,' said Duncan, checking his phone.

'Don't worry, I'll get the train.'

Clover got home at midday. Usually she arrived home around half-past four, bone-tired. Her knees, back and arms ached. It didn't seem to have got any easier in the five weeks she'd been working. Sometimes she wondered if she was mad to take up such a physical job in her fifties.

However, despite the low wages and the uncomfortable working conditions, she was proud of what she was doing. She liked having two hundred pounds at the end of the week.

But an early knock-off was an early knock-off. It was exciting. She made herself a cup of tea and, fired up by the story of Lola's father, switched on her laptop to see if there was any other news about it, checking her e-mails first. She scrolled past the latest Baxtersblog without even opening it because, after weeks of silence, there was an e-mail from Alice.

Dear Clover,

Thank you for your message, although I feel an apology might perhaps have been more appropriate. I warned you that Ben was a bad influence on Lola when we last met, and you refused to take any notice, or to do anything about the situation. Now, not only is Lola traumatised by her father's rejection, but I have also lost the monthly payments that he had been making on condition that her paternity was kept a secret. This will cause me considerable hardship, as you can imagine. And it's all Ben's fault. He has encouraged her in this quest.

You've always undermined my relationship with Lola, and you've also always been openly curious about who her father was. I imagine that Lola's spending so much time in your house has fed her own curiosity. You always dive into things without any thought for the consequences, and now this has happened, presumably as a result of repeated questioning from you to Lola about who her father is.

I don't think you or Laura have ever really understood how difficult it is to bring up a child without a father. Both of you have very strong, supportive men in your lives, who put their families first. You're in a very privileged position – which I don't think either of you fully appreciate. And, of course, it has been particularly hard on Lola, to spend so much time with friends who have good fathers when she has none.

I also still feel very bruised about the way I've been deeply resented by everyone because I've needed more help than families with two parents do. We've all laughed at Sheila Lewis, and the way she paints me as a 'scarlet woman' but I've often thought she was only being open about what the rest of you really thought. Not surprisingly, I feel hurt and unsupported, especially as this has all been so damaging for Lola.

I'm keeping Lola away from Kent for the foreseeable future, as she is in a terrible state and needs to settle properly at Oxford. I trust you'll make sure Ben keeps his word not to pester her. I've rented out the cottage in Pilgrim's Worthy on a long lease – to a very nice couple of lecturers at the university – but do pop in any time you're in London. I'd love to have coffee or lunch some time.

Love Alice.

Clover gazed at the screen in horror. It felt like being punched in the stomach. This wasn't just a swipe of irritation at Alice's secret being revealed. This was long-term resentment and fury.

Clicking on 'reply' she began to type. 'I wouldn't dream of asking Lola about her father. I never have and never would.' She stopped. If there was to be any future in her relationship with Alice – although after such an e-mail it seemed very unlikely – then she had to think very carefully before replying. She pressed 'cancel' but, after a moment's thought, forwarded Alice's e-mail on to Laura, and then, after another moment's thought, George.

First she needed to find out what Ben's involvement in it all was. 'Pester' Lola, indeed. Burning with indignation on his behalf, she called him.

'Hello,' he whispered.

'Why are you whispering?'

There was a silence, the sound of footsteps and a door opening and shutting. 'There,' he said in a more normal voice. 'I was in the library.'

She supposed she should be pleased at the sign of work

being done. 'I've had a furious e-mail from Alice. Saying that you encouraged Lola to look for her father.'

Ben sighed. 'When I started my course, Lola wanted me to do a bit of investigative reporting and help her find out who her dad was. She'd collected bits and pieces of paperwork over the years – she'd copied the odd bank statement and kept a few letters she'd found in the bin. So I said that I didn't think a first-year media studies student was quite at Watergate standards, and why didn't she just take it to a tabloid newspaper, who'd be able to do some proper digging. I mean, Alice is getting really quite famous, so they'd probably get a story out of it.'

'Ben! How could you?'

'How could I what? Lola's perfectly capable of thinking that up for herself. She is at Oxford, after all. I did add that I thought that her mother would be upset and that it might not be the best way of going about it. But she said she didn't care, that it was her call and her right to know. I kind of agree with her. But it's none of your business.'

'Alice is making it my business. By saying you'd encouraged Lola to do this.'

'I didn't encourage her. We talked about all her options and, ultimately, I advised her against it. But it still isn't anything to do with you. Lola and I can do what we like.'

'*I* know that, but Alice has asked me to make sure you don't . . . see Lola.'

'I don't think you *do* know it, judging by your tone of voice. I'm an adult now. And so is Lola. You can't put us on the naughty step any more. Nor can Alice. You two have got to resolve whatever's going on between you without bringing us into it. I'm going to put the phone down now, Mum.' She thought she heard a gruff, muttered 'love you', then the line went dead.

She stared at her handset in frustration. It was the most loquacious speech she'd heard from him for years. And he'd sounded completely calm and in control.

She called Laura. 'Are you anywhere near your computer?'

Laura sounded out of breath. 'Um, not now.'

'Could you check it when you get back?'

Laura gave a gasp.

'Laura! Are you all right?'

'I'm fine. I just tripped on something. Call you later.' Laura's voice was suppressed, as if she were trying not to cry.

Clover looked at her mobile again, puzzled. Then, although she didn't normally call George at work, she decided to try. She had to talk about this to someone. But his phone was switched off.

Feeling very alone and close to tears, she decided to call her father, to check up on him. But he wasn't answering either.

Chapter 28

After showing Clover the article about Lola's father, Laura left the town house in Canterbury. Passing the railway station on her way back to the car park, she saw a poster for getting away. The train was so quick, it declared. She could go anywhere. There were special prices.

On an impulse she bought a ticket and sat, numb, leaning her face against the grimy train window. She would get out at her destination, and if she found a hotel she would take a room. If there wasn't a hotel within ten minutes' walk it would be a sign. She would take the train back again. There would be no harm done. Her hands trembled in her lap.

There are always hotels near railway stations. She paid for a night.

'Do you have any luggage?' asked the young woman at reception. Her uniform was smart. She had dark hair in a chignon and a name badge. This wasn't a hotel where people made assignations.

'No, um, it was a very last-minute decision to travel. Um ... a family emergency ... I'll have to buy some ... er ... things.' Laura treated the receptionist to what she always thought of as her 'star smile'. The smile she gave when she wanted to look radiant for the cameras. 'There seem to be lots of shops around here.'

The receptionist smiled back, practised and incurious. 'Certainly, madam. Would you like anyone to show you to your room?'

On shaky legs, Laura managed to find the room, fumbling over the way the key worked in the door. Once inside, sitting on the huge, impersonal bed, she sent a text, giving the hotel name and address and her room number. She didn't sign it. You never knew who might come across a mobile phone. Then she opened the mini-bar and took out a quarter bottle of champagne. She would sip it very slowly, enjoying it, leaning against the massive padded headboard, cushioned by six different-sized cushions, arranged geometrically. If he wasn't here by the time she had finished the bottle, he wasn't coming. His mobile might not be on. He might be anywhere.

But she knew, in her bones, where he was. There was an electricity between them, that meant she knew he had summoned her. Somehow, somewhere, he had known she was walking past a railway station poster and he had transmitted the idea into her head. He knew she would come.

When he tapped lightly on the door she opened it. They didn't need to speak. She found herself unbuttoning his shirt before he had kicked the door shut behind him.

'Laura.' He held her face in his hands. 'Say my name.'

'No. I will never say your name. If I don't say your name, this isn't happening.'

'But it is happening.'

She shook her head, pushing his shirt back over his shoulders. 'If anyone ever asks, I will lie. Is that clear? I will lie and

212

lie, and say this never happened.' She undid his belt as he pulled her sweater off.

She was stripped to the waist when her phone rang. She answered it without thinking, desperate to stop it ringing. While she talked to Clover he continued to undress her.

'This is about as wrong as it could possibly be,' she said as she turned the phone off.

'But you are shameless, are you not?' He stood up.

She licked her lips nervously. 'Yes. I am shameless.'

'I love you, you know. I always have, ever since I set eyes on you.'

'Don't.' She steered him back on to the bed. 'Don't speak of love. Not here. This isn't about love.' And she silenced him with kisses.

Later, she picked her clothes off the floor and looked at her watch. 'I must go. I have to pick Tim up at four. From the hospital.' She stepped into the shower.

He stepped in with her, turning it on.

She shrieked. 'You're getting my hair wet.'

'I'll shampoo it for you.' He picked up one of the tiny courtesy bottles and squirted shampoo onto his hand.

She let him, luxuriating in the strong, smooth strokes across her scalp, and the way he kneaded her neck muscles.

'When is Tim's next chemo?' He spoke close to her ear.

'Three weeks today. But we can't . . .'

He turned her round, his eyes fierce. 'We can and we will. We can't let this go.'

'This was just once. The one and only time. Well . . .' she remembered New Year '. . . the second time, anyway. We can't do it again.'

His soapy hands ran down her body, making her gasp. 'I think you'll find we can.' He grinned down at her, turning the shower on to rinse her off, then taking her hand and leading

213

her out of the shower. Towelling her dry like a small child, he wrapped the towel protectively around her shoulders and kissed her nose. 'Now get dressed like a good girl, and I'll see you here in three weeks.' He stepped into the shower and turned the spray on.

As she stumbled back to the station, too late to dry her hair, she felt sick with guilt. All she could think was that she couldn't wait three weeks. And that she should never do this again. But this forbidden sweetness was addictive.

She picked Tim up outside the hospital. 'Your hair looks nice,' he said. 'Have you been to the hairdresser? It looks different.'

'It got wet in the rain. I didn't have time to dry it properly.'

He accepted the explanation. 'Just shows, you have no idea what's going on in the outside world when you're having chemo. I didn't even notice it had rained. But maybe you should do it like that more often. You look ...'

Laura turned to look at him, terrified he was going to say 'you look as if you've been shagging all day'.

'You look beautiful,' he concluded.

Laura rested her head in her hands on the steering wheel. 'I can't be beautiful,' she whispered. 'I'm fifty-two.' She began to cry. 'And I'm horrible. Horrible, horrible, horrible. Horrible inside and out.'

'Hey.' Tim put an arm round her shoulders. 'I know this whole cancer thing has been tough on you too. But you've been great.' He opened the glove compartment, and took out a small packet of tissues, handing her one. 'Here. You've been fantastic. Please. Believe me.'

She blew her nose. 'If you knew what I was really like, you wouldn't say I was fantastic.'

'I do know what you're really like. Now, I don't feel too

bad, and you seem to be in bits, so shall I drive? It always takes the chemo a good twelve hours to kick in.'

She got out of the car and they swapped seats, Laura trying to tidy up her eyes in the passenger shade mirror.

Chapter 29

George came home late, whistling. Laura still hadn't called Clover back. Clover also had another nagging worry about her father, who she had rung several times and who had not replied. He was in his eighties; surely he would be home at eight o'clock at night?

'Alice sent me an e-mail today,' said Clover, as soon as she could. George was still taking his coat off, and didn't seem to hear. 'I wanted you to see it,' she added.

'I'll have a look after supper.'

'Actually, I was wondering if you could look at it before. Then we could talk about it over the food.'

He looked sharply at her. 'You're always so impatient.'

'Why shouldn't I be?' she flashed back. 'This is something that matters to me, and I can't think of anything else. Why should I pretend otherwise?'

With a sigh, George opened up his laptop and logged in to his e-mail account, reading Alice's message while Clover put the rice on.

'Hmm,' he said eventually. 'Tricky things, e-mails. I think she's written it in rather a rush, because she's upset about Lola. To be honest, I don't really think it is about you, I think she's dissatisfied with some of the choices she's made in her life.'

'Well, she's making it about me, and I'm upset about the way she seems to consider Ben a nuisance who isn't worthy of Lola. And about the allegations she's made. I've never asked Lola about her father – I wouldn't dream of it.'

'Could Lola have overheard you asking Alice? She seems to think you've raised the subject quite often.'

'Directly or indirectly, not more than about five times in ten years. Not even that, probably. And not all that recently.' Clover dished casserole and rice on to their plates, and began to fork hers indignantly into her mouth.

'Hmm,' said George. 'Some people might call anything more than once a bit too nosy.'

'Well, it's been partly practical. You know – will her father be coming to the leavers' ball, that sort of thing.'

George raised his eyebrows. He began to eat.

'Well, I can see why *you're* not upset,' said Clover. 'She's called you strong and supportive and a good father, so you're presumably rather flattered by the whole thing. But even if you don't care about my feelings, I can't believe you're not angry on behalf of Ben.'

'I do care about your feelings, but I think she has a point, if badly made. It is important that they settle into their universities – whether they're at Oxford, Leeds or Gwent – and make friends and get involved. Any romantic involvement from home is bound to get in the way of that.' He chewed another forkful. 'I wouldn't like Holly to be visiting a boyfriend miles away every weekend instead of making the most of uni.'

'*You* wouldn't like Holly to have a boyfriend full stop. Whereas you don't care about Ben. It's all Holly, Holly, Holly as far as you're concerned, but Ben needs a' – she wiggled her fingers in the air – a "strong supportive father" too, you know.'

George's face darkened. 'I think you should think very

carefully before you turn this into an issue about me and Ben. I love both my children very much indeed.'

Clover took a deep breath. He was right. 'I'm not talking about fault. But I think you're too hard on Ben.'

'He needs someone to be hard on him. I don't want him to be a failure because he won't get off his arse.'

'I think his self-esteem is low, and that's not helped by having a father who constantly criticises him, and a family friend who openly says he's not good enough for her daughter.'

'I don't think that's actually what she is saying.'

'I'm also hurt that I've put a lot of effort into helping her over the years, and all she can say is that I've never really understood how difficult her life is. I've tried to understand. I've tried to help.'

'Hmm. Gratitude's another very tricky thing.'

'I'm not asking for gratitude,' snapped Clover. 'Just a bit of respect for my feelings. And I'd like to feel that you were on my side over all this.'

George started to say something, then stopped.

'What?'

'Nothing.'

'Say it!' Her heart ticked faster.

He sighed. 'Really, Clover, there's nothing to say. I agree that Alice's e-mail is tactless and badly worded, and not entirely fair on either you or Ben. But it does make some reasonable points underneath it all. You do dive into things without thinking.'

Clover was stung. 'In what way, exactly? Marrying you because I was pregnant, for example?'

There was a hush. She wished she could call the words back. She had sometimes wondered whether they would have married at all if it hadn't been for Ben. And if you married for the children, what did you do when those children left? Her heart froze.

He looked pale and tense. 'I don't think we should talk about this when you're upset about Alice's e-mail. Which I think you should treat as a silly outburst. She's having a very difficult time over Lola and, ultimately, I still don't think this is about you. Ignore it.'

Clover knew that she had taken a risk. She had dived into the cold sea and was swimming away from the shore. She had questioned the very basis of their relationship. She felt sick. I don't want to ask these questions, she thought. I might not like the answers.

She tried to concentrate on the words 'silly', 'tactless' and 'not entirely fair', finishing her meal and ringing her father again. There was still no reply. 'Do you mind if I pop over to Dad's? I'm worried that he's not answering the phone.'

George looked at his watch. 'Going nearly to Tunbridge Wells is scarcely "popping over". And it's nearly half-past eight. Won't he be going to bed?'

Clover shook her head. 'No, he doesn't sleep much. I'm sure he's fine, it's just that it worries me because he usually has his mobile with him and I've been calling him since lunchtime. I just have a funny feeling about it.' She waited for George to offer to come with her, but he just smiled vaguely.

'I'll do the washing up,' he said.

'I might stay and chat with him.'

He smiled a bland, remote smile. 'Do that.'

Clover drove badly, her thoughts treading and re-treading the same grooves. Alice. Lola. Ben. George. Tim's cancer. Her father.

Her father was very much alive, and snappish. 'Really, Clover, don't you have anything better to do with your time now that the children have left home? Anyone would think I was a little old man who could hardly get out of bed in the morning. I've spent the day with a friend.' He emphasised the word 'friend'. 'And it's all been rather tiring, so I'm having an early night, if you don't mind.' He began to shut the door on her anxious questioning. Clover thought she could hear a querulous high-pitched voice from inside the bungalow.

'Who's that? Are you entertaining?' Clover almost put her foot in the door to stop it closing.

'That's none of your business.' He must have seen her face crumple because he added. 'You can come over on Wednesday as usual, if you like. If you're bringing lunch, there'll be three of us.' He patted her shoulder kindly and proffered his cheek for a kiss.

Chapter 30

George looked surprised when Clover got back, having been gone for not much more than an hour and a half. 'Dad's terminal illness appears to be love. I think he's got Poinsettia Woman in there and won't let me in the house.'

'There was a woman there when I went over.'

'Why didn't you say? What was she like?'

He shrugged. 'It didn't seem important. Can't remember much about her.'

'How old was she?'

'Well, I don't know, do I? Seventy-something?' And he drifted off to do some e-mails. Clover felt very alone. Nobody needed her, not even her father.

She rang Laura. 'I've just had a row with George. And Alice has sent me the most horrible e-mail.'

'I've just seen it.' Laura sounded slightly drunk. 'It's awful. Everybody's awful at the moment. I've been awful to Tim.'

'What have you done?'

'Oh, you know.' Laura was vague. 'I'm just an awful person. Awful wife. Awful mother, awful friend. What was your argument about?'

Clover wasn't sure that there was much point in going on with the conversation, but she had to talk to someone. 'He accused me of diving into things without thinking, or, at least, he said he agreed with Alice. And I said that maybe that was why I'd married him. I was pregnant with Ben, you see. I've sometimes wondered if, secretly, one or both of us regrets it. That maybe that's why he doesn't seem to love Ben as much as he loves Holly. He says he does. That he loves them both.'

'I'm sure he does love them both. And you'd probably have married him anyway, wouldn't you?'

Clover clutched the phone so tightly her fingers hurt, as she paced around the kitchen. 'To be honest, I don't really know. But we've always veered away from talking about all that. We've concentrated on the children, but now the children have gone.'

'It's still all about the children, isn't it?' Laura's voice was definitely sounding slurred. 'Alice is behaving with all the tact and diplomacy of a wounded buffalo, presumably because she's distraught about Lola. And you could forgive her anything, except criticism of Ben.'

'But they've left home,' cried Clover in frustration. 'It's like being back in the playground again. When are *we* going to grow up?'

She heard Laura take a gulp of something. 'Did you know I always thought adultery was something you could only do when you were an adult, and that's why it was called adultery? Something you do when you're grown up.'

'There are other things, apart from adultery, that we could be getting on with,' said Clover through gritted teeth. 'Like being civilised to each other.'

'Clover, you've got so fucking serious. You've got to get your mojo back.'

'My mojo? Me?'

'You need to find your mojo again,' repeated Laura.

'I don't need a mojo,' Clover replied. 'I need a pension

plan. In fact, I can't think of anything worse than suddenly finding my mojo. I'd have to lose it again immediately.'

'Not true.' Laura sounded as if she was falling apart. 'Alice has found her mojo. Going up to London. Buying socking great flat.'

'Alice has found her evil twin. And you sound a bit tired.'

'I found my mojo. Didn't have any lunch. Had mojo instead.' Laura began to laugh. 'Can't remember supper.'

'That's the doorbell. Must go.' Clover looked at her watch with a start of alarm. Half-past ten at night was not the time for anyone to be dropping round. She peered through the spyhole to see a slim frame and long hair.

'Lola!' She opened the door. Lola was panda-eyed with misery.

George came down the stairs behind her. 'Who's that? Lola, what are you doing here?' He stepped forward to catch her as she almost collapsed on the doormat.

'You need to tell me about my father,' she said, bursting into tears on his shoulder.

'Drink this.' Clover handed Lola a mug of hot chocolate, as she sat at the kitchen table, the sleeves of her black sweater pulled down over her hands. Her hunched shoulders were as thin as coat hangers.

'Mum won't tell me anything.'

'She won't tell us anything either. Nothing at all.'

George signalled to her to be quiet as he sat down opposite Lola. Clover took a seat next to her.

'How can I be me if I don't know where I come from? Mum doesn't care, she just wants me to be exactly like her.'

'Your mother does care,' said Clover. 'She loves you very much. She just isn't very conventional in the way she shows it.'

Lola glared at her with scorn. 'No, she just wants someone who'll look good beside her in photographs. Or in the catalogue. I've been in that catalogue ever since I can remember. We don't have a family photo album, we have a pile of catalogues with a sort of fake family in them. Me, Mum and a whole lot of models. In a house that's rented for the day and styled up for the photographs.'

'I think that's why she stayed here in Kent, even though she could have afforded to move to London earlier,' said Clover. 'To give you a sense that there's somewhere you belong.'

Lola stared into her lap, pulling at the cuffs of her sleeves so that one end almost unravelled. 'It's all right for you two, you've got a proper family and you came from proper families.'

'In fact, I didn't,' said George. 'My father died when I was three. I don't remember him at all.'

Lola looked at him as if he might save her life. 'How did you get over it?'

'I didn't have to. I didn't know any different. My brother and I were brought up by our mother, who worked, because our father left us without much money, and that's how we were. My mother was amazing, but she wasn't always there. Like yours.'

Lola wiped her face with the back of her sleeve and Clover passed her a tissue. 'Sorry.' She blew her nose. 'But at least your dad was a good man. Mine's a shit.'

'I've no idea what sort of a man he was. My mother never talked about him. People didn't in those days.'

'Listen, Lola.' Clover leant forwards. 'The most important thing is that you go forward, not look back. Your mother really does love you, whatever you feel now, and you're bright, beautiful and lots of people love you. You can't throw all that away. If you're consumed by bitterness you'll spend all your time thinking about what you could have had, not how you can make the most of what lies ahead. You'll have a family yourself one day.'

Lola shook her head, but didn't reply directly. 'Has she told you anything? Either of you?'

'No, nothing,' said Clover.

'She said he was a very good businessman,' said George. 'And that she was keeping it all a secret to protect you.'

Clover swallowed down a hundred questions.

'I don't know how it could protect me,' said Lola, but the fear had gone out of her eyes. 'She is silly.'

'We all are, sometimes,' said Clover, trying not to think about when Alice might have told George about Alice's father. She had always refused to say anything at all about him to Clover. 'None of your friends have perfect parents. And life is never quite what you want it to be, sweetie. You just have to make the best of what you've got.'

Lola nodded, but didn't seem to be listening. 'Didn't you ever wonder about your father?' she asked George.

Clover thought, for a moment, that he wasn't going to answer.

'No point,' he said, getting up. 'There really is no point. Now, I take it you're staying in your usual bed?'

'I'm really tired,' admitted Lola.

'Do you want to tell your mother you're here?'

Lola shook her head. 'She doesn't need to know.'

'Text her,' advised George. 'And say you'll be getting back in time for lectures tomorrow morning. That means getting up at six. I'll drive you to the station. I'm going out around then anyway.'

Once Lola had closed Holly's bedroom door Clover and George went to bed.

'Well,' she said. 'I don't think Alice could possibly accuse either of us of undermining her relationship with Lola. I think you really got through to her.'

George shook out a newspaper, looking at her over it. 'Thanks.'

'But I can't help wondering if Alice is trying to undermine our relationship by telling you things that she wouldn't tell me.'

George held up the newspaper. 'It's too late to dissect the meaning of all this now. I don't remember when Alice talked about Lola's father. As you can see, she didn't say very much. And I simply forgot about it.'

'I've never really thought about it before, but do you think that some of your problems with Ben are because you didn't have a father yourself?'

'I don't have problems with Ben. *You* have problems with my relationship with Ben.'

Clover picked up her book. He was right. It was too late to talk. They were at a critical juncture, and it would only take one of them to say one more thing and the fabric of their lives would be torn irreparably.

She woke up at three o'clock and couldn't get back to sleep. There was a wind outside, tugging at the trees and wailing down the street. She heard the crash and tinkle of a roof tile being blown off, and the sound of a bottle rattling down the road. I'll huff and I'll puff and I'll blow your house down, she thought, remembering the stories she used to tell Holly and Ben when they were tiny.

Clover looked at her mobile. It was time to take control of her life. She needed to deal with Alice.

She sent a text to Alice. 'Let's meet. It would be good to talk.'

Chapter 31

Laura found herself staring at her phone every few minutes, and carrying it around with her like a talisman. The house was empty and silent without Jamie. Tim was determined that his chemotherapy was going to make no difference to his life and was still working, although he was taking an increasing number of days off. Outside the sky was flat and grey, with the earth beneath it sodden and muddy. Laura found her hand sliding into the biscuit tin more often than it used to.

The doorbell rang. Laura jumped, and put the biscuit back. It would be someone to read a meter, she supposed, wiping crumbs away from her mouth and checking her reflection for chocolate marks. In case it was a burglar, checking if someone was in by knocking but determined to force his way in, she looked through the spy hole.

As usual, she couldn't really tell who it was through the tiny aperture. He – she thought it was probably a man – was leaning on the doorframe, so all she could see was a bit of dark jacket. 'Who is it?' she called.

'Who do you think?'

Laura leant on the wall, winded. 'You can't come here.' But she opened the door.

'Yes, I can.' He was grinning as he put his foot firmly on

the doormat, preventing her from shutting the door. 'I'm a family friend, after all.'

'But what if someone saw your car?'

He shrugged. 'What if they did? Anyway, it's parked round the side.'

She craned her head round. It was tucked in beside the garage. 'What if Tim didn't feel well and came back?'

'Does he do that?'

'Occasionally. But he's in Cambridge today. They've got a project in—'

But he had covered her mouth with a kiss.

'No,' she pushed him away. 'Not with the front door open.' She pulled him in and slammed the door. 'We shouldn't be doing this.'

'But we are.' He kissed her again and began to lead her upstairs.

'Not in our room.'

'You do have a very conventional idea of what is and isn't acceptable behaviour, my dear little hypocrite.'

'I am not going to sleep with another man in my husband's bed. That is where I draw the line.'

For a moment, she thought that he would take it as a challenge and make her give way on that too, just as she'd given way on everything else. But he put a hand on another door. 'Here?'

She shook her head. 'No, that's Jamie's room. The next one. The spare bedroom.'

There was something comfortingly anonymous about a spare room, the nearest they could get to a hotel. It was the same as it always was: desperate, greedy, abandoned, breathless. 'We should be calming down by now, taking things a bit more slowly,' she said, gasping, just five minutes later as they lay undressed on top of the dove grey silk bedspread she'd so

228

carefully chosen. Without realising what she was going to do on top of it.

'I can take things slowly if that's what you'd like.' He turned on to his side and began tracing the shape of her face with his finger. 'Starting now?'

'Now?' She rolled over to lie flat, laughing. 'I don't think I could do anything now. Except learn how to breathe again.'

Her phone began to ring from the pocket of her jeans on the floor. 'Leave it,' he said.

'Suppose it's Tim, saying he's on the way back?' She jumped off the bed and began to fumble through her pockets with clumsy hands, finally locating it. 'Hello?'

It was an unfamiliar female voice. 'Is that Mrs Dangerfield?'

'Yes?' Her voice was high with anxiety. She thought of Jamie. 'What's happened?'

'Tim's all right,' said the voice. 'I'm Marianne, one of his colleagues—'

'Oh yes, of course, Marianne, hello. Tim's mentioned you. Lots of times.'

'—but he's been admitted to Addenbrookes. Here in Cambridge. He's running a very high temperature.'

Her heart flipped in terror. 'Why?'

'I can hand you over to one of the doctors now.'

A young, serious, reassuring voice told her that sometimes the chemotherapy that Tim was having destroyed the neu-trophils in the blood, lowering the body's immune system to dangerous levels. '. . . when he can pick up any kind of infec-tion. But we're treating it now.'

'How ill is he?'

There was a pause. 'It's potentially serious, but he's stable. We're looking after him. Luckily his colleagues insisted on calling an ambulance. He was insisting that he'd be fine to take the train home and call a doctor from there.'

The phone was handed back to Marianne and Laura thanked her, promising to get to Cambridge within a couple of hours.

'This is all my fault,' she said, ending the call and stepping into the shower. 'I'm a bad wife. This is what happens to bad wives. It's a punishment.'

He raised his eyebrows. 'I hadn't got you down for a religious maniac. What are you? Catholic?'

'I'm not anything,' she said sharply. 'But if you behave badly, bad things happen. Everyone knows that.' She thought about Jamie. Suppose it had been him? Suppose God had chosen to punish her by hurting Jamie? Pain swept over her in a wave.

She towelled herself vigorously. 'We've got to stop this. It's all wrong.'

He was lying back against the pillows, looking at her appreciatively. 'How can this be wrong? It's love.'

'It's not love,' she hissed. 'Love is what I feel for Jamie. Love is me and Tim. Not this.' She stopped, astonished at what she'd said.

'*Excuse me.*' He rolled off the bed and pulled his trousers on. 'I think I might be forgiven for thinking that you had very much fallen out of love with your husband many years ago. Having seen your behaviour to him on holiday.' He zipped up his flies and began to edge his feet into his shoes.

Laura emerged from the neck of her pullover and tugged it down. 'What? Oh, that. You can't tell from the outside what goes on in a marriage.'

'You certainly can't.' He shrugged his jacket on. 'Goodbye.'

'Stop!'

He turned round, halfway down the stairs. 'Yes?'

She thought of Tim lying in hospital. 'Nothing,' she forced herself to say. 'I'm sorry.'

He ran down the stairs and slammed the front door behind him. She could hear the wheels of his car skidding on the gravel.

With a whimper of pain Laura slid down the wall, and curled up in a ball on the landing. She had to get to Tim; he was waiting for her. And the floor was so hard. Eventually, she managed to straighten out her limbs and pull herself to her feet, holding on to the door.

She felt hunched, like an old woman, as she picked her way around the house, forcing one step after another, switching off lights and locking windows, finding a change of clothes from the laundry room and hunting for keys. It would be a two-hour drive to Cambridge; she had to concentrate. At least she had stopped this madness.

Laura had been afraid that she was going back to the sort of person she'd been before she met Tim and had Jamie. She had been wild, promiscuous and unhappy.

She wasn't going be that woman any more. Tim had rescued her once. Now he needed her, and his need would rescue her again. She was hardly aware of the tears that streamed down her cheeks as she drove. Or of whom the tears were for.

Chapter 32

That evening Clover went up to London to talk to Alice.

Alice seemed blithely unaware that her e-mail might have upset Clover. 'Yes GR8' she had texted back, when Clover asked. They established the date.

'Shall I pick up some food from M&S at the station?' texted Clover.

'GR8. See you at 8.'

In fact, it was nearer to eight-thirty when Alice appeared round the corner. 'Oh hi.' She kissed Clover. 'I was hoping you'd be late as usual. I got completely trapped by a call from China. He just wouldn't get off the line and it was a problem we had to solve.'

Clover, who had been sitting on the doorstep for half an hour, mentally rehearsing adult, sensitive ways of addressing the issues between them, was taken aback. 'Am I usually late? I didn't think I—'

'Oh, don't worry about it, it's just lovely to see you. How are the kids? Oh, hey! Josiah!'

Josiah, handsome in a dark cashmere coat, came up behind them and held the door open over their heads. 'Alice.'

After a squeaky, excited exchange of kisses, Alice re-introduced Clover. 'You remember Clover, my great, great friend from Kent.

She's brought some gorgeous takeaway food from Marks and Spencers – why not join us?'

Clover opened her mouth but, as 'it would be good to talk' didn't specifically mean a private discussion, she didn't think she could say anything.

'There's masses,' said Alice, looking at Clover's bags. 'And I've got some stuff in the fridge.'

'I've got some champagne,' said Josiah. 'Just let me change and I'll see you in about twenty minutes.'

Alice and Clover unpacked the salads and Alice pulled some ham, olives and cheese out of her fridge. 'There!' she said. 'A feast.'

Clover looked at the clock. Would they have time to get a 'proper' talk in? 'How's Lola?' she started.

Alice looked up sharply. 'Fine. She's great. Loving Oxford. How's George? He was in great form the last time I saw him.'

Clover decided to ignore the reference to George. 'I'm glad she's settled. I was a bit ... worried by your e-mail.'

'Oh, that. I didn't mean to worry you but, obviously, I couldn't let the situation with Ben go on any longer, and you clearly weren't prepared to do anything about it. Not that I blame you – the mother of the boy is always fairly detached, isn't she? It's the mother of the girl in any relationship that ends up holding the baby.'

'Ben hasn't got Lola pregnant?' Clover was horrified.

'Of course not. I was speaking metaphorically. Now, do you want a glass of wine to keep you going before Josiah comes down with his champagne? He usually stocks awfully good stuff.'

Clover said that she would wait. 'I wanted to say ... I really don't think I've ever undermined your relationship with Lola.'

'Well, I'm sure you didn't mean to, but with all the time she spent in your house it was pretty inevitable, wasn't it? I mean, it was typical that she came down to see you after the story in the paper, wasn't it? She said George was wonderful, by the way – thank you – and that you didn't give her too much of a lecture, considering. But, you know, it needs to be me she comes to. Don't you think?'

'Well, of course, but—'

'I knew you'd understand. And I think these things are much better out in the open. I know it helps enormously when people give constructive feedback, and I'd hope you were too much of a friend to see it in any other way.'

'But how? Can you give me an example of a time when I've undermined you?' Clover furrowed her brow.

Alice took her head out of the fridge, straightened up and sighed. 'Look, Clover, it's such fun to have you here, and I don't really want to rake up past arguments. That phase of our life is over, and it's been pretty difficult all round, but now the kids are at uni we can put it all behind us.'

Clover was about to ask what Alice meant, when her phone rang. It was Laura, hissing because she was on the staircase at the hospital and she wasn't sure if she was allowed a mobile phone. 'Tim's got some terrible infection. His immune system can't fight it. I'm in Cambridge for a few days, but I left the house in a bit of a hurry and wondered if you'd pop in each morning to make sure everything's all right.'

'No problem,' said Clover, moving out of earshot into the bathroom. They talked about Tim's condition. 'I'm with Alice, by the way.'

'No! What does she say?'

'She says that she doesn't want to rake up past arguments, and that I've undermined her with Lola, but that that phase of our lives is over and we can put it behind us.'

'No!' Laura almost sounded gleeful. 'The cow. The phase she's talking about is the one where we provided free childcare for her daughter while she jetted around the world becoming frightfully rich.'

Clover instinctively wanted to defend Alice. It was a habit. 'Well—'

'Don't you dare say "poor Alice, she's had a difficult time". Life is difficult for all of us.'

'Actually, I wasn't going to,' said Clover. She smiled. 'That phase of my life is over. As it were.'

'Attagirl!' Laura rang off.

Clover needed a few moments alone to collect herself, and opened the bathroom door.

'Don't use the main one, by the way,' said Alice, spotting her. 'It's not flushing very well at the moment. Go to my en suite.'

Clover picked her way through Alice's untidy bedroom and into the sandstone and glass en suite. This phase of my life is over echoed in her head. Everyone is spinning off in different directions. Mum is dead. Dad has a new girlfriend. Ben and Holly have their own lives. Alice and Lola don't need me any more. Laura and Tim are bound up in Tim's illness. And George?

While she was washing her hands, she looked at herself in the mirror. Who am I? The question she'd asked herself so often when she was younger, staring into mirrors, and which had, since she married, been answered by 'George's wife. Ben and Holly's mother. Alice and Laura's friend. Stalwart of the PTA. Organiser of the school run.' But the question had popped up again, as if those years had never held any answers after all.

Her gaze strayed idly along the bathroom shelf. It was surprisingly tidy for Alice. A bottle of smart liquid soap and a matching one of shampoo. From an upmarket hotel, judging by the small print on the label. Clover couldn't help smiling.

235

Alice might be lauded in the press as the face of go-getting business today, but she still nicked the soap and shampoo from the hotels she stayed in. As she put the shampoo bottle down she spotted a cufflink. It was similar to one of George's, one of those jokey resin designs with an image of Superman on it. If you held your wrists up to the light in one way, it read 'Zap!' and if you moved the legend changed to 'Pow!' George had been given them by Holly when she was ten (although, of course, Clover had bought them, and they had not been quite as cheap as she had expected). He wore them all the time. Or had done. She hadn't noticed recently.

It couldn't be George's. There must have been hundreds of thousands of pairs sold. She picked it up and studied it to see if there was any distinguishing feature about it. There wasn't. She placed it back, carefully, where it had been on the shelf. Someone would be missing it. Alice presumably had a man with a similar taste in cufflinks to George.

She was about to ask Alice a bit more about Josiah when she realised that he had arrived, presumably letting himself in as she hadn't heard the doorbell. He moved round the kitchen in a familiar way, pulling glasses out of the cupboard and pouring champagne. 'Cheers.'

Clover lifted her glass. 'I've just had a phone call from Laura, by the way, Alice. Tim's got an infection. He's in hospital in Cambridge.'

Alice's face was bland. 'What a shame. Look, Josiah's brought down the skiing photos from Christmas. Do look.' Once again, Clover had the impression that anything to do with Tim's illness made Alice uneasy. It was as if Tim and Laura had been airbrushed out of her life.

Clover obediently thumbed through them while Alice gave an excited commentary, teasing Josiah and laughing. She was suddenly impatient with them both.

It was simple. She could make an excuse, and leave. She didn't have to be here, and Alice was clearly not interested in repairing their relationship. 'Look, this has been lovely,' said Clover. 'But I must go back. Thank you for the champagne, Josiah.' She could see Alice looking surprised.

'I'm sorry,' Clover improvised. 'Laura asked me to check the house. She had to dash out in a hurry because of Tim being taken ill. She needs me to . . . check that she hasn't left some washing on the hot part of the Aga. She's worried about fire.' It sounded weak, but it would have to do.

'Don't you want some supper?' Alice sounded disconcerted, as if Clover wasn't sticking to the script.

Clover didn't want anyone to think she was flouncing out. 'No, really, it's fine. I just need to get back. We'll catch up soon.'

'Give my love to George,' said Alice, her eyes glinting as she got up to show Clover out. 'Tell him I've just had some great news about Pets & Things.'

'Oh, what? I can pass it on.'

Alice leant forward to kiss her, holding the front door open. 'Actually, I'd like to tell him myself. If you don't mind. I'm sure you understand.'

'Of course.'

Somewhere along the line, friendship had turned into war.

Chapter 33

Laura always got lost in hospitals. There never seemed to be any logic about the way departments led into each other. She clung on to Tim's ward name and floor number, repeating it over and over to herself like a mantra, but still found herself in the Oral and Maxillofacial Unit, then outside the front door again.

Eventually, close to tears, she found Tim hooked up to a drip. His eyes were closed.

She sank down in the chair beside him. He looked different. Not just ill. Different. He opened his eyes and she took his hand. 'Be careful,' she said. 'I've only just found you again. I don't want to lose you.'

He smiled weakly. 'You won't.' He fell asleep.

Laura rootled out the ward sister, who told her that they'd have the results of a series of tests over the next forty-eight hours, but he was on a broad spectrum antibiotic and as test results came back they'd be able to put him on more specific medication. She spent the next few hours sitting in the chair beside his bed, reading.

It was a long time since she'd spent so much time sitting still, without talking. At six, Tim woke up, but didn't want anything to eat.

'You don't have to stay here,' he said. 'Go home. You'll be more comfortable.'

'I'll stay up until I can take you back. It'll only be a few days.'

His hand crawled across the sheet and she took it, moving her chair closer so that she could sit holding his hand. It was the least she could do. Tim's features – his aquiline nose and long, sculpted face – seemed more distinct, as if the flesh was melting off the bones. Eventually she was chased out of the ward as it closed for the night. She drove uncertainly into the centre of Cambridge, getting lost in the pedestrianised areas and one-way systems before finding herself a bed-and-breakfast in a terraced house run by a tall, booming woman with glasses.

'I've come out without ...' She stopped and blushed, remembering the last time she'd checked in to a hotel. But at least this time she had her clothes and toothbrush. 'I've come out without anything to read, and I presume the shops are closed.'

'We've got a shelf of books for people to take or exchange. Upstairs in the hallway outside your room. We ask people either to leave a book in exchange or put a donation in the RNLI box on the top shelf.'

It seemed a curious charity to support when you were about as far inland as it was possible to be. Laura thumbed through a series of paperbacks. She didn't want anything about war, crime or killing – there was too much pain in her life as it was. Politics bored her. There were some therapy books. She picked up two, along with *Warleggan*, the Poldark novel, which she remembered loving as a child, and pushed a ten-pound note into the box. She wanted to be generous. If she was generous to Fate, Fate might be generous to her.

She sat beside Tim for a second day, flicking through

Warleggan and the self-help books, which were easier to follow. She couldn't take in a continuous narrative, or remember who the various Poldarks were in *Warleggan*, so she dipped in and out of the psychological theories. We all have a script, she read, which we concoct for ourselves by the time we're about seven. We spend the rest of our lives living as if the script could never change. But we're too young and small to understand the full story. We write our scripts based on the scraps of experience and information we had then. Often we're wrong.

She saw, in her mind's eye, the little Laura handing her report card to her father and him throwing it into the wastepaper basket. The pain of being unloved reached out over the years and squeezed her heart so tightly she couldn't breathe.

Doctors, nurses and cleaners came and went, and she found out where a kettle was kept. Downstairs in the café, she bought a croissant and ate it slowly, savouring every mouthful. The hospital came to seem like home.

She called Jamie. 'Dad's fine, but he's had to go into hospital suddenly.' They agreed that Jamie probably didn't need to make the cumbersome journey over from Wales. 'How's the course?'

Jamie groaned.

'Darling, you must talk to someone about it. You can get special help, I'm sure—'

'Mum. Stay off my case. OK? I'm busy. I've got to go.'

As she sat and waited by Tim's bed, she heard the voices of the past. Her father shouting about Laura and her brother: 'That boy's got to support a family one day. All she has to do is catch a husband, and men don't like clever women.' Her mother replying, 'I know, I know. All you have to hope for is that your daughter is a pretty fool, or she'll be very unhappy. And she's pretty but she's no fool.'

None of it had made any sense to her at the time. It was just shouting and anger. At her. All her fault. Now she recognised fear in their voices. The kind of fear that Jamie heard in her voice when he said he wasn't happy at university. The desperation of parents who had grown up with a war and feared that their children would be ill-equipped for peace.

Words like 'fool' and 'unhappy' had echoed in her head. Now she also remembered 'pretty' and 'not a fool'. The image, again, of her father's back as he read the report before putting in the waste-paper basket. Then, retrieved from some memory cell, that he had grunted something that might have been praise.

They came from a different world, but they were trying to do the best they could for me, she thought. Just as I'm trying to do the best for Jamie. They didn't do the right thing. Maybe I'm not either.

She thumbed through the books again, but there were no answers there. Her memories shifted, like sand dunes, so solid one moment, altered in shape the next. It was as if she'd looked at her life through a different window. Looked east instead of south and found a completely different view. She was still the same person and in the same place, but what she could see had changed. Then she looked again, and saw what she'd always seen.

Clover called to find out how Tim was. 'I think he'll be OK. He looks hot and uncomfortable, but is mainly sleeping. How are you?'

'I'm fine.' She tried to share some of the theories in the book with Clover. 'It could help you understand these problems with Alice.'

But Clover didn't want to know. Laura got the impression of someone who had curled up into a ball, prickles outward, at the mention of Alice.

I used to be like that, thought Laura in another flash of insight.

'Do you know what?' she said, changing the subject. 'My wheat allergy has disappeared since Tim got ill. I've been living on sandwiches and croissants ever since I got here. And I feel fine.'

'Why do you think that is?'

'I'm ashamed to admit that it might have been what one of these books call a power play. It gave me a reason to slink off to my room when I was cross with Tim. A sulk, in other words.' The image of what had happened when she'd last done that rose up. 'I'm so very sorry,' she added, almost without thinking.

'Hey,' said Clover. 'We all get through any way we can. Maybe you needed to be alone. Maybe it was the only way you could get that space.'

'I never went to see a doctor about it, you know.'

There was a pause from Clover. 'Yes, I did know,' she admitted. 'I asked you once what tests you'd had. I could tell you hadn't had any.'

'So were you all laughing at me all that time?' Laura was surprised at the hurt. 'Did you roll your eyes every time I took to my bed?'

'No! Of course not . . . I think we just thought you were—'

'What?'

'Unhappy.' The word dropped into the conversation like a stone.

'Unhappy,' repeated Laura. 'Yes, I suppose that's fair. And now . . . I'm not unhappy. I'm terrified.' She tried to make a joke of it.

'Of losing Tim?'

'Of losing Tim.' There. It was out in the open. Losing Tim. It was the first time Laura had acknowledged, even to herself, that he might die. A shot of sadness, as pure and fine as polished steel, sliced through her, marking her for ever.

'The treatments are very good now.'

'I know.' But Laura had heard too many people say bland, meaningless phrases like that to be comforted. 'Anyway, it's probably that I'm worried about Jamie, too. It's not going well at Gwent, and I'm not sure what to do about it. But you don't need to cheer me up. You've got your own problems.'

'Alice, for example.' Clover sighed.

'I really do think you should talk to a professional about this. It's clearly affecting you very deeply.' This was as close as Laura dared get to telling Clover to 'get proper help now'. Reading between the lines, Alice had clearly set her sights on George, and she was a determined and capable woman.

Clover made an explosive noise. 'Why is everyone making Alice's behaviour my problem? And my fault? I've no idea why she's behaving as she is. And I can't see that my talking to someone will make any difference to it. If you think therapy is so wonderful, why don't you go for some?'

'Because I'm working things out in my own way.'

'And so am I. So am I.'

Laura got the impression that if Clover hadn't been speaking on a mobile she would have slammed the phone down.

I could have handled that better, she thought. The awareness of the old Laura, the old, selfish Laura, washed over her like a cold wave. There was the Laura who betrayed people, and the Laura who looked after people. She still couldn't make them feel like the same person, however many different windows she looked out of. It was easier to escape.

Tim's hot hand felt for hers, anchoring her down.

Chapter 34

Mrs Dundy decided on the purple for the spare room, and liked it so much she wanted the master bedroom repainted. 'Get that girl, the one who's been to Chelsea. I want her advice.'

Chris reported that Clover was required by the Devil. Clover rummaged in her huge bag for her paint charts and went upstairs to where a furious Mrs Dundy was screaming into her mobile phone. She hung back until the conversation was over, trying to avoid catching the eye of Dave, who'd been called in to re-plumb the shower five millimetres to the left. He was bent over and she could see a deep cleavage at the top of his baggy jeans.

Mrs Dundy snapped the phone shut. 'You. What's your name?'

'Mrs Jones.'

A pair of tweezered eyebrows shot up. She frowned. 'Haven't I met you somewhere before?'

'Yes, we talked about colours for the spare room.'

Mrs Dundy flapped a hand. 'I know that, for heaven's sake. Not then, not then. Somewhere before.' She peered at Clover. 'I know. Aren't you Alice Fanshawe's friend? From St Crispian's?'

Clover considered saying 'not any more', but simply nodded.

'Alice is such a darling. And so talented.' Mrs Dundy took her arm, and drew her towards the window. 'My youngest is at St Crispian's. In the junior school. Now, as we're all friends together, what's your first name?'

'Clover,' she conceded, wishing she didn't have to.

'And I am Eleanor. As we're friends,' she repeated, darting a look at Dave, who had straightened up and was viewing the exchange with barely concealed amusement. 'Have you sorted that shower out?'

Dave turned back to his work.

'Now, this gardenia-type colour Chris and Duncan have done in here is just too insipid. Don't you agree? Men always play it safe, don't they? What do you think Alice would say? Is there any way she'd pop in, do you think, as you're such great friends? I'd really value her input.'

'Alice is in Shanghai,' hazarded Clover, marvelling at how Devil Dundy had shifted the blame for the colour to Chris and Duncan. Eleanor Dundy was clearly not a woman who took responsibility for her own mistakes. 'But perhaps I can help.'

After half an hour of deliberation, rejection and roundabout discussion, returning to rejected colours, then rejecting them again, they agreed to test a number of blue shades for the master bedroom and its en suite. After a few more sharp exchanges with Dave and Chris, Eleanor clattered off in a haze of Chanel.

'She handled that woman well,' commented Dave to Chris as he lumbered down the stairs. 'Got her listening by insisting on being called Mrs Jones. Devil wasn't having any of it, of course, but it stopped her short, didn't it, Clover?' He winked at her.

'It was just politeness, that's all.' It was the first time he'd ever got her name right, having called her Daisy, Rosie,

Poppy, Daphne and every other flower name he could think of.

'She handles you well and all,' said Chris, with a level look at Dave.

It was the nearest thing she'd had to a compliment in seven weeks of arduous work. Clover was surprised at how pleased she felt.

Her good mood only lasted until she got home, where George was frowning. 'Anidrug is in takeover talks with Petfast,' he said. 'Yet another round of mergers. Another round of redundancies.'

'You got promoted in the last two mergers.'

'Yes, well, my luck will hardly hold for ever, will it?'

'What if it's more than luck? Maybe you're good at your job.'

But George had picked up the telephone and was punching in numbers. He seemed to know them by heart, Clover noted. As it began to ring, he withdrew into the study, sitting down in his swivel chair.

Clover couldn't resist trying to listen.

'Hi, Alice,' she heard him say. 'Is it a good time to talk?'

The answer must have been yes, because she heard George swing away from the desk and push the door shut. The conversation sounded like a series of growls and mumbles. Not one word was discernible. She decided to cook supper while she was waiting, just to give herself something to do. A cold feeling spread through her. She could just hear George laughing. He hadn't laughed at anything she'd said for so long.

Her mobile rang. 'Yes?' It was Laura. 'How's Tim?'

'Fine, much better. His temperature went down quite suddenly and I was able to take him home. He's in bed, but talking about getting up tomorrow. The doctor said it was probably just one of those things. He might even be able to have his next chemo on Friday, if his blood count stays up. But that wasn't what I was calling you about. Are you anywhere near a computer?'

'Yes, mine is on the kitchen table.'

'Go to Alice's blog.'

'Alice's blog? I didn't even know she had one.'

'I read about it in a newspaper. It was an item called "top ten retail blogs" or something like that. shirtsandthings is number three in the list of blogs we should all read.' Laura dictated the address to Clover, who called it up. 'Go to "Alice's Top Tips". The one dated just before Christmas. On having guests round.'

'I love having friends to stay,' read Clover out loud. 'And now that I live in London, everybody seems to find a reason for testing out Sheets & Things' latest 800 thread count Egyptian cotton bed linen. My motto is "spoil your guests". I always add one of our cashmere throws as well as a duvet in case guests get cold in the night. You need three pillows per guest: two ordinary ones, plus a little neck pillow for reading (see our *Pillow Talk* page). We've got a new "hotel" range of towels, which coordinate with the sheets, so that your guest room will look extra inviting, and, finally, of course, a good reading light, and a pretty bunch of flowers on the bedside table will make your guests feel both comfortable and welcome. Your only problem will be that they'll all keep wanting to come back.'

Laura laughed. 'I'm not sure I remember you mentioning the reading light or the bunch of flowers on your bedside table when you stayed there about two weeks after this blog was written.'

'A bedside table would have been nice. I had to put my glass of water on the floor.'

'Don't you think it's delicious?' Laura was amused.

'I suppose some people would say that everyone lies to sell

stuff. That it's not really a lie, just promotion. And maybe she does spoil everyone else. Perhaps it's just us who get treated like we do.'

'And now go to the "Alice's Diary" slot.'

Alice's Diary had a number of glamorous photos from the skiing holiday, describing 'our great friend Josiah', as an 'Olympic-standard skier'. 'Then home to Kent for New Year,' she trilled 'with lots of old friends round for one of those informal gatherings I love so much. I don't do formal dinner parties: I just like to take us back to all our student days, with lots of red wine – served in Sheets & Things' new "College" wine glasses, of course – and great mounds of shepherd's pie and chipolata sausages. There are all ages, with my daughter Lola welcoming all the friends she's made down here in Kent. Everyone always seems to congregate in the kitchen or on the stairs, talking about books or films and we all stay up far too late! Then off to New York to help Lola spend her Christmas money.'

'How odd,' said Clover.

'She's describing your party and pretending she gave it.'

'Maybe she had another party without inviting any of us?'

'No, she spent ages telling me what a tight – and important – schedule she was on. She trapped me in a corner, declaimed what a busy life she was having, then went off to talk at someone else without asking me anything. I know every detail about what she was doing over those few days. Anyway, we'd have heard via someone else, even if we weren't important enough to be invited.'

Clover didn't say that George was on the phone to Alice at that very moment. She didn't want to hear what Laura thought about that. 'I'm not sure that we were all talking about books and films. I think mostly we're all talking about Alice. Or the way everyone seems to have changed since the children left. How's Jamie, by the way?'

'Not sure,' said Laura. 'I haven't spoken to him for a week, since I told him his dad was in hospital. I texted that he was better, of course, and he texted back, but no actual news.'

'Well, maybe no news is good news, particularly in this day and age.'

'Mm. If, this time last year, you'd told me I wasn't going to speak to Jamie for a whole week, and that I'd hardly notice it, well, I wouldn't have believed you. But it's fine.' Laura's voice seemed lighter and freer, as if the sun had come out and she'd shaken off her heavy winter coat. 'I can't wait to have him back, but there are compensations, such as enjoying not having to buy six loaves of bread a week.'

'Good.' Clover was glad, but she had one eye on the study door as she put the phone down.

It was another ten minutes before George walked out of the study. Clover steadily peeled potatoes. Keep yourself busy. Don't think. Everything will be all right. A little heartbeat of panic ticked away inside as the pile of potatoes stacked up beside her. It had been a long conversation, and there was a finality in his face that chilled her to the bone.

'We need to talk.'

'OK.' Clover was determined not to let him see how frightened she was. If this was her home being wrenched apart, she intended to be brave about it.

'Alice and I . . . what are all these potatoes? Are we expecting people?'

'What?' Clover heard her voice sharpen. Her nerves were at screaming point.

'All this.' He pointed to the mound on the table beside her.

'Never mind the potatoes,' she snapped. 'What's this about Alice?'

He sat down. 'Alice and I . . . I want to join Alice. Be MD of Pets & Things. She's got the funding for it—'

'No!' The peeling knife slipped and Clover cut her hand. She jumped up, shaking it, and ran it under the tap. 'I mean, no, I don't want you to.'

'Sorry?' He sounded bemused.

'Don't leave your job. Please.' She could feel the soreness of the cut coming through the cold water.

'My job might well leave me.' George ignored her hand. 'If these takeover talks go through, which they probably will, there'll be a restructuring, and—'

'Go when it happens. Wait to find out if you are going to be pushed.' Clover tore off a square of kitchen paper and wrapped it round the cut.

'But Alice will have another MD for Pets & Things by then. She wants an answer in a week. Whoever comes in as the first MD gets equity. She was very clear about that.'

'I bet she was.'

'What does that mean?'

'I think Alice is only offering you this job to get at me,' she blurted out. 'And then we'll be dependent on her, and she'll be able to do what she likes. She wants us in her power.'

'Have you any idea how insulting that sounds?' George sounded incredulous. 'Alice and I have been going over plans and figures for months now, but all you can say is that it's all about you. We are both professionals, unlike you.'

'What do you mean, unlike me? I work, too, you know.'

'You now work twice the hours for half as much money as you did before. I call that unprofessional. And while I am consulting you over this, rather than just going straight ahead with it, I didn't hear you consulting me before you took this . . . this labouring job.'

'Is that the problem? That you think my being a decorating apprentice is below your dignity?'

George slammed his hand on the table. 'No, it is not the

problem. The problem is that you appear to have little or no faith in my professional ability, and to believe that Alice has some kind of a vendetta against you. I have to say, I am seriously questioning your sanity on this one. This is a business deal, and business is something you know very little about.'

'Don't you condescend to me,' Clover shouted back. 'I may not know a huge amount about business, but I do know about Alice, and in this case I don't trust her. Look. Here's her website. It's up now. Look at it. We've stayed there. We know what it's like. And here, see, she's pretending to have a fully equipped guest room—'

'She probably does by now.'

'Look at the date on that entry. It was written a few weeks before Christmas. We went to stay the first week in January. She doesn't have any bedside tables. And she says she does.'

'Am I hearing this right?' George's face coloured. 'Are you seriously suggesting that I don't go into business with Alice because she's pretending to have bedside tables when she doesn't?'

'It's not the bedside tables. It's the principle. The lying. Look at this entry, from after Christmas. She's describing our party and making out that she gave it.'

'That's a compliment, you idiot.'

'It would be a compliment if she'd made it clear it was a party she'd been to rather than one she'd given. Or if she'd rung me up and said, "You had a great party, do you mind if I pretend to have given something similar when I'm writing my blog?" But she didn't, did she?' Clover put her hands on her hips. 'Or did she ask you? Maybe that's the explanation. Maybe she talked to you about it, and you said go ahead?'

George looked away, picking up the kettle for some tea. 'She may have done.' He sounded evasive.

'Wouldn't you have mentioned it to me?' Clover tried to

look him in the eye, but he gazed at his reflection in the dark window.

'For God's sake. We're not all obsessed with trivia, you know. I might not have remembered. If she did say something.' He turned to her. 'You know, you have really got to stop getting wound up about minor issues like sheets, bedside tables and parties. It is all so unimportant compared to our future. So unimportant.'

'This is our future. Throwing our lot in with someone who lies and who uses us. And who doesn't care about our well-being. I don't happen to think that's a good idea.'

'You clearly have no faith in me.'

'No, it's *you* who doesn't have faith in me. In my judgement. I know something has gone terribly wrong in our relationship with Alice. And, as a result, I don't trust her.'

'You are simply not making sense.' He turned round and leant on the kitchen table. 'Ever since the children left, you've had this downer on Alice, as if it was all her fault that you're not Mother Hubbard any more.'

'Mother Hubbard?' They leaned towards each other over the table. Clover could see a vein pumping in George's forehead. 'Is that how you see me?'

'Yes. Having a house full of children, and their friends, and their friends' parents, and being needed was who you were.' His voice softened. 'Look, Clover, I know it's hard for you to accept that those days are over, and you'll never be at the centre of their lives the way you were—'

'That is *not* what this is about,' hissed Clover. 'This is about someone who I thought was a friend, who I now know I cannot trust. And if *I* can't trust her, *you* can't trust her. Because we're a team. And that's what she hates. She absolutely hates the fact that we're a team. She'll destroy it, even if it means damaging her own interests. That's what she's like. She's self-destructive.' It all suddenly seemed so clear.

'I can't believe I'm hearing this.' George shook his head in bewilderment. 'Alice has created a life – for *herself*, I might add, without relying on someone else's salary the way you have – and it's a very rich, full life. While the rest of you are flailing around talking about empty nests and personal fulfilment, she's made a success of herself. How you could consider her self-destructive I can't imagine.'

'She *has* had another salary. She's been getting money from Lola's father all along. While saying that she wasn't. And she's had help from us. Probably as much help as if she'd actually been married to one of us. But, once again, without much in the way of commitment in return. Or any kind of acknowledgement of what we – and I mean everyone, all the mothers who've helped her out over the years, not just me – have done for her. Don't you understand, George?' Clover raised her voice. 'Alice is a user. She'll use you and she'll drop you when she's had enough. Or when she wants to hurt.'

'I think you're turning a molehill into a mountain. You're basing your judgement on a few bits of bed linen, and what she's written to promote her company. People write anything in their blogs. No one's expected to believe it.'

'Really? So what am I expected to believe then? Maybe people say anything to their wives, too. And no one's expected to believe that either?'

'What does that mean?' George's voice was low and cold.

'You know exactly what that means.' Clover's heart was being wrenched out of her body. 'You may not have done anything illicit with Alice – not yet – but she has bewitched you, and you will say absolutely anything to me to get me to go along with all this.'

George picked his briefcase and coat up from a kitchen chair and headed towards the door.

'Where are you going?'

He turned round. His eyes were red with exhaustion. Or emotion. 'I don't know. I just know that I have to get away from here. I can't think straight with this kind of noise going on around me. Because that's what it is: white noise.' He slammed the front door behind him. As she heard the car door open and shut, and heard the engine start, she wondered if she should go out there and stop him. She could ask him about the cufflink.

Instead, she went upstairs to their bedroom and opened the box in which George kept his cufflinks. One 'Pow' cufflink sat there. The other one seemed to be missing.

She went downstairs and picked up the potatoes again. Mashed? Boiled? George would come back. George always did. George was the rock on which her life was built.

She picked up a potato, looked at it, and at the rest of the pile. There were too many. She'd peeled the amount of potatoes they'd needed when Ben and Holly, usually along with Lola, had been living at home.

Perhaps that's what was wrong. Perhaps George was right. She was peeling three pounds of potatoes for a life that only needed one. The blood from her finger ran over the white flesh of the potato, contaminating it. She threw them all away.

Chapter 35

Tim's next chemo day dawned, with a sky that threatened snow. 'Cathy's going to pick me up when she drives past,' said Tim as he opened the curtains. 'You don't need to bother. If my bloods aren't up to it I'll get a taxi back. Or I'll call you.'

Laura stirred in bed, not quite opening her eyes to the greyness. Did she need to go with him to the hospital and make sure everything was all right? As soon as Tim had been diagnosed, she'd moved his things out of her dressing room. She realised she'd missed him when she'd slept alone. Mentally she assessed the day for danger, but heard only the birdsong outside the window. Tim was in good hands. The hospital wouldn't let him have the chemo if his blood counts weren't good enough. 'Fine. Good.' She snuggled under the duvet, reluctant to leave its warmth.

'So what are you going to do today?' He strode across the room towards the en suite shower. He was still a lean, strong man. From her mound of fluffy duvet she appraised him through half-closed eyes. The image of another strong, lean physique came into her mind and she tried to banish it. She was so lucky, she told herself. She had so much. She had a second chance with Tim that she must not endanger.

'What are you going to do today?' Tim repeated, sounding amused. 'Are you meeting your lover?'

'What?' She struggled up from the bedclothes. 'What are you talking about?'

'Well, that got you up.' Tim laughed. 'I was beginning to think you might have died under there.'

She shook her head. 'I'm ... um ... going to think about work.' The words sprang out of her mouth. She didn't know where they'd come from.

Tim laughed again. He paused by the shower-room door. 'What, back to acting again?'

'Don't be silly. I've been away for nineteen years, and there aren't enough good parts for the really good middle-aged actresses who've been working pretty steadily over that time.' She propped herself up against their giant headboard, realising that this was the first time she'd actually said, out loud, that she was no longer an actress. It was like a ray of sunshine hitting her eyes. So painful that she couldn't look directly at it.

But when she adjusted her head she was able to open them again, and could see a world of rosy possibilities. She couldn't be an actress – that stabbing pain again, but less this time – but there was so much else she could do.

'Are you all right?' Tim peered at her. 'You look a bit pale.'

'Actually, I think I'm better than I have been for years.' She hopped out of bed, looking forward to her first cup of Lapsang Souchong. Very weak, with a drop of milk. Heaven. If it wasn't too cold she might put a coat over her pyjamas and listen to the birdsong outside. 'You know how I always used to say that when Jamie went to school, or when he went to secondary school, or when he left home ... just when, when, when ... then I'd go back to acting? Well, those whens have run out. I'm not an actress any more. Finito. Over.' She smiled back at him over her shoulder, feeling the world open out ahead of her. 'But I'll be something else, don't you worry.'

'I have complete faith in you.' He returned her smile.

'I know you do.' And she did. A year ago, she would have heard that remark as sarcastic. They would have argued, snapping away at each other, each determined to win or, if not, to hurt.

Downstairs in the warm kitchen, she poured boiling water onto a teabag, then whipped it out of the cup almost immediately, luxuriating in having the drink exactly how she liked it. Her mobile phone vibrated and she seized it, anxious that Tim might suddenly appear downstairs. Of course, it would be Clover. Or Sheila Lewis. Or Leila Marchandani. With some practical arrangement. Or maybe Jamie telling her that Gwent was working out after all. Her heart sped up. This was Jamie's future, and it didn't seem to be going very well.

But there were no more practical arrangements requiring texts at seven-thirty in the morning and, with the exception of Clover, there was no reason why anyone should text her. Jamie would certainly be asleep.

She knew who it was as soon as she read the number. 'See you at midday. Usual place.'

'No' she texted back. 'It's over. Over. OVER.' She stuffed the phone into her pyjama pocket and made a mug of tea for Tim, laced with more tannin than hers, and carried them upstairs. The new, strong Laura did not need a man's hands running over her body to validate her. She did not need admiration in order to function.

'Laura! Laura!' Tim's anguished cry nearly made her trip.

Slopping the tea in her haste, she hurried along the landing to find him naked in the shower, holding a handful of hair in his hands.

'It just came out,' he said, holding it in amazement. He ran his hands over his head again, and another clump came out in his fingers.

Laura gazed at his scalp. Some places had tufts of scrappy hair and in others tendrils barely covered the pale skin. 'Tim, stop it! You're pulling it all out.'

He looked at himself in the mirror, at the sparse strands across his scalp. He was very pale. 'No, I'm not,' he said. 'It's coming out the minute I touch it. Look at the shower.'

She let out a cry of revulsion. The plughole was thick with hair.

'You need to get rid of that.' He pointed at it. 'I haven't got time. I'll shave the rest of it off.'

Laura stared at the drain with horror. She didn't do that kind of thing. Tim did it. She thought she might be sick, but went downstairs to get rubber gloves while Tim shaved his head.

This is what marriage is about, she told herself. Practical. Working as a team. She managed to get all the hair out of the drain without retching, then Tim snapped at her because he didn't have any clean socks.

It was while she was searching through a pile of clean laundry, finding a pair of socks that matched so much more quickly than she used to when Jamie's pile of clothes doubled the washing pile, that the second text came through.

'I will be there', it said.

Well, he'd be waiting for a long time. She switched the phone off without replying to the message, and stumped upstairs with the socks.

'You've been a long time. What kept you?' Tim's voice was harsh and complaining, jarring her.

Laura stared at him. A completely different person stood there, a man with a shiny, pale head. This wasn't the Tim she knew.

258

'What are you staring at? I know it looks hideous.'

She shook her head slowly. 'It doesn't look hideous. Just . . . ' She tried to tell herself that this was still her beloved husband standing there.

She failed. This was an angry, bald man she had never met before. 'It just looks different,' she said.

He turned away from her and walked to the window. 'There's Cathy. I don't want to keep her waiting as she's been so kind to come and pick me up.'

'She didn't have to. I was quite prepared to take you to the hospital.' Laura tried to sound normal, but she knew she'd failed. She could hear herself sounding defensive and snappish.

'I wouldn't like to get in the way of your perfect life,' snarled Tim. 'I know what a nuisance all this is for you.'

Laura bit back a reply, but the words stung her like thrown stones. Sharp, painful, unexpected. Leaving bruises. She watched him from the window, leaving the house muffled up in his coat, his scarf flying as he crunched over the gravel. He was wearing a woolly hat, but as he opened the car door he leant in to say something to Cathy and pulled the hat off.

Laura saw him smile at something she'd said, and noted the easy way he got into the passenger seat. They both belonged to a club she wasn't a member of. She didn't want to be a member – of course not – but she felt left out. Diminished. I did the wrong thing. I wasn't there for him. I let him see my revulsion. The tickertape rattled through her head.

This, too, is marriage, she told herself. Seeing their sunny side shining on someone else while you get the rainy days. This is the lonely bit of marriage.

The new strong Laura could deal with that. But the text message burned in her pocket.

Chapter 36

Clover slept restlessly. George had sent a text about two hours after he'd left. 'Thinking things over. Will stay out tonight. Hope that's OK.'

Maybe thinking it over was what he needed. It was not an angry text. She told herself, over and over, that George would be bound to see sense. Nobody would leave a well-paid job for a start-up with a friend. Surely? Expecting to wake up at three, worrying, she was surprised to wake at six, having slept through the night. But she had a sick feeling in the pit of her stomach. Where had George spent the night? Her mobile phone lay still. There were no further messages.

She remembered the time she'd re-met George properly once they'd left school, as opposed to simply acknowledging him as part of her wider group. They were all in a pub – for someone's birthday, she thought – and he'd been in a trio of men, just another bloke with a pint in his hand talking about cars. They'd nodded. George had lifted his glass in a brief salute to her, and she'd started chatting to someone else.

Until an argument broke out between two of their party. She couldn't remember any of their names now, but there'd been a short, pretty girl hissing furiously at her boyfriend that she'd found mascara marks on a towel in his flat. As everyone backed off or slipped away, Clover realised that she and George had got trapped in a corner behind the argument, which was deteriorating into insults about each other's performance in bed, who paid for what and beyond.

They exchanged glances of amusement and embarrassment. He put down his pint and took her hand. 'Come on, let's escape.' He propelled her through the shrieking couple and out on to the street. 'Phew,' he said. 'Someone shoot me if I ever get like that.'

'They're nuts about each other,' Clover replied. 'Apparently it's true love.'

He shook his head in mock despair. 'Love should be about being kind to each other, not scoring points over who's best in bed, or who's paid for what. I was enjoying that pint — shall we have a drink across the road?' They had stayed, drinking and chatting, until closing time. Four hours had slipped by, and they'd discovered so much in common. They both loved walking in the countryside more than going to nightclubs. They liked boiled eggs and toast soldiers for breakfast, long, lingering baths and early Sunday mornings when the streets were almost empty. Neither of them ever carried an umbrella. They both enjoyed the feel of rain on their faces.

At the time discovering these little details in common had been like finding precious, sparkling diamonds, but now she wondered if they were both running away from their passionate side. She and George had never screamed at each other the way that couple in the pub had. Maybe that meant they didn't really care enough. He was like a cosy sweater, someone to keep her warm on cold nights.

And maybe, she thought, that wasn't enough any more.

It was the last few days of the Dundy job. Duncan picked her up at seven-thirty, and she cleared the usual collection of newspapers, old sandwich wrappers and empty drinks bottles off her seat.

'After this job finishes,' she asked him, determined to distract herself, 'have you got any work for me? I know Sean's due back now his wrist's mended.'

His face crinkled up in a smile. 'Do you want some?'

'I'd like to learn more specialist treatments. If you'd be willing to teach me.'

He nodded slowly, as if thinking it over. 'It would certainly make sense to have someone else who could do them. I get tied up with actual decorating when I should be out finding new business or project-managing the other jobs. But if we're going to get serious – how's George about the idea of your becoming a painter?'

'Oh, George doesn't mind what I do.' But she saw, again, her younger self plunging into the sea and ignoring the cries of everyone else on the shore.

One day she would be caught by the current.

This might be that day.

'Actually,' she said, the words so glued to her mouth she could barely speak, 'George and I had an argument last night about what we both do, and he spent the night away.'

Duncan flashed her a quick look of concern and checked his watch. 'I could murder a quick coffee. How about you?'

'Won't we be late?'

He grinned, as he parked the car in front of a café. 'I'm the boss.' He made a call to Chris, established that they'd be on site in an hour, and ordered two coffees.

They sat at a tin table, Duncan spooning sugar into his mug. 'Tell me.'

He was a good listener. Clover mapped out the increasing distance between herself and George since Holly had left, George's belief that he would be made redundant, and her own hurt at Alice's behaviour. 'I'm frightened,' she admitted. 'I get the feeling – and I don't know why – that Alice is actually out to create trouble. Which is why I don't want George to go into business with her. But all I can do is point to things that he regards as silly, such as her not making us very welcome when we visit her flat, or seeming to pretend that she'd given our New Year's Eve party on her website. Which are all so trivial it seems ridiculous to base a life decision on it.'

Duncan was silent for a few moments, stirring his coffee. 'Well,' he said eventually. 'One thing I do know is that she's very jealous of you.'

'Jealous of *me*? But why? She's got a multi-million-pound company – she's in every article about successful women I ever see. She's brought her daughter up on her own, so she's really a modern mother, and she's got two homes, both of which also feature in every magazine article going. And I'm just an ordinary country housewife with a scruffy house and a seven pound an hour job!'

'I was going to talk to you about that. But it's another conversation.'

'Sorry, I wasn't grumbling. That's what the job's worth.'

'She's got two houses, not two homes. You've got a real home, with friends coming in and out, and George. And Ben and Holly. It smells of cooking and good times. It's almost tidy but not quite. You've got it looking nice – really ...' He touched her hand briefly, the back of his hand against the back of hers. 'I like the way you use colour, and the bits and pieces you've picked up everywhere. Her places are both picture perfect, but they've got no real warmth about them.'

Clover thought about it. Even when she and Alice had been close, and Alice had been living mainly in Kent, she'd spent relatively little time in the extended modernist glass bungalow. Clover sometimes thought she liked what Alice

263

had done with it more than Alice did herself, from the way the views seemed to come right in through the huge plate-glass windows to the sense of space. It was a great place for parties, although Alice rarely threw them. But had it ever been redolent of the smell of frying onions or roast beef? Had there ever been muddy boots strewn along the wall by the back door, coffee mugs left on the perfect slabs of polished wenge, or books sprawling, face down and open among crushed cushions? There was a stillness about the house, as if even the air rarely moved.

It had a glossy black open-plan kitchen, which Alice rarely seemed to use, preferring to heat up microwave meals in the scruffy little pantry. Otherwise she and Lola seemed to watch television in their bedrooms, which were usually quite untidy. It was as if they actually lived in the same square footage they'd had in the original bungalow.

'But if Alice wanted to make her homes more homely, surely she could just live in them more? Instead of travelling so much. It's such an amazing house – it just needs living in.'

'I think if you lived there it would be a home. And that's what she can't forgive.' There was a gentleness about his eyes that made Clover blush.

'But all of this is within her power,' she said. '*I* can't turn myself into a hotshot businesswoman, but if *she* wants to be able to cook, or to entertain more, or have people around, then all she's got to do is make an effort. There's no point in hating me because I have people to supper. She should just have people to supper herself. They'd be delighted to be asked.'

Duncan laughed. 'Well, it's not so simple for someone like her. I think she's too busy, constantly looking over her shoulder to see if someone else has a better, more sparkly toy. There isn't always the time or the energy to grab every sparkly toy as it goes past. Essentially she sees herself as a victim. And everyone else as lucky.'

'It still doesn't make a lot of sense to resent me for it. Surely she must look at my life, and at hers, and realise that, although we have very different things and different characters, she really doesn't have less than me. And if you're talking material goods she's actually got more.'

Duncan drained the last of his coffee and put the mug down. 'I don't think she counts what she has, only what she *hasn't* got. And she hasn't got a husband like George.'

Clover stared at him, feeling the current get her at last. It was dragging her out into the cold, merciless sea, towards the higher waves. 'He's a middle-ranking executive,' she said. 'A rather shambolic, practical middle-aged man who likes a lot of sport, and would look like a camel at Ascot races if she took him to any smart parties. Please do not tell me that this is all about wanting my husband.'

'I don't know how much she does want him. She just knows she hasn't got him. And one of the things she really minds is that Holly and Ben have him. I know that Lola has said – and I'm sure she's said it quite often – that she wishes she had a father like Ben and Holly's. And, sometimes, when she's angry with her mother, she throws that in her face.'

'But Lola and Alice are – well, they were – so close. They don't need a father,' protested Clover. 'Alice pretends to be cool about it, but she's absolutely devoted to her. Lola is the centre of her world. The other mothers used to criticise Alice for being away so much, but she was always at the end of the phone. And, as Lola got older, Alice seemed to grow closer and closer to her.'

'Yes, and that's the last thing Lola seems to need at the moment. Lola wants a daddy, but not a mummy.'

Fear clutched at Clover's heart. If Lola wanted George as a

father, then Alice would stop at nothing to get him for her. She was the most determined woman in the world. Especially if she thought it could restore the mother–daughter closeness she'd so enjoyed. 'Is this all about Lola finding her real father? I mean, none of this ever came up before Lola left school. Alice was always friendly and appreciative. Or was I just being very stupid?'

He shrugged slightly. 'I don't suppose any of us notice envy until it slaps us in the face. And slap us in the face it does. Alice and I had a brief affair, which is why she invited me out to France. Just to make my role in all this clear. I ended it at the end of the holiday. I didn't think that Alice really cared for me, one way or the other. She was just looking for a Mr Alice, someone to carry her handbag and pick her up from places.' He grinned. 'She makes out that she's so independent, but she hated being a single woman among a whole lot of couples. She really hated it. She felt left out. She thought you all felt sorry for her, as if she was some kind of poor relation in a Jane Austen novel.'

Clover was astonished. 'Well, she wasn't. We invited Alice round because she was huge fun, and we admired her enormously. She was part of the family, and so was Lola.'

'Well, these things are always tricky.' He made a pattern on the table with some spilt sugar. His hands looked strong and dark, with the inevitable grimy nails of the professional painter. 'She said one or two things that made me realise how bitter she was. As if she was just tamping down resentment until Lola got to uni and didn't need a second home any more. That kind of thing can be corrosive. I don't like being around it.'

Clover was struggling to reconcile the casual, laughing Alice she remembered with this underlying bitterness. Yes, there had been sharp remarks, but they were often funny or self-deprecating, so Clover had assumed they were just part of

Alice's way of making the best of things. 'But she seems pretty wrapped up in this Josiah man, doesn't she?'

'Gay,' Duncan replied. 'His boyfriend, Pete, was there when I went up to do a quote on Alice's flat. He was charming, but works part of the time in New York. I got the feeling that Alice and Josiah are both very insecure. Talented, hardworking, successful and insecure. Maybe quite similar personalities, which is why they get on. But Josiah is her Plus One – someone she can take to parties when Pete's away – not her lover.'

Clover frowned. 'I'm sure she said . . . ' But what had Alice said? Probably nothing that couldn't be explained as a misunderstanding.

'Are you going to paint Alice's flat? I don't think I could work on it if you did.'

He shook his head. 'I was surprised she even asked me, to tell you the truth, considering that I was the one who ended it between us. She didn't really want me, but she certainly didn't like it when I pulled out. So I got the feeling that she wanted me in her power, and clients can be very, very difficult when they want to be. I gave her an outrageous quote and told her we were booked up for six months.'

Clover was relieved. 'Did she ever talk about Lola's father? And how she got into the situation where she couldn't tell anyone who he was?'

'A bit. She told me that she hadn't realised he was married – he hadn't told her and she thought they were an item. According to her, she'd been terribly in love with him and he let her down badly.'

'But Alice always kind of implied to me that she'd rather be on her own, and that men who wanted commitment bored her. I've never felt she wanted to be a couple.'

'I think she says different things to different people. Who knows the real Alice?'

Clover tried to digest it all. If Alice really resented her so much, then their friendship was over. In fact, it had never properly existed. That hurt. It hurt a lot.

Maybe Alice had wanted it to hurt. Perhaps she had been damaged so badly that making other people feel pain was the only way she could function.

And there was George. Clover stared into her empty mug.

Duncan's mobile rang, and he answered it, flicking a quick look at Clover. 'Mm. Yes. OK. I'll ask her. Mm. Bye then.' He snapped it shut and put it back in his pocket.

'Well, that was another call for Mrs Jones.' He smiled at her and stood up. 'Eleanor Dundy has a friend called Cherry Williams, who is also doing up her house. Rather to my surprise, Mrs Dundy has recommended us because of our design expert, Mrs Jones. Who went to Chelsea.'

'I'm not a design expert.'

'No, but you have an eye for colour and can handle people like Devil Dundy – sorry, I wouldn't normally speak like that about a client.' He shrugged on his battered flying jacket and raised an eyebrow. 'Back to work, Mrs Jones?'

She made herself smile. 'Back to work,' she agreed, suppressing the horror of knowing that someone she had thought was a friend – for so long – actually wished her ill. It was a shock, like a bucket of water in your face. Inside, she was still gasping.

She wondered what George was doing, and whether he was back at work too. And how she could stop him making the worst mistake of his life. Of their lives.

Chapter 37

Laura was sickened by herself, as she checked his room number with the hotel receptionist. He was there. In Room 28. Expecting her. The receptionist gave her a second key. She couldn't even pretend this was a spur-of-the-moment thing. She'd had to take a train. Buy a ticket. She'd even, to look less furtive to the receptionist, packed a small case.

He was lying on the bed watching TV when she let herself in to the room. 'Hi doll.'

She sat down carefully on the bed. 'I'm not your doll. I've only come to talk, because I didn't want to end it badly.'

'I don't want it to end at all.' He smiled. 'You're wearing too many clothes. Take them off.'

She knew what she had come for. 'If we do this, now, do you promise you'll never contact me again?'

He put down his bottle of beer and took hold of her wrist. 'This is not the sort of relationship where you exchange promises,' he said, looking amused as he pulled her down on top of him. 'And if you did, you wouldn't expect to keep them. Now, am I going to undress you or are you going to do it yourself?'

She pretended to consider it, as she stood up and turned her back. 'Let me see. I think, perhaps, today . . . I'm Duchess

Laura. I couldn't possibly undress myself. And as my lady's maid is fucking a stablehand in the hayloft, I'm going to have to ask one of the footmen to oblige.'

'Certainly, Madam.' She heard him laugh softly, as he stood up and lifted her hair from the nape of her neck, planting a kiss on her bare skin. 'And how does Madam like her kisses? A little bit lower?' He unzipped her dress a few inches.

'Just a little.' She stood there, imperiously, as he slowly undressed her, kissing each area of skin as it was exposed, thinking herself into the role of a Duchess being undressed by a footman, playing for an invisible audience and revelling in the glory of not having to be herself.

But later, as they lay side by side, she turned to him. 'Tim lost all his hair today.'

He turned on one side, resting on his elbow. 'Just today?'

'I think it's been thinning for a while, but so slowly we haven't noticed. But he went on a new drug a few weeks ago and it came out in clumps.'

'And he doesn't look like Tim any more.' It was a statement, not a question.

She nodded, surprised to feel a tear trickle down her cheek.

He wiped it away with his thumb. 'It's not easy for you, all of this.'

'Oh, it's fine for me. I'm just hopeless at it all,' she explained. 'I'm a useless nurse, not at all sympathetic, and much too selfish. He deserves a wife who would really look after him.'

'And you come here, because you need to be yourself,' he suggested. 'Where you're not expected to be a nurse or a supportive wife?'

She turned over, her back to him. 'No. I come here because it's the only place I can get away from myself.'

She felt him lift her hair again, gently away from her ear,

then his lips against her skin. 'Laura,' he whispered. 'You are one seriously fucked-up lady. You need to find some help. Before you destroy yourself completely.'

She rolled onto her back and looked up into his eyes. 'You're funny,' she said, tracing the rough stubble across his chin. 'You come over all Big Bad Wolf, but underneath you're a great big soppy St Bernard rushing in with a flask of brandy around your neck.'

He pretended to look affronted. 'Hang on, I've got my reputation as a heart-breaker to consider. You can't go around saying things like that.'

She smiled and looked at her watch. 'I need to go.'

He picked up the half-drunk beer bottle, and switched on the TV. 'I meant it, by the way. Get some professional help.'

She shook her head as she pulled her dress up and zipped it up behind her with a practised wriggle. 'I keep thinking that if anyone finds out who I really am they'll hate me.'

'I know who you really are,' he replied. 'And you are infinitely loveable.'

She put her coat on and looked at him, lounging against the huge cushions, channel surfing to find the football.

She believed him. She had never really believed anyone else.

'Thank you,' she said as she let herself out. But he'd turned the volume up, and probably hadn't heard.

Chapter 38

Clover spent the day putting the last touches to Devil Dundy's en suite shower room, listening to Radio 4. Dave had been recalled yet again, to replace a tap, and Chris was chasing an ever-changing list of tiny snags.

'Oi, Mrs Jones,' called Dave. 'Can you make good that paintwork by the shower? I've scratched it and my life won't be worth living.'

Mrs Jones seemed to have turned into her name. Clover quite liked it.

When she got home the house was still empty. There was no sign of George having returned, and Clover had to restrain herself from phoning him.

At six-thirty she cracked. He answered immediately. She kept her voice light and even. 'I just wondered if you'd be home for supper.'

'I'm in the drive now.' He sounded remote.

Annoyed with herself for not hanging on slightly longer, she began re-heating a casserole that she'd taken from the freezer. It would be difficult to concentrate on cooking something new from scratch. 'Hi.'

He didn't meet her eyes. 'Hi. I'll just pop up to change.'

When he came downstairs he picked up the paper. Clover

told herself she wasn't going to ask where he'd spent the night.

That lasted all of five minutes. She had to break the silence between them. 'So,' she said, as cheerfully as she could, 'did you find somewhere decent to sleep last night?'

'No,' he replied, still holding the paper up. 'I drove around.'

Clover gasped. 'What, all night? That's so dangerous! You might have had an accident. You could have been killed.'

'Well, at least you could have claimed on the insurance.' He folded the paper up and walked to the window.

'George! How could you say that? You know I wouldn't think like that.'

'I'm not sure I know what you're thinking.'

'Oh stop all this sulking! It's like dealing with Ben or Holly aged ten. Only with less maturity.'

He turned to face her. 'I'm not sulking. I'm trying to make some very difficult decisions about what to do with my life.'

'What, whether to work with Alice? I've been talking to Duncan. As you know, he went out with her ... ' Too late, Clover realised her mistake.

'And what does Duncan say about our marriage or my career? And Laura's view? And maybe you've e-mailed Sarah Baxter for hers? Leila Marchandani? Sheila Lewis? I don't suppose you've asked Alice, though? She doesn't have any bedside tables, which puts her outside respectable society.'

'George, you are being absolutely horrible and very unfair.'

'At least I'm not discussing our marriage with half of Kent.'

'Neither am I. I haven't spoken to anyone apart from Duncan. He and I did have a discussion because I wanted to be fair to Alice. I wondered if he thought it was dangerous to go into business with her, and he said—'

George thumped his fist down on the table. 'If I want Duncan's opinion on who I should go into business with, I will ask him. Clover, do you never think more than two minutes ahead? Of course Duncan's going to support your view of Alice. She dumped him and he wasn't best pleased. He's an extremely attractive man who's not used to women saying no.'

'She didn't say no. *He* dumped *her*.'

'Really? And you believe him?'

'It's no stranger than your believing Alice.' Clover felt like crying. Or screaming. 'I've worked with Duncan for a couple of months and I have never known him lie. While the evidence that Alice lies is there on her website, in black and white.'

'I see we're back to the bedside tables again. The ones she doesn't have. Shall we drive up there together and ask to see her spare room?'

'No!' shrieked Clover. 'You're the one who keeps banging on about bedside tables. I don't care.'

'You seemed to care very much indeed when we were first talking about them.'

'George, you are twisting everything I say, and you are not talking about what is really going on.'

'So,' he said, neatly pinning her into a corner. 'What is really going on?'

Clover didn't want to put it into words. They stared at each other. 'I think you're tired,' she said eventually. 'And that you should have something to eat and a decent night's sleep. And we should talk about it tomorrow.'

'Fine by me,' he said, opening the paper again.

Chapter 39

When Laura got home, Cathy and Tim were drinking herbal tea in the kitchen.

'Oh, hello.' She was surprised. 'Did your chemo finish early?' She couldn't quite look at Tim's head, which was like a large, shiny egg.

Tim looked at his watch. 'No, normal time. What have you been up to?'

The words branded her with guilt. 'Oh, nothing much, just shopping.'

'Did you get anything nice?' She could see Cathy looking around for carrier bags.

'I couldn't find anything I liked.'

'Laura's shopping is legendary,' said Tim. 'She can spend all day looking at eight different pairs of jeans in eight different shops and not buy any of them.'

Cathy laughed – light and merry, and directed at Tim. He smiled back at her, shutting Laura out. She felt as if they were laughing at her.

If Cathy didn't have cancer she'd have been jealous of her, Laura realised with a jolt. She felt the old fear and insecurity rise up like bile in her throat as she left the room to hang up her coat. This is *my* husband, she felt like saying, and we will deal with his illness together. We don't need you getting in the way.

But she forced herself to think differently. To look out of another window, and see how you could still be in the same place but have a completely different outlook. She smiled when she came back in. 'Would you like some supper, Cathy? It's only ham and salad, but we've got lots.'

Cathy looked at Tim. 'Do stay,' he added.

'I'll make it early,' said Laura, 'so you're not late getting to bed. I'm starving, myself.' She forced herself to smile again. Act, Laura, act. You're good at acting.

She must have been, because Cathy looked pleased and accepted.

They ate, with Tim and Cathy swapping anecdotes about the nurses and some of the other patients. 'It's funny how everyone needs something to blame, isn't it?' said Cathy. 'People look at me and say "But you don't smoke, you're not overweight – why did *you* get it?" They want an explanation.'

'They want to hear a reason why it couldn't happen to them,' said Tim. 'Tall, thin people want to hear that cancer only happens to short, fat people, and the other way round.'

Laura thought she knew why Tim had cancer. Because he had an awful wife. That's what happens if you misbehave. Terrible things happen to you and the people you love. She fiddled with a piece of bread, breaking it up into crumbs. She heard the words 'you're infinitely loveable' in her mind and tried to hold on to them, but it was like trying to catch snowflakes. Sometimes she tried to look out of those different windows, but they'd been bricked up while she had her back turned.

'I feel I'm a sitting duck for every zealot,' added Cathy. 'There's a woman I knew vaguely at the school my children used to go to, who I haven't seen for years. She insisted on coming round and healing my chakras. She spent ages holding her hands just above the top of my head, then down my body a few inches away from me, flicking her fingers away from time to time, and telling me there was a lot of heat over the area that stands for jealousy. Then she charged me eighty pounds. I'd thought she was going to do it as a friend, but, in a way, I'm glad to have paid. Then, I don't have to be grateful.'

'That finger-flicking is getting rid of the negative energies,' said Laura. 'Speaking of jealousy, I spoke to Clover today, and apparently Duncan thinks that *Alice* is jealous of her.' She addressed Tim, then turned to Cathy. 'Alice is this super-successful friend of ours. Clover is a country housewife who works as a jobbing decorator. Alice is clearly bonkers if she's jealous of Clover.' She offered the salad to Cathy again. 'But then again, Alice is bonkers.'

'Perhaps it's not about what they've both got, but what they haven't,' said Cathy. 'I remember when the children were little, and one of them would be furious about some toy the other had got, and no amount of saying "but you've got one of your own" or making sure that everything was equal would ever sort the arguments out. I think they were often just doing it for my attention.'

Tim laughed. 'Well, I wonder whose attention Alice is trying to get, then?'

'George's,' said Laura immediately. 'Who is, apparently, sulking like a spoilt toddler. He wants to go into business with Alice.'

'He talked it over with me,' said Tim. 'He's pretty sure he won't survive another round of redundancies at Petfast, and Alice is offering him a fantastic opportunity to start something from scratch and get some equity.'

'Clover thinks Alice is out to get them. She thinks it would be a huge mistake.'

'What do you think?' Cathy asked Laura.

'Personally, I think George would be absolutely mad to throw in a well-paid job, with benefits, to go into business with someone as unstable – and dishonest – as Alice.'

'I don't agree,' said Tim. 'Alice has a difficult personality, especially where women are concerned, because she's so competitive, but she's got an enormous amount of drive and she has made a great success of her business.'

'I think I should go.' Cathy got up. 'I'm so tired. Thank you so much for supper, Laura.'

Tim got up to show her out, and Laura heard murmuring in the hall. She wondered what they were saying. Jealousy flickered inside again, burning her. Even if he was ill and angry, Laura did not want her husband talking like that to another woman.

Tim came back into the room, his head still seeming alien. 'You can hardly bear to look at me, can you?'

'What? Of course I can, it's just that if I do you accuse me of finding you repellent. And I don't. But it is different. If you'd lost your hair gradually, over the years, like most men do, I'd be used to it. But I'm not. And if that makes me a bad person, or a bad wife, well . . . '

She got up to clear the table, keeping her eyes fixed on the plates and glasses. Because she knew that when she did look at Tim, she didn't see a bald head. She saw a sick, frightened man. And if Tim – who had always been so strong, her knight on a white charger – was sick and frightened, then who was going to look after her?

Chapter 40

Clover decided to give George an ultimatum. Choose Alice or me. Choose between the security of your job and marriage or going it alone. She tossed and turned all night, then told him in the morning once they had both showered and had breakfast. They stood in their farmhouse kitchen, the children's drawings still tacked to the noticeboard and 'hope u miss us' spelt out in magnetic letters across the fridge. Outside, the first tulips reached for the sky and the trees were starkly outlined against the clouds. This beloved landscape was what she stood to lose if George didn't see sense.

'You'd leave me if I joined Alice's company?' he asked, his eyes red-rimmed.

'No. I wouldn't want to. I would do everything I could *not* to leave you. But I don't, in reality, think our marriage could survive. If you do this, it means you don't trust my judgement. And trust is what our relationship is built on.' She couldn't believe that they'd got this far.

'But you don't trust me. Or you would never have issued this ultimatum.'

'No, it's Alice I don't trust.'

She had honestly expected him to understand. Everyone

always said how difficult it was to go into business with friends. Surely he could see?

'Well,' he replied. 'I suppose I should be used to you driving all the main decisions of our life without paying any attention to what I think. Just remind me, by the way, of that accidental pregnancy that meant we had to make a sudden decision about our future. Tell me again exactly how that happened. Because I've never been quite clear about it.'

Clover stared at him, her stomach falling away. 'What?'

'I'd just like to know, once and for all, if your first pregnancy was genuinely an accident, or whether you were just so determined to have a baby that you went ahead without discussing it with me.'

'I did not trap you into marriage. If you remember, I was the one who wasn't quite sure.'

'That's not what I asked.' He picked up his coat and gloves. 'But sometimes no answer is an answer of sorts. I'm going into the office. I got very behind last week.'

Clover wanted to call him back. To call it all back – her words, his angry replies, even the ultimatum. She was sure she was right, but she knew she'd handled it wrong. She should have been more clever, more patient.

In search of distraction she fired up her laptop, only to find an e-mail from Alice. She opened it, still hoping against hope that it would contain affection, an apology, or even just an explanation that might make sense.

'Hi guys,' she read, noting that it was a group e-mail sent to all the class mothers from St Crispian's.

Hope you're all fine. This is just to connect you all with what's been happening with Lola. As you've probably read, there have been stories in the press about who her father was. This kind of publicity is the price we have to pay for success, I suppose, but it's been a rough ride for Lola, and I'd be really grateful for your support. She needs to put everything behind her so she's agreed to shut down her Facebook account and not get in touch with anyone while she settles down properly at Oxford. So if you've contacted her but haven't had an answer from her, don't worry. We'll be back! But, just for the time being, she needs a bit of space. Could you all make sure your kids understand this too? A couple of them (no names, no pack drill, as my father used to say!) have been texting her and she's been quite upset by it all.

I'm spending this week in a hotel in Oxford so that I can see her every day, to make sure she's all right, so if there's anything anyone needs to say, do contact me and I can pass it on.

Thanks all, and kisses, love Alice.

The phone began to ring. It rang and rang all morning, as the St Crispian's mothers, many of whom had barely seen each other for nearly a year, got in touch to fume over Alice's missive.

'This is so unchristian,' said Sheila Lewis. 'I know Alice has always been a friend of yours, but this is not a kind e-mail.'

'No, I don't think Alice is kind. She certainly wasn't thinking about how we might feel when she was writing it.'

'She was thinking about her daughter,' said Sheila. 'Which is right and proper. I know Alice thinks I'm a fussy old fool, and that I don't know half of what Ruby gets up to. But Nigel and I have to trust her: she's living her own life now. We've done our best to impart our values to her, but it's up to her whether she accepts or rejects them.' Her voice rose with

281

indignation. 'We wouldn't dream of going behind Ruby's back to talk to other people about her, although she does worry us. We'll always love her, whatever, and she knows that.'

'I think you're quite right.' Clover felt guilty for presuming that the Lewises were so unaware of Ruby's behaviour.

'Funnily enough,' Sheila went on, 'Ruby sees quite a lot of Lola. She says she's handling it fine now. She was more upset about Ben dumping her.'

'My Ben?' Clover was horrified. 'Don't tell me Ben's dumped her just when she's so down.'

'Oh, I'm sorry, I'd have thought you knew all about it. No, Ben didn't break up with her recently – it was ages ago, just after the summer holidays – and I don't think he really, as such, dumped her. He just told her he wasn't ready for a relationship and wanted to stay friends. And I think they have. But Ruby says Lola definitely holds a candle for him. He's gorgeous, isn't he? I know he's very quiet when adults are around, but he's quite the centre of that little group as far as the kids are concerned.'

Warmth flooded through Clover. She rarely heard compliments about Ben. He was gorgeous. She knew he was. She was a bit puzzled, though. 'But they spent the night together here at New Year.'

'Yes, Ruby told me, but she said nothing happened. It was just a couple of old friends sharing a bed.'

'And Alice has made a huge fuss about Ben distracting Lola from Oxford.'

'I don't know anything about that. I think Lola's been up to York – and Leeds – once or twice, with the others. But it's a gang thing, as far as I can see.'

'I sometimes think I know absolutely nothing about anything when it comes to my children,' said Clover.

'Join the club. I suspect that's the way it's supposed to be. I must go, the vet is coming to look at the goats. Two of them are pregnant. It's so exciting: apparently nobody has bred Mongolian goats successfully round here. Not on any scale.'

Clover put the phone down, liking Sheila more than she ever had done before.

The phone rang again immediately. 'Talk about helicopter parenting!' shrieked Laura. 'Spending a week in Oxford to keep an eye on Lola. That's hovering over your adult child in a big way. Not to mention all these machinations to try to stop her communicating with us. Whose life is it anyway? Hers or Lola's?'

'Oh, Laura, guess what I've done.' Clover mapped out her conversation with George.

'Oh no, Clover, you didn't! Not an ultimatum. They're so destructive.'

'Um, thanks, Laura, I was hoping for a bit of reassurance.'

'I'm sorry. I'm not really in a fit state to reassure anyone at the moment. Tim's kind of . . . just somehow . . . gone. All I can see is this sick, frightened man who I barely recognise. The old Tim drove me crackers, but at least, well, even when we weren't speaking we were a unit, and he was in charge somehow. Now it's just me on my own. And because he's ill I feel that anything *I* need or feel isn't important. And Jamie is just not connecting with me any more. Every time I ring he says he's busy and puts the phone down.'

Clover decided that Laura's problems were much worse than hers, and talked to her for a few minutes.

Once Laura had rung off, the phone rang again. It was Sarah Baxter.

'Sarah! I thought you were in India.'

'Ken is still out there, but I've come back to talk to Adam's tutors.'

'Oh, why's that?' Clover was disconcerted. If people like

Alice and Sarah saw their children's tutors on a regular basis, should she be haring up to Leeds or York? She didn't even know who Ben and Holly's tutors were.

'Well, Adam hasn't really settled in very well, and he doesn't like his course. He's thinking of dropping out and joining us on our empty-nest adventure for a while.'

'Ah.' Clover suppressed an unsupportive giggle. It would be ironic if the parents who made the most fuss about enjoying an empty nest were to be the ones to actually have a gap year with their child.

'Of course, we think it's very important that the children make their own decisions in life, but ... ' Sarah let the sentence hang.

'Of course. Jamie Dangerfield seems to be having much the same problems, although he's not really talking to Laura about it.'

'Well, Laura is always hovering over him and organising him, so I expect he doesn't want to communicate too much. I mean, that's what you get if you don't let your children make their own decisions.'

Clover refrained from pointing out that Sarah herself had flown back from India for just these reasons, while Laura was restricting herself to a couple of phone calls a week. Which were mostly ignored or briskly terminated.

'The thing is,' Sarah added, 'I was wondering if I could beg a bed for a few nights. I'm also coming back to try to sort out my back, which hasn't really been great. I'm also not sure that going through the menopause and spending nights on Indian trains really combine well. I wake up boiling hot, then never get back to sleep again.'

'Of course. We'd love to see you.'

Clover looked at her mobile phone and thought about George. Eventually she sent him a text: 'I'm sorry.'

One came back immediately. 'So am I.'

But she suspected that neither of them wanted to say what they were sorry for.

A tanned, very skinny Sarah Baxter sat at their table a few hours later. Clover and George wore their host faces – amiable, interested, working as a team. They'd had enough practice over the years.

'What would you like to drink, Sarah?' asked George.

Sarah accepted a glass of red wine and sipped it eagerly. 'Oh, lovely red wine. I've dreamed of sitting at a kitchen table with a bottle of wine and a few good friends. We've met some fascinating people, but there's nothing like old friends.'

'Aren't you enjoying it?' asked Clover. 'The blogs sound such fun.'

'It is fun, but it's all a bit relentless. Ken is happier than I've seen him in years, but to be honest I'd quite like it all to be a bit less full-on. And I'd like to feel that the children had some kind of base. I can't help wondering if we did this all a year too early, and that if Adam had been able to come back to his childhood home he'd have settled better. His grades aren't very good.' She sighed and filled up her glass. 'How are Holly's and Ben's grades? Do their universities let you have them directly?'

'No, I've never thought to ask.' Clover was surprised.

'Well, I asked Adam's tutor, and was given the brush-off. I ask you! I have to say that the biggest difference between me now and me when I used to commute to the City every day is that when I wore smart clothes, and had a job title and a briefcase, people actually respected me. Now I feel completely invisible. Sometimes I can make a suggestion and no one even bothers to reply.'

'Well, I don't think the tutors—'

'How are we supposed to make sure that he actually does his work if we don't know his grades?'

Clover was puzzled. 'I don't think you are supposed to make sure he does his work. Isn't it up to him?'

'Oh well, yes, in principle. But we don't want him making mistakes about something important when we could help him. I mean, I'm sure you're the same. Of course, none of us can bear the way everyone is far too protective these days, but you can't just leave them completely stranded, can you?'

George and Clover exchanged glances. There didn't seem to be a tactful, true, coherent answer.

'Well,' said George smoothly. 'Perhaps it's a bit like when they were all younger, and each set of parents was fussy about something different.'

Sarah looked uncertain, then clearly decided to change the subject: 'What's all this from Alice then? She wants us to stop our children talking to Lola, because Lola's upset about find-ing out who her real father is? As I said, I can't bear helicopter parenting. Get a life, Alice!'

Clover didn't dare look at George. She must, must, must stay out of the Alice conversation, so she focused on the pepper pot.

'I Googled the story about Lola's father,' added Sarah, 'because, of course, we hadn't heard anything about it. It turns out that my sister lives in the same village as what's-his-face, the father. In fact, I spoke to Julia yesterday and she's great friends with the wife.' Sarah forked in pasta as if she hadn't eaten for a year. 'Great pasta, Clover. God, I've dreamed of pasta.'

Clover couldn't resist saying something. 'According to Duncan, Alice told him that she had no idea Lola's father was married at the time, and that she'd thought they were the real thing.'

Sarah spluttered into her glass. 'What? That's ridiculous.

Alice was his secretary. They worked from his house, where his wife was very much in residence. The story in the village was that Alice had got to thirty and was determined to have a child, and picked him because he was so rich. He was the main initial investor in her company, but at least he's been richly rewarded for it. It's very successful, apparently: they've bought a villa in Tuscany on the strength of the annual dividends. He wants Alice to turn Shirts & Things into a public company, as he'd like to sell out, but she says she's not quite ready.'

Clover carefully avoided George's eye. Bingo! Surely, after this, he must realise how deceitful Alice was. She concentrated on the pepper pot again.

'Yes, that's exactly what she told me,' said George, leaning back to drain his own wine glass. 'She said that she panicked about time running out for her fertility and was on the rebound from a terrible relationship so, on the spur of the moment, she decided she'd go it alone. I think the boss made a pass at her at about the same time, and that was that. She says she knows she was too impulsive about it, but she's tried to shield Lola from the consequences as far as she could.'

Clover looked up, shocked.

'Perhaps Duncan got the wrong end of the stick,' added George, fixing his eyes on Clover's.

'Or perhaps Alice should have trusted Lola with the truth from the start rather than covering everything up,' Clover managed, aware that, once again, they were not quite answering each other's points.

'I think we can all see how we could have managed things better when we look back on them,' said George. 'And trusting people with the truth seems to be a particularly difficult thing to do. I don't think Alice is exactly alone in that, do you?'

'I've dreamed of a proper bed,' said Sarah, who was drooping over her plate.

Clover led her upstairs. 'Fluffy, white sheets and duvet and crisp, clean pillowcases! Heaven, Clover, heaven. It was like sleeping on a shelf on some of those Indian trains.' She kicked off her shoes and flung herself on her bed with a sigh. Clover had a feeling she might fall asleep in her clothes.

'The next ten years are so important,' mumbled Sarah. 'We mustn't waste them. We've got to live them to the full.'

Chapter 41

Laura was terrified. Her hands were shaking as she put money into the parking machine. As she checked the city map the edges of the paper trembled. Number four. It was a Victorian terraced house with two stone steps leading up to the door. There was only one bell.

She hesitated before ringing it. She didn't need therapy. She was fine. She certainly didn't need anyone holding a mirror up to her, showing her how awful she was. If she left now, without ringing the bell, she could pretend that something had come up with Tim, that there'd been a crisis of some kind, and then she could always make another appointment when she was feeling a bit stronger. Maybe this wasn't a good time for therapy, not with everything Tim was going through. The last thing she needed was to stir things up and to start thinking about herself. Everything was fine. Really. Her hand dropped. This was silly and self-indulgent. A waste of money. She could do it, if necessary, when things were a little better.

She turned round to go, and suddenly hit a wall of despair. If she left here she would die. Before she could change her mind, she pressed the bell, hard, and counted to ten. If no one opened the door before she got to ten it wasn't meant to be. She would go.

'Hello.' A pleasant-looking woman, who rather reminded her of Sarah Baxter – even features, brown bobbed hair, medium height, middle-aged – welcomed her in. 'I'm Erica Collins. Call me Erica.'

Laura shook her hand 'Thank you so much for seeing me.' She was back in role again, the charming actress. 'I do hope I won't be wasting your time.'

Erica showed her into a sitting room, and indicated a chair beside the fire. Laura accepted water, and sipped it as Erica explained how she worked.

'I work a lot with transactional analysis, which is a system based on three important principles. Firstly, I believe that people, including you, when you're functioning at your adult level, are fundamentally OK.'

'I've read about that,' interrupted Laura excitedly. 'OK and Not OK. But I'm Not OK, am I, or I wouldn't be here? I just feel desperately, desperately guilty, but I can't stop myself from doing the things that make me feel guilty.'

'Well, that leads onto my second and third beliefs, which is that everyone has the capacity to think, and that we can all decide how we're going to deal with what happens to us. And we can change how we do that. You're here so that I can help you think that through. There are parts of you, just as there are parts of everyone, that are Not OK. You are OK enough to work out why they're there and what function they may have played for you in the past. And you can decide what you want to do so that the Not OK parts make you less unhappy in future.' She smiled. 'But if this is going to work, then it's *you* who is going to make it work. This isn't like going to a doctor, getting a diagnosis of something like "depression" and then being given a prescription for something you have to take every day.'

'But even if I was given a prescription, I'd still have to do the work by taking it every day, wouldn't I?'

290

Erica laughed. 'Laura, I think you're going to be very good at this.'

Laura felt absurdly pleased for a moment, her heart swelling with the compliment. Then she remembered why she was there. 'The thing is,' she said, 'I'm just an awful person. I wrapped myself up in my son for years and years and years. I've been the most pushy mother you could possibly imagine, but now my son's left home for uni, leaving a hole the size of California in my life. And my husband's got cancer, and I'm having an affair with ... well, I'm sorry it's all just so awful I can never say who I'm having the affair with, but I'm having one. And now my husband's friendly with a woman on the same cycle of chemo that he's on, and I'm jealous of her. Jealous of a woman with cancer! But there you are, I'm a typical actress – what do you expect?'

'I don't expect anything,' replied Erica, not seeming at all shocked. 'I'd only like to ask you what you expect of yourself.'

Laura looked at her in astonishment. 'I expect to feel ... guilty, and bad and wrong for wanting to ...' She came to a halt.

'What is it you want?' asked Erica gently.

'I suppose ...' Laura crossed and uncrossed her legs, then concentrated on the picture over the fireplace. It was an oil painting of a bowl of flowers, and she thought she could see Erica's signature in the corner. 'Did you do that picture yourself, by the way? It's awfully good.'

'I think we need to stay on the subject. What is it that you want?'

'Well, I suppose it's just what everyone wants, really.' Laura raised her hands, palms outwards. 'You know.'

'I can't know anything unless you tell me.'

'Well, I suppose ...' Laura took a deep breath. 'I want ... well ...' She dredged up the last shreds of courage from the depths of her soul '. . . to be loved.' She stared at a point in the middle of the rug.

'And you don't feel as if you are?'

Laura rubbed her face. 'Not by my parents, certainly. They always preferred my brother. And Tim had an affair.'

'But your son loves you?'

'Well, he's off on his own life now. I suppose he does. He doesn't get in touch much, and doesn't want to talk to me when I call. And I think he's unhappy, but he won't let me help him. It was all so much easier when he was young. It filled a hole. He was someone to love, and who I knew loved me. But he's gone and . . . ' she dropped her voice to a whisper. 'All I can see is emptiness and despair. And the only way I can fill that emptiness is with this terrible affair.'

'But remember, you did find something to love in him. And he loved you?'

'Of course.'

'So you know you are capable of being loved, and of finding something to love?'

Laura shrugged. 'I suppose so.'

'But you *expect* to feel guilty and unloved? In fact, it seems to me that you are very loved. You get on well with your son, essentially, although he seems to be pushing you away at the moment. Your husband had a choice of another woman but stayed with you—'

'He didn't really want to. That was financial,' interrupted Laura.

'Have you heard of life scripts?' Laura nodded, so Erica continued. 'We all write ourselves a life script, which is what we expect to happen to us and how we can best survive it, by about the age of seven. We write it from what we observe around us, and how we fit into that environment. For the rest of our lives we unconsciously live up to that life script, and

292

tend to discard any evidence that contradicts it. Like saying that Tim has only stayed with you because you can't afford to break up.'

Laura focused. 'So if I had decided that I was unloved and guilty by the age of seven, I probably wouldn't take any notice of anything that proved otherwise later on in life. I'd just say "ah, that was because of . . ." I'd discount it and stick to the script.' She felt something click into place. She knew she'd come home. 'So you mean that Tim and I might have actually stayed together after his affair because we wanted to be together?'

'That's up to you to decide. But it's certainly as likely as any financial reason. After all, lots of people with the same amount of money as you, or less, split up. And you may not have been right about the reasons for your parents' apparent lack of love either. You just had to evaluate it when you were very young and very vulnerable.'

'They praised my brother over me every time,' said Laura, feeling the sharpness of the pain now. 'They kept telling me that women had to stay in the kitchen and that no one wanted women who were bluestockings. So they ignored my A grades at school while praising his much worse ones.' The unfairness of it still burned, deep down inside.

'That doesn't, for that era, necessarily mean lack of love. If they believed that you would be safest and happiest as a traditional housewife, then they would have done anything to make sure you stayed in that role. Because they loved you.'

'But why couldn't they let me decide for myself? Let me be who I am?'

'How easy do you find it to allow your son to decide things for himself?'

'Well, Tim and I try to help Jamie make decisions because obviously he needs help, but it's up to him in the end.'

Erica smiled. 'Why is it obvious that he needs help?'

Laura felt a chasm open up in front of her, a drop of thousands of feet on to hard rocks. 'Well, it's my job to bring him up safely and, well, I have to . . . ' her voice trailed off.

'He's an adult,' said Erica. 'In most societies and most eras your job would have been over several years ago.'

'But . . . ' Once again she had the sensation of seeing her life out of a different window.

She looked at her fingernails. 'But if he no longer needs us, then where does that leave me?' Her voice had dropped to a whisper.

Erica smiled. 'We can't change the facts of your life, such as your husband's cancer or your son leaving home. But what we can do is re-write that script into something that works better for you and reflects the reality of your life more accurately.'

Chapter 42

Sarah Baxter spent the following day on the phone to Adam and his tutors, before setting off to Manchester in the evening 'to sort it out in person'.

Clover and George waved her off.

As he closed the front door, George looked amused. 'If I'd been asked to guess which St Crispian's mothers would hang most tightly on to the control of their kids, I'd never have predicted Sarah Baxter and Alice.'

'I presume you'd have said it would be either me or Laura,' replied Clover tightly. 'Mother Hubbard or the world's most dedicated stay-at-home wife.'

'Give me a break. Just, occasionally, give me a break.' He went into his study and closed the door.

I could have taken that as a compliment, Clover told herself. I could have accepted that tiny sliver of criticism of Alice as an olive branch. She had to decide whether to tell George the truth about Ben's conception, and to accept that if that broke up their relationship, the relationship was broken anyway.

She tapped on his door, then opened it. 'When I got pregnant . . . ' she had to force the words out.

George swung his chair round. His face was tight with tension. 'Yes?'

It would probably be better to lie, she thought, wavering. Or to fudge it. To save his feelings. But he knew her well enough to know if she was concealing something. Otherwise he wouldn't have brought this up.

She began again. 'Do you remember we went away to Berlin about two months earlier?'

He nodded.

'I forgot my pills. I genuinely did forget them.'

His eyes stayed on hers, willing her to go on.

'But,' she added reluctantly, 'I didn't want to tell you I'd forgotten, because—'

'Because you didn't trust me?'

'I don't know,' she admitted. 'I just felt it was best not to say anything. I really didn't think I'd get pregnant and I told myself that if, by some extraordinary chance I did, and you didn't want the baby, I'd manage on my own. I did so very much want children.'

'And time was running out for your fertility. Like Alice. Who you condemn so much.'

'This isn't about me and Alice,' Clover forced herself to say. 'It's about me and you.'

He nodded, and sank his face into his hands with a sigh. 'Clover, I don't regret any of it. I love Ben. I love Holly. Beyond anything. Our family is the best thing that ever happened to me. But I needed to be included in on the decision to create it.'

'You were. You *were*. You didn't have to marry me. And now the choices are all yours. Whether to join Alice and what it will do to our relationship.'

'Clover,' he said. 'An ultimatum is not a choice.'

Chapter 43

Laura returned home, buoyed up. She was going to be different now. Not the needy old Laura, who had been so frightened when her long-running television series came to an end that she'd accepted a couple of parts in plays that she knew weren't any good. The Laura who was so afraid of being alone and unloved that she'd deliberately hunted for a husband who ticked all the boxes. A Prince Charming who would carry her off to his castle so that she could accept only the best roles. Handsome. Ambitious. Well off. Someone who could keep the unlovable core of her warm.

Well, Prince Charming had now lost all his hair and had a permanent metallic taste in his mouth. He needed to get up in the middle of the night to change the sheets, sometimes twice, because he was sweating so profusely. She hoped the new Laura might be strong enough to change the sheets for him, rather than migrating to the spare room. For a moment she felt all the self-loathing flood back, but reminded herself that she was loved, she had been loved, and she was capable of loving and looking after someone without being so frightened any more.

Tim's face was ashen. He was waiting at the door for her.

'Tim! What is it?' Her heart turned over. 'Has the hospital rung? Is there a problem with your tests?'

'No,' he said. 'It isn't me. It's Cathy. She had the results of her scan today and the cancer's spread. To her liver and her lungs. The chemo hasn't worked.'

Laura held her arms open and embraced him. 'I'm so sorry,' she whispered. She rocked him quietly as they stood in the hall.

Eventually he pulled back. He seemed haunted.

'But *your* scan was fine last week,' Laura comforted him. 'So far every chemo session has reduced the swellings. *You're* still on course for the stem-cell transplant.'

He nodded. 'But she's so brave. She needs to live. She loves her life. Some people are miserable all the time and grumble about everything, but she never does.'

Laura felt like snapping. Tim never showed that kind of concern about her.

But he did. She made herself remember the times he'd driven to an all-night chemist because she had a headache, or taken the baby Jamie out to the park so she could rest. Tim, she realised with a slight shock, was someone who cared about other people.

Another window opened in her mind, and Laura could feel the warmth of the sunlight it let in. 'Do you want to go to her?'

But every fibre of her being wanted him there with her, talking about how she'd started to unravel the knots inside herself.

'Do you mind?' Tim was already pulling on his coat, along with the woollen hat that protected his bald head from the cold. 'I won't be long. Her sister is coming down from Northamptonshire as soon as she can, and her children will be coming back in the next few days, too.' He stopped, as if sickened. 'She's talking about weeks.'

'Go. With my love. Stay as long as you need to.'

He kissed her forehead, and took his car keys off the tray in the hall.

'Tim?'

He turned round, halfway through the door. 'Yes?'

'Nothing.' She had wanted to say that she loved him. But she couldn't. And when the door closed behind him she grabbed the phone to call Clover. 'Keep me talking, Clover, stop me panicking, I think Tim really cares about this woman and I think she's going to die, and I don't know what that will do to him . . . to us.'

'Hold on,' said Clover. 'Which woman?'

'Cathy. You know her.' Once Laura had gone through the story, and told Clover about her therapy session, she felt calmer. 'I've got to tell myself that Tim doesn't care more about Cathy than he does about me. That it's only me interpreting things through what I believed as a child – that I would always come second.' Laura swallowed down fear. 'But if I trust Tim, it'll be all right. That's what the theory is. I just don't see how it can be. She is going to die, and that will affect him very, very badly. I know it will.'

She didn't notice that Clover was barely replying.

'We have to use our adult reasoning,' added Laura, 'to help the bits of us that aren't OK to change. Because we're all capable of being OK, if that's what we decide we'll be. You can choose despair or you can choose life.'

'I don't see how everyone can be OK, as if they were we wouldn't all be in such a mess,' commented Clover.

'Yes, but it means that you can sort yourself out. In fact, you *have* to sort yourself, not expect someone else just to hand you the answer. We all have Not OK bits, but we have to work out why they're there, and whether things are really as bad as we think.'

'Well, I can tell you that George will not be OK if he goes to work for Alice. It will be a complete disaster.'

'Maybe he can deal with it.'

Clover paused. 'Well, in that case Tim's going to be OK with Cathy,' she snapped. 'And you're going to be OK with whatever Tim does about Cathy, which doesn't, to me, seem likely to be very much. In fact, none of us have any problems at all.'

'I think it's about trust,' said Laura. 'It's about first trusting yourself, then trusting everyone else to run their own lives.'

At ten o'clock that night the phone rang again. Laura grabbed it, thinking it might be Tim. It was Jamie. 'Darling! How lovely to hear from you.'

'I'm just ringing to say that I'm giving up law at Gwent.'

'No, please don't. I'll drive up tomorrow and we can talk about it then. If you drop out now you'll have to go through Clearing in August, and there's no guarantee you'd get a better place or a better degree.'

'Mum, you can't drive up here.'

'Why not? It'll only take me three or four hours— Just a second, that's a ring at the door, hold on, don't hang up.' Tim must have forgotten his keys.

She opened the door to find Jamie, with three days of stubble and somehow taller yet again, standing at the door, grinning, with two friends behind him.

'Jamie!' He wrapped her up in a big bear hug, and she revelled in the feel of him. 'But Jamie, what's all this?'

'This is Luke and Tom.' Two – she wanted to call them boys, but they were undeniably men – stood behind him: a small one with a goatee and one who was so tall that she could barely make out his features, who nodded down at her, smiling amiably. 'We've brought my stuff back in Luke's uncle's van. Then they're going to take it on to buy some wine at Calais. I'm staying here.' Just for a moment his confidence wavered. 'If that's OK.'

'Of course it's OK. But what about your—'

The boys began to bring in carrier bags and suitcases. 'Upstairs, second on left,' directed Jamie. 'Let's get all this in, then we can talk.'

When the van had been emptied Jamie offered Luke and Tom a beer, and Laura bustled around cooking a fry-up, listening to their banter and their easy laughs. She placed three plates on the table. 'Right,' she said to Jamie. 'Let's hear it.'

'I've left Gwent. Law wasn't right for me.'

'But—' bleated Laura.

'I'm going to do sports science at Loughborough instead,' he interrupted. 'I've got it sorted. I've been talking to them since before Christmas. And, if it's OK by you, I'm going to spend the rest of the year at home, saving some money. I've contacted the gym you go to and have got a really ground-level job with them – I think it involves cleaning and answering the phones, mainly – and I'm volunteering with the rugby club as an assistant trainer. I'm just going to do as much as I can to do with sport, and save as much money as I can.' He squeezed her hand. 'And I'd like to be around while Dad's ill.'

'But we didn't want it to affect your life, and—'

'It isn't the reason I made the decision. But it's another reason why it's the *right* decision.'

Laura tried to smile. 'We all thought you'd be such a good lawyer because you were always so good at arguing.'

'I'd be a crap lawyer,' Jamie said flatly. 'Come on, Mum, this stem-cell transplant's a pretty major operation, and I don't want to be miles away in Gwent when he's having it.'

'Well, it's not that major.' Laura still wanted to protect him.

'Come on, Mum.' He patted her hand. 'I may not be bright enough to be a lawyer, but I can look stem-cell transplant up on the internet, and I'd like to be around when my father's having one.' His teeth flashed white as he grinned at her and forked in the last mouthful of bacon and egg.

'I suppose we did it all wrong,' sighed Laura. 'We should have realised, and then we could have found the best place for a sports science degree.'

'Mum, I had to do it for myself.' There was a warning in his voice. 'And Loughborough is the best place.'

She nodded. 'Yes, I can see that. Well done.'

'Just like that?' He sounded surprised. 'I thought we'd have to talk about it much more than that.'

She looked at Tom and Luke. 'Don't tell me you brought these two to protect you from me throwing a hissy fit?' The three boys looked uncomfortable, but Laura burst out laughing. 'You great wuss.'

'We did want to come and get some wine from France anyway,' said Tom.

'Where's Dad now?' Jamie suddenly looked around.

'He's just popped out to see a friend he's made during chemo. She's just had some very bad news and he didn't want her to be alone. He'll be back as soon as one of her family gets there.' Laura was surprised at how easily the words came out. Of course he'd gone to keep Cathy company while she waited for her family to arrive. Why shouldn't he?

The boys accepted it and continued chatting. Laura felt so relaxed in her own skin that when a text came through from the familiar number she deleted it without reading it. As soon as she did, a text came through from Tim. 'Cathy's sister has arrived, so leaving now. See you 20 mins.'

Chapter 44

George told Clover he was joining Alice's company, as he walked in from work, before taking his coat off. 'I've already given in my notice at Petfast.'

Clover's world dropped away. 'Without discussing it with me?'

'We have discussed it,' he reminded her. 'You issued an ultimatum. I don't function well with a gun to my head.'

'Oh, so it's my fault? You've got a gun to your head so you *had* to leave Petfast? You can't blame me for the stupidest decision you've ever made in your life.'

'I don't think we're talking about fault or blame here,' he said wearily. 'But I have to be responsible for my own decisions.'

'Not if you've deliberately gone *for* something because *I* don't want it. That's just sulking, not responsibility.'

'I'm not deliberately going against you. And I know that, in accepting Alice's offer, I'm taking a risk. But now that the kids have left home we can take those sort of risks. Or rather, *I* can take those sort of risks. And I want to. It's my last chance to do something that I really believe is mine, rather than working for a big corporation.'

'Are we back to Ben again? And you having to take the job

at Petfast because I was pregnant?' Clover couldn't believe her ears. 'Are you going to beat me over the head for ever because I didn't mention I'd forgotten my pills for *two days*?'

'I don't know,' he said. 'I hope not.'

'So where do we stand?' Clover looked around her beloved kitchen. She was going to lose it either way, whether she and George split or Alice used George to get Pets & Things going, then found an excuse to dump him.

'I really don't know,' he repeated. 'We seem to have gone a long way down a certain path, and I'm not sure that either of us knows the way back.'

'I don't think there is a way back,' she whispered. 'I can't see one, anyway.'

His face looked old and crumpled. 'I've always looked to you for the way,' he said. 'And if you can't see it, there isn't one. Do you want me to move into the spare room? Or out of the house completely?'

'No, no, don't go completely, it would be silly to spend money on rent.' Clover grasped at the practical aspects of the situation. If you got them right, you'd be fine, wouldn't you? She and George were civilised people, they'd never behave the way people who were getting divorced often behaved, grabbing at possessions and using other people as pawns. A bleak, dark emptiness overwhelmed her.

There wasn't really a lot of point going on, was there? Holly and Ben no longer needed her, and George didn't want her.

Chapter 45

Cathy died three weeks later. Tim got the news when he was hooked up to drips in both arms, harvesting his stem cells. He'd had six days of injections of growth factors, to strengthen the stem cells as much as possible. Then he and Laura had come in to spend the morning at the hospital. The nurse had explained that blood would be taken out of one arm, then 'cleaned up' and the stem cells extracted, after which it would be returned to the other arm. 'It'll take three to four hours,' said the nurse brightly.

Tim's phone rang, and Laura handed it to him. She'd brought in a pile of reading – mostly about transactional analysis and cognitive behavioural therapy – and she was buried in ways of getting her Adult to function properly and wisely, rather than her wilful Child or her judgemental Parent. She still found it muddling, until she came to the words: 'You can't teach navigation in a storm.' Another lightbulb lit up in her mind, and she looked at Tim. Change would take time. It would take conscious thought. She wasn't wicked because she couldn't, overnight, become the balanced, confident person that she could occasionally see in her mind's eye, walking across a sunlit meadow in a flowery dress blowing in the breeze. She and Tim were in the middle of a storm, and it would take time for them to learn to navigate their way out of it.

As long as they didn't sink in the process.

'No.' Tim's response to whatever he was told on the phone was almost a groan. 'When?'

Laura could hear high-pitched agitation on the other end, and strained her ears.

'But she seemed good when we saw her.'

It must be Cathy. Laura and Tim had been to see her the day before. She'd been sitting up in a chair, very frail-looking, with a rug over her knees, but smiling. Her two daughters rushed in and out with cups of tea and coffee, her toddler grandson was eating at a high chair, and she was surrounded by cards and flowers. She grasped Tim's hand when he sat beside her. 'Big day tomorrow? They'll be harvesting the stem cells, no?'

He nodded, and they began to chat about the hospital and the consultants. Tim made her laugh, but she began to cough. Laura got up to find one of the daughters and a glass of water. When she came back Cathy and Tim were talking intensely, too low for her to hear. She handed Cathy the glass and Tim stood up, kissing her on the forehead. 'I'll let you know how it goes. I'll see you before I go in for the big one.'

Cathy smiled and clutched his hand. 'You're braver than I am, going through all that. I'm just so relieved to have no more treatment.'

'No one is braver than you are,' said Tim, leaving the room abruptly.

Cathy smiled and took Laura's hand, pulling her down so she could speak softly to her. 'Tim loves you very much,' she said. 'It's very special, what you two have got.'

Laura was embarrassed for a moment, but decided to be honest in return. 'I'm afraid, though, that he will give up. He seems to be preparing himself for . . . '

Cathy began to cough again, and a daughter came in, fussing.

Laura had hoped that Cathy would know how to get through to him. Somehow Cathy's future and Tim's seemed inextricably linked. If Cathy couldn't make it, then how could Tim?

Back in the hospital she heard Tim ask when the funeral was in a strangled voice.

There was more squeaking at the other end of the line.

'Tuesday at three. I'll be there. And I'm so terribly sorry. Thank you for calling.' The phone fell from his hand and clattered to the floor. Laura scrabbled to get it.

'Cathy?' she asked.

Tim nodded and closed his eyes. 'Apparently she had a heart attack in the middle of the night, probably because she wasn't strong enough for the treatment she'd been having. It seems ... unbelievable.'

'Well, we knew she was not going to have long, so maybe it's not so surprising after all.'

Tim's eyes snapped open. 'You know absolutely nothing about all this, so please don't pretend you do.'

Laura was stung, but reminded herself to keep reasoning like an adult rather than allowing the frightened, hurt little girl inside to take over. 'I do, in fact, know about—'

'You don't know about *me*,' he shouted. 'Cathy did. And now she's gone, and however much you know someone is going to die, it is still a fucking shock when they do, especially *today*, especially *Cathy*, especially *now*.'

A nurse opened the door gently. 'Is everything all right in here?'

'It's fine.' Laura felt like getting up and storming out of the hospital, but she looked at Tim, with a drip in each arm, and told herself that now was not the time. Very Adult, she told herself, as she tried to concentrate on the books again.

The words danced across the page until they counselled her

to focus on 'What's important here? What is the loving thing to do?' She suddenly looked at Tim. The loving thing would be to support Tim. He would be fighting for his life in a few weeks, and that was undoubtedly the most important thing. She must focus on that.

But where did that leave her? She felt lonelier than she had ever felt in her life.

Tim sank into depression over the next six days. Most of the time he lay on his bed, staring at the ceiling. Laura gave him some books, carefully chosen – the latest architectural work, some books and magazines on sailing and a raved-over novel. He barely opened them. She brought a television up to the bedroom but he said he found the comedies too silly, the news too sad, he couldn't follow the soaps and all the crime and thrillers were too full of death.

'Game shows?' she suggested.

He nearly laughed.

Conversation didn't work either. He just smiled distantly, in the wrong places, or was clearly not listening. Jamie breezed in with his tales of the rugby club or the gym, and got slightly more response. 'See if you can find a match to watch with your father,' counselled Laura. 'Or some racing, maybe. Or golf?'

While Jamie was there he watched, but on his own he seemed to have lost interest. 'I don't suppose I'll ever play golf again,' he said.

'Of course you will! Don't be so self-pitying,' snapped Laura, before she could stop herself.

'Sit down.' He pointed to a chair.

Laura sat.

'I don't think I'm going to make it through this.'

'Yes, you are. Just because Cathy died, it doesn't mean—'

'Laura, I need you to listen to me properly, not pretend that everything is all right. We have to have this conversation.'

Laura stared at her hands, reminding herself to focus on what was important. The loving thing. She was so determined to behave that she nearly missed what he was saying.

'If I die, I want you to stay in this house until Jamie has properly taken off. Finished his studies and got a flat somewhere. Is that OK?'

'Of course it's OK. It's my home, but you're not going to—'

'My will is in . . . ' Laura vaguely took it all in, while thinking about what to cook for supper. Tim was not going to die. He couldn't.

Cathy's funeral, the day before Tim was finally admitted to hospital in London for the stem-cell transplant, was on a bright sunny May day. Everything seemed bright and fresh – the tips of new leaves on the trees, the riot of purples, reds and yellows in every front garden and window box, and the busy chirruping of the birds as they flew to and from their nests bringing back tasty morsels for their chicks.

The crematorium was so full that people were standing round the edges of the room and out on the steps, their faces taut and grey. Laura sang her way through a few standard hymns, conscious of Tim standing silently like a block of stone beside her. He usually loved singing.

Then Cathy's daughters got up, one to tell the story of her mother's life: how she'd won scholarships and sports prizes, and had then gone on to be a research scientist, wonderful mother and friend, and how much courage she'd shown in her last few years. 'We never knew we were going to have so little time with her,' she concluded, with a catch in her voice. The second daughter read a poem, but had to stop in the middle to collect herself.

After that, Laura couldn't stop crying. She was crying – almost silently – for Cathy and her bereft daughters, for the scared-looking nineteen-year-old boy sitting next to them who must be Cathy's son, for Cathy's elderly mother, bleak at losing a child so late in life, crying for all the friends who were never going to sit round Cathy's table again, for Tim who had lost the person who had really got through to him. Then she cried for herself and the lonely weeks that lay ahead, and for how Jamie would suffer if his father died. She cried silently, using five tissues and trying to control the shaking of her shoulders, hunching herself almost into a ball. Tim, stranded in his own misery, barely seemed to notice.

Finally, as the curtain closed in front of Cathy's coffin, Laura managed to collect herself. This was not her grief, she told herself, not she who deserved sympathy. She had hardly known Cathy. There were too many people here who had lost too much. She sniffed and straightened her shoulders, thankful that she'd worn a broad-brimmed black hat so that no one could see her eyes.

She and Tim agreed that they didn't want to go to Cathy's house afterwards. 'I wouldn't feel I belonged,' said Tim. 'What Cathy and I had was between us.'

The words cut Laura deeply, but she found one of the daughters and explained that Tim was going back into hospital the following day. 'Thank you so much for coming,' she replied, looking at Tim. 'You really made a difference to Mum. You gave her back the self-respect she lost when Dad walked out.' She kissed Tim on both cheeks and, rather as an afterthought, kissed Laura too.

They walked away from the crematorium in silence as people, either sobbing or with their spirits lifted, returned to their cars.

'The thing that worries me,' said Laura when they got

home, 'is that you're about to go through a very high-risk, physically demanding operation. You're going to need all your will to live.' She faced him straight. 'And you don't seem to have any.'

'I know,' Tim said heavily. 'Do you think I don't know that?'

'There's us. We need you. Me and Jamie. Don't leave us.'

He smiled distantly, as if barely registering her words. 'I'll try not to.'

Laura made herself a cup of tea to give herself time to think. She made one for Tim, too, and took it to him in the sitting room.

He frowned when she put it down. 'I've gone off tea.'

She felt like slapping him, but forced herself to sound calm. 'Is there anything else you'd like?'

He agreed, somewhat begrudgingly, to a hot chocolate.

She brought it in and sat down beside him. 'Tim, please don't go into this believing it will fail.'

'I'm just being realistic,' he said, looking into the middle distance. 'A few people don't survive because they get some simple infection while their immune systems are down. It could be blown in on the wind or come in on someone's shoe. It could be something that a well person would barely notice.'

Laura tamped down fear. 'Even so, most people do survive that stage. It's important to acknowledge that.'

'Then,' he continued, 'some people relapse within a year or so.'

'Most don't,' insisted Laura.

He smiled the distant, remote smile again. 'I think you should be clear-sighted about this.'

'I agree. Clear-sighted. As opposed to negative. Listen.' She leant forward and took his hand in hers. 'Whether you've got

311

a terminal illness or not, there's a point in everyone's life when they have to choose between life and despair. That's what you admired about Cathy. She chose life, right up to the very end. I was there, I saw her. She went on thinking about other people and the future right up to the end.'

'What frightens me,' said Tim, 'is that I'm not as good or as brave as Cathy.'

'You are,' Laura tried to tell him. 'You are.'

But he retreated back into his lost world.

Chapter 46

Clover dreamed the solution. She dreamed about having another baby, a sweet little girl who popped out with George's brown eyes and George's curly brown hair, and a dear little button nose. It completed Clover to give birth to her – the third child they'd never had. This was what had been missing.

As the dream went on, she kept wondering where she'd left the little girl. Every time she made a phone call or went shopping she realised she had to take her with her. In the dream she turned round – so often – to realise she'd left her under a table or dangerously close to the edge of a bed. She even needed to take her into the loo. The old anxiety – the terror of keeping a child safe – snaked up her leg and curled around her torso, tightening until she couldn't breathe. There was no one else to help: her mother had died and all her friends' children had grown up. Then she had to go back to school as she had her old job back again. But she couldn't take a baby. Even as she was about to leave for work she hadn't solved the problem of where she would leave the baby. Who would look after her? What would she eat? How could Clover carry her books, shopping and a baby? She would have to employ a nanny or a childminder, but who could she trust? And how could they afford it? Her freedom – so brief, so precious, so filled with light in spite of everything – had ended. The prison door shut with a clang.

By the time this baby had grown up she would be in her seventies. The lightness of the past year was over. She had a twenty-four-hours-a-day, seven-days-a-week responsibility for another tiny beloved, vulnerable person who deserved all the love and care that Holly and Ben had had.

She couldn't do it. But you can't give a baby back. Clover stared into the small, defenceless face and watched her love drain away.

She woke up sweating and terrified. It was a dream, she told herself. It was a dream. I am so, so thankful it was a dream. She looked at the empty side of the bed. No George. She wanted to go running in to him, to tell him about the dream. That was what the dream was telling her, that the last year had been pointing in the right direction. That this stage of their lives was right for them.

She tapped on the door of the spare room. There was no reply. The bed was made. George had gone.

Downstairs, on the kitchen table, was a note. 'You were asleep when I got in last night. Alice and I are going to Malaysia to source some suppliers. I'll be away about eight days. Let's talk afterwards.'

A trip to Malaysia, even in Alice's world, was not planned in one day.

Clover went to work and tried to distract herself by learning about marbling from Duncan. It didn't work. 'Are you OK?' he asked.

'Actually, I don't feel too well.' Making excuses, she went home and called Laura.

Laura was spending four or five hours a day at the hospital. 'Tim is on day five of the strongest chemo imaginable. There's

314

so much liquid going into his body that he's swelled up to eighteen stone. And I can't get through to him. It's as if everything I say is either too trivial or too complicated. Cathy was the only one he wanted to hear from.'

'And Alice is the only woman George seems to want to spend time with,' said Clover. 'I think I need to see a lawyer. Just to find out my options. He's gone to Malaysia with her, sneaking away without telling me. So for the next five days he's spending twenty-four hours a day with her, and even if they're not together now I think she might be difficult to resist. Especially as we are, I suppose, technically almost separated. At least, he's sleeping in the spare room, and we don't know where we're going next.'

Clover was surprised to be able to get an appointment for the following day. Laura agreed to go with her, and to visit a lawyer herself immediately afterwards. 'I need to write a will. Tim keeps talking to me about his, and where it is, and what I should do after he dies. I'm terrified that he just wants to die, that I'm not enough to keep him alive. Then I thought, well, what if I die instead? Nothing ever seems to happen the way you expect it to. I'd better get it sorted so that Jamie doesn't have to deal with huge complications.'

The solicitor's office was in a Georgian town house, built in the time of Jane Austen to impress the newly wealthy middle classes.

The front door had strips of mirror glass inset into its panels and Clover could see slices of themselves – her own thick red hair tied up, and the neat dark edge of Laura's bob. They looked good in thin strips, as if in avant-garde photographs. Petite Laura was a flash of camellia-pink, and Clover, taller and slimmer than she really was in the slivers of glass, wore the soft greys and creams of a pebble beach.

Perhaps everything looks good if you don't see the whole picture.

Behind them was a bustling street. People hurried about their ordinary lives, thinking about what they would buy for dinner.

Clover pushed the panelled door open. In front of them was a quiet pastel hallway, its whispered secrets and pain all bundled up into neat files. This was where those ordinary lives were torn up into tiny pieces.

Once they stepped into that hallway, there would be no going back. 'Are you ready?' she asked Laura.

Laura nodded. 'And you?'

A mother rushed past, a child in school uniform trailing in her wake.

'Late for school?' suggested Clover, still hesitating.

'Perhaps the child has a dentist's appointment.' Laura's voice was wistful. She turned to Clover. 'I feel like warning her, don't you? Make the most of it now. The day your children leave school, your life changes for ever.'

'It hasn't been all bad, though. I think we've learned more about ourselves in a year than in the whole twenty that went before it.'

'Hmm,' said Laura, pulling a face. 'Trust Clover to look on the bright side. Do you remember the leavers' ball? We actually felt a sense of relief, didn't we? We thought we'd done it. Finito. Over. Job done. I remember Alice saying that, don't you?'

Clover didn't want to talk about Alice. The sense of betrayal was still too deep. They watched the woman turn round and chivvy her son on. 'Come on,' she shouted. 'We haven't got time.'

Clover looked at her watch. 'Neither have we.'

Laura nodded.

They turned left, into a room where a receptionist sat at a big modern desk.

'Good morning,' she said with a polite, practised smile. She looked from one to the other, obviously trying to identify the client. 'Can I help you, Mrs . . .?'

'Jones,' said Clover. 'I've come to see Janice Clare.'

The receptionist would know that Janice Clare did divorces. All day long. She spoke down a phone in a hushed voice. 'Mrs Jones to see you.'

'And Dangerfield,' added Laura. 'Although my appointment is an hour later. I'm going to accompany my friend, but then I need to do my will.'

They sat, nervously flicking through magazines.

'Are you sure that George is actually having an affair with Alice?' Laura said, looking up from *Kent Life*. 'I mean, couldn't it just be business?'

'No, of course I'm not sure. Although if not, I don't know why he couldn't have talked openly about the Malaysia trip. And I think I found one of his cufflinks in her bathroom. But it shows what it's going to be like. He'll go travelling with her for five or six days at a time, and eventually it will happen. Alice will make sure it does. She's already got us lying to each other and arguing, and this is just the first month.'

'My therapy books would say you have to use rational thought to sort it out. It's no good just sticking to tried and tested beliefs, such as "when people keep secrets they're up to no good" or "men and women can't work together without shagging". They're just the sort of things your parents would have told you when you were young. They're not universal truths. And you can't let the frightened child deep down inside run the show either. You've got to keep thinking about what's really true. All you actually know is that George is on a business trip. You've no real evidence that there's any more to it.'

'It's a bit difficult to explain in any other way. Why not tell me beforehand?'

317

Laura shrugged. 'Nervous of your reaction? Too busy? You can ask him when he comes back.'

'Mrs Jones?' A young woman clutching a huge pile of folders appeared. 'Would you like to follow me?'

Clover got up. 'No, I wouldn't. Sorry, Laura, you'll have to find another witness to your will. Oh, and if you could pay Janice Clare's bill for today, I'll pay you back.'

'Where are you going?' shouted Laura as Clover left the room.

'Malaysia.' Clover paused at the doorway.

'You can't just go to Malaysia like that,' Laura shouted after her. 'All you have to do is wait till George gets back.'

'It might be too late by then.' Clover stopped for a moment. 'And Laura?' she called back.

'Yes?'

'Could you train as a psychotherapist rather than picking up bits and pieces of theory and throwing them around to see where they land? I think you could be very good at this, but I'm not sure you know what you're doing most of the time.'

Chapter 47

Laura returned to the hospital after doing her will, with a sense that, whatever happened, she had at least set her affairs in order. Tim had reached the lowest point of the procedure, and the stem cells had just been returned to his body. They now had to wait for them to take hold and grow into new cells to rebuild his immune system.

Until then, the slightest cold could kill him. But it was not just germs he couldn't withstand. It seemed to be everything. Her perfume was too strong. The smells from the corridor sickened him. The sound of her turning the pages of her book were too loud, so she bought an e-reader. He didn't want one because he couldn't follow more than one line of text. He couldn't watch television. He couldn't bear to eat. He didn't even sleep. He lay there, hour after hour, as if in an invisible coffin. He didn't speak to her, and she had to feed him with a spoon. He never wanted more than two mouthfuls. Eventually Laura found some very gentle classical music for his CD player, hoping it didn't have any sudden clashes of cymbals. He didn't want headphones, they were too close, too irritating.

The nurse said he was responding normally.

'I'm worried that he's grieving over a friend of his who died recently, and that it's slowing his recovery.'

'No, it's physical,' she reassured her. 'I sometimes feel it's almost as if the immune system isn't something that only keeps infection at bay, it's like your barrier to the whole world. He has no barrier and everything is too bright, too loud, too fast.'

'Too smelly?' added Laura, smiling sadly.

She spoke to David Craven, the consultant. 'I'm frightened that, because he doesn't seem to want to live, he's just going to let go.'

David Craven shook his head. 'You hear a lot about "fighting spirit" and "the right attitude", but most of us think that's a myth. Statistically, there doesn't seem to be a difference in survival between those with the so-called fighting spirit and those without.' He looked concerned. 'We're keeping a close eye on him.'

She took off the disposable apron, cap and surgical gloves that she always had to wear when she entered Tim's room and threw them away, retracing her steps along the long, familiar linoleum corridor towards the lift. And bumped into Holly.

'Holly!'

Holly kissed her. 'We know we can't all see Tim, because we don't want to take germs in there, but we've come to take you out to dinner.'

'Take me out? But you can't—'

Jamie's arm went round her shoulders. 'Hi, Mum. We thought you'd like a plate of pasta.'

'And Lola! Why aren't you at Oxford?' The last thing Laura wanted was Alice on her back, blaming her for distracting her daughter.

'I am,' said Lola, flicking her long shiny hair out of her eyes. 'But it's Saturday tomorrow, so no lectures.'

'Is it?' Laura was bemused. 'I've lost track of the time.' She allowed Lola, Holly and Jamie to lead her to a small Italian restaurant.

'Eat,' ordered Holly.

'You're going to turn out like your mother if you're not careful,' said Laura. 'Looking after everyone all the time.'

'Good. I like my mother.'

'I like mine too,' said Jamie, with a grin.

They all looked at Lola.

'OK, OK.' She raised her hands in mock surrender. 'I've come to terms with mine. I've told her she can't see my essays before I hand them in. And restricted her to one phone call a week. She seems OK about it, actually.'

'You just have to be firm with mothers,' advised Jamie. 'It's part of growing up.'

'And let's not mention fathers,' said Lola. 'Or you'll all get a joint boss-o-gram from my mother, ticking you off.'

'The thing is,' said Holly, 'mothers are always there for you, so you can forgive them almost anything.'

'Almost,' said Jamie. 'Except wearing pink while waving wildly.' He gave a shudder. 'It was the major embarrassment of my primary school days.' His eyes met Laura's and she giggled.

'I like my pink jackets.'

Every day, for four days, they took blood tests, but there were no signs of the key indicators climbing. 'It doesn't mean nothing's happening,' said the consultant.

Laura fingered her mobile. 'I know it's tough', read one message. 'Call me if you need me', was another. 'I am here.'

She needed a strong, healthy pair of arms very badly indeed. She talked to Erica about it, and she was quietly non-judgemental.

On the fifth day Tim, who had not spoken for forty-eight hours, snapped at her for shutting the door too loudly. The consultant seemed dismissive of her fears. The nurses were too busy. Jamie, who alternated at the hospital with her and helped out by shopping and cooking, had a double shift at work. The dialling tone on Clover's phone indicated that she was indeed out of the country, and Laura wasn't sure about the time zones and the costs of phoning. Nor did she have the emotional strength for talking about Tim and what he was going through to anyone else.

So she texted that number. Him. 'Usual place. I'll meet you in the bar. Six-thirty this evening'.

He immediately texted his agreement. She arrived early, taking pleasure in getting dressed for the first time in weeks. Velvet trousers. A cropped cashmere cardigan with little sequins sewn on to it. Her favourite earrings. She smoothed away the tired, anxious look with make-up.

She was Laura again. Sparkly, social-butterfly Laura, ordering a drink with complete confidence.

He strode in, wearing battered jeans and an open-necked white shirt, the sleeves rolled up to show his powerful forearms. 'Hi doll,' he said, leaning in to kiss her.

'Hello Joe.' She moved her face sideways, so he kissed her cheek.

He froze. 'You said my name. You were never going to say my name.'

'And there's something else I have to say too.' She placed her hand on his arm and, just for a moment, was overwhelmed by the strength and warmth it offered her. She took her hand away. 'It is over this time. I'm old enough to be your grandmother.'

'So? You've always been older than me. What's different?' He ordered a beer, some of the cockiness returning.

'I'm different,' she said softly. 'You've done me a lot of good in some ways—'

'Hey, I'm not, like, on the NHS.' He tried to make a joke of it, but she could see he was knocked back.

'I love Tim,' she added. 'Even now, when he is certainly at his least lovable. And my best friend's daughter is interested in you; she would be devastated to think we were in any way involved—'

He almost spluttered over the beer. 'Holly? But she's drop-dead gorgeous.'

Laura couldn't help laughing. 'Joe, dear, you are drop-dead gorgeous. You're all gorgeous. But you're my son's friend. A little girl I used to take home from school and serve fish fingers to would like to get to know you better.'

'I'm not a kid, you know. I'm nearly twenty-one.'

'And I'm nearly fifty-three. But it's not the age. It's the people we both care for, and how they'll feel if they know. You've been enormous fun, Joe—'

'Yeah, well, that really puts me in my place, doesn't it?'

'I hope I've been fun, too.'

'Yeah,' he conceded after a pause. 'You've been fun.'

'So.' She held her hand out for him to shake. 'Friends? Or rather a friend's parent. From now on, I'm Jamie's mother, just boring old Jamie's mother.'

He grinned and shook her hand in assent. 'Do you really think Holly might be interested?'

'I think she might well be.' Laura picked up her bag. 'But there's one thing you might think about. Maybe you were missing an older woman in your life.'

She saw the defences come up in his face. 'I don't think you need an older woman as a lover, Joe, I think you're missing someone else, someone very much more important. And if you want strong, healthy relationships in the future, and to build a family of your own one day, I think you should probably address the issue of losing your mother. Get professional help. Instead of getting involved in relationships you know will go nowhere.'

He looked at her and, for one moment, she saw the lost little boy behind the swagger.

'I mean it, Joe.' She handed him Erica's card.

He looked at it, then put it in his wallet. 'I'll think about it.'

She left him ordering another beer, punching a number into his phone.

It was only seven o'clock. She could still get to the hospital.

Tim opened his eyes. 'Hello darling,' he said in a whisper. 'My tests are good. My neutrophils are climbing.' His hand moved on the white sheet, fingers stretching out towards her. It was the tiniest of movements, but more than he had been able to manage for over a week.

She took his hand gently in hers, rested it there quietly for a few moments.

He was the first to speak. 'I had a choice,' he said, each word dragged slowly out, his voice low and hoarse. 'And I choose life.'

She saw the ghost of a smile as he closed his eyes again.

Chapter 48

Clover started with George's office and Judi, the secretary he shared with Alice. 'Hello, it's Clover Jones, George's wife. He said that you'd be forwarding his schedule so that I could contact him, but I don't seem to have it yet.'

'I don't know anything about that,' said Judi, sounding slightly affronted. 'He didn't say anything to me about it.'

'Typical George! He must have forgotten. Could you forward it all the same?'

'Well, I'm really sorry, but only if he tells me to.'

'I'm his wife.'

'Yes, and I'm his PA. I can only do what he asks me to do.'

Well, can you give me the telephone number of the hotel they're staying at?'

'I can leave a message for him to pick up when they get to Penang tomorrow evening. He can call you then.'

Judi was obviously either a stickler for protocol or had been very well briefed. Maybe she knew that something was going on. 'Never mind,' said Clover. 'I'll ask him myself when he calls this evening.'

She had, at least, narrowed it down to Penang tomorrow evening. Calling up Penang on Wikipedia, Clover was briefly discouraged by how large and modern it looked. There was no question of going there and walking about looking for a Mr Jones.

On the other hand, Alice was very fussy about where she stayed. It would have to be bookable from the United Kingdom, and it would have to be a boutique hotel – classy, comfortable and not too big. It would have to have high standards of service, but also have character. It would either be *dernier-cri* modernist or historically authentic. There would be no anonymous international corridors, but neither would there be ramshackle bathrooms and creaky beds.

Oh Alice, thought Clover, as she typed 'boutique hotels Penang' into the search engine and got five results. Cross-checking with other websites and discounting all the larger, tower-block style hotels and anything with three stars or less, she whittled the choices down to three.

She rang each of them asking to leave a message for Mr Jones or Mr and Mrs Jones. Each time the receptionist told her there was no Jones staying. She had to ask several times because it was difficult to understand their accents and they spoke so quickly. 'No, no Jones here,' was rattled out at machine-gun speed.

Next she tried Fanshawe. 'Mr and Mrs Fanshawe,' she said, her heart speeding up. 'I'd like to leave a message for Mr Fanshawe.'

'I can put you through to their room now, if you'd prefer,' gabbled the receptionist at the first hotel she tried.

Clover dropped the phone and went online. She bought the cheapest ticket for Penang, flying Air Asia, leaving at ten o'clock that night, her cursor hovering over whether to pre-order her meal and 'comfort pack'. Stuffing some linen trousers and a couple of T-shirts into a wheeled carry-on suitcase, she booked a taxi to the airport, arranging to drop Diesel and the cats off at the kennels on the way. They all looked at her reproachfully.

Surely there must be more than that? Lock doors? Well, of course. It only took a few minutes.

It seemed an age before the taxi came. Was it really that easy to go halfway round the world on a whim? She checked her passport for the tenth time. It was in her bag. Visa? She had a moment of panic before she discovered that you could stay ninety days in Malaysia without one. She'd be home before then. Probably. In spite of her worry about George, the sense of adventure leapt in her.

As soon as she stepped onto the Air Asia flight she knew she'd left Britain. There were no special reclining beds or in-flight entertainment, just straightforward seats. When Clover saw what the woman next to her was having, she was relieved she'd pre-ordered the Asian meal, which was curry and noodles. 'Mine's the International Meal. Lasagne,' explained the woman. 'But it's made with minced chicken, because there are so many different dietary requirements with meat, depending on what people's religion is. My daughter lives in KL, so I go out twice a year.' She smiled.

A long and uncomfortable night followed. Clover didn't like to switch on her reading light because it illuminated everyone around her. Eventually the blinds were raised and the crew began to serve curry and noodles again. Her neighbour had ravioli, made with minced chicken. 'There isn't really any distinction between breakfast, lunch and supper,' she explained with another smile.

Clover stepped out on to the steps and was hit by the heat and humidity. Her T-shirt clung to her back by the time she'd walked three steps. 'It's about ten minutes' walk to the terminal,' added the helpful woman as they were beckoned towards the distant building by a series of smiling faces. Her flight to Penang left in two hours, by which time Clover realised she was a long way from home. Her journey seemed like madness.

At Penang she got to the head of the taxi queue, only to discover she didn't have a voucher. 'Voucher! Voucher!' shrieked the Chinese taxi driver. 'No trip without voucher!' Clover couldn't understand what he was saying, but people kept smiling and pointing back towards the arrivals hall. Feeling utterly travel worn, she retraced her steps and discovered that she had to buy a pre-paid voucher for taxi journeys from a little booth.

Eventually she rejoined the queue for a series of battered red and white taxis. This was a very bad idea. What would she say to George and Alice if she did find them? Maybe it was another Mr and Mrs Fanshawe who were staying there.

She lowered herself on to a bumpy back seat and gave the name of the hotel to the taxi driver. He set off without acknowledgement, a grim expression on his face. The journey seemed more and more perilous, especially as the road, apparently made up of a series of concrete blocks, and the erratic way everyone was driving, didn't exactly fill her with confidence. The seat springs had long since expired and she was jolted from one side of the taxi to the other, occasionally being thrown against one of the driver's large collection of dangling charms.

Scrubby bush and overhanging palm trees gave way to kampong-style wooden bungalows, with old cars and untidy gardens in front of them. They were punctuated by occasional tiny mosques, barely twenty feet square, with their distinctive gold onion domes. A few more bone-shattering jolts got them into streets flanked by Stalinist high-rise blocks, then into the older part of town, a riot of pattern, colour and ornament. Great white wedding-cake colonial buildings faced terraces of narrow two- and three-storey shophouses painted with slashes of pink, turquoise, yellow and red. Eclectic Chinese, Victorian and art deco influences emerged in their louvred shutters, rooflines and archways. Clover pressed her face to the window.

'Historic area,' snapped the taxi driver, his first comment of the journey.

'Mr and Mrs Fanshawe checked out half an hour ago,' said the receptionist.

Clover sagged. She should have realised that they were probably on a whistle-stop tour.

'But their luggage is still here. They may be eating breakfast.' Smiles and pointing indicated the way.

Clover, recognising, with a lurch of panic, George's suit carrier – piled next to Alice's almost equally familiar Gucci case – decided to wash before she confronted anyone. Splashing cold water on her face and looking at herself while she brushed her hair, she realised that she recognised the person in the mirror. It was someone she'd known a long time ago.

She had lost weight, probably because the decorating was so physical and, without children to cook for, she hadn't been nibbling so much. She had collarbones. She looked tired, but the shapes and lines on the face in front of her reminded her of who she had once been. She smiled. 'Hello there,' she said to her reflection. 'I've missed you.' Her reflection, travel-weary, wiser and more resilient than it had been twenty years ago, smiled back.

Clover quickly twisted her hair up with a clip, put on some make-up and strode into the breakfast room. Her heart dropped out of her body when she saw Alice and George eating breakfast together.

'Oh hello,' said Alice. 'To what do we owe the honour? Have you developed stalkerish tendencies in your old age?'

'George had to leave before I woke up,' said Clover. 'And

I wanted to know when he would be back.' She pulled up a chair and sat down, determined to look cheerful.

'Are Pilgrim's Worthy's phone lines down again?' enquired Alice sweetly.

'No, it was rather a cold, rainy day so I thought it might be nice to take in some sunshine. And I've always wanted to see the Malacca Straits.'

'It's just sea. Over there. Like Margate, but hot.' Alice signalled to the waiter. 'A coffee, please, for my friend.' She almost snapped her fingers. 'So how did you find us? Judi has very clear instructions never to reveal my whereabouts to anyone. I'm afraid that now I've got so successful I have to be careful about kidnapping and other security issues.'

'If you're worried about that, I suggest you try to be slightly less predictable in your choice of hotel,' replied Clover. 'Although, presumably, you're not expecting to be kidnapped by anyone who's looked after your daughter.'

'I don't know,' said Alice with a quirky smile. 'You all seem to have rather taken against me since the kids left school.'

'In fact, Alice, we – or rather I – feel hurt at how irrelevant we seemed to have suddenly become to you since Lola left school.'

Alice looked genuinely surprised. 'Really? I don't think I've changed in any way. If you think about it, you'll realise that the person who has changed is you—'

George cleared his throat. 'Clover, I take it you'll be wanting to check in to my hotel.'

Alice's cup froze halfway to her mouth and she held herself still, signalling that she wanted to return to the conversation after George's interruption.

'Your hotel?' asked Clover.

'Yes, there weren't enough rooms here.'

'They didn't understand Judi when she asked for two

330

rooms,' interposed Alice. 'They put us down as Mr and Mrs Fanshawe, if you can imagine! Their English is really not very good.'

'It seemed superb when I rang. Sorry, George, what were you saying?'

'I'm staying in one of those international chains not far away. I've got a huge room with a vast bed so there's plenty of space, but I'll need to check you in and we've got a meeting in half an hour so there's not much time.'

Alice finally put her cup down, as if withdrawing from the conversation. 'You two go ahead. I'll meet you there, George.'

'And you had better have a decent explanation of what you're doing here,' muttered George as he marched her to his hotel, grim-faced. 'I do not appreciate your coming halfway around the world to check up on me, and I am not a toy to be fought over by you and Alice.'

'That's not what I—'

'We'll talk this evening. I want to concentrate on the day's business.'

'According to the guide book I bought today, Penang is one of the best places in the world to eat street food,' said Clover when George returned that evening. 'I thought it would be nice just to stroll and see what we find, rather than going to a restaurant.'

He nodded. 'Seems a good idea.'

They wandered towards the evening food market, jostled by the crowds, dodging bicycles and mopeds. Hundreds of steel stalls, each selling just one dish and adorned with banners or signs proclaiming satay, hokkien char, rojak, cuttlefish or rice noodle soup, lined the street. Round tin tables and plastic chairs crowded the pavements. Clover saw every kind of face: Chinese, Indian, white tourists and expats, whole families and single travellers, people on their way back from work and sight-seers, busily lifting chopsticks to their mouths. 'Apparently, Char Kway Teow is the local speciality,' said Clover, pointing to a sign on one of the stalls.

'Char Kway Teow it is,' agreed George.

They both ordered small bowls of what turned out to be a mix of noodles, shrimp, squid and sausage, sizzling hot and spiced with chilli.

'The other local custom is to drink a yogurt drink or lime juice,' added Clover, deciding on a frothing jug of laksa.

George took a mouthful, then laid his chopsticks down. 'Clover, I am fully aware of what Alice is up to. I know perfectly well that she's used us – well, most particularly you – with the whole business of bringing up Lola. But she does know which side her bread is buttered. She is an excellent business-woman, and I have taken enough legal advice to make sure that she is not in a position to get vindictive for the sake of it.'

'I—' Clover tried to interject.

'Look. She's up to everything. Booking us a double room "by mistake" is only the half of it. She's made it quite clear to me, on a number of occasions, that our relationship could be more than professional. But Clover, I am married. I do not have affairs while I am married. And if you and I cease to be married, I will still not have an affair – or any kind of roman-tic relationship – with Alice. This is about trust, and you have to trust me to make good decisions, you trust me with infor-mation that is important to both of us and you have to trust me not to go off with Alice. Without that trust, we do not have a relationship worth saving.'

'If you'd even said a fraction of what you've just said to me now, I would have known you understood. I wouldn't have been so. . . frightened by it.'

'I didn't want to make things worse. You and Laura had

gone into anti-Alice mode, and if I joined in I thought it would get out of hand. I felt I had to counteract it.'

'You can't counteract something by pretending it doesn't exist. *You* didn't trust *me* to have a sensible conversation about it all.' Clover looked into George's eyes. 'You thought you had to control the situation.'

'We're both trying to control things, in our own way,' he acknowledged.

'I've been thinking about what Alice said today. About me being the one who'd changed and not her. I think she's right. While the kids were at home I was Mother Hubbard, looking after everyone, rescuing people like Alice, getting my satisfaction from knowing I was being the best mother, neighbour, teacher and friend I could be. It's what I learned from my own mother: be nice, sacrifice yourself for other people. What Laura calls my script.'

George nodded, looking reflectively across the crowded street as if reading the mishmash of brightly coloured neon signs in Malay and English above each street vendor: 'Best Penang Asam Lakso' and 'Chicken Gizzards'.

'But now the kids have gone, I don't *want* to give more than I get in return. If someone does ask for my help I expect them to do as much work as I do, and then to say thank you at the end, or to do something roughly equivalent for me. That was the difference between painting Jamie's room with Laura – who worked alongside me and actually did about twice as much as I did, then gave me a lovely silver bracelet afterwards to say thank you – and us painting Lola's bedroom. It would have been fine if Alice had painted it with us, instead of constantly checking her e-mails, then being ill, or had at least said thank you, and had then devised some kind of treat or favour in return. But she expected me to do what I always do, which is help out because I need to be needed.'

'I can see that. But I can assure you that I have drawn up a contract with Alice, which gives me rights to shares, and to compensation if I have to leave. Alice does not expect me to do something for nothing, and that's the difference between you and me.'

'It isn't any more,' Clover pointed out. 'I want to be valued as Mrs Jones, the decorator, not as Ben and Holly's mum. I'd love an equal relationship with Alice, because she's really good company and losing her has hurt. But I don't see any evidence that she wants that, and I don't know what she does want – if anything – now that I'm no longer useful for Lola. So I think she was right. I'm different. She's not.'

She wondered if George was still listening. She took his hand. Behind them the cry of the street vendors and the sizzle of frying noodles and garlic mingled in the warm night air.

'Please believe me. I didn't come all this way to find out if you were having an affair with her, although I thought it was a strong possibility. I came to say that I understand why you need something different.'

George stroked her hand.

'And to say that Mother Hubbard wants a divorce,' said Clover softly.

He stared at her for several moments.

'But *Mrs Jones* would be very happy to accompany Mr Jones on a new adventure. If he feels the same way.'

A huge smile spread across his face. 'Let me see. Well, if Mrs Jones is happy to take another twenty or thirty years on trust, I think Mrs Jones and I would do very well together.'

'By the way,' she asked as they wandered hand-in-hand among the street vendors, wondering whether to try black bean ice-cream, 'did you lose one of your Zap–Pow cufflinks?'

He shook his head. 'No, Alice thought we might be able to get cufflinks made with pets heads on them, so she asked me if she could borrow one. I tried to lend her both, because it's so irritating having them separated, but she insisted she only needed one.'

'I bet she did.' Clover put an arm round George. 'She left it in her en suite shower for me to find when I went up there.'

George threw back his head and roared with laughter. 'Well, if she uses even a fraction of that cunning in business, we'll be millionaires in five years' time.'

Chapter 49

Baxtersblog. 15 July

Hi guys! Well, now here's a thing. The Baxters have called it a day. Sarah and I have enjoyed twenty-seven wonderful years together, and we have two gorgeous and successful children. However we feel that the time has come to give each other some space for a while. Maybe not for ever, but Sarah is buying a small cottage back in Kent. Although she's not going to stop travelling, she and I want different things in different places. We've realised that the kids don't stop needing us just because they leave school, and that they'll be wanting a base – and someone to dump washing on – for a few years yet. And Sarah needs to sort out a few health problems – we won't be saying the 'M' word in a public blog, will we?

Having said that, we know that the next ten years are very precious. We met when we were travelling – bet none of you knew that! – and there are still so many places we want to visit. They just, sadly, aren't the same places. You know how it is. But one thing we've learned in the past year is that no matter how far you go, you take yourself and everything you are with you.

This has been an amazing year and nothing has turned out quite how we planned. Adam has dropped out of his history degree, and was going to 'gap year' with us. That lasted about three weeks. He doesn't enjoy travelling. He just doesn't. We do. Hey, we're all different. He's going to do an IT degree instead, and has been accepted at Kent. He'll probably be living at home for some of the time. Milly is still on course to be a doctor. We – and for the last time I can say 'we' – are so proud of them both.

As I said, I think I've learned a lot. Most of it from our kids and the rest from our friends. Just kick me in the backside if I ever stop learning. Thanks, guys.

'So, Alice's "one couple at each table will divorce" statistic was right,' said Clover to Laura over Saturday-morning coffee.

'It could so easily have been us,' replied Laura. 'If I hadn't decided – really decided – that I needed to sort myself out rather than blame Tim all the time.'

'Or us,' agreed Clover. 'If I hadn't finally worked out that trust was more important than trying to control things.'

'It's rather sad. I suspect Sarah initiated the split. She seemed very glad to be back, and we never heard her voice in the blogs. I think the permanent travelling was probably Ken's dream, not hers. And, although he would never, ever admit to regrets, he sounds pretty down at losing her.'

'Except that there's a pic of him with two girls in bikinis.'

Clover and Laura peered at the fuzzy shot at the bottom of the blog entry. It showed three people beside a pool, raising huge cocktails to the camera. The women were blonde, young and bikini-ed. Ken's grey chest hair was just visible.

'It's not very ethnic,' said Clover. 'I mean, that could be a poolside in an international hotel anywhere in the world.'

'Anywhere in the world that's hot. But you're right, it's not quite the "getting to know the real country" lifestyle Ken has suggested.'

'Oh, here's an e-mail from Sarah too.' Laura opened it quickly. 'It's just a change of address notification. "Sarah Baxter and Mark Warrenden will be living at"'—

'Who on earth is Mark Warrenden?' shrieked Clover. 'Let's hit the phones.'

Epilogue

Clover and George drew up outside the black timber-shingled house, set amidst the bleak desert landscape of Dungeness. With the sharp angles of its roof and striking plate glass windows it was, if you looked carefully, quite different from the other cottages dotted around the landscape. But it also respected their size and scale, echoing their black tar weatherboarding and the way they hugged the stony ground. From a distance it could have been one of them.

'It's like us,' said Clover, pulling her bags out of the car. 'Different, but recognisable. Linked to the past. But not the same.'

Laura came racing out. 'Isn't this fun? It's the most extraordinary place – look, the power station is just there! And two lighthouses.'

George hefted two more bags out. 'Food,' he said.

'Wait till you see the kitchen. I've never known a holiday rental that actually had a better-equipped kitchen than I have at home. It's just amazing. And all the surfaces are made of polished concrete that looks like limestone.'

Inside, the tongue-and-groove walls were painted white, with full picture windows and wide glass slits that turned the eerie landscape into a series of works of art. The scrubland

and shingle stretched for miles around the house. Desolate and windy, it had a bleak beauty all of its own in the fading afternoon light. 'It's Britain's only natural desert, apparently,' said Tim, following Laura out. His hair had grown back into its well-cut crop. He did not look like a man who had been into the jaws of death. After six months of painstakingly slow recovery, he was due to return to work.

'Who else has arrived?' asked Clover.

'We're the first. Sarah and Mark have just called to say they're about fifteen minutes away, and I think Duncan and Cherry will be here around six. They're bringing supper.'

'Alice asked me what I was doing this weekend, just before I left,' said George. 'I got the feeling that she would have loved to be invited.'

Clover's first instinct was to make it better for Alice – to call her up on Monday and arrange a similar weekend. Then she realised how easy it would be to go back to being who she was then. 'If Alice wanted to spend a weekend with us,' she said instead, 'she could have organised one herself and invited us.'

George touched her shoulder and smiled. 'It's OK. That's what I thought. But I just told her it was all Sarah's idea, which it was.'

'I don't think I've quite recovered from seeing those pictures of Alice's fiftieth birthday party in *Tatler*,' said Clover, with a pang. 'If she didn't invite us to that, she'll never invite us to anything.'

'Well, with my professional involvement in the company, it's probably just as well to be off her Christmas-card list.' George handed her a crate of fruit and vegetables.

All the bedrooms were small, with huge beds and equally easy access to a bathroom, so there didn't seem any reason to fight over them. 'Fabulous,' said Laura, bouncing on one of the beds. 'Someone had better help Tim with the fire – he's read half the instruction booklet and still can't work out how to open its door.'

They agreed that women unpacking the food and men tackling the fire divided the labour up nicely. 'Although Tim's brought his trademark tagine for supper tomorrow night,' said Laura.

'There's meant to be a great fish shop-cum-smokery nearby.' Clover found somewhere to stack various boxes of tea and coffee. 'So our contribution will be to get lots of fish and smoked fish for lunch tomorrow.'

'And Sarah says that Mark is an amazing cook, so they'll do Sunday lunch,' concluded Laura, filling one fridge with bottles of white wine, lager and fruit juice.

'So we've only really got to cook one meal each,' said Clover. 'And the rest of the time is our own. It all seems so easy.'

'Yes, do you remember when holidays were much like being at home, only hot? All shopping and cooking and laundry for loads of children?'

Laura smiled, and looked outside at the low rumble of a car. 'Oh look, here's Duncan and his fancy woman. Just remind me – who's this Cherry?'

Clover only had time to whisper that Cherry had hired Duncan's company – along with Mrs Jones – to decorate the new house she'd bought after her divorce. At some point in the renovation Duncan and Cherry had become more than client and decorator. 'I don't know much more than that.'

There were cries of delight as everyone enthused over the contemporary design of the light-switches, the sunken slate bath ('Who's going to be first to fall in and break their neck?' asked George), the suspended washbasins, and tried to work out how to open the sliding doors on to the various timber decks. 'Surely we don't need to open anything?' shrieked Laura. 'It is December, after all.'

But Duncan and George were determined to find out how everything worked, while Cherry brought her own big basket of food to the kitchen to unload it. 'It's incredibly kind of Sarah to treat us all to a weekend like this, isn't it?' she said. 'I mean, I hardly know her – apparently Duncan's wife used to be on a school run with her at primary school.'

'Really? I didn't know that.'

'She was always so generous. We tried to persuade her that we could all pay our share of the rental, because if there are only two of you it's really not expensive.'

'So did we,' said Clover. 'But she said it was in return for all the help we gave her when the kids were growing up and she was working full-time. Not that I remember having to pick up the pieces all that often, and she always did something for us in return.'

'Yes, whenever you think about Alice and whether she had to use people the way she did, you only have to think of people like Sarah,' added Laura. 'She worked just as hard, but always found a way of saying thank you or doing something in return. It's the difference between helping someone and rescuing.'

'I'm afraid you get a lot of psychological jargon from Laura these days,' joked Clover. 'She'll analyse all of us.'

'I think it's really nice to help people. It's important. Otherwise, we'd all find life much more difficult,' said Cherry.

Clover opened the other fridge and began filling it with vegetables, so that she was out of Laura's eye line.

'Helping is good,' explained Laura. 'If you help someone, firstly they need to ask for help, then they should either do at least fifty per cent of the work themselves, or if they can't at that point they need to do something equivalent later. For

342

example, if you said you needed to clear your attic, you could ask Clover to help you, but you'd still have to be responsible for how it went, and do as much work as she did or more. That's helping. But if Clover turns up, unasked or almost unasked, and starts clearing the attic all on her own, or while you paint your fingernails and leave it all to her ... That's a rescue.'

'You don't need to lecture,' said Clover, straightening up. 'I know you think it's only a question of time before I slip back into my old ways of looking after Alice, then getting upset when she doesn't reciprocate, but I'm pretty clear about where I stand now.'

Sarah Baxter and Mark Warrenden were the last to arrive. Mark had worked in Sarah's office in the City, and neither of them, even to Laura, seemed prepared to admit when their relationship had started. ('But it was obviously before Ken and Sarah went away. I'll get it out of them this weekend,' promised Laura in an aside to Clover and Cherry).

Sarah pulled champagne and good red wine out of boxes, stashing the champagne in the fridge. Duncan found a place to stack a crate of beer. Laura, as penance for her old non-existent wheat allergy, had stocked up on bread, croissants and muffins. Cherry tentatively laid out a cheeseboard. 'I wasn't sure what people would like,' she said, 'so I brought a bit of everything.'

Soon they had opened bottles and laid a huge black-stained table with simple white china ('*Très chic*, don't you think?' said Clover approvingly). As soon as they raised the first glass to their lips, the smoke alarm went off because George hadn't quite secured the door of the wood-burning stove. ('A fire that can defeat George,' muttered Duncan. 'This I have to see.')

'Try the instruction booklet,' suggested Laura.

'I've *tried* the instruction booklet.' George sounded ratty. But only slightly.

Tim began to read from it. 'The house has a solid internal core of polished concrete, comprising the hearth, the chimney, stove and bathing rooms. The chimney is the only concrete element seen from the outside and reflects the colour of the landscape in contrast to the tarred external walls—'

'We don't want to know what it's made of, just how to use it.' Laura snatched it from him. 'Oh, listen ... sage green seakale, blue bugloss, red poppy and yellow sedum give bursts of seasonal colour in the stony desert landscape of Dungeness, but it is the purple viper's bugloss in August ... how exciting! In August all the landscape out there ...' she waved at what was now darkness, illuminated by the ocean-liner brilliance of the power station '... more or less matches the purple floor in here. Isn't that clever?'

'I'm feeling a bit smoked out,' said Duncan. 'Can we have the architecture lesson later?' He picked up something that looked like a spanner, quickly and easily shutting the door of the stove.

George looked disappointed. 'Well, that's modern design for you. Really difficult to work out until you know how to do it, and then it's easy.'

'The whole point of these houses is to get British people finding out what it's actually like to sleep and eat in an ultra-modern homes,' explained Laura to Cherry. 'To make us think differently about how we live. It's a charity called Living Architecture, and there are about eight houses around the country so far.'

'What fun,' replied Cherry. 'Do try this hummus.'

Duncan and Cherry worked so efficiently together over supper that Clover suspected they were closer than even she knew.

'Amazing breadknife,' said Cherry. 'I didn't think there could be differences in bread knives.'

'Extraordinary,' commented Duncan, wielding a lemon. 'A grater that actually grates.'

'I thought this was going to be such a cheap weekend,' bemoaned Laura, 'but it's obviously going to cost a fortune because we'll all have to re-equip our kitchens with everything they've got in here.'

Duncan and Cherry were trying to work out how to use the hob. 'The cooker thinks it's intellectually superior to me,' muttered Cherry. 'The hob turns itself off when you lift the pans off.'

'I refuse to be bossed about by a hob,' agreed Duncan. 'I shan't be getting that one in a hurry. It's ready, folks.'

George banged the table, and raised a glass to the cooks.

'The cooks,' they chorused.

'And we've got a couple of announcements.' He looked at Clover. 'You first.'

Clover blushed. 'Mrs Jones Decorating is now open for business. I'll still be working with Duncan, but I'm also operating solo as a colour advice service and specialist effects expert. With a particular expertise in Empty Nesters. They – we – always end up redecorating. One way or another.'

Cherry smiled. 'That's true. I wouldn't have met Duncan if I hadn't got divorced, and had to have my new house repainted.'

'And we've redecorated to have a special project,' admitted Laura. 'I feel different. Tim feels different. Jamie feels different. So redecorating the house seems a way of acknowledging that.'

'No, you're a Life Changer, not a true Wallpaperer,' said Clover, rather enjoying lecturing Laura for a change.

Laura raised her eyebrows. 'And what does that mean?'

'Wallpaperers are the ones who paper over the gap left by their children by starting a new decorating project. Something like new bathrooms or converting the loft. But it only keeps them busy for the first year because, of course, the builders do go eventually. But Life Changers are the ones who train for new careers or give up their old ones.'

'Like us,' suggested Sarah.

'Oh, you're Grown Up Gappers. Instead of the kids going off travelling, the adults do. You're no good to me as a client until you come back again. Which I suppose you have.' She smiled at Mark.

'What do we think about the Lewises and their obsession with Mongolian goats?' asked Tim.

'Ah, that's Fifty is the New Thirty – But with Hobbies,' said Clover. 'I ought to think of a snappier title, but they don't do a lot of decorating. Too busy pursuing their interest in snowdrop trails, compost, entering politics or seeing every production of *Hamlet* around the world.'

'I can think of another category: the Husband-Swappers,' said Sarah. 'People like me who look at each other when their children leave home and find they've got nothing left to say to each other. Or who go off and have affairs for some other reason.'

'We've covered that one with Cherry,' said Laura hastily. 'I think everyone should raise a toast to Mrs Jones Decorating.'

'Mrs Jones Decorating.' Everyone lifted their glasses again.

'And George, you should say too.'

George looked pleased. 'On Monday morning I take over as managing director of Shirts & Things, Sheets & Things and Pets & Things, because Alice has finally decided to take the company public. She's going to concentrate on design and new development.'

346

Everyone banged the table in approval and raised their glasses again. 'We'd like to say something,' said Duncan, putting an arm round Cherry. 'Cherry and I are moving in together.'

Cherry beamed as Duncan kissed her, and they all toasted 'Duncan and Cherry.'

'Laura!' said Clover, nudging her. 'Your turn.'

'Me? Oh, me. Well. OK. I've been accepted on to a year-long course to begin my training as a psychotherapist. I am so excited I can barely sleep. I've never been so fascinated by anything in all my life.'

'So now you're going to sort out all our problems?' queried George.

'No! You're going to sort out your own problems. But I can facilitate your doing that. Now Tim. Your news is pretty important.'

Tim admitted, to cheers round the table, that he'd just had a clear scan, and that, for the first time in a long while, he also felt really well. He topped up their glasses.

'Well,' said Sarah sheepishly. 'I suppose we'd better admit to a bit of news ourselves. We've been keeping it all a bit quiet because we don't want to upset Ken, but ... Mark and I got married yesterday. That's why we thought this weekend would be such fun. A second-time-round wedding can be a bit of a minefield, but we thought that to spend some time with a few old friends—'

'Less of the old,' interjected George.

Sarah smiled at him. 'I wanted Mark to meet the people who've been with me through the thick and thin of bringing up the children. It's lovely to meet the newcomers ...' she raised a glass, with a smile in Cherry's direction '... but most of all I want to raise a glass to the empty nesters. For, as Ken would say – perhaps, rather cringingly,' she acknowledged, wrinkling her nose at her former husband's prose, 'Thanks for sharing the journey.'

The champagne was not quite cold, but it had to come out of the fridge anyway.

Reading Group Discussion Points

What do you think of the choices each woman makes in *The Empty Nesters*?

What does this novel say about female friendship?

Alice is accused of 'using' Clover and Laura. To what extent is friendship an 'exchange', and is it important that the exchange is seen as equal – that there is an approximate give and take on both sides? Do you think Clover is as responsible as Alice is for the situation between them?

How does this novel explore the family dynamic, especially when children leave it?

What does *The Empty Nesters* say about taking responsibility for yourself, especially once you've spent twenty or more years being responsible for your children? Does having children help you deal with your own problems, or do problems from your past reassert themselves once your children leave home?

What is the central theme of the book, and how did it resonate with you?

There is much colour imagery in this novel. Can you explain why imagery is so important in the story and how effective it is?

How are relationships between the three central women portrayed in the book? What do you think of the choices they make?

What do you think of the men in the book?

Who is your favourite/least favourite character and how true did each of them feel?

Author Q&A

Have you always wanted to be a writer?

I used to write little stories with my father from the age of four or five. When we moved to the Caribbean, there was only one small library and no bookshops. School was intermittent as the island (the Dominican Republic) had several revolutions and the electricity supply was too unreliable for TV. So when I ran out of books to read, I had to rely on my own imagination, and wrote.

How did you research *The Empty Nesters*?

The Empty Nesters has its basis in my own life, as both our children, and many of our friends' children, are now at uni – although I never put 'real people' directly into any novel. I talked to lots of empty nesters, and have also done psychological research in building the characters and their situations, occasionally discussing them with a psychologist friend, Penelope Williams. The books I've read include *I'm OK, You're OK* by Thomas Harris, *Games People Play* by Eric Berne, *TA Today* by Ian Stewart and Vann Joines, and *Scripts People Live* by Claude Steiner.

All these books – and many others I've read – are about trans-actional analysis (TA), or our patterns of relating to other people. They look at how we re-enact the same scenarios and make the same mistakes throughout our lives. TA encourages you to understand these patterns and use your own intelli-gence to help you stop repeating them. I felt TA was particularly appropriate to *The Empty Nesters* because I think that the issues you had before having children don't go away: they just get subsumed in childcare and being busy, so they re-emerge – sometimes like a slap in the face – once children leave home.

What is your process for writing each novel?

I try to work during the day, Monday to Friday, with week-ends off. After walking the dog, I start at around nine o'clock in the morning, and probably close down at around half-past six. But, like most writers, I only do a maximum of about four hours of actual writing (and often less) in that time. The rest is tinkering, re-reading, admin, fiddling about on Twitter or e-mail, day-dreaming or chatting to people on the phone – which is where I get lots of my ideas, so I pretend it's work. Towards the end of a book I get up earlier and earlier and write in my pyjamas.

How did you become a novelist?

I always wanted to be a novelist, but while I was working as a full-time journalist my writing and creativity was wrapped up in that. When my children were five, I went part-time, and that freed up some mental space (although, with two small children, it didn't free up a great deal of time!). Sometimes I got halfway through a book, then threw it away because I could see it was no good. Eventually, I went on a five day Arvon Foundation course where I was encouraged to finish my novel about office politics, *The Office Party* (now out of print). It was bought quite quickly by a publisher, so I didn't have lots of rejections, but I think that was because I threw away so many novels before they could even be rejected.

What advice would you give to aspiring novelists?

Just keep going. Keep writing, re-writing, reading, reading about writing, listening to your favourite authors speak, reading their blogs and following them on Twitter, and, if you can manage it, go on the occasional creative-writing course. Then back to writing and reading again. It's always very difficult to get published, but almost everyone I meet who really keeps going seems to get published in the end. (I would say everyone, but I know someone will pop up and say 'I haven't!') You do need luck, but keeping going will mean you're ready to make the most of opportunities when luck strikes. Finally, don't get too hooked on writing one particular book. You may have to try several styles or genres before you find your real writing voice.

Where do your characters come from, and how do they evolve?

My characters aren't based on real people, but they do come from real-life situations. I build them the way a painter or sculptor creates a figure. My inspiration for Clover, for example, was someone who was very involved with school and her children's lives, so in some ways, she's like me and lots of friends. But then I start to sketch in other details, such as her artistic side. At this point, I decide on my character's career, so I can interview specific people to ask them, 'What kind of personality would a female decorator need?' 'What kind of things would a former actress worry about?' These may be their own characteristics or they may have observed them in colleagues. This is the painter's equivalent of beginning to add paint to the sketches or a sculptor finally chipping away at the stone.

Then, once the characteristics seem to fit, I do extra research, which provides detail and background – for *Lovers and Liars* I interviewed people who worked with victims of domestic abuse, and for *Sisters-in-Law* I joined an Army wives' coffee morning, interviewed social workers and talked to people who run radio and TV production companies. For *The Inheritance* I talked to countless professional riders. I also read biographies and autobiographies of people working in the worlds my characters inhabit, as well as books on psychology.

The rest is just instinct. Some characters stride into a book fully formed, apparently from nowhere, and others need constant re-drawing and re-researching, even into the second draft. I find 'wicked' characters much easier and more fun to write than heroes and heroines.

Do you have a favourite character?

In *The Empty Nesters* I think my favourite might be Laura, who I found irritating at first. Although she's spoilt and self-indulgent at the beginning of the book, she faces up to her problems, and has the courage to take responsibility for herself by the end.

What do you enjoy reading?

I love all kinds of books – *Middlemarch* by George Eliot is my all-time favourite novel. But I have a particular weakness for thrillers about ordinary people in extraordinary situations – Harlan Coben, Nicci French, Peter James, Sophie Hannah, Rosamund Lupton and Stieg Larsson, for example. I love fiction about women's lives – it's not just entertaining, but helps us work through issues of our own. The ones I'd buy in hardback (can't wait for the paperback) are Elizabeth Buchan, Dorothy Koomson, Jodi Picoult and Joanna Trollope. I've just discovered Lucy Dawson, too, and like what I've read so far. And, although I wouldn't think of myself as a fan of historical fiction, I do occasionally love it when there's a vintage or historical background, such as Sarah Blake's *The Postmistress*, many of Penny Vincenzi's glorious blockbuster sagas or – new to the intelligent historical thriller genre – Andrew Williams. I think Fiona Mountain is now a name to watch in proper historical fiction too. Finally, no one can beat Marian Keyes for humour and compassion interwoven with accurate research on serious issues.

If your book was made into a film, who would you cast?

If *The Empty Nesters* was made into a film, Caroline Quentin would be my number one choice for Clover. She's such a funny, versatile, talented actress and everyone loves her. I'd have Helen Mirren as Alice and Helena Bonham Carter for Laura.

George is a James May–Jeremy Clarkson type (although I know they're not actors, so maybe Kiefer Sutherland?), and Tim is pure George Clooney.

Of the novels you've written, do you have a favourite character?

I feel a great affection for the characters in *The Inheritance*, *Sisters-in-Law*, *Lovers and Liars* and *The Empty Nesters* who, in their different ways, are just trying to get on with their lives and do the right thing, but who don't spot the game-playing of the other characters soon enough. That's Bramble Kelly in *The Inheritance*, Kate Fox in *Sisters-in-Law*, Paige Raven in *Lovers and Liars* and Clover Jones in *The Empty Nesters*. Clover's probably my favourite of those four, because she's a lot tougher than she first appears, and she's less of a worrier than, say, Paige (although Paige has been forced into a very difficult situation).

Read on for the opening chapter of
Nina Bell's *Sisters-in-Law*

Chapter 1

Kate Fox and Jonny Rafferty were late getting Sunday lunch ready. This often happened because they tried to crowd too much into their days.

'We should have done this weeks ago,' said Jonny, hefting his tool box up from the tiny cellar tucked under their narrow Victorian terraced house. 'People will be here in a minute.'

'We've got about an hour. We can get these hung in that time.' Kate unwrapped a series of family photographs, each in an identical matt black frame with a huge cream mount, transforming the image from a happy memory into a work of art. They had just finished having a modern kitchen extension built, and instead of the jumbled, friendly collage of colourful snapshots she'd crammed into frames or pinned up on the noticeboard in the old kitchen, she'd decided – no, *they'd* decided, because she and Jonny discussed everything – that it would be nice to choose one or two really beautiful photographs of each family member and frame them dramatically on the new white walls.

But they were all due round for lunch at any moment and the photographs lay on the floor, in their packaging, the 'washed and ready to eat' salad was in bags in the fridge and the rice was still in its packet, although at least there was a hunk of meat, marinated in Turkish spices, roasting in the oven.

'We couldn't do it any earlier, we had that awards ceremony, three parties, two parents' evenings at school, the Lovelace Conservation Committee meeting and we both had deadlines at work.' Kate handed Jonny the first photograph, a deliciously retro black-and-white image of her mother and father, Ella and Michael Fox, as bride and groom circa 1966. Under her pillbox hat and above his kipper tie their faces looked unrecognisably young and innocent. 'Let's start with this one in the middle, shall we?'

The earliest photos were the easiest – a studio shot of Kate and her brothers Simon and Jack, aged five, seven and three, respectively, with gap-toothed smiles, and another on Jonny's side, of him and his sister squinting into the sun with buckets and spades. Kate had tried to exclude anything that resembled a traditional family photo, rejecting the garish colours and muddled composition of everyone crammed on to a sofa in their Sunday best, with unrealistically neat hair and bright smiles. She wanted simple backgrounds and casual clothes, pictures that really gave an impression of the person behind the image, like the head-and-shoulders portrait of her mother, Ella, her chin jutting out in determination, her sharp eyes seeing everything. Well, almost everything.

She'd found a good one of her father, in his late forties, with a wry smile on his face, urging them on to be the best they could be, encouraging them all every inch of the way, taking their childish worries seriously and sorting out their scraps and bickering.

Until a drunk driver on the A3 wiped him out of their lives overnight when Kate was fifteen. He had been on his way home after working late, as personnel director of an industrial components firm.

After that, the sunny childhood had become muddled and grey. They moved to a smaller house, with a back yard instead of lawns and three bedrooms instead of five, in a less 'nice' area. While Si won a scholarship to finish his A levels at the private school all three had attended, Kate and Jack had to leave, and found themselves in the school none of their friends wanted to go to. For Kate it was easier – she was starting her A levels and, higher up the school, the rebellious element had left – but, Jack, aged thirteen, had to prove that he wasn't a 'toff' and he learned to prove it with his fists. Ella, who had always been at home, checking their homework and cooking meals, had to go out to work, and the heart went out of the household. Kate cooked the boys fish fingers or sausages and beans. Simon became 'the man of the family' at seventeen. Jack, the youngest, became loud and scrappy in the school playground and was suspended three times. Kate and Si persuaded him to clean up his act, and managed to cover up a certain amount of his bad behaviour. The three of them made it work. That's what their father would have wanted. To keep the worries away from their mother. They tested each other at exam time, supported each other over boyfriends and girl-friends, and tried not to think about their father.

Si got into Oxford and became embarrassed about coming from the suburbs, then married Olivia, his long-term university girlfriend, a few years later. Kate, whose exam results were less stellar, went to London after leaving school, to become a radio journalist. Jack grew up and dropped the bad boy act, joining the army. Eventually Ella bought a tiny cottage in Thorpe Wenham, a picture-perfect Oxfordshire village. She had done her job. The family was launched. And so well. Everyone said so.

Kate took another photo out of its bubble wrap. It was a beautiful one of Si and Olivia at their wedding reception at St

James's Palace – she was, according to Ella, who was impressed by these things, 'terribly well connected'. Si was the taller of the two Fox brothers, and his hair was darker than Kate and Jack's mousey blond. Kate teased Si that he should put 'dark mouse' under 'hair colour'; Jack joked that he should just write 'rat'. Olivia was tall too, and gangling, a string bean in a frothing meringue of a dress, with a generous mouth and long chestnut hair.

Then the photo of Jack and Heather: Jack was stockier than Si and tawny in colouring. Heather was strawberry blonde and tiny, like a very pretty pixie. She had a hesitant gaze, dimples and wrists so slender that they looked as if they might snap. She married in a slim silk sheath with a twist of flowers in her hair – the photo showed her peering nervously up at Jack's fellow officers as they crossed swords above the couple in a guard of honour as she and Jack left the church.

Kate and Jonny had chosen three photographs of their sons, Luke and Callum, from a serious-faced Callum with baby Luke in his arms to a pair of cheeky boys grinning at the camera to the one taken last year of them sitting back-to-back in white T-shirts and frayed jeans, with Callum's spider-long legs and arms twice the length of his brother's more rounded limbs. Luke and Callum had Jonny's blond wavy hair and penetrating blue eyes, combined with the Fox jaw. Luke was ten. Kate still ferried him to and from school, and knew all his friends, while Callum, empowered by going to secondary school, ambled off on his own, taking a bus, and the names he referred to at the end of the day were unfamiliar to her. He often begged Kate to walk on the other side of the road from him if they were anywhere near school, because she was so 'embarrassing'.

'Should we put the boys' pictures in some kind of age order?' she asked, 'or just dot them around wherever?'

Jonny, who as a television director had a strong visual sense, spent a few minutes experimenting, then tacked them up in exactly the right place. Kate kissed him.

'And now,' he shot a teasing look, 'we've actually got some representation of my family to go up. I didn't think you were going to allow them on the wall.'

'Of course I am. Don't be ridiculous. It's you who barely keeps in touch with your sister. It's none of my business if you don't.' But it had been with secret reluctance that she'd rummaged through his photographs, although she'd found a wonderfully nostalgic-looking photograph of Jonny's parents, both now dead, looking rather like the Duke and Duchess of Windsor and another she quite liked of Jonny's sister, Virginia, as one of the 'girls in pearls' in the front of *Country Life* when she got engaged to Angus. Such photos did look great in huge frames, even if she wasn't terribly fond of the people in them.

But the most difficult task had been to find the right photographs of herself and Jonny. There was an arty shot of the whole family tangled round a ladder, all with bare feet (no conventional line-ups for the Fox–Rafferty household), and a heavenly close-up of Jonny outdoors, with his lazy, beach-bum smile and creased blue eyes.

When she'd first met him – she'd interviewed him as the hot new director of a cult documentary series – the first thing she'd noticed was a pair of tanned and muscular legs emerging from shorts. In November. And she'd thought that any man who smiled like that instead of speaking and had hair down to his shoulders might well be both stupid and vain. He's got a lot of women after him, she thought – accurately, as it turned out. He needn't think I'm going to be one of them.

But she soon discovered that he used his smile to give himself time to think, and that, far from being vain, his hair was long because he could only be bothered to have it cut once a year, when he would have it virtually shaved off. And those shorts had been the first thing that came to hand when he'd opened the wardrobe that morning.

He was certainly a man who needed looking after. Kate had risen to the challenge, but had made it clear that she wasn't going to pander to his every whim like all the Jennys, Janes, Jamilas and Janelles that seemed to clog up his answering machine. The relationship would be on her terms, and if he didn't like it, he knew where the door was. If he wanted someone adoring, or even a histrionic diva, he could go and find one.

So far, he hadn't. She thought of the first time she'd 'accidentally' left her make-up at his flat. He hadn't said anything, so she left a pair of jeans, then some shoes, kicked under the bed so they could seem to be there by mistake. Over the next few weeks, her possessions crept into his place under their own volition, like guerrilla fighters sneaking over the border, and draped themselves over bits of furniture, challenging the now invisible Jenny, Jane, Jamila and Janelle, until he suggested that she have a drawer and a corner of the wardrobe.

She'd seen that drawer as an interesting sign that they might have some sort of a future together, and that, for the time being, the Js were in retreat. So she brought out the big guns, inflicting damage invisible to the naked male: two little dark smudges on the corner of a towel to signify 'mascara-wearer was here' or flowers in a vase. Men never put flowers into vases. Women knew that.

There was no answering fire: no single earrings on the floor near the bed or discarded female razors in the bathroom waste-paper basket.

Her first pregnancy had been an accident – she had been

quite frightened by its suddenness, barely a year after they'd first met – but Jonny seemed unfazed, and they'd decided to buy a place together. 19 Lovelace Road.

So here they were. But she couldn't quite identify a photograph that said 'this is us'. They'd never married – they'd talked about it, but somehow there'd never been the time or the money. Throughout her twenties, Kate had come away from weddings storing away little details that she liked or making mental notes as to what had been wrong. Your wedding day was the most important day of your life, and she didn't want to do it until she was ready to do it perfectly. And not, of course, until she was down to a size ten. And Jonny agreed. Or rather, he didn't really seem to care.

Men didn't. Thinking about this, Kate suppressed a very faint worm of unease. Very few people got married these days. There was no point. It was absurd to abide by old-fashioned conventions. It just meant there were no photographs. And none of the pictures of him looking cool and her in a big, unfortunate hat at various friends' weddings would do. There were several photos of them on holidays, but Kate thought she looked like a fat, white slug next to the tanned, relaxed Jonny. In the end, she'd discarded the beach-bum shot because there was no equivalent one of her, and decided to frame a stylish photograph of him taken for a media magazine after he'd won an award for one of his series, and one of herself in the kitchen at 19 Lovelace Road taken when she'd been interviewed by a woman's magazine about one of her programmes. Both had the right kind of relaxed, cool seriousness and were well composed.

It was only when they were up that she realised that she and Jonny were not only in separate photos but they seemed to have defined themselves purely in terms of their work. She shot a look at him. Had he noticed?

'That looks great,' he said, looking at his watch. 'So who's coming?' He put away the tool box and moved over to the wine rack, recently installed in the sleek new kitchen. 'Do you think we'll need more red wine or mainly white?'

Kate whisked a bag of carrots out of the fridge and began to grate furiously, a new Middle-Eastern cookbook propped up in front of her. 'Olivia and Si. Olivia drinks white, but don't forget that she hates Chardonnay, and Si likes really good reds. Don't give him any rubbish, you know what he's like, he'll get pompous. Heather barely drinks . . .' Kate put down the grater. 'I get the impression that her parents might have been teetotallers or something, maybe a big ban on wicked alcohol in the house when she was growing up, what do you think?'

Jonny shrugged. 'She's never mentioned any of her family to me.'

'Don't you think that's odd?'

'I think we need to get on with sorting out lunch.'

'Oh, OK.' But Kate frowned slightly as she picked up another carrot. 'Jack, of course, knocks back anything, and the children will stick to orange juice. Mumma likes sherry. Oh, and I've invited Sasha Morton. That woman I met at the drinks on Thursday. She's the daughter of the painter Roderick Morton, so she could be quite interesting. She's going through some hideous divorce and is on her own this weekend, so I felt sorry for her.' Kate flicked hair out of her eye. Her arm ached and there were still seven carrots to go. 'And she's trying to get into "the media".' She put down the carrot and wiggled her fingers to indicate quote marks. 'She said she'd love some advice. She seems really nice.'

'Just don't put me next to her.' Jonny's voice came from the fridge, where he was having difficulty finding space for a few extra bottles of white wine. 'The weekends are my time off, and I don't want to have to give the ten reasons why it is almost impossible to get into TV.'

'Me too. But to be fair,' said Kate, who was always trying to be a better person, and rather guiltily feeling that she'd failed, 'I thought she was rather interesting. And her ex-husband sounds awful.'

Jonny rolled his eyes. 'You never stop, Kate, do you?'

'What do you mean? I'm just trying to be nice. If you walked out, you wouldn't want people to leave me on my own all weekend.'

'If I walk out, it'll be because you invite people round the whole time.' He began opening the red wine, shaking his head in mock despair.

The doorbell rang twenty minutes later. Ella was always the first to arrive.

'The traffic was terrible.' She handed over the pudding that she'd made as her contribution to lunch, plus a bunch of daffodils from the garden. 'Really awful. I think I'm going to have to stop driving. I'm getting far too old. I'm seventy this year, you know.' She delivered these lines in crisp tones.

'Oh, no. Seventy is nothing nowadays. Just the right age for trekking in the Himalayas or taking up parachuting.' Kate was disconcerted by Ella's admission of frailty. She wanted Ella to go on exactly as she was, the mainstay of the Thorpe Wenham allotments, a demon bridge player and, twice a week, a volunteer at the charity shop.

Luke came racing up to kiss his grandmother, and her face softened at the sight of him.

'Come and see the new extension.' He took her hand and pulled her towards the back of the house.

Ella nodded, conveying approval. 'I love the light. And it's so big. But wasn't it very expensive?'

'Oh, not really.' Kate knew the question of how much they'd spent would be a hot topic amongst the family for weeks to come, with lines being drawn and sides being taken. She would be labelled extravagant. Quite unfairly. This was an investment. She avoided the question. Ella settled herself on one of the huge dark sofas, and accepted a sherry from Jonny. 'Tell me who's coming.'

'Everyone. Si and Olivia, and Jack and Heather with the girls, and someone I met last week called Sasha Morton. She's the daughter of the painter Roderick Morton. She's getting divorced, and doesn't have her children this weekend, so she's a bit lonely.'

Ella frowned. 'I thought we would just be family. It's not a good idea to invite divorced women round, you know.' She indicated the stairs. Jonny had disappeared with Luke, to check something on the computer. 'I mean suppose *he* fancies her? You're not married, you know.'

Why were mothers so infuriating? 'Mumma, that has absolutely *nothing* to do with *anything*, and the reason why Jonny stays with me isn't about a meaningless piece of paper, but because he knows that we're both free agents.' She picked up the carrot she was about to grate, held it as if it were a microphone, and tried to sing. 'He knows my door is always open and the sleeping bag . . .' She couldn't quite catch the tune. Or the words, for that matter. Ella looked perplexed.

'What *are* you doing?' Jonny came back into the room.

'Karaoke with the carrot.' Kate began grating again. 'Trying to remember that song that says how your sleeping bag stays rolled up behind the sofa because the door is always open. "Ever Gentle On My Mind", that's it. That's what I am, Mumma.'

'Kate, you're many things when you're on my mind,' said Jonny, 'but ever gentle is *not* one of them.'

'You never could sing.' Ella was thoroughly disapproving. 'Si and Jack both have lovely voices, but you always sounded like a frog trying to get through a grating.'

Kate giggled. 'Mumma thinks this new friend of mine might be after you, Jonny, because she's a divorcee, and therefore, by definition, must be looking for a man. I was saying "so what?"'

Ella's cheeks went pink. She firmly believed in keeping secrets from men. And any kind of female machination. Then she raised her chin towards Jonny. 'Well, she might be after Jack, he's got no sense, or Si, because anyone who works that hard is bound to have an affair at some point.'

'It sounds like fun.' Jonny laughed, leaning against the chunky black granite 'island' they'd installed in the middle of the room. 'But as Si and Jack are so busy, shouldn't we worry more about Olivia and Heather – they're obviously on their own so much?'

'Don't try to tie me in knots, you know what I mean.'

'I look forward to being fought over,' said Jonny. 'Bags I, in fact. Jack doesn't deserve it, and Si only thinks about money anyway.'

'Dream on,' said Kate, squeezing lemon over the carrots and adding caraway seeds. 'She can have you if she wants you. Which she won't unless you shave before they all arrive, you look as if you've slept on a park bench.'

Jonny saluted and went upstairs.

'Anyway,' said Kate, feeling guilty about teasing her mother, 'I don't believe that someone can just walk in and destroy a good relationship. There'd have to be something wrong to start with, so she won't get far with any of us. I mean, both Si and Olivia and Heather and Jack are really strong together. Don't you think? In their different ways?'

Ella regarded her steadily over the rim of the glass with a

knowing expression. She was not going to be persuaded. 'Where's Callum?' she said, changing the subject. 'And isn't that the doorbell?'

'I hope we're not late,' said Heather, edging in the door nervously, kissing Kate, hugging Luke, and proffering a large flat box, slightly dented. 'Sorry, Molly sat on the apple tart. It's a bit squashed. Sorry. Sorry.'

Heather's constant churning anxiety made Kate want to shake her. She was beautiful, bright, slim and nice – why did she have to apologise for herself the whole time? 'Don't worry, Heather, it's fine. Callum . . .' she called upstairs, 'everyone's here.' An indistinct snarl from the top floor indicated that Callum had heard.

'Molly sat on the tart!' shrieked ten-year-old Daisy, as she was towed in the door by Travis, their chocolate labrador. 19 Lovelace Road's long, narrow hall had little space for enthusiastic labradors. He barrelled past Kate, almost knocking her down, dragging Daisy behind him as a motorboat tows its water-skier. 'The tart was on the seat and she just didn't look. She sat right down on top of it!' Almost everything Daisy said had exclamation marks.

'It wasn't my fault.' Twelve-year-old Molly followed, the image of her pale, slender, strawberry-blonde mother. 'It's not very sensible to put a tart on a seat, is it?'

'Well, where else you would you put it? Not on the floor,' said Jack, coming in last with his arms full of bottles of wine and a jar of Heather's home-made marmalade, which he pressed on Kate. 'Can you pump up the apples somehow?'

Kate kissed him. 'I'm sure I can do something with it. How lovely. I adore Heather's marmalade.' She expected this sort of thing from Jack. He was the family hero – he was in military intelligence, which he self-deprecatingly referred to as 'a contradiction in terms', completely at home with obscure snippets of information from tribal elders in terrorist-infiltrated villages, but vague about domestic matters. How he had managed to persuade the immensely competent Heather to agree to marry him was a mystery to them all, but it proved that he did have some sense, as Heather was, everyone agreed, the perfect wife. They had lived in a series of army quarters, which varied from depressing 1960s boxes on windy estates to the current rather pleasant – even lavish – 1930s colonel's quarters in Halstead Hill, just inside the M25 in Surrey. Their various houses were usually too small – or too far away – for full family gatherings, and Kate's other sister-in-law, Simon's wife Olivia, hated cooking and was too busy 'sorting out the world' as the family legend had it. So family celebrations were usually directed by Kate and centred round 19 Lovelace Road.

'Oh, wow!' Heather stopped. 'This is amazing, Kate. What a transformation.'

'How much do you think it cost, Heather?' asked Ella. 'Kate never tells me anything.'

Heather paled. She always seemed terrified of Ella. 'Oh, I . . .'

The new extension stretched out before them, all thirty feet of it, with its width spanning the entire twenty feet of 19 Lovelace Road's plot. There were lantern-windows in the flat roof and a full wall of glass ahead of them, flooding the room with light, and, along one side, a steel double fridge, range and line of units. Daisy and Molly rushed round the chunky island unit in the middle, shrieking. Their voices bounced off the hard surfaces.

'It's amazing,' repeated Heather. 'And, oh, look the photographs. Aren't they lovely? You're so clever.'

'Are you sure we're not too grubby and stained to be

allowed in?' asked Jack. 'Now I can see all sorts of things I would never have noticed before. Like your roots.' He grinned at his sister with brotherly venom.

Kate blushed. 'I haven't had time to have my roots done,' she said. 'Or the money. We went over budget.'

'So it *was* very expensive,' confirmed Ella, with triumph in her voice. 'I thought so. Now where is Callum?'

'Have a drink. We've got some elderflower cordial and there's masses of wine.'

Jonny kissed Heather and shook hands with Jack. 'What can I get you?'

'Mm. This is a smart bottle of red, Jonny,' said Jack. 'Have you won the Lottery?'

'Jonny, this is lovely,' said Heather, accepting her glass of elderflower cordial, and looking round again. 'You must have added so much space to the house.'

'Not to mention the space you must have added to your bank account,' added Jack.

'I would like to see my other grandson,' declared Ella. 'I've been here for half an hour and there's been no trace of Callum.'

'Callum!' Kate screamed up the stairs. 'Granny's here. And everyone else.'

Callum slouched down around ten minutes later.

'You look terrible, darling,' said Ella. 'Are you getting a cold?'

'No, Gran, I'm fine.' He kissed her, glared at Kate, then poured the entire contents of a carton of orange juice down his throat.

'Goodness,' said Ella. 'You must be about to start growing. It's so important for men to be tall. Now where have you been?'

'Out.'

'And what have you been doing?'

'Nothing.'

Ella smiled indulgently. 'Jack was exactly the same at his age,' she said to Heather. 'Boys will be boys.'

Acknowledgements

Thank you so much to: Penelope Williams, Suzanne Church, Jacqui Eggar, Cassandra Chubb, Victoria Dickenson, Emma Duncan, Emma Daniell, Deborah Baker and Julian and Amanda Mannering. At Little, Brown I'd like to thank my terrific editor and publisher Joanne Dickinson, as well as Zoe Gullen, Hannah Hargrave in publicity, Carleen Peters in marketing, Rob Manser, Sara Talbot and Andy Coles in sales and Jenny Richards for a great cover. And at David Higham Associates, thank you so much to Anthony Goff, Georgia Glover and Marigold Atkey.

And, as always, David, Freddie and Rosie.